Spark and Shadow

Trisha Thacker

Desert Cats
PUBLISHING

Contents

Chapter One

Chapter One

Situated in the woods, within walking distance of the city, Etana's house was far enough away that the noise of the city didn't reach it. Wakana was busy with all walks of life and no one knew about the fae that lived among them. At least, Etana hoped that was the case. It would ruin things if people knew he and his brethren were out in the world, quietly guiding humanity down the pathway they wanted them to go down. It was a thriving environment and could almost be mistaken for one of those cities that didn't have magic. But there were still the fae outside of the city limits causing problems. Etana ran a thriving business in raw and worked metals to protect the humans who wandered outside the city bounds.

Etana liked his house; it was a simple single-story, wide-spaced house with plenty of large windows that let in the light. Shadows pooled on the ground in the wake of such bright lights. He also had a secondary light source for when the weather didn't cooperate. The extra light was perfect for opening pathways to different parts of the world. It was useful when he had visitors as well. The fae, like Tabor, who had the key to his pathways were always welcome here and Etana enjoyed the company. He was a social creature but had few close friends.

Tabor was one of the few he counted on as being more than just a friend; he was close with him in a way that wouldn't have occurred to him half a century ago. It was a shame that he now came with baggage.

Still, Tabor found a fascinating kid, Etana mused to himself. Half of him is human, the other half aodhamair. An interesting combination, but the fire would win in the end. It had a way of overpowering humanity. For all he knew, Fateh would eventually have fire for hair instead of sprouting it when he was angry. He might change in other ways as well, unable to stand the touch of water, metal, or salt. Fire was a primal force, much stronger than a human.

Etana liked the kid, for the short time he knew him. The kid was familiar with Tabor and had a friendship with him, but they only went back three years. Half of those years was Tabor acting as if he worked for the Shadows. Why he had waited so long to let Fateh know he wasn't one of the Shadows, Etana didn't know. He might have tried to protect Fateh. He had known Tabor for half a century and still couldn't figure him out.

For the time being, Etana was content. He saved Tabor's life long ago. They later became friends and then lovers, Etana having cashed in part of the debt owed with Tabor's willing participation. He didn't think he could ask for the same type of payment from Fateh, though, age difference aside. The kid said he didn't care about sex; he said something about being asexual. It had to be disappointing for Tabor, who was a very amorous individual.

Etana even considered helping them, instead of interfering with them. Not because it could be more fun to be on the losing side, and he did think the kid and Tabor would lose—but because he liked Fateh and wanted to see him succeed even a little.

Etana lived a mostly quiet life in the city he chose as his home base. He established rules early on and the humans he trusted enforced them. They weren't so obvious as to be wearing uniforms, but everyone knew who to avoid if they were up to something. Nothing was perfect, but things were less chaotic overall. There were the odd sets of humans here and there that didn't like being ruled by the fae, but they never caused much trouble. Not that they had much opportunity to cause mischief; Etana and his brethren weren't allergic to metal like the rest of the fae were. Even Fateh felt the 'burn' of metal, as much as he tried to hide it. It was almost adorable how much he tried to pretend to be as human as possible.

"So." Etana clapped his hands together and smiled brightly at Tabor and Fateh. "You're planning a rebellion of your own against the Shadows. Tell me, how well has that gone for the humans in your town?" He saw Fateh tense and he knew he struck a nerve. Humans were too easy to read. It wasn't like he cared about the fate of the Shadows; they were the dregs of the fae world.

"They've had some successes." Fateh's tone was guarded, as if he didn't quite trust Etana. That reticence would serve him well in the future, but right now, Etana visibly pouted, making a show of it, as if Fateh's distrusting nature hurt him.

"Now, now—you can tell me all about it. It's not like I can go running to those Shadows of yours and tell them all your plans." Etana spread his hands wide. "May I remind you we're on the other side of the world from where you come from?"

"And didn't you say you had paths in the shadows?" Fateh shot back, fire sparking in his hair briefly. "It's not like everyone in town doesn't know about the Shadows and how to fight them. What happens here won't affect what happens there." He considered Etana. "Not that their method of attack would hurt you, I suppose."

"They used metal, then," Etana said in satisfaction, as if he had cleared up a mystery he had been trying to solve. "Good weapon against the Shadows and other fae, bad against my kind. It would only make us stronger."

"It was a bomb." Fateh's tone was bland and he eyed Etana sidelong. "Even a bomb would make you stronger?"

"The shrapnel from the bomb wouldn't hurt me." Etana said, confident. "It might piss me off, but it wouldn't hurt me. So if you were planning a full-scale rebellion against my kind, you best think of a different way." He grinned widely at Fateh's obvious dismay. "Not that you could use metal in the same way anymore. It'll hurt as badly as it would hurt the Shadows once you fully awaken."

"You mean I'm going to get worse?" Fateh demanded, looking towards Tabor for help. "I already lit myself on fire. What else is going to happen?"

"You're going to learn how to gain control of your magic." Tabor sounded firm and kind, and Etana mentally rolled his eyes at the way Tabor obviously cared for Fateh. It was a good trait to have as a protector, but Etana privately thought he never should have gotten as involved as he did. "So when you set things on fire, it will be on purpose. Eventually, you'll be able to have nightmares without setting the bedding on fire." His lips widened into a smirk. "Should we buy you sheets made of asbestos so that we don't have to worry about it?"

That earned a rude gesture from Fateh, which only made Tabor laugh. Etana looked rather serious and his tone reflected it.

"Yes, I would appreciate it if you learned control sooner rather than later, especially if you're going to be hanging around here." Etana didn't know how much longer Tabor and Fateh planned to stay, but it would be wise to take advantage of Etana's hospitality for as long as it was offered. It wasn't always a guarantee and they still had supplies to get before they decided to travel any-where. The kid couldn't go around wearing the same clothing for however long Tabor dragged him around. While Tabor would be fine, the kid still retained most of his human characteristics. They liked some variety in their lives.

"We're not planning on staying that long." Tabor raised an eyebrow at Etana. "I don't want to be caught out when your hospitality comes to an end. It never goes well."

"I told you, I wouldn't hurt you. I swear it on my honor that I won't turn you into the Shadows that linger on this pathway or others. I'm invested now." He tried to make his tone as sincere as possible; he was telling the truth after all. Fateh was a weird kid and he said that there were more like him out there. Etana wanted to see where this would all end up. Tabor and the kid didn't have a prayer on their own; they were too vulnerable. Their very natures made them shine like fireworks to the Shadows; bright as a sunrise and a temptation too tantalizing to resist.

"Invested in my little spark?" Tabor looked disbelieving, but voiced no more protests. "Maybe we can trust you to be able to come back here at times when we need a safe haven. You won't burn Fateh, you like him."

"You're the one that likes him." Etana couldn't help his bright smile as he teased Tabor about how he felt about Fateh. It was obvious to anyone that he had a crush on the teenager.

"I do not." Tabor protested loudly and entirely untruthful, in Etana's opinion.

He grinned even wider. "Come on, you can't lie to me."

"You realize I'm standing right here." Fateh made a face. "Can you not talk about me like I'm not here? So what if Tabor likes me?"

"Why, you like him back?" Etana showed his interest now and he leaned forward to give Fateh a more penetrating look. "You were the one loudly protesting any sort of sexual relationship."

Fateh's ears turned red. "That's a different thing altogether." His voice grew sharp. "Does it really matter anyway?" he asked. "We have more important things to think about, like finding the other fae-touched kids and asking if they want to -- want to..."

"With your powers combined, fight the bad guy of the week?" Etana offered helpfully. "And it absolutely does matter. How will my gossip train work if I don't get information?"

"You don't have to put it quite that way." Fateh's cheeks were scarlet now. Any moment he was going to catch on fire from embarrassment. Etana watched with avid curiosity. "And really, hut up." Fateh groused. "You're like an old man, wanting the latest gossip."

"That's because Etana is an old man." Tabor was brutally cheerful. "Isn't that right?"

Etana huffed and rolled his eyes. He didn't need to put up with them being ageist of all things. "I'm more mature than the both of you combined." That was his argument and he stuck with it.

"Whatever." Fateh squared his shoulders. "So you'll have pathways open for us?" He switched topics rapidly, going back to the original crux of what he was trying to do. "I don't know how to open the shadow paths--" His tone said he clearly didn't want to learn. "And I don't know where Tabor can go."

"I can take you back to Mokosh's little pond and you can hunt down the lost children in the place they were last." Tabor spoke up and ruffled Fateh's hair. "That's the logical thing to do, even if going back to Mokosh's territory isn't the best thing for either of us. Still, it may be the best start."

Fateh visibly shuddered, and Etana could feel some semblance of sympathy for him. He didn't know Mokosh personally, but Tabor said she was a water spirit and Fateh nearly drowned while in her clutches.

"Sometimes that hardest step is going back to where it all went south," said Etana, leaning back in his chair and closing his eyes. "I can open a pathway back to where you came from, but that's all I can do. I can't join you on your happy little jaunt. I have a town to protect." He didn't miss Tabor's look of raw envy. Etana knew Tabor's weakness really got to him too. He had been the protector of Fateh's town. Instead, the Shadows nearly consumed him.

Fateh probably didn't know Tabor's past and it would be interesting to see his reaction once he found out that Tabor would have been the one looking over Felinheli in the same way Etana looked after Wakana. He probably would have had cousins, siblings, or friends helping him out. They would have been lost to the darkness and Tabor left alone, fighting a battle he couldn't help to win.

"We appreciate you opening a pathway." Tabor was smooth. "As long as it goes both ways for a time, we won't be caught flat-footed."

"Oh trust me, I'm very curious as to how this is going to turn out." Etana grinned widely. "But let's not worry about pathways for now. You still have some time left in my company and I'd hate for you to leave so soon."

Fateh gave him another distrustful look, as if suspected him of an ulterior motive. Etana didn't mean to sound threatening. The words came out that way.

"Come on, tell me more of what you found in town. Did you meet with any of the locals? Fess up." Etana suspected that a rebellion grew here as well, but he didn't know what they were rebelling against. He treated everyone fairly and so what if they were a little closed off from the rest of the world? It kept them safe.

Having a group of fae look after you couldn't be a bad thing.

Fateh looked hesitant for a moment and then shrugged, flicking his gaze towards Tabor for a moment. "There were a group of kids." He began slowly, obviously weighing his words and what he should tell Etana. "Mind you, they were kids. They were probably like eleven or twelve, some of them were younger. But they noticed what the fae had done and they wanted no part of it. I guess they wanted things back to the way they were." His smile turned lopsided. "They tried to recruit me."

"And how did you get out of it?" Etana asked curiously. "It's not like you could lie your way out." Fateh would learn to get around the restrictions of his fae nature soon enough, if Tabor was teaching him how to lie. It would be difficult to use his words cunningly enough without learning what to say. "You certainly didn't tell them the truth or else you wouldn't be here."

"I'm not stupid." Fateh's tone was sharp. "I didn't tell them everything. I declined against being part of their little group and they said they'd keep an eye out for me, since I obviously don't know what's going on here."

"And they don't trust you." Etana knew this for a fact. "New boy shows up out of nowhere when they usually don't get visitors? I'll be surprised if they didn't send someone to follow you here." Etana glanced out the window, thinking he would be able to spot such a figure. There was no one in sight, but it didn't mean someone hadn't been there.

Tabor smirked. "You think I wouldn't be able to tell if we had a tail?"

"Yep." Etana replied bluntly. "If they know the city, they could follow you and you'd never know. This isn't your territory, you don't know the landscape or the people."

"Fair enough." Tabor tone was laid-back. "But I did check to make sure there was no one near us as we made our way back. How much trouble could a bunch of kids be? Like you said, their principal weapon is metal, which certainly won't hurt you and I doubt you'd let them get close enough to you to have salt thrown at you." Tabor grinned, probably at the image he conjured up.

"Please don't tell me you think salt will hurt me like that." Etana said. "I'm not some little Shadow that will die at the taste of salt."

"You mean salt doesn't offer us protection?" Fateh's obvious dismay reflected his reaction to this new information.

"Oh, you can line your home with salt and the fae can't cross the barrier." Etana shrugged. "The lesser fae are more repelled by it, but I'm not going to melt if someone blows a bunch of salt at me."

"You'll get blisters." Tabor pointed out. "Salt can still irritate if used correctly, little spark. But most people don't know how to use it." He grinned widely. "And don't be scared of eating anything that has salt in it. You won't die. If humans could get us that easily, we would have been defeated long ago."

"You have to watch out for iron." Etana went deadly serious. "You are going to be, for lack of a better word, allergic to the stuff. Some other metals may bother you as well, but iron is the big thing." He suddenly grinned. "Don't you wish you were me and not have to worry about such pesky things?"

"I wish I were human." Fateh's tone went flat. "I wish that none of this had ever happened. I want things back the way they were." He crossed his arms defensively over his chest, the fire appearing in his hair again.

"You're sparking." Etana brutally pointed out. "There is no going back to whatever life you had before. You were always different. It was just a matter of time before you changed. You're still going to change. Get used to it."

Fateh's hands went to his hair and he scowled, hands patting out the fire. "If Tabor hadn't shown up..."

"Then you'd probably be dead." Etana wouldn't play games with Fateh. "Tabor saved your life, him being here and knowing what you are. What if you manifested in front of a group of humans? Hurt those you cared about when you couldn't control your fire?"

Fateh blanched and Etana nodded in satisfaction. "Accept what you are, little flame and be grateful that you have Tabor here to help you." He clapped his hands together. "And now that's out of the way, who's ready for food?"

Fateh looked like he wanted to argue further, but Tabor placed a hand on his shoulder, as if to reassure him. Fateh looked up at Tabor and sighed, giving in. If only for the moment and with little grace.

Etana knew the fight was far from over, but he didn't push it for now. It would be Tabor's job to convince Fateh.

Chapter Two

Tabor watched Fateh sleep, making sure there would be no more accidents. He was curled up in the fetal position, hugging his middle as if trying to hold onto himself. One nightmare and he could set himself on fire again. It wouldn't be a pleasant experience and it would piss Etana off to see more damage to his house. He couldn't help but think of when he first met Fateh. The kid stuck out in his mind and Tabor hadn't been able to figure out his secrets then. It had been too early for Fateh to manifest, but there had been something different about him. Maybe it was the way Fateh treated him:after their initial meeting; teasing and joking with him. That first meeting wasn't the best, but it luckily didn't set the tone for when Fateh talked with him later. It wasn't until the Shadows came where everything messed up.

***

Three Years Ago

Felinheli wasn't overly large, but the clustered homes echoed with the sounds of laughter and chatter. The size of the town made it ideal for protection. There were a few outliers that lived up in the woods. But it didn't matter. As long as they came into town, they would be under his protection. He would invite his cousins and they could make it their home. Being too young to remember life before the humans settled here, he relied on the stories he heard. There was a sense of satisfaction in reclaiming what had been taken away from them. They once wandered freely and had their own homes established across the lands, until humans came with their metal and salt and protection spells.

It would not be like before. He wasn't going to have the same problems. He was stronger now than he was half a century ago. The scáthach weren't around and he could take care of everyone without worrying about them mucking things up. There were whispers that they were going to show up again but he would be ready for them this time. With more of his cousins around, they could fight back any incursion. There were multitudes of them, all with as strong or stronger fire magic than his own. There would be an advantage in having the numbers.

He ignored the little voice in his head that said that his cousins didn't help the last time. They lost the fight that he hadn't known was happening. He still didn't believe that the scáthach could have harmed his older kin; the ones that were stronger and older than he had been. Their deaths were all lies.

He felt a strange, familiar, power in the bookstore next to him so he investigated. He blended in well with the people in town. This was his home, after all. They didn't even suspect that one of the fae was in their midst, and wouldn't know it for a while, if Tabor had anything to say about it. He didn't want to scare the humans, after all. He looked human enough, it wasn't as if his hair was actually fire, like some of his relatives.

The clerk behind the counter looked up at the tinkling bell which rang from the door when Tabor came in, but other than a smile and a nod, he didn't make a fuss. This was the type of shop where you did your own thing. Tabor hated pushy people and this suited him fine.

He noticed the kid lingering by a stack of books; one he saw before selling vegetables in the farmer's market downtown. There was something peculiar about him, a mysterious aura that piqued curiosity. He sparked Tabor's interest before, but now he found himself truly fascinated by him. It may have been something about the way he viewed everyone else around him.

"What are you reading?" Tabor looked down at the teenager, intent on figuring out the puzzle and also simply wanting to bug him. Tabor was bored and this random stranger was a perfect target.

"A book." Ooh, a real genius there.

"Oh, really. What kind of book?" he leaned over to see better the words on the page. Driven by curiosity, he gave in to peer over his shoulder. He sought something to add excitement to his day. The town wasn't exactly full of excitement.

"A book you read." The kid turned the page, clearly intent on ignoring Tabor. "Find one of your own."

"Got a smart mouth for such a shrimp. What if I wanted to read the book you're reading? Is it good?"

"It would be better if you weren't here, annoying me." His irritation was obvious in the way his shoulders tensed, showing his annoyance as well.

"I want to be entertained, though," Tabor smirked. "You entertain me and so I can't see how me leaving you alone will continue to do so. ." He nudged closer to him.

"Go away and bug someone else now."

"Aw, you wound me, shrimp—and here I thought we could have such fun together. You were much friendlier in the farmers market." Tabor watched him, eyebrows raising as the kid's hands clenched around the book he was reading. The pages were starting to curl inward, as if they were lying next to a fire.

"Fateh, is this guy bothering you?" The clerk regained some life as he focused on Tabor and his victim. At least now had a name to go with the stranger; he couldn't keep referring to him as the kid, especially if he wanted to get to know him in the future.

"No, I'm fine." Fateh waved off his concern. "This jerk was just leaving." His gaze bored into Tabor's. "Weren't you?" The book smoked faintly and Fateh spared it a dismayed look before hastily putting it down.

My... there really is something more to this kid than meets the eye. He didn't think humans had that particular trick with heat, but he didn't know everything. Once upon a time, humans possessed their own brand of magic, but it had been ages since it last revealed itself. It was a pity he couldn't extend his stay to unravel Fateh's enigmatic secrets.

Tabor couldn't stay in town the way he wanted to, much less spend the time annoying Fateh. He needed to talk to Etana first to see what was going on and what he could do. Tabor knew time was running out, and he had to set up his routes quickly so he could escape if it came down to it.. He didn't want his home tainted by the looming presence of the scáthach coming back.

He would come back as soon as he had the information he needed. There was a feeling he should stick around Fateh; a reaction like the smoking book encouraged him. He always enjoyed riling up people. The results could be so amusing.

"Well, it's been fun." He grinned, but he couldn't resist a parting shot, since the kid looked so hopeful at the idea of him leaving.

"I'd watch the book, though," Tabor grinned and waved at Fateh. "I'm guessing you only want to borrow, not buy it." He waved as he left the shop, keeping an eye on Fateh. Once he felt secure, he understood the importance of keeping a close eye out for him once more. There were too many opportunities to exploit there. He would have to investigate to see if other humans could do the same trick. He didn't know any humans that could produce heat or fire like himself, but it was obvious that Fateh had done something with the book.

***

"So you think the scáthach are coming back to the town you claimed?" Etana lazed on the couch, seemingly not bothered by Tabor's important news. "What makes you think they'll go to your town? It's a bit damp and cloudy for them. Feeling special, are you?"

"They'd do it just to spite me." Tabor said, making a face. "They're still pissed that I got away all those years ago. They'd take my town just to prove a point; that I'm not strong enough to protect what I've claimed."

"You have a point." Etana sat up straighter. "Have you established your pathways out just in case an incursion happens? You can't count on me bailing you out all the time."

"How do you think I got here?" Tabor raised an eyebrow. "But yes, I have several pathways I set up, because I'm not going to get caught again." His smile turned fierce. "Not like I'd be as easily taken as I had when I was younger. I'm much stronger now than I used to be. I have more allies." He gestured to Etana.

"You needed those allies to get yourself out of the mess you got yourself into." Etana observed. "You're lucky I haven't decided to collect on my favors yet. I don't think you're ready."

"Because having a debt hanging over my head is so preferable." Tabor rolled his eyes. "You're going to strike when I least suspect it, I'm sure." He shook his head. "But let's not talk about my debt; I have a question for you. Do you know of any humans with magic?"

"Humans are too dull to have magic." Etana waved the possibility away. "I don't know of any humans who have magic, unless they've made a contract with one of us." He sat up slowly, eyeing Tabor. "Why, have you found something interesting?"

"Maybe." Tabor rested his chin on his hand, thinking. "There is a kid in my town. He did a neat trick with heat and I want to investigate him further. If he's made any deals, I want to know who he's been talking with. I don't think any of my cousins would make a deal with a human kid. They usually go for older prey."

"But kids are so gullible and stupid." Etana grinned. "They're easier prey. They want the world and all the magic that it offers and they're willing to pay anything for it. It doesn't have to be one of your cousins. It could be an elder fae came to town before you did and made a deal. It wouldn't be the first time."

"They leave a mark." Tabor dismissed any wayward deals out of hand. "They usually do fancier tricks, too. Wealth, success, those sorts of thing. The kid works in a farmers market, selling vegetables. It doesn't look like he's got an easy life a fae wish grants you."

"An easy life until the price comes home to roost." Etana's tone turned serious. "Then we have broken contracts and the scáthach appear like mice in the cupboard. You best make sure your little trick hasn't gone making deals he shouldn't make. You'll want to make sure he fulfills the terms of his contract before he loses his soul."

"I'm not that interested in some random teenager." Tabor protested, waving the topic of Fateh away. "I think the kid has some natural magic of his own. It's not entirely unheard of. If he has eyes which can see through illusions, who's to say they don't have magic of their own as well?"

"It sounds like you're very interested in some random kid."

"He's just interesting in a sea of humans which are dull, that's all." Tabor feigned unconcern at Etana's insistence. "Besides, like you said, I should keep an eye on him to make sure he hasn't made any deals."

"It's not like you to be so interested in a random stranger. He must have really caught your eye." Etana grinned. "Should I be jealous?" He batted his eyes at Tabor, who only made a face.

"He's like ... thirteen. I don't think you have anything to worry about." Tabor leaned forward and stole a kiss. "Maybe I can pay my debt back through more pleasurable methods." He gave Etana an arch look.

"You'd enjoy it too much." The offer got dismissed out of hand and Tabor pouted.

"Worth a try." He shrugged. "Can't blame a guy for trying." He leaned back again and rested a hand over his eyes. "Give me some warning before you spring it on me, hm? I'd rather also like to say we were friends rather than enemies when it happened."

"I'll do my best." Etana grinned. "Come on, Tabor. We've been friends for a long time and I haven't had anyone come to sway my alliances from you. Of course, if the scáthach actually do appear, our friendship may change."

"You wouldn't work with them, would you?" Tabor asked, aghast. "They're disgusting; the remains of human souls. They're not even properly fae."

"They're fae enough." Etana pointed out. "Salt and iron hurts them and they can't lie. They have all the same restrictions some of our older cousins have and they love to make deals."

"It's in their nature to try making a deal that is better than the one they failed at." Tabor didn't like the idea of it. They were dangerous creatures, using their shadows to absorb power and life, making it part of their own. Humans were their favorite victims to make deals with, because as Etana pointed out, they were susceptible to the deals offered by the fae.

"But they can be good allies if you play with them right." Etana eyed Tabor. "You may consider working with them instead of against them for once and see how far you get."

"It'll take a lot for me to consider them an ally." Tabor didn't trust the scáthach. "But I may consider working with them if only to save my own life." He didn't want to be trapped again. He barely escaped last time and it was only because of Etana he survived. He owed debts to a lot of people, even if his family wouldn't collect the same way Etana would eventually.

"Saving your skin is all you have to do." Etana stood up and leaned over Tabor. "Now, what's your plan if the scáthach actually come? Run like hell and leave the humans defenseless?" There was a calculating gaze in his eyes. He knew Tabor too well.

"No. I'll keep an eye on them and make sure it doesn't go completely to shit." Tabor tugged Etana down and kissed him again. "But let's concentrate on other things before I go home."

"I thought you'd never ask."

***

So began his friendship with Fateh. Tabor would stop by the vegetable stall where Fateh worked and hung around him until the teenager finally caved in to Tabor, The initial meeting was not an indication of how charming Tabor could be, and Fateh started talking back to him. He learned Fateh was fourteen, not thirteen like he originally thought. Tabor only seemed to be a few years older than Fateh, which make it perfect for him to establish a friendship. He didn't live in town, but up in the woods with his mother and his grandparents.

"I have fresh milk for you." Fateh plunked a basket of vegetables and a bottle of milk in front of Tabor. "You're too skinny, you need to eat more and drink more milk." Fateh gave Tabor a sly grin. "Not that I have any room to talk, but maybe you'll grow if you drink it."

"Yeah, you really have no room to talk, shrimpy." Tabor snickered and accepted the basket. Fateh began saving fresh vegetables and milk for him, the same way he did for his favorite customers.

"Hey, I'm still growing. You could give me a little leeway." Fateh pointed this out with inescapable logic. "What's your excuse?"

"Don't worry, I still have some growth left in me." Tabor pressed a hand to his chest. "Keep plying me with milk and vegetables and maybe a miracle will happen."

"I'll do it just because you need it." Fateh stuck his tongue out. "I told you, you're too skinny. It's not just your size, you're skinnier than me." Fateh clearly saw Tabor's lankiness as a goal one shouldn't meet.

"Maybe you need to eat more junk food instead of just fruit and vegetables. It's not normal for a kid to not eat junk food."

"And you eat so much of it, I'm sure." Fateh shot back. "You turn sideways and you disappear. Maybe you should be the one eating junk food, not me. I'll grow out of this eventually. You're stuck the way you are."

"I told you, miracles can happen." Tabor stuck his nose up in the air. "You'll see."

It wouldn't ever happen of course, Tabor burned fat the way he would any other fuel and he would be short and skinny for his life. Most of his cousins were the same way; it was their nature.

He wanted to say more when he noticed the shadows next to him moving. He hissed out a breath and backed Fateh into the booth. "Stay back." He gave out a warning, but didn't know if Fateh would heed it. Maybe it was his imagination--the scáthach couldn't be here. There should have been more warning, some sign they came back.

The shadows surged without warning and suddenly Tabor and Fateh weren't alone. There were screams from all over the farmer's market as the shadows came to life and formed into the smoky figures of human nightmares. Tabor could see people collapsing all over the market as the shadows subsumed human bodies and left a husk in their wake.

"Hello Tabor."

Tabor winced and took a step further back, crowding into Fateh, shielding him from the scáthach at the same time. It wasn't just human nightmares; the scáthach were a regular feature in his dreams as well. "Hello Ilianda." He remembered the name of the scáthach who had cornered him long ago. It wasn't something he would forget. "So you're alive after all."

Fateh made a sound of frustration, prompting Tabor to move slightly and alleviate the boy's discomfort. But the choking noise was not a result of Tabor pressing into him, but something else entirely.

"You know this thing?" Fateh demanded. "Tabor, what the hell?"

"I--" Tabor winced as Ilianda leaned closer and brushed a grimy hand over his cheek. "I can explain."

"Tabor knows us from long ago, don't you?" Ilianda asked, her eyes dark pits in her already smoky form. "I knew you missed us. It's been ever so long, after all."

Tabor jerked away before she could steal his power again. He wouldn't fall for the same trick twice. But first, he needed to get her away from Fateh before he ended up like so many others in the marketplace. "Should we go somewhere to talk?" he asked.

"Oh, we have so much to catch up on." She spared Fateh a look. "I'll even spare the little tidbit."

"How gracious of you." Tabor meant it, too. The shadows could have easily subsumed Fateh. Someone could easily take out that interesting little spark of his in an instant, and Tabor would not only lose a friend, but he would lose the most intriguing human he ever met. "Let's leave and catch up on old times." He could fight, he could stand his ground, but there were too many of them for him to fight on his own. If he had his cousins or even Etana, he might stand a chance, but he was himself, alone. He had to play their games for his own survival.

He could practically feel the betrayal coming from Fateh as he walked away from the booth and Fateh, leading Ilianda away. He could apologize and explain later. Fateh would understand.

Chapter Three

Fateh hadn't understood Tabor's reasoning and once the rest of the fae started popping out of the woodworks and people started going missing, he blamed Tabor even more. Fateh trusted him even less since and he kept up the antagonistic side of their relationship. Fateh never grew out of his smart mouth, even if he saw Tabor as one of the enemy, and Tabor couldn't stop trying to win his friendship back.

Unlike many others, Fateh had never been involved in the growing rebellions which arose after the fae arrived, which brought Tabor a sense of relief. Too many of those people died, and Tabor didn't want Fateh to become one of them. Tabor kept close tabs on Fateh, making suret the scáthach didn't go after him. It was the least he could do. Fateh living outside of town, in the woods, helped. It was where some of the wilder fae roamed, but the larger of the scáthach didn't venture. The scáthach liked being around people; it meant fuel and food and the vehicle to make their bargains.

He knew Fateh's grandparents were some of those who left the town all together before the borders shut. He never could figure out why Fateh and his mother stuck around. They could have left at the first opportunity.

So life had gone on for two years until everything exploded when Fateh's mother had been killed. Her death woke up Fateh's latent talents. Tabor suspected Fateh showed the traits of an aodhamair, but he couldn't figure out how or why. However, he realized it too late—Fateh had been taken away to live in one of the group homes which housed fae-touched children. It didn't matter whether they had traits of the fae themselves or simply were caught on the wrong side of their wrath.

***

Fateh stirred and woke up slowly, blinking up at Tabor. "Were you watching me sleep?" he demanded. "You're not creepy at all."

"I agree. I'm not creepy." Tabor added a forced cheerful note to his tone. "Have to make sure that if you had any nightmares you wouldn't set the bed on fire again. Once was enough."

"You're telling me." Fateh rubbed the sleep out of his eyes and focused on Tabor as he became more aware. "You weren't the one who woke up in flames."

"Yes, but I got to see you on fire, which while thrilling in a way, didn't do my heart any good. I didn't know if it wouldn't damage you until recently." Tabor pressed a hand to his heart as if he demonstrated the toll it took on him. "What if you hadn't been fireproof after all?"

"Then you would have had one less problem to deal with." Fateh was grumpy. "What are we planning to do today?" he asked. "I never got to do the shopping I planned to do and I am not going to imitate you, wearing the same jeans for weeks on end."

"How do you know it's the same jeans?" Tabor asked with a grin. "I could have dozen pairs which all look the same and you would never know."

"And where do you pull them out from? Your bag of holding?" Fateh snorted. "You didn't exactly carry anything with you, anymore than I did." Not that he had a chance to carry anything away from the prison he stayed in. Mokosh made escape almost impossible and the idea of Fateh running to his room to grab what little he had in the way of clothing was laughable.

"I do have something like a magic bag." Tabor grinned at Fateh's open-mouthed astonishment. "But I don't have it with me, unfortunately. It's back at my house."

"You have a home?" Fateh asked in bewilderment. "I thought you were some random fae who just wandered in and out of people's lives."

"Of course I have a home." Tabor huffed and crossed his arms over his chest. "I have to have a place to sleep and eat, after all. I wasn't going to rely on anyone for shelter." He gave Fateh a look. "You think the price the scáthach extract from humans is high? It's nothing compared to what they do to our kind."

Fateh shuddered. "I don't want to know." He lowered his words to a whisper. "It's bad enough they suck the souls out of people."

"Yeah, well, they do the same to us, only they absorb our power until there isn't anything left. With humans, there's a chance they could come back to some semblance of life. With us, once they drain our power, we're no more."

"Didn't Etana imply they drained your power?" Fateh asked. "How did you escape from death?"

"I owe Etana a debt for saving my life. He and the scáthach don't get along, because of all the metal he grows on his body. When I first met him, I found out he can produce and work any kind of metal. All he has to do is touch one of the scáthach and they recoil from him. If Etana does anything more, he can kill them with little effort." He considered Fateh. "And that's all I'll say on my past for now. Maybe I'll tell you more later." He winked. "If you're good."

Fateh ignored the comment about 'being good' and instead focused on Etana. "So why doesn't he?" Fateh demanded. "He could destroy the nest of Shadows where it stands and he doesn't do anything?"

"Not his territory, not his problem .You notice there aren't any of the scáthach here, hm?" Tabor pointed out. "They're scared of Etana."

"I wish he could come back with us and destroy the Shadows." Fateh looked towards the bedroom where Etana slept. "It would be so much easier."

"You don't want to be in his debt." Tabor said firmly. "Putting his life at risk to save a handful of humans isn't something to go into debt for. You can ask him for weapons--if you could handle them without getting poisoned."

"Right." Fateh looked uneasy and gave a slow nod. "It's like making a contract, right? You don't want to make a deal you won't come out on top of."

"You're asking a favor, which is worse." Tabor said seriously. He wanted to make sure Fateh understood. "Etana may be a friend, but friendship can have its price as well. Etana's help doesn't come cheap."

Fateh swung his feet over the side of the bed, clearly preparing to get up. "So what can we do? I know I said a lot of big words last night, but I do want to get rid of the Shadows. Do we have any advantages other than being a torch?"

"We can burn them when they're solid. Usually it's after they, ah...eat." Tabor carefully picked out his words. "When they're in the shadows, we can burn away their light source so they have nowhere to go and they'll be trapped in a void." He raised an eyebrow. "I know it's not much, but you have raw power, Fateh. You can do a lot of things with it."

"Hopefully my friends can do more." Fateh rubbed at his nose and made a face. "It all depends on who I find and who wants to come with me." His tone sounded wistful, as if he missed the other kids at the prison.

"You've all got raw power, still growing and untapped." Tabor was confident in this. "All jokes aside, with your combined power, you could wreck a lot of havoc." His grin turned fierce. "I look forward to seeing what you can do."

"Why didn't you destroy the scáthach when they first came?" Fateh asked. "You instead went with them, as if you were long-lost friends." His tone was bitter and Tabor couldn't blame him. Fateh lost friends the day the scáthach appeared.

"I was outnumbered and lacked the strength to confront them all." It was unlikely the humans would work with the fae. They saw them all as one great big enemy, at least the ones in Fateh's town did.

"The humans, we, I mean, they-- are already fighting." Fateh stumbled over his words. "They have weapons they've concocted and I taught them about salt and metal." He winced a little. The knowledge he taught them could be used against him now. "They just need more metal." He gave Tabor a searching look. "Is there any way to handle it without getting hurt ourselves?"

"Recruit humans to your side, find the metal in town and have them carry the metal into battle."

"Battle?" His tone went almost high-pitched at the word. "What battle?"

"You think it will be as easy as walking up to one of the scáthach and killing them? It's going to be a fight and people will lose their lives over this. Be careful who you ask for help, make sure they know the risks before taking them with you."

"I hoped we could attack them with stealth." Fateh pursed his lips together. "I don't want it to be a battle. We'd never win if it came to that. I don't know many people who could help."

"Stealth it is, then. Although your cover will be shot the first time you set one of the scáthach on fire." He appreciated Fateh trying to look at this from different angles. He knew it was going to come down to a fight in the end.

"I can take the risk." Fateh stood with his arms crossed, his entire stance radiating stubbornness."So--let's get what we need to get, plan some more and then get going. I don't want to be on the wrong side of Etana's hospitality when it runs out."

"Knowing your limits is very wise, but are you prepared to go back so close to the town where you grew up?" Tabor asked seriously. "I know the end goal is to go there and fight the good fight, but you're going back to a town where you they kept you as a prisoner and it's right next door to your home. Are you truly prepared for the consequences?"

"Maybe not going home quite yet." Fateh allowed himself that much. "I'm sure there are other places we can go, more people we can find. Maybe we can find another one of those prisons and free the kids there."

"Now you're thinking." Tabor said approvingly. "Gather as many allies as you can afford and then you can sort out what you want to do in the end."

"Am I going to be one of those allies?" Etana asked as he emerged from his bedroom. "Ask away, little flame, and maybe you'll get a suitable answer."

"I'll need weapons I can give to people who can handle them." Fateh said decisively. "I'm going to gather some human allies and maybe I'll find some of your family." He had a crooked grin. "You can't be the only miotal around."

"Aw, he's thinking." Etana stepped over to Fateh and ruffled his hair. "Yes, you might find some of my family willing to help and I'll do what I can, while my alliances lay with you." He considered it. "I don't foresee myself aligning myself with the scáthach any time soon, so you're safe."

"Being on our side is good at least." Tabor gave an exaggerated sigh of relief. "So you can supply Spark with weapons?"

"It doesn't cost me anything to provide metal." Etana shrugged. "I won't even charge you. You have to find a way to get those little humans to a spot where I can supply them."

"Or you could put yourself in a place where we can reach you." Tabor pointed out dryly. "You don't have to lock yourself away here forever, you know."

"We'll see what you do first and it will determine what I do." Etana was cheerfully brutal. "Maybe it's my way of extracting payment. I need you to prove yourself first. Make sure you pick strong allies who won't turn on you."

"There's a few people I have in mind." Fateh ran a hand through his hair. "I have to go back to Caergybi."

"You're excused." Etana blinked. "Oh, is that actually the name of a town? You and your Welsh names. I can never understand them."

Fateh mimed a punch at Etana, but he didn't follow through with the gesture. "I'm sure your New Zealand names are completely normal." He sounded extra dry. "Wanaka, really? Isn't it too simple?"

"To me, it's just right." Etana grinned. "To you, maybe you have a hard time pronouncing names which don't twist your tongue in a knot."

"Haha, it's like I've never heard the same joke before." There used to be tourists who would come to Felinheli and they would make fun of the name of the town and the other Welsh towns they visited. Messing up the names of the towns Fateh saw as normal seemed to be a big game to those who didn't live there. The tourists had stopped after the Shadows had appeared. Fateh idly wondered if they were living normal lives or if they had their own incursion of fae to think about. It was an uncomfortable thought, but Etana and his city were proof the fae had spread to the other side of the world.

"Keep up your sense of humor, little fire. You're going to need it in the future." He looked up at Tabor. "Do you need another hold all my shit bag? I notice you don't have yours on you."

"Is that the technical term we're using these days?" Tabor asked. "I liked Fateh's bag of holding. Much simpler."

"He stole 'bag of holding' from Dungeons and Dragons." Etana rolled his eyes. "Fine, fine--would you like a new bag of holding? This way you and Fateh can carry around all you need without loading yourself down with packs of clothing and food."

"I would appreciate it, but what is it going to cost me?" Tabor asked suspiciously.

"Nothing. Call it a freebie, since I like the kid." Etana disappeared back into his bedroom for a moment, emerging with a small backpack. "Voila, one bag to hold your shit." He handed it to Tabor. "Now do me a favor and actually go shopping before you dither around my city for longer than you planned?"

Fateh gave the bag a doubtful look, mixed with curiosity. "Is there anything in it already we have to worry about?" he asked. "And how will we get things out if it's an infinite space?"

"You have to think about what you want, so if you want apples one day, you better be thinking apples and not blue jeans when you stick your hand in the bag." Etana gave the bag an experimental shake. "And it's empty, waiting for your use. Make good use of it."

"A magic bag." Fateh's tone was flat, disbelieving. "What other tricks do you have up your sleeves?" he asked.

"So many." Etana grinned. "You'll have to get to know me better to learn any more of them, though. Now go, shoo. Buy clothing and food and then plot insurrection. I'm sure if you hunt long enough, you'll find more little rebels to join your happy band, other than the ones you've already handpicked."

"Gathering more allies is the plan." Tabor said cheerfully, clapping a hand on Fateh's shoulder. "What do you say? Shall we go and buy out the city?"

"This is just too weirdly ordinary." Fateh complained and shook his head. "Shopping for clothing and food--it's normal."

"You have to find your normalcy somewhere." Tabor shrugged. "Take it as it is and don't look back."

Fateh shrugged and nodded. "I guess you have a point. Let's go shopping."

Chapter Four

After the third shop, Fateh noticed they were being watched. They were in the middle of buying jeans when he felt a prickling on the back of his neck. "Don't look now." Fateh lowered his voice as he spoke to Tabor. "But we're being followed."

"Oh, I noticed after we bought the trail mix you insisted was a must for the road." Tabor shrugged it off. "Didn't you say you had those kids interested in you? They're probably keeping an eye on you now, watching what you do and where you're going."

Fateh's decisive tone made it clear. "I don't like it. How can we shake them?"

"Aw, they're only seeing you buying normal shit, like clothing. You're new in town, it stands to reason you'd buy clothes when you first got here. The fact you didn't actually do it yesterday probably stands out more."

"Standing out is what I'm afraid of." Fateh muttered and looked uncomfortable.

"Just keep doing what you've been doing, so they don't know you know you're being followed. They might get hostile if they find out you know."

"I'd rather they come out and say they're suspicious." Fateh huffed out the words, sounding almost petulant. "All this sneaking around is creepy."

"Yes, because you go and tell someone you're suspicious of them." Tabor rolled his eyes. "Just act normal." He steered Fateh towards a rack of jeans. "What do you think? Should I up my pair to two?"

"I thought you already said you had ten pairs that were all the same." Fateh couldn't keep back the sarcasm.

"I also said I didn't have them with me." Tabor pointed out. "Fine, fine, to assuage your sensibilities, I'll buy more than one pair of jeans. But I don't need a lot of clothing." They were more likely to find shorts and t-shirts, some helpfully emblazoned with "WAKANA" on it, as if one could forget where they were. There were some warm weather items, which could be good if they went to colder climes. It couldn't be for tourists; did they even have tourists here? By the way the Meg reacted, visitors were a rarity, but Etana said the town wasn't closed off.

"At least buy a shirt so you don't stick out so much." Fateh begged. Tabor wore one now, but only because the store's signage proclaimed there would be no service if you weren't wearing shoes and a shirt. The note underneath stated 'yes, this means bottoms as well', as if someone tried to come in with only a shirt and shoes.

"You're too hung up on appearances." Tabor laughed and ruffled his hair. "But fine, if you don't want me sticking out so much, I'll wear a shirt for you. Don't want to scare away the people we're trying to recruit after all."

"That's the plan," Fateh said with forced cheerfulness, imitating Tabor. He wondered if he should recruit the tricycle brigade, having them keep an eye on things in the city. He had Etana, though, and he didn't want to start a rebellion and piss off an amazingly strong ally.

They spent the rest of the afternoon hopping from store to store, buying clothing, non-perishable food, and the equipment to cook it in. Fateh watched it all vanish in the bag in bemusement. "I didn't think you had an actual bag of holding," he said. "This is probably the most awesome thing I've seen yet."

"I'm hurt I'm not the most awesome thing you've seen, I am pretty amazing, after all."

"Are you a thing now?" Fateh asked, giving Tabor a sidelong look. "I can demote you, if you're wanting to be considered a thing instead of a person."

"No, no--I like you thinking of me as a person and not as a nuisance."

"Didn't say I didn't think of you as a nuisance." Fateh grinned.

"And here I am, hurt all over again." Tabor gave a dramatic swoon, as if Fateh's words were all too much. Fateh poked him in the side so he actually toppled over. "Ow."

"Come on, get up and stop clowning around. We have a tail to shake before we lead them directly to Etana's door. I think he'd be annoyed."

"Or grateful you brought the rebels onto his land," Tabor suggested and leaned against a restaurant wall, watching as people went by. "This is a good city, Spark. Etana doesn't need trouble and he'll stomp it out if he gets the chance."

Fateh couldn't help but compare this city to his town, how the people acted and how alive the city was. There were no Shadows, lurking and waiting to consume people. There were fae, but they weren't harming anyone Fateh could see. He supposed there still might be deals and contracts and conversations, but it wasn't visible on the surface, as it had been at home.

"And does it mean killing people?" Fateh asked, low and abrupt. "Would he be the type to kill little kids because they're worried about monsters in their town?"

"No, he wouldn't go so far," Tabor reassured him, to Fateh's intense relief. "He'll make sure they don't rebel, but he won't kill them. There are ways of scaring people so they obey you. There's also talking to them reasonably and letting them know who the real monsters are."

Fateh considered this and then nodded. "Alright, let's go back to Etana's and figure out the next step of our plan. I don't want to go back to Mokosh's pond, but the city around it should be okay. I have a feeling we'll find some of the kids there. It's not like they could go back to their homes."

"You're probably right." Tabor pushed off from the wall and slung an arm around Fateh's shoulder. "It'll be okay, Spark." He spoke with a calm and self-assured tone. "We'll find your little friends and take out the nest of Shadows plaguing your home. Maybe we'll even be lucky and take out a few more trouble spots as well. There is the little troll bride friend of yours. I'm sure she would love the help in taking care of such pests."

Fateh swallowed hard. He didn't know if he was ready to fight trolls, but for Randi? He wanted to try. "Let's go," he repeated. "We'll figure out what to do next."

***

"So you're ready to go?" Etana surveyed Tabor and Fateh critically. "You're all provisioned, have a plan and all the good stuff?" Etana still claimed they were allies and he was willing to help out as long as necessary. He said it could be more fun to be friends than to be enemies. This way he could see what Fateh could do firsthand. The option of meeting more like Fateh couldn't be discounted either. Half-fae and half-human children, trying to survive in a world where the odds were stacked against them.

"Yeah, I guess we are. We can't think of any other reason to stay here. Fateh is getting antsy and I think it's time we gather his little group of friends." Amusement filled Tabor's voice. "It'll be interesting to see what we'll turn up. I think I'm even going to be surprised."

"You won't act surprised, though, You'll act as if your findings are something you expected all along, playing it cool for Fateh." Etana found Tabor's reaction even more amusing. "Just don't act so self-assured to where you come off as a total dick."

"I'll try not to." There was a dryness to his tone that even made Fateh smile, even with him being so nervous. "We'll come across something truly bizarre and even I'll be shocked. I'm sure Fateh is the type to attract the truly unusual. After all, look at where he ended up."

"It's not like I try to find weird people," Fateh protested. " It wasn't my fault they put me in prison for the fae-touched. I just had bad luck a fae wanted to collect us."

"You need all the allies you can get if you're going to be fighting the scáthach." Tabor said. He shook his head. "Your weird luck may end up helping you."

"I hope they want to help." Fateh ran a hand through his hair. "They may be perfectly happy where they are and not want to get involved in my battles." He wouldn't blame them. He felt safe with Tabor and away from the Shadows, but he wanted to go back to save the people of the town he lived in. Felinheli didn't deserve to be swallowed by the Shadows any longer. The other fae--Fateh knew they were here to stay. But the Shadows were a danger to everyone, fae and human alike.

"You may be surprised at what people are willing to do for one another," Etana reassured. "It's why I helped Tabor, after all. It was a necessary thing, even if I did claim a debt from it."

"You could forgive the debt," Tabor suggested with a grin. "I wouldn't hold it against you if you did. In fact, I'd be most grateful if you did."

"Nope, I plan on collecting on your debt one day." Etana didn't even blink. "I'll promise you it won't involve Fateh, though." He put a hand to his heart. "He's under your protection, it would be wrong of me to use him against you."

"So glad you have some standards," Tabor said dryly. "It does provide me some relief you won't hurt Spark, though."

"Great, I won't be used as a pawn in your games." Fateh crossed his arms over his chest. "I hate to see what you'll do to Tabor otherwise, but I'm glad I won't be involved."

"It wouldn't be fair, you're not in my debt." Etana gave him a look of surprise. "It would be different if you messed up and you got a favor from me. You're hands off, as far as I'm concerned."

"Good. I'll make sure I won't be in your debt. The way you talk about it, it's going to be the worst thing in the world." He gave Tabor a worried look. "You really won't hurt Tabor, would you?"

"Trust me, my debt doesn't involve hurting him at all." Etana made sure his point was clear. "I like Tabor, I don't plan on doing anything to damage him." He grinned down at Tabor. "Tabor knows, you don't have to be worried on his behalf."

"I'll be fine, Spark." Tabor reassured him, "The payment for his favor will be a pain in the ass, but it won't hurt me."

"Alright." Fateh squared his shoulders and stared at the shadows in the corner of the room. He took a deep breath. "I'm ready to go."

Tabor took hold of Fateh's hand, squeezing tight. "Take a deep breath, it'll be over before you know it."

Fateh nodded and turned to Etana. "I appreciate your help," he said carefully. "I hope I'll see you again soon and we'll still be friends."

"I'll always be your friend, little Fateh." Etana faintly radiated sincerity. "I like you too much to be your enemy."

"Good to know. I look forward to working with you in the future." Fateh reached forward and gave Etana an unexpected hug. "You're a good friend, Etana." The thank you went unsaid and it was a good thing, but Etana understood.

"Take care of yourself, Fateh."

Tabor nodded and without any fanfare, dragged Fateh into the shadows.

***

It wasn't as bad of a trip as it had been the first time Fateh traveled the shadows. The pathways were open to him now, so instead of feeling like he would be turned inside out, he felt only the cold and it didn't last as he and Tabor stepped out into a space outside of the town, away from the prison. They were as far away from the pond as they could get, for both their sakes.

"You alright there, Spark?" Tabor rested a hand on Fateh's shoulder. "You don't look like you're going to be sick this time." He grinned. "See, traveling by shadow isn't bad once the pathways are open to you."

"It's still not natural." Fateh grumbled. "I admit, it's quick, though." Moving through the shadows made him think of the Shadows and how they appeared out of nowhere to attack people. You couldn't even trust your own shadow; for fear they would be hiding there.

"Easier than taking a plane or a boat or whatever travel you're willing to take to cross countries." Tabor nodded. "It's good when you have paths between allies. I'll teach you to open your own pathway one day, because it was part of my favor from Etana. He opened the pathways for me and taught me the secret of the shadows."

"You must really owe him, then." Fateh gave Tabor an impressed look. "I thought he just saved you." His look turned curious. "One of these days, you'll have to tell me the story, you know. I would hate for it to bite me in the ass when I least expect it."

"I'll tell you when I think you're ready." Tabor murmured. "Now is not the time to spill my sordid past. Right now, you're on the hunt for your ragtag bunch of friends." He raised an eyebrow. "Where are you going to begin?"

"Ask around for rumors of weird things happening." Fateh gestured to the town. "This isn't that big of a place. Rumors are going to spread about the kids who escaped from the prison. They're probably keeping an eye on them; they're probably with someone of high authority, like the mayor or somebody similar."

"Good idea. Let's go hunting."

Chapter Five

I t didn't take them long to find the mayor's house. The person waiting outside the house surprised them. Marisa, on the steps of the house, calm and staring off into space. Once Fateh and Tabor came into her line of sight, she stood up, smiling.

"I knew you would come back." Genuine cheer colored her tone. "I knew the shadows would return you to where you were last. You're here to look for the missing children and take us all on an adventure."

Tabor stared at her and whistled slowly. "You made friends with a Seer?" he asked. "She's someone who could be useful, Spark." He held out a hand to Marisa. "I'm Tabor, Fateh's friend."

"Friends, maybe." She gave him a quizzical look and took his hand. "You hold one end of a chain which connects you both. His hands can be on the chain as well, but he chooses to defer to you." She gave him a dreamy look. "Your hold on the leash is light and held with affection. Fateh may not see you as a friend, but you want to see him as much more."

Tabor turned red. "Forget what I said, Seers are a pain in the ass." He released her hand in a hurry. "They See too much and are entirely too willing to spill everything."

Fateh snickered. "Etana said much of the same thing." The insinuation didn't bother him, Tabor grew on him and Fateh was willing to admit he felt some sort of affection for Tabor. He wasn't as bad as he seemed at first; the betrayal of not knowing of his fae nature had passed. He could fall back into the camaraderie he had when they first met.

"Yes, and it doesn't change the fact it's embarrassing to have your secrets spilled." Tabor shot back. "Girl. What's your name?"

"Marisa." She brushed off her skirts; she wore as many layers as she wore when she was in the prison. A scarf still hid her hair, even if wisps of it escaped to fly in her face. "I will go with you on your mission to gather allies and enemies alike."

"Wow, I didn't even have to ask." Fateh raised an eyebrow. "How long were you waiting for us?" He couldn't rid himself of the image of Marisa hanging out on the steps for days on end, waiting for Fateh to come back to Caergybi.

"Since today." She shrugged. "The stars said last night you would return in the shadow of the town and come to search. I know where everyone is. You'll want me along. You need a human to hold the weapons you need to fight the Shadows."

"Who's to say I'm not human?" Fateh demanded, feeling a chill go down his spine. "I could..."

Marisa shook her head. "The fire inside of you has grown." She rested a hand on Fateh's. "It was like sparks before, shiny and sparkly and glittery. Now it's more like a wildfire, waiting to break free and consume everything in its path." She patted his hand. "It came loose from you once before, but with Tabor helping you, the firestorm can be controlled."

"I---" Fateh found himself speechless and sharing Tabor's sentiment about Seers. It had unnerved him when Marisa had seen the fire inside of him before. He hadn't known what she meant then. It was another thing for her to know about the fire nearly consuming him when he had his nightmare. "We appreciate your help."

"Of course you do. But you can't say thank you for me lending a hand, but I understand." She twirled around, once, twice and then faced the both of them again. "Some of whom you seek have traveled, others have made their nests here.

Do not seek out Jonathan, he's too wet for you to go near. He'll put your fire out without you even knowing, without him even trying."

"We weren't planning to go to Mokosh's pond." Fateh shuddered at the thought of it. "I plan to avoid the pond as much as possible." He nearly drowned--and Marisa? Had she been caught in the water or had she seen the pathway out before the water closed in?

She saw his look and she gave him a serene smile. "I didn't float or drown in the water. I went outside our prison walls when the water closed in and took so many of our companions." Her eyes were wide. "I told you your sparkle was going to go out. Why did you stay?"

"I didn't expect it to happen so fast!" Fateh protested. "No one did, or else we all probably would have escaped." He felt a pang of sadness for those who didn't make it out. It wasn't like he had been friends with them, but he hadn't wanted them to drown by Mokosh's hands, either.

"Still, Jonathan saved you and now he swims to his heart's content in the cold, cold waters with only Mokosh to keep him company." She tugged on his arm. "Let's go and find others before the Shadows grow stronger and consume more than just your town. They're like ink on paper, bleeding into everything."

Fateh shuddered at the premonition. "You know where the others are?" he asked. "Do you know where Randi is?"

Her expression grew solemn. "She is caught in the same trap she was before; the sun holds her captive and the trolls more still. You'll have to face the king to take her back." She placed her hands behind her back. "The sun is your friend and enemy of the trolls. Fire can crack stone if it's hot enough."

"Good to know." Fateh shuddered at the idea of facing trolls. They were a fae he read about, but not experienced in his town. Randi said it was for the best.. Now he planned to go into their territory and face them to save a friend. She had been his friend while in the prison and she deserved saving.

"Well, let's see the people in town first." Fateh ran a hand through his hair. "We'll gather as many people as we can and then we'll go from there."

"They might not want to leave their nests." Marisa warned. "They're safe here, even if they are watched. Going into the vipers nest will only scare them; they see no value in risking their skins when they have nothing to offer."

"I'm all about not scaring people." Fateh kept his tone evenly measured. "I don't want to drag Mari into the Shadows; she was..." She had been a pet, a living doll for the fae to play with. It would be cruel to drag her into the nest of Shadows when terror would be all she felt.

"She is content where she is. You'll find your friends for your mission further along than the pathways of this town." She held out her hand, smiling brightly at Fateh. "I have to grab my bag of tricks and I'll be ready to go."

Fateh didn't ask what 'tricks' she would be bringing, he wasn't sure he wanted to know. It could just be clothing; it could be scraps of metal which would burn him if he decided to stick a hand in her bag. "We'll wait for you."

"I know you will, You won't get far without me to lead the way. The trolls are closer than you think, though." She left with them as she went inside the house and Fateh wondered how close they were to danger.

"Are you ready to face trolls?" Fateh asked Tabor. "I know we talked about this before, but now it's a reality--"

"I know how to face down trolls. Fire can work, but it'll work better if we have a sledgehammer for the daytime. At night, you have to be quick. It's when they're awake and at their strongest."

"Marisa said fire can crack stone if it's hot enough," Fateh said slowly. "If we combine our power--" Fateh gave a self-deprecating laugh. He didn't even know how to control his power, much less combine it with someone else's.

"I'll teach you how to reach for your power before we go facing trolls," Tabor promised him with a reassuring smile. "I won't leave you defenseless." He jerked his head towards the house. "We'll have to go the long way around, though. We can't take a human through the shadows. She may be strange, but she's not fae."

"Not going on the shadow roads is fine by me." Fateh stuck his hands in his pockets. "I told you, I'd rather walk than use the shadows. I don't know where they lead and unless it's going to Etana's, it could be going right into a trap."

"I only have pathways to friends, so no worry about ending up in a nest of Shadows." Tabor patted Fateh on the head. "So I don't mind the overland route as well, It's fraught with its own dangers, but we'll get to see more that way. The world outside your town is vast, little Spark. You're going to find out how wide it is."

"I've already been to the other side of the world.'" Fateh pointed out. "I think I'm getting the picture." Still, he hadn't been to so many places. Wakana was the furthest he had ever been from home and he hadn't explored as much as he could have. He stuck close to Etana's, afraid his magic would get out and he'd out himself and hurt someone at the same time.

"You have no idea."

He hadn't been able to say anything more before Marisa came back out of the house, a bag slung over her back. It wasn't as big as Fateh thought it would be and he was glad Marisa decided to pack lightly. It would be easier if they were going to be on the move a lot.

"We should find a safe place to practice your fire." Marisa said without preamble. "The trees won't appreciate it if you practice in their domain and Sam would be most displeased if you hurt the trees. They will never come with you if you set the forest afire."

"How did you know I needed to practice?" Fateh asked, then shook his head. Marisa Saw it, of course. He didn't know why he bothered asking.

"I'm sure we'll find a place which doesn't contain trees." Fateh said, looking back up at Tabor for an answer.

"I'll find a place, Spark, don't you worry. It's important you learn control before going to face an enemy. I don't want to see you squashed flat because you rushed in to rescue a friend before you could fight."

"Good. Let's get going. The sooner I won't accidentally set myself on fire, the better." He looked at Marisa. "You're sure you want to come with us?" he asked. "The Shadows are dangerous."

"Danger is what danger is and it's best to stop the Shadows before they spread to places even I can't escape." Marisa gave him a comforting smile. "I know what I'm walking into, but I know by the end of it, we won't be walking alone."

The tension bled out of Fateh's shoulders at her words. Whatever happened, he wouldn't be fighting by himself. He didn't know who would come with him or what they would offer, but he would have people by his side to face the enemy.

***

They didn't find anyone else in town who wanted to come with them. As Marisa said, the people who survived the pond were happy where they were and didn't want to go into enemy territory. Being near Mokosh's pond was bad enough. They heard plenty about the Shadows from Fateh and didn't want to deal with it.

Chapter Six

Fateh kept Marisa's words in mind. They wouldn't be alone in the end. He didn't know how long it would take to gather everyone or who they would be, but he had a feeling it would be more than Sam and Randi.

They made their way to an abandoned part of town and Tabor stopped and directed Fateh toward a side of cinder-block houses. "Here's where we'll practice. You won't burn down the town and you'll see what your fire does to stone at the same time. It's a win-win situation."

With a worried expression, Fateh looked at Marisa, fearing the fire would spread and harm her. He had no idea what he was doing, and it was too simple to get out of his control.

"You won't burn me." Marisa's confidence showed in her words and tone. "You'll get a hang of it faster than you think." Still, she stayed well out of the way of the houses and Fateh's uncertain aim.

Tabor stood behind Fateh, resting his hands on his shoulders. "Feel the fire inside of you. Don't be scared of it. I know it's hard, but you can't be scared of yourself. You'll never gain control if you don't trust it."

Fateh nodded, but still worried. Fire could be both terrifying and comforting at the same time and he tried to hold onto the comforting feeling. The fire couldn't hurt him, and he could use it to help others. He imagined the fire inside of him; it was a part of him, Tabor said.

He held out his hands, wanting to form the fire there, acting like some sort of wizard preparing to do a fireball spell. Thinking of creating a spell, he acted out the motions before when he was younger and played D&D with his friends. He never thought he would do it for real.

Slowly, a small ball of fire appeared in his hands and he beamed at Tabor, grateful it was small and not some huge fireball which could engulf them both.

"Good job, Spark." Tabor praised him, squeezing his shoulders. "Can you make it bigger without losing it? That little bit of fire isn't going to hurt a troll and it's what we're facing next."

Fateh made a face and bit his lip. "I'm not sure. Making this is hard enough." The fire rested in his cupped hands, swirling a bit and sending warmth racing through his body. It energized him and he took a deep breath. He could do this. He concentrated and imagined the fireball growing larger. He added more heat to the fire, swirling it around as he formed a bigger ball. It suddenly grew too large and he panicked, throwing it away from him. It smacked into the nearest house and smoldered against the wall. It blackened, but nothing caught fire.

"People build fire pits out of stone and brick and cinder blocks." Tabor observed. "It'll take more than a runaway fireball to damage these houses." He sounded pleased with Fateh. "Look at you, creating fire on your first try, and hitting a target besides."

"I threw it like a baseball." Fateh looked at where the fire went out, shaking his head. "I thought I was going to catch fire again. I just wanted to get rid of it."

"Don't discount what you did." Tabor scolded him. "You just did something against what you've always known. So what if it got a little out of control? You're not going to do it perfectly the first time. I'd be surprised if you did."

"I guess so." Fateh concentrated on his hands again, twirling them around to grow a new fireball. He drew on his imagination and his childhood and smiled to himself at how jealous his friends would be that he could create a real fireball.

His smile faltered a moment later. If they didn't run me out of town and tried to burn me with metal first.

Fateh decided not to think about being harassed and threatened by his friends, and instead focused on what he the now. He was a—what did Tabor say? An aodhamair and could create fire to save Randi and the people in his town. Not all of them had been involved in killing his mother, there were so many innocents. Fateh could save them, but didn't know what he would do when faced with those who changed his life forever, like Meira and Tobias.

The fire grew exponentially at the thought of his old friends and Fateh struggled to hold it. He didn't want to keep losing control. Fearing the fire would spread and hurt Marisa, Fateh couldn't keep the fear out of his eyes. At least Tabor wouldn't get hurt from catching on fire.

He finally closed his hands around it, putting it out entirely. He looked back up at Tabor, panting slightly. It was hard work, controlling the fire. It wanted to rage and spread.

"You're doing good work." Tabor ruffled Fateh's hair. "Let's take a break, breathe. You don't have to do everything at once." He looked down at Fateh, bemused. "Why a fireball, though?" he asked. "Creating a flame would be easier to control."

Fateh turned red. "I always wanted to make a fireball." He confessed. "I used to play a game when..."

"Ah, yes." Tabor grinned widely. "Wasn't there also an anime with a character who used a fireball?" Tabor paused and then shouted. "Fireball!" He threw his hand out and a fireball appeared and he flung it toward the nearest house. After a whooshing sound, the wall collapsed on itself, smoldering from the force of the fireball Tabor created.

"You want to explode the trolls."

Fateh was too busy staring at him. "You know what anime is?" he demanded. "I didn't think you knew something like anime."

"I haven't lived under a rock my entire life. I have interests outside of tormenting you." Tabor grinned widely at Fateh's open-mouthed surprise. "Is it so shocking I'd like such a human thing?"

"I didn't think you had the time, honestly." The idea of Tabor sitting down and watching anime was an image too bizarre to contemplate. Fateh shook his head to clear it of the picture and instead focused on the broken wall instead. "Hate to see what you'd do if you used Dragon Slave."

"Oh, we'll work up to such powerful attacks." Tabor winked. "For now, let's stick to a single fireball. It'd take too long to do the incantation if you wanted to do Dragon Slave. You save the attack for when you have time."

"You're acting like I've memorized it or something." Fateh raised an eyebrow at Tabor. "It's not like I'm that big of a nerd."

"Yet you want to create fireballs like some magic wielding hero from one of your games." Tabor laughed at the indignant look on Fateh's face. "You forget, I've been in town since before the Shadows appeared and messed everything up for you. I've seen some of those games that you're referencing." He smirked at Fateh. "You're a big nerd, admit it."

"It's fun and it helps me visualize what I'm creating." Fateh defended himself. He held out both his hands, trying to create fire in both of them. He wanted to learn fast, he wanted to be strong enough to fight trolls and not get 'squashed' as Tabor said. Fateh wished he had the sledgehammer Tabor talked about. It would be much easier to break the rocks the trolls turned into. Fire sprouted in both palms and he gave a pleased grin, letting them go out. In a way, it was enjoyable; knowing he would utilize this ability to save Randi was helpful.

Marisa clapped nearby, clearly impressed with the both of them and not showing a hint of fear. "Wonderful!" She called out. "I knew you could do more than just sparkle, Fateh."

Fateh blushed and waved the compliment off. Having someone other than Tabor or Etana felt peculiar. He couldn't help but think how strange a human was watching him. *When did I start separating himself from the humans when I remain partially human?* Fateh drooped a little, uncertain all over again.

"It's okay, Spark. Take a breath. You're adjusting just fine. Just take this one step at a time." Tabor wrapped an arm around Fateh's shoulders and turned him around, looking down into his face. "Think about how much fun you were having. Don't think fire is a bad thing."

"I forgot about my humanity." Fateh admitted quietly. "I...I thought about Marisa and her being human and forgot about myself. There was only the fire."

"Humans get scared, so you don't want to think about your humanity."

"And aodhamair don't?" Fateh scoffed. He knew Tabor was scared of the Shadows, he just didn't show it like everyone else did. They did something horrible to him, He and Etana hinted at but didn't elaborate on.

"Of course we get scared." Tabor rolled his eyes. "But we have weapons to use when we're scared. We have the fire we can not only we can use as a weapon, but can create shields out of fire to protect ourselves."

"Let's do protection next, then," Fateh said decisively. "I want to learn more than creating fireballs and I have a feeling we'll need fire shields when we're facing the trolls."

"It's a good assumption to make." Tabor nodded. "It won't stop you from getting stepped on, but it'll protect you from their magic. They can't use fire against you." He considered Fateh for a moment. "I think we need to create lightning."

"Lightning?" Fateh blinked up at him. "You think-- oh, wait. There's a legend trolls run from lightning."

"Exactly." Tabor smiled at him and Fateh felt a little flutter at Tabor being so proud of him. He knew things which would help him fight and if he could harness his powers correctly, he could do more than just cower behind Tabor.

"Let's do this." He looked towards Tabor for guidance. Fateh had a feeling all he would produce would be sparks when he first tried for lightning and he wasn't disappointed when it seemed more like sparklers appeared rather than lightning bolts.

"It's going to take you longer to create lightning, but we have days to work on this. We'll take breaks for eating and sleeping, but by the time we leave here, you'll be able to produce your own lightning."

"What about fire tornadoes?" Fateh suddenly asked. "I've read about those; they create their own weather."

"You don't think small, do you?" Tabor whistled. "Yes, there are fire tornadoes. I'm not sure you're ready for something as large as a fire tornado and we don't want to hurt anyone in town if your tornado gets out of control and decides to break free of your control."

"You have a point." They weren't far from the populated part of town, after all. This was a section that had been left for reasons unknown. It could be anything from Mokosh's reach to other fae who decided to take over and then left again. "Okay, let's work on lightning first."

Fateh bounced from accepting to denying his power; it almost made him dizzy with the way his feelings switched. He had to accept this, he couldn't accept this-- he needed to make up his mind. If he didn't accept this, then he'd never be able to save his friends and save his town.

"I know I have a point." Tabor grinned. "Listen to your elder in fire magic." He gripped Fateh's hands, pouring fire through them, stretching it out so his hands formed lightning. "Feel what it's like to hold lightning."

Fateh watched as lightning formed in his hands, a small ball of it, like how he started with the fireball. "You're doing this, not me."

"Yes, but you can feel the difference between fire and lightning." Tabor said firmly. "You can do this, you need to do this. Fire is one tool, lightning is another. Both are valuable."

"Aren't we going too fast?" Fateh asked. "I don't think I'm ready to start throwing lightning yet."

"You will be by the time I'm done with you." Tabor promised. "It's not as hard as you think it is. It's another form of fire, just more concentrated. It's fire from the sky, using air and heat together."

"Okay." Fateh took a deep breath and tried to pull out lightning, but all that came out was more fire.There were big sheets of fire, instead of the small lightning he had been going for. He absorbed the fire with a frustrated huff, not even realizing what he did until he finished.

"I just set myself on fire, didn't I?" he asked Tabor, who looked at him with amusement.

"You certainly did." Tabor laughed. "And it felt good, hm? You don't have to be scared about setting yourself on fire anymore. You know it won't hurt you."

"Yeah, I guess you're right." Fateh took a deep breath and cupped his hands again, determined to master this. He might be here all day and into the night, but he would get this. Randi was depending on him.

Chapter Seven

It took several days, complete with napping in the remains of houses, before Fateh could produce a credible strip of lightning. It wasn't as large as his fireballs were, but he found he could combine the two, for something truly frightening in its ferocity. Even Tabor was impressed and said as much.

"You're going to be a force of nature, Spark." Tabor looked pleased at his progress. "All those gaming sessions of yours as a kid paid off."

"Would you stop bringing them up?" Fateh groaned. "I get it, I was a nerd, okay? I had fun imagining being able to do magic and now I can do it, it's something I have to get used to."

He could only produce fire and lightning, though. Any great feats of magic were beyond him, so he couldn't quite live out his fantasies of being a wizard and using magic spells. "We're not the great fae, Spark." Tabor shrugged and sat cross-legged on the ground in front of Fateh. "We can't do magic the way they can, but we can produce illusions out of fire."

Tabor began producing balls of flame, juggling them and then doing something to twist their shape and create birds of fire. "Simple party tricks, but if you're ever invited to a fae gathering, they're amused at what we can do."

"Yeah, that'll be the day." Fateh snorted. "The only fae I saw were the lesser fae. The higher fae never came to town." And he was grateful for the fact he never saw the higher fae; he didn't know what he would do if he met one of them. The little ones were trouble enough.

"You may be surprised at what you find along the way." Tabor remained calm. "You could just as easily run into one of the higher fae as you would an elemental, once you really began looking. Get one of them on your side and you'll have better luck with the Shadows."

"You have some high hopes for me." Fateh tried to imitate Tabor's birds, but only produced more fireballs instead. "I can't do as much as you can." He sounded disappointed he failed to keep up.

"And I would be dreadfully disappointed to find out all my years of work could be discounted by a prodigy in under a week." Tabor flashed him a grin, producing a wavering image of a person out of the flame. It was different shades of fire; blue and white and gold. Fateh couldn't even create a hotter fire yet, though it wasn't for a lack of trying. "You'll get there, Fateh. You have to keep practicing."

"We don't have time for me to keep practicing, though." Fateh made a frustrated face. "Randi is in trouble now, the people in my town--"

"Hold off on thinking about the people in the place you lived. You're nowhere near ready for something like going back home." Tabor was dead serious. "You'll be snatched up and sucked dry before you know it. The Shadows don't play around. You need strength in numbers to fight them."

"And more than Marisa's bag of tricks." Fateh agreed. "I know, I know--but am I least ready enough to fight the trolls for Randi?" He didn't relish the idea of burning the trolls while they were still flesh and bone; it turned his stomach to imagine burning anything alive. But a few well placed lightning strikes to crack stone in half, maybe one of the larger, more destructive fireballs Tabor wielded.

"I'll teach you how to make stronger fire first." Tabor compromised. "I'll teach you how to do the hottest. The type where you can melt stone."

Fateh gulped at the idea of holding so much power, but nodded. "I guess it's the next logical step." He brushed his hands off on his pants and faced Tabor, who stood up behind him again, resting his hands on his.

"One breath, imagine how hot a fire can get." Tabor lowered his voice as he instructed Fateh and he listened; remembering Tabor's fire and wondered if he could even produce such a powerful flame with him only being half fae. He knew fire; it was a part of him and in his dreams he could produce wonders.

Slowly, bit by bit, the fire increased in intensity in his hands, glowing first orange, then white and then finally blue. In the end, he held a small globe of blue fire and he threw it at the wall of the house with all the force he could muster, causing a smoking hole to appear. He stunned even himself.

"See, you don't need the incarnation to do damage." Tabor wrapped a hand around Fateh's shoulders in a one-handed hug. "You're producing miracles, Spark."

"Guess I can do it." Fateh rubbed his hands together to get rid of the lingering heat and beamed up at Tabor. "You think I'm ready now?"

"You're so eager to throw yourself into danger. Remember, you have to guard your Seer friend of yours as well as rescue the little troll bride."

"Their names are Randi and Marisa, which you know." Fateh said, nettled. "It's not a bad thing to remember people's names. For instance, I'm Fateh, not Spark,"

"But it's so much more fun to assign names to people than use their real ones. It's only polite in some circles, after all. For instance, you'll never use my true name and I'll never use yours. Spark is something only I'll call you, no one else."

"And should I be grateful for the privilege?" Fateh snorted. "Just use my name once in a while, so I know you know it."

"Ab, but Spark, I like my little nickname for you. You turn such interesting colors when I use it."

"Whatever," Fateh shook his head and turned to Marisa. "Have you Seen enough to know if we're going to succeed?" he asked. Sometimes asking her a direct question got direct answers and she observed them playing with fire for days. Her watching them had to induce something in her Seer abilities.

"Your spark won't go out if you face the rocks and not the trolls." Marisa said calmly. "If you face the trolls head on, it will be a much more fierce battle and you'll forever hold the image of what it's like to use your fire against a living creature."

"No thanks.' Fateh shuddered at the image. Rock would be harder to destroy, but he could do it. The only thing was Randi. She could be so far gone as to actually turn to stone in the sunlight as well? If she turned to stone in the sunlight, they would have to travel by night, carefully protecting her during the day.

"The bride is weaker by the sun, but the sun doesn't hold her still." Marisa twirled around. "She is strongest at night, capable of hurting the troll king himself if she was so inclined, but the sun saps her strength until all she wants to do is stay still."

"I hope that by breaking the troll king, it'll break their hold on her and she'll be more free." Fateh didn't know how it would work, he could only guess.

"She'll always be weaker by daylight, it's in her nature now." Tabor shrugged. "But she'll be a powerhouse at night. It may be good to move at night sometimes to harness her strength."

"Huh." Fateh considered her words and then nodded. "Alright, enough with the fireballs, Let's go find us a Randi."

"I think you're ready for almost anything." Tabor agreed. "It'd help if we had more allies before facing trolls, but you're determined to save your friend."

"Where would I pick up more allies?" Fateh asked. "It's not like I have a homing beacon which leads me to other fae kids. Marisa knows where the trolls are."

"I know where other sparks are, too." Marisa offered. "Not as sparkly as you, but they shine in other ways. I can find them for you." She fell into a moment of silence. "Our prison wasn't the only one to hold the shiny ones. There are many more out there than you can imagine. Tabor is right, you need more allies before facing down such an implacable enemy."

"But—" Fateh wanted to save Randi before she got even more entrenched in the trolls, but if Marisa and Tabor were both saying they needed more help, then he supposed they should wait and see what allies they could conjure up.

"Okay, where do we go find the shiny ones?" he asked Marisa. "Can you See where they are?" He tried not to show his frustration; what had all the practice been for if not to face down the trolls?

"Not as far as you think." Her scarves fluttered around her face, the wind catching the ends of them. "But we'll have to traverse the darkness to get to the light."

"Tabor said you couldn't travel the shadows." Fateh protested and looked up at Tabor, who was eyeing Marisa with an interested look.

"You think you can travel the shadow paths?" Tabor asked her seriously. "It'll make things easier if you can travel them and find a pathway out of them to where we need to go. I don't know much about Seers, except they see through the illusions we cast."

"I can open a path in the dark." She said, complacent. "This way it's not as dark as it could be and the pathway to where we need to go will be much easier to see." She wrinkled her nose. "I can't travel the dark alone, but with someone who knows the paths--"

"I don't have pathways everywhere, you know." Tabor said in amusement. "Are you sure you can light the way so we won't get lost in the darkness?"

"It's part of what a Seer does." She looked up at him calmly. "Trust me and I'll trust you and together we'll get Fateh to where he needs to be to gather those who are willing to help."

"Alright, little Seer." Tabor held out a hand to both her and Fateh. "Let's step into the darkness together." He indicated a patch of shadow cast by the lee of the house they were practicing against. "I've never traveled with a full human before."

"I'm not human, I'm a Seer." She raised both eyebrows at him. "You have to trust my light will guide us out of the dark."

"Let's go, then," Fateh suggested, tugging the two of them towards the shadows. They were inert, but Fateh could almost see the opening in them that would allow them to travel. His eyes could have been playing tricks on him.

"Alright, let's go." Tabor tugged them both into the shadows and this time instead of things turning on their head and it being a nothingness between two points, there was a light that shone all around Marisa, illuminating a path for them to follow.

Tabor looked astonished at Marisa, then just shook his head and followed the light to where it led them. It never took long to travel in the shadows, but they were cold and before now, pure darkness. Only minutes passed by before they were stepping into a completely different part of the world. The fae had obviously touched this place. There were their marks all around, in the sight of crumbling buildings where houses once stood.

"Guess we're in the right place." Fateh pointed towards a building off in the distance, surrounded by thick greenery. "I sure hope this place isn't held by a water fae."

"I don't sense them here, so we're relatively safe. I hope no fae at all holds this place and it's just a collection the humans started, not knowing what they have." Fateh didn't hold up high hopes for not being held by a fae, anything that held strong against the onslaught of the fae had to have a patron in some way.

He was making his way towards the building, Marisa and Tabor close behind when a familiar voice called out to them.

"Fateh?"

Fateh turned at the sound of Sam's voice, plainly astonished. "How did you get here?" He asked. "Where is here?"

"You're in my forest." Sam gestured with wide arms to the expanse all around them. "And as to how I got here, all forests are one forest if you're attuned to them enough." They looked at Fateh critically. "Glad you got out of the water, but something about you has changed."

"Where is your forest?" Fateh asked. "I've traveled all the way to New Zealand, so you can't surprise me."

"Even if I told you were now in Japan?" Sam asked with a grin. "You're going to become a regular world traveler, Fateh. You'll have to tell me how you got to New Zealand, you're not attached to the forests like I am."

"Good thing I know some Japanese." Fateh was two years out of lessons, having not been able to take classes since the Shadows took over, but he practiced for years after his lessons were over. He would speak Japanese with his mother, and with Meira and Tobias, much to their amusement.

"You can learn languages quickly with your fire." Tabor observed. "You can absorb it. Maybe that's why you were so inclined to learn a language in the first place. I bet you were better at it than you thought."

"Never thought I'd need it for more than watching anime." Fateh shook his head. "Guess it's a good thing I decided to learn the language."

"Aw, look, anime does have a purpose other than rotting your brain." Tabor smirked.

"Shut up, you admitted you watch anime, too." Fateh shot back.

Sam looked between all of them, a bemused expression on their face. "So you're friends with one of the actual fae, Fateh? Good for you. I made friends in the forest, too. The other gwyrddni are welcoming and have taught me a lot."

"So you've accepted you're half fae?" Fateh asked with interest.

"I've known it since I left the prison." Sam confirmed. "Had a suspicion before we left. We were all too weird to not have something wrong with us."

Marisa giggled. "Nothing wrong with shine and sparkle and the quiet spaces in between."

"Marisa, glad to see you're here, too. You always had words of wisdom for the rest of us, even if we realized it too late."

"You've grown and spread your roots." Marisa gave him a solemn look. "Are those roots up to traveling? We have a plan and it involves gathering as many people as possible to help rid Fateh of the Shadows which plague his town."

"The Shadows are a nuisance." Sam made a face. "They're spreading further than their origin point, which seems to have been your town, Fateh. If we get rid of them there---they'll stop. I'm for it, if you're willing to have me." They looked shy all of a sudden. "Not sure what help I'll be, but I'll do what I can."

"You can turn the trees and the ground against them." A new voice spoke up, stepping from between the trees and looking at Sam with fondness. "Your power with the trees and plants of the forest is more powerful than you know."

"This is Kikoumi," Sam bowed slightly to the tall and willowy forest spirit. "She lives here and has been taking care of me." Kikoumi's face was seamed with wrinkles and she looked as weathered as an ancient tree.

"I'm not the only one with the care of Sam." Kikoumi exuded serenity. "There are others of our kind who look after them." She spoke English with an accent. Fateh tried to show his gratitude. He was still getting over the shock of seeing Sam again and with them knowing what they were.

"You're awfully accepting of this." Fateh said bluntly. "It took me longer.."

"You had a much more dramatic awakening, I'm sure." Kikoumi said with a smile. "Fire tends to get out of hand quickly. The forest is slower, less inclined to rouse itself to a fury. The trees are patient."

"Guess you got lucky." Fateh observed. "I got raging fires and you got a religious experience."

"Not quite like a religious experience, but I suppose it's a fair comparison." Sam's grin was quick. "But isn't there something about being baptized by fire?"

"If so, I think I'm fully set for a long time. "Fateh shuddered."I don't need to go through being set on fire again."

"You'll burn much brighter than you have before." Marisa bushed her hands over her skirts and smiled up at Fateh. "You won't burn out, though. Tabor will make sure of your shine."

"Have any prophecies for me?" Sam asked. "I miss hearing your dire portents about what's going to happen to us."

"You're going to sprout and grow like a massive tree." Marisa faced Sam now. "You'll be a walking forest, able to travel paths we cannot, but you will always have a home in the forest."

"Glad to know." Sam saluted Marisa, who gave them a bright smile in return. "Now what's this about going to the Sanctuary? Planning a jailbreak?"

"Something like a jailbreak." Fateh shrugged. "I hope I'd find them in town, while they were on a day off and try and convince them. They can't want to stay in a place they're forced to."

"They aren't fae at all, but Japanese spirits or spirit-touched, hurt by the yokai, and are looking for a haven. We try to make it as safe a place as possible for them, but..."

"But if they go beyond the boundary of the forest, we don't know what's waiting for them." Kikoumi said solemnly. "I hate to lose any of our children on a wild adventure, but if they agree, I'm sure you'll find them strong companions."

"You watch over the prison?" Fateh asked in surprise.

"We don't call it a prison." Sam corrected Fateh. "It's a school, a safe haven. The forest protects them."

"Well, we'll see who we can find who's willing to take a trip." Fateh looked towards the large building, running a hand through his hair. This might be a good place and the forest fae might have good intentions, but it was still a place where they were locked up.

"Do they wear metal?" Fateh asked. "Or are they free from what can scar them?"

"We don't have any iron in the forest." Kikoumi wrinkled her nose. "But we also aren't as scarred by it as you are. I am telling you the home we offer is a safe place. The children can leave any time they want. I'll have Sam show you to the front doors, even."

Fateh held back disbelief after his own experience, but perhaps Kikoumi and Sam were right. He might not find anyone here willing to leave the safe boundaries of the forest, but he wanted to try.

Chapter Eight

The sanctuary, as Sam called it, was a low building surrounded by towering trees, closing in the place. The sun barely peeked through the foliage of the trees and Fateh hunched his shoulder, feeling very small. Sam showed how much they were in their element, perfectly at home and looking more content than Fateh remembered them being before.

"Visitors?" Someone called out from the front of the building. Fateh understood the Japanese. "How lovely."

Fateh looked up at the girl in front of him and blinked. There were two fluffy ears on top of her head and a fluffy tail. "Hello?" he asked, hesitantly in Japanese. "I'm Fateh. This is Tabor and Marisa."

"I am Hana." The girl bowed to Fateh, who gave a clumsy bow back. "What brings you here to our fair home?"

"We're looking for companions." Fateh's words were measured and probably only halfway correct,, but Hana seemed to understand him. "We're fighting the Shadows."

She recoiled at the name. "They are evil." She hissed. "They create a blight across the fields and forest alike, till everything in their path is nothing but darkness." To Fateh's intense surprise, he understood everything she said. No matter what Tabor said about being able to understand languages, it was one thing to hear about it and another to see it working.

"Their evil is why we want to fight them." Fateh spread his hands out. "If you can walk the shadows, we have a pathway to lead us to them and their nest of vipers."

"This is a big thing you ask of strangers." She held open the door. "Won't you come inside so we won't be strangers any longer? You can introduce yourself to the other residents of the house and see if you have anyone who will be willing to come with you."

"What about you?" Fateh asked boldly. "What can you do against the Shadows?" He noticed Hana had taken off her shoes before she went inside and he followed suit. He didn't want to drag mud inside.

"I am blessed by the gods themselves." Hana spoke serenely. "I can bring down storms on them so there are no shadows for them to hide and they are exposed. I have killed such Shadows before, but never a nest of them." She gave him a look as she led the group down the hallway to the main room. "But I have not said I will be helping you."

"True, you haven't, but a kitsune wants to make mischief and what better mischief is there than in upsetting a regime?" Sam asked. "I'm going; I thought you and Haruki might both want to go."

"Leaving will be up to Haruki, if he thinks it's wise to leave our own nest for dangers well-known."

Fateh blinked as the pieces fell into place. "You're a kitsune." He was vaguely ashamed he hadn't figured it out before this; the ears and tail should have given it away immediately. He wasn't used to Japanese fox spirits; there were none in Wales and so his grandparents didn't have an emphasis on studying them. They touched on them, in case Fateh ever encountered the yokai, but his grandparents only made an extensive list on fae that were 'native' to Wales.

"Of course I'm a kitsune. I never said anything different. I would have thought my nature obvious." She swished her tail from side to side, obviously proud of it. "Kitsune are beloved of Inari; we protect the rice crops and protect travelers." She eyed Fateh. "Maybe I will come with you. You will need a kitsune's luck on the paths you walk."

"We already have one Seer, we don't need another spouting cryptic words." Tabor groaned. "Spare me."

"You are not open to words of wisdom?" Hana teased wickedly. "I should think someone like you would appreciate knowing as much as possible. You look as if you do your own brand of mischief. That has to be tempered with wisdom or else it will be nothing but chaos."

"A little chaos is good." Tabor protested. "Believe me, I'm going to make sure things don't spiral out of control."

"You are a fire user, you would have had to learn control in the cradle." She cupped her hand and a blue flame appeared. "It seems we have something in common."

"You can light the dark paths as well," Marisa said approvingly. She had been quiet up until now, observing the house around them and the strange kids that peered at them from behind doorways and around corners. Some were showing horns and tails, others looked as ordinarily human as Marisa did. He blinked at the number of cats which were around. She obviously didn't understand the language, but she understood the intent of the words.

"Those are nekomata." Hana saw where his gaze turned and smiled. "There are a number of shapeshifters in this house and the cats are the most numerous of them. They like to travel in packs and keep close to each other. I doubt you will get a cat to go with you, but who's to say? Cats are contrary by nature and might go with you because I said they wouldn't."

"I like cats." Fateh reached out a hand to one of them, kneeling down. He didn't care if this was a shapeshifter, if they were cat enough to look like one, then they probably enjoyed pets just as much as an ordinary cat would. A tabby came up to him and nuzzled his hand. "We have cat shapeshifters where I come from as well, but I've never met them."

"You probably have and don't know it." Hana smiled indulgently. "They are the best at hiding in plain sight. If you get a cat to come with you, they make excellent spies."

"Can you change forms as well?" Fateh asked. "A wild fox will stand out more, but we are going to remote places before we go to my home."

"I can shapeshift into any form, even one of the Shadows." Hana's form shimmered and one of the Shadows stood there in her place, smokey and indistinct, the edges bleeding away. "It is how I infiltrated their number before and took them out with sacred fire."

"Can you please not?" Fateh asked, shuddering. He hadn't seen a Shadow in over a year. He hadn't quite forgotten how creepy they were, but he couldn't help but react to the strangeness of Hana changing into their form. "I'm not ready to see them quite yet."

"Although your talent will be very useful if you come with us." Tabor put in "Why not come with us for a bit of adventure?" he asked. "You'll get to see many other lands as we travel. The Shadows don't nest here; this way you get to see the world."

"I will think about it. For now, let us get acquainted with one another." Her form shimmered again and she went back to looking like the fox-eared girl she first appeared as. "Would you like some tea?"

More people came into the kitchen as Hana prepared tea, grabbing mugs and joking with each other. This place did seem like a sanctuary; maybe Fateh would have to travel further afield to find a place that wasn't so well-loved and filled with people who were safe. It couldn't be a stronger contrast to the prison he came out of.

"Do you stay here, Sam?" Fateh turned towards the other. "Or do you live among the trees?"

"I stay here occasionally. I still like to eat and Hana makes the best cup of tea in the area."

Hana spooned powder into the bowl in front of her, pouring a measured amount of water in with it. She whisked tea into a front as the others waited, a smile on her face. She seemed peaceful and relaxed and while Fateh would like to have her come with, she seemed perfectly content to stay here.

He wondered about the who and what of the mysterious Haruki, then a boy with dark black wings and a prominent nose came down the stairs, yawning and focused on Hana. She lit up when she saw him.

"Haruki!" She set aside the tea and swept the shorter male into a hug. "Were you sleeping the day away as usual?"

"You know me too well." Haruki said with a sheepish smile, then focused on Fateh, Marisa and Tabor. "We have visitors?" He spoke with a lilting accent and immediately switched to English when he saw Marisa wasn't understanding any of the conversation.

"We do indeed." Hana looked vaguely embarrassed. It seemed she hadn't realized Marisa would be ignorant of what they were saying and she switched to English as well. "They come from far away with a proposal to get rid of the Blight. But first, we are getting to know each other before we go on any strange adventures."

"Getting to know each other is a good idea." She moved back in front of the tea, inspected it and then began pouring it into the waiting cups. She poked at one boy who eagerly put a mug in front of her. "You wait until I make a second batch." She scolded him. "This is for our visitors first."

"But Haruki gets some."

"He is going to be listening to the proposal our visitors are making." Hana said calmly. "Plus, you know he is my favorite." Her tone was impish and without a hint of being self-conscious. "I will make tea for all of you after I speak with our new friends."

There were general grumbling about this, but each person assented and left the main room, leaving Hana and Haruki alone with Fateh, Tabor and Marisa.

"Now we drink tea and talk about where we began and how we came to be where we are now." She pointed to Tabor. "You seem like you have the most interesting story. Why don't we begin with you?" She sipped her tea. "It's best to know the whole story if we are to work with you."

"Not the way I wanted to spill my story to Spark here." Tabor made a face. "But I suppose it's best you all know about my ties to what you call the Blight."

Fateh perked up at this, he wasn't going first and grateful for it, but to know what happened to Tabor with the Shadows? Tabor had been closed-mouthed about.

"It's a short story, but not a pretty one." Tabor spread his hands. "I'll spare you the grisly details, but know this. I was once taken captive by the Shadows. They found me when I was young and vulnerable, without the allies I have now. They used me as one would use a toy, playing with me and taking my power bit by bit, every day." He grew quiet, shuddering as he relived those memories.

Fateh winced. This was the fate Tabor had said might befall him. He didn't know Tabor had been captured.

"I fortunately came across a metal-worker fae who was amenable to saving me and I escaped on the shadow-paths." Tabor shrugged. "Being young and stupid is how the Shadows found me. I'm stronger now and I'm ready to burn them out for what they've done to me and my family."

"How interesting...what made this metal working fae so important?" Hana asked.

"The Shadows are burned by it. ." Fateh provided. "I...me and Tabor, it doesn't do so well for us either."

"We don't have the same limitations with metal as you do. We're from the earth, so we can use it. We're not fae like you, we're yokai." Haruki took a sip of his own tea, making a pleased noise as he drank it.

"I brought metal to use as a weapon." Marisa held out her bag. "Maybe it will be best if you go in my stead. You can light the pathways and hold the metal that burns Fateh and Tabor."

"You are a Seer. We need you and your words of wisdom." Tabor looked at her in surprise. "You're invaluable, Marisa."

"You know my name." Her tone showed her surprise and she beamed up at him. "I thought you were allergic to names." She held out a hand to Tabor. "I'll still go with you if you want a human along."

Hana nodded at Tabor and looked at Fateh. "What is your story?" she asked. "I'm sure it's not as fraught with peril as Tabor's is."

"You may be surprised." Fateh muttered. "Up until three years ago, things were normal while I lived with my mother. One day while I was in town, the Shadows came and ate people. They consumed them with shadow while I watched. They destroyed the technology in town and left us without much of what we were used to." Fateh's eyes closed briefly. "There were contracts in our town, people would chain themselves to the Shadows for a bit of safety. One year ago, my mother decided to sign a contract and they killed her for itt."

"And where did you end up after such a tragedy?" Hana asked gently. "You did not come here, or else you'd still be here." She looked up at Tabor. "Maybe with your companion in tow, but you'd be in a safe place."

"I went to a place like this one, filled with half-fae children and some who were hurt by the fae, but it was a prison. We didn't have the safety you have here. We wore iron bracelets and we were harmed by the metal." He took a deep breath, trying to steady himself.

"But you got free and your power is obviously being nurtured so it can grow." She looked at Tabor. "He helps you control your power, as the other kami do for us."

"I nearly drowned. The fae who was watching over the place took it over and turned it into a pond." Fateh shuddered at the memory of all the water. He still remembered the near-drowning all too well.

"What are your plans before you fight the Shadows? Are you planning to go straight to your home on the pathways to fight or are you gathering more allies?"

"There's a friend we want to save first." Fateh said slowly. "Her name is Randi and she's been trapped by trolls for the last couple of weeks. They've held her in their thrall before and she got trapped again after we escaped from the prison together."

Haruki nodded. "Trolls sound like a worthy adversary."

"So you find yourselves here, with one who sees clearly." Hana looked toward Marisa next. "You are a companion on their travels, helping them to safe harbors and opening their eyes to dangers they would otherwise miss. I don't need to know your story, it's written all over your face."

"But it's a good story." Marisa said dreamily. "Filled with meeting people which sparkle and grow and swim like fishes. Fateh, Sam and I shared the prison Fateh spoke of. I saw the pathway out before the water closed in."

"Where were you before?' Fateh asked curiously. "You never said." The other kids shared what happened to them with the fae, but not Marisa. She instead just spouted prophecies and insinuations.

"When the fae came, I was with my family." She held out her hands. "I was much younger and knew the fae would consume us and wipe our kind out. So I tried to convince my family to run with me, but they laughed and said I had nightmares. I didn't want to be consumed by the dark, so I ran until I found the prison, with its iron walls and bracelets."

"You lost your entire family to the fae that took over?" Fateh asked, shocked. "What kind of fae were they?"

"I lived on the coast and the fae from the water came up onto land and drowned all who lived there. They expanded their territory, but erased ours." Marisa gave a faint shrug, as if it didn't bother her, but there was sadness in her eyes as she spoke of the family she lost. An entire community of people who didn't listen to her paid the price.

"Water fae are the worst." Fateh huffed, crossing his arms against his chest. "They don't realize the rest of us can't breathe underwater when they create their homes."

"Some of them were children, following in the wake of their parents. The oceans were poisoned, so they made fresh areas so their children grew up and had a chance to thrive." Marisa shook her head. "I wish we could have coexisted, but fear prevented both sides from trusting each other."

Everyone grew quiet after her story.

Chapter Nine

Fateh finally broke the uncomfortable silence, gesturing to Hana and Haruki, "What's your story?" he asked. "If we have to play show and tell, so do you."

"Like I said, kitsune are beloved of the gods; we are their messengers on earth. Some of us run into more mischief than others, but those are the yako. Those are cousins who cause harm to humans and other spirits." Her face closed off briefly. "I was living with my kitsune kin when a group of yako came and played a prank with fire that got out of hand. We all survived, but we scattered. I found my way here; my personal fire showed me the path to a sanctuary where I could live in peace and protect others of my kind." She shrugged. "They have since made a new home, but I am comfortable here and do not wish to go back at this time."

"I'm a tengu, one of the bird yokai." He offered. Haruki shrugged and explained, "My nest grew too small for so many mouths, so they set me free to fly where I wished and claim new territory. There were many dangers along the way, but I slew the enemies."

"And we've been together ever since." Hana dimpled at Haruki. "He is my protector and I do not go anywhere without him. With my fire to light the way and my illusions to confuse, he can slay the darkness that comes upon us."

"So will you come and help slay the Shadows for us?" Fateh asked. "The town I lived in got taken over by the Shadows and as far as I know, they're still there. Like I said, people died and others are under their control. I want to rid the world of the nest so they don't spread further."

"It's an interesting proposal. How does one slay shadow?" Haruki asked.

"You have to wait until they've fed." Tabor said softly. "Lives are going to be lost in the fight, but many more are going to be saved if we get rid of them."

"Are you offering yourself as a sacrifice or are you speaking for others that are not here?" Hana asked sharply. "Lives will be lost, yes, but there should be a choice in the matter."

"The other way is to find their base and cleanse it with fire, but I don't know if they'd be stupid enough to have their base where anyone could wander upon it." Tabor made a face, taking the chastisement. "It's sure to be guarded by the strongest of their kind. Again, it would be difficult to fight them."

"But that is why you are seeking allies with powers beyond your own, are you not?" Hana asked. "Maybe Haruki and I can lend an edge to the battle that your fire cannot do alone. There are many ways to defeat shadow; the easiest is to do it in the dark, where there are no shadows except what is cast by the light."

"You have a point there." Tabor looked interested in her words. "So based on knowing about us and learning our stories, are you willing to lend a hand'?"

Hana and Haruki exchanged a glance, asking each other without words what the other wanted to do. After a long silence, Haruki spoke up.

"We'll go with you, but we won't fight your Shadows until you have more companions and stronger magic to fight them with. You have the Earth with Sam, the air with Haruki, and fire with yourselves." She gave him a severe look. "As much as it pains all of you, you have to make amends with one of the water folk, or else you don't have the full range of power on your side."

Fateh made a face; he didn't want to deal with any more water fae. Mokosh has been bad enough. "Water puts out fire."

"So does the earth, yet you are still coming to us for help."

"The earth is also fuel for fire." Tabor put in. "But water is our nemesis."

"And air is the enemy of earth, yet I still work with Haruki and he is more than just my friend. We find ways to work together, to compromise. As long as you withhold your fire, the water will not drown you to put it out. You have lightning, do you not? Lightning on water kills all life within."

"I never thought of using lightning in the water." Fateh admitted. "But I got some control over lightning a few days ago. I don't think I could produce more than a sizzle on the water." It was nice to know he did have a weapon against water, however.

"Water is weak to Earth, so with us as a balancing force, you don't have to fear the water as much." Haruki put a hand on Fateh's and smiled at him. "We are allies, as air and fire work well together. But you need one of the water spirits as your friend as well."

Fateh thought of Jonathan, but he was happy in his pond and with Mokosh. He didn't want to go near all the water and the place where he nearly drowned just to see if Jonathan wanted to take a stroll outside the water. "What about the gwragedd annwn?" Fateh suggested to Tabor. "They come from lakes and rivers and they can walk without the need of drowning the world."

"The maidens?" Tabor considered the suggestion. "They're not vicious like some of the other water fae are. Having one of them as a companion might not be a bad idea." He grinned at Fateh. "They're known to take human men for lovers, though. You better watch out." It was obvious that he couldn't help but tease Fateh.

"I don't think I'm human enough to entice them." Fateh said flatly, producing a small ball of flame in his hands. Hana clapped her hands together at the sight.

"Marvelous. You are gaining impeccable control over your fire. Yes, you will be a good ally and if we can find these--" she made a face and waved her hand. "Forgive me, I cannot say the words you spoke. These 'maidens of the water' will suffice to be a good choice. You only need their power over water to protect you."

"Who would have thought fire would be protected by water of all things?" Fateh asked no one.

"Make yourselves comfortable in our home before we go on any travels. We have to let the household know of our decision so they are not left in the dark when we leave." Hana stood up gracefully, tail swishing from side to side. "This also gives them the opportunity to join us if they want to. Some of those who reside here were hurt by Shadows and it may entice them to fight for you."

"I'm not going to force anyone." Fateh was firm. "We appreciate you coming with us to fight."

"It should be an adventure and a chance to stretch my wings." Haruki said with a smile. "I look forward to the battle ahead."

Hana simply rested a hand on Haruki's shoulder and left the room, leaving him to show Fateh, Tabor and Marisa to rooms where they could stay in while they rested that night. Tabor insisted on staying with Fateh, just in case there were any accidents.

"This place is far more flammable than Etana's home." Tabor pointed out when Fateh protested the lack of privacy. "It's not been so long since you escaped your prison and only a year since you left your home under less than ideal circumstances. You might still have nightmares and I can put out a fire faster than you can."

"I'm not planning on going to sleep anytime soon." Fateh rolled his eyes. "It's daytime, after all. I think they just gave us rooms so we could relax in private without tripping over everyone in this place."

"Still." Tabor didn't budge. "I want to keep an eye on you, Spark."

"Can't you leave me alone for like a half an hour?" Fateh begged. "You've been in my pocket for the last week, I need a break. The prison let me have more privacy."

"When you put it that way, I suppose you have a point." Tabor patted Fateh on the head. "Alright, but no falling asleep on me. I don't want to wake up with the room in flames and you hysterical because you set yourself on fire again"

"Gods, you're such a mother hen. Cluck your way somewhere else for awhile. I need a moment to myself."

"Fine, fine." Tabor heaved a sigh as if it were a monumental thing Fateh asked. "I suppose I can give you your privacy. You deserve it after everything you've been through." He left Fateh alone.

Fateh flopped down on the bed, staring up at the interwoven branches of the ceiling. This place reminded him of a giant tree and he shook his head at the image of being trapped inside one of the great redwoods he read about that were in America. Not this early in the day, he wasn't going to sleep. He wanted to close his eyes and puzzle through everything that happened, everyone he met. From Etana's metal-covered body to Hana's ears and tail; he met a number of the strange and fantastical. He only read about them in stories. His life had taken a strange turn.

He wished his mother was here to see this, too see him interacting with so many fables. He wished he knew where his grandparents went; like Marisa, they were Seers and they left the town before the Shadows came. Like Marisa's family, he and his mother ignored their warnings and they paid the price for it.

He wondered if Marisa could find other Seers, if she could find his missing grandparents. He wanted to show his appreciation for them teaching him so much. It was because of them he survived as long as he did. If it wasn't for their teaching him 'fairy tales' he wouldn't have known how to survive against the Shadows.

Of course, the books he learned from never taught about Shadows. Numerous types of fae, both ill and good, existed. According to Etana and Tabor, they were closely linked to humans; the result of contracts gone sour.

Fateh had his doubts about fighting the Shadows, but if they gained enough elemental powers, could they honestly defeat them? The fire in him said to burn away the Shadows, overload them with fire until they evaporated under the strain, The human part of him remembered all too well the Shadows swallowing humans whole and dissolving them into darkness. He was terrified and wanted to stay here, safe among the trees, refusing to go back. Would it be so bad?

Then he thought of Randi, trapped by the trolls and unable to break free. They gathered more allies to save her, even if they had to stop by one of the lakes in Wales to find a gwragedd annwn. He didn't even know if Randi was still in

Wales. The trolls weren't native to Wales and they could have dragged her on the shadow roads to Finland for all he knew. His ambition was to explore the world, yet Fateh wondered if he would like every person he met. It wasn't likely; based on people he knew from home.

Hana and Haruki were okay, as was Etana, but trolls were definitely not on his list of things to see. But he would do it for Randi, who had been his friend through all Fateh's problems in the prison. She deserved better than to be taken by trolls.

Restless, he rose from the bed, resisting the urge to be comforted by sleep. He wanted to explore the house and meet residents to gauge their happiness. There might be others that were touched by Shadows and he could see if he could offer help.

As he left the room, one of the cats, who was lounging in the hallway, suddenly changed form. The cat transformed into a young man, similar in age to Fateh.

"So you're the one who wants to take away Hana and Haruki." He spoke without preamble, facing Fateh down, staring at him as if he could dig out all his secrets. "I don't like the idea of them leaving."

"It's their choice." Fateh defended himself. "They said they wanted to come and fight with me and my friends. They're allowed to make their own choices."

"But they're our friends, too. We don't want them hurt. They're safe here." The cat-person spoke rapidly and Fateh struggled to keep up.

"They want to get rid of the Shadows."

"The Shadows killed my family." The man spat. "There is nothing good about them."

"Why don't you come with us and keep an eye on Hana and Haruki and fight the Shadows yourself?" Fateh suggested. "You can take revenge on the Shadows that hurt your family."

"I already killed those Shadows, while they were still full from power they took from my family. It's harder than you think, the sword alone won't do it."

"Good thing we're going to have more than swords." Fateh tried to make his tone as casual as possible. "What's your name?"

"Akio."

"Well, Akio-- you're welcome to come and teach us what you're supposed to do when you fight the Shadows, or you can stay here in safety. I know which I'd pick." *Safety all the way. If I had a real choice, I'd stay here and never leave.*

"Can you promise I won't get hurt if I come with you?" Akio sounded small and scared and Fateh shook his head.

"I can't promise anything. I don't even know if I'll make it out of there alive." Fateh was nothing if not honest. He didn't want to give Akio or any of the denizens here any illusions about what they would be getting into if they decided to come.

"I'll show you what to do, but I won't come with you. I like my home here, I like the other cats and the safety this place represents. The Shadows can't follow me here." Akio gave Fateh a regretful look. "I'm sorry you might die."

"I hope I won't." Fateh grimaced. "It's not in my plan to die as a martyr." He would live to see his town and surrounding areas free of the Shadows.

Chapter Ten

"So no one except Haruki and I have decided to come." Hana carried a bag over one shoulder. "It is expected; this place is a true safe house away from the Shadows and the humans who seek to hurt us."

Fateh never thought about the humans being the danger, but he thought of how people in his town acted about the fae. He had to agree a safe harbor was necessary for the kids who were half of one and half human. In Japan, they didn't consider them fae. They were kami. Keeping the names and classification correct could be difficult.

"Akio read me the riot act about taking the two of you away." Fateh was glad no one else decided to come. It somehow got ridiculous, and they were still picking up more people. Randi, for one and the gwragedd annwn, if they would even agree to come. Did the Shadow taint their waters or were they safe from such dangers?

"Akio is protective of everyone in this household." Hana said calmly. "Scarred by his history with the Shadows and does not want those dear to him to fall to the same fate."

"He knows how to fight the Shadows, he would be useful to take along." Fateh could get all the lessons he needed, but without the strength behind them, such lessons could be considered useless.

"This place is better suited for his power. There are still dangers, even if the forest protects us. He has to go out foraging and a Shadow can be anywhere. You do not hold all the Shadows in the world, but you hold the origin of them."

"Lucky me." Fateh held a wry tone with his next words. "I'm so glad to have the honor of having the blight on the world in my hometown."

"We'll take care of the blight soon enough, but first we have a friend of yours to rescue, yes?" Hana asked. "I have read up on the menace; it's best if we go in the daytime, but we may have to fight at night, to strike the heart of the king of the trolls."

"Going to fight at night is what we were thinking." Tabor looked at Fateh. "Trolls aren't native to where we are either and we may have to travel to find them. Are you up for visiting other countries?"

"More than your native Wales?" Hana looked curious. "I knew we would be traveling far, but this is interesting. I am prepared for anything." She squared her shoulders, looking determined. "We have committed to this venture, we will not step away now."

"The pathways we tread are shrouded in darkness, but with you and I to light the way, we will find our way to where we need to go." Marisa spoke calmly. "We walk in shadow to fight the Shadows and there will be enemies along the path."

"Great, so we're going to run into the Shadows on the way to where Randi is?" Fateh asked. "Marvelous, I always wanted to test my abilities before the big fight in the end." He was secretly grateful. It would show him how much he could actually do before there was no turning back.

"Take this opportunity for what it is. We can show the Shadows what we can do together." Haruki said firmly. "This is a blessing in disguise; a calamity that will make us stronger."

"When you're right, you're right." Hana agreed and smiled at the small group. "Is everyone ready?" she asked. "We will return here once we have your friend, I don't think it is wise to take her beyond to where the Shadows wait. She is vulnerable in daylight and she will need a safe place to stay."

Fateh looked at Hana in surprise; he didn't think she would offer a haven. Despite his doubts, he still hoped. He didn't think Randi would be up for fighting after being freed from the trolls. *If we save her. Nothing is guaranteed.* "I appreciate it."

"Of course. We would offer you safe harbor as well if you weren't so determined to fight the Shadows at their source." Hana gestured to the house. "If you ever change your mind, our doors are open to you."

Fateh thought about the peaceful room he spent part of the afternoon in and it was so very tempting. It would be good to relax in a place that wasn't trying to kill him with metal; to not have anything to worry about. He wanted to be surrounded by cats and other half-human kids. It sounded like a paradise.

"Yes, I'm sure Spark would love to stay here in your happy little home, if he didn't have other obligations and ties." Tabor rested a hand on Fateh's shoulder. "Isn't that right?"

"Yes." Fateh's shoulders sagged as Tabor reminded him of the chain binding the two of them. Tabor didn't need to stay in such safe harbors and, for better or worse, Fateh couldn't get away from him.

"Don't be so down, Spark. Once we clear the nest, then we can both go home."

"I don't want to go home." It wouldn't be the same; his mother was gone and his friends were a part of the rebellion that had killed her. He would carve a new life for himself, traveling the shadows with Tabor.

"Yeah, well. We'll see where we end up." Tabor squeezed his shoulders and sighed. He obviously wanted to do his best by Fateh and support him in whatever he chose in the end. "There are plenty of places to explore and people to meet."

"Exploring other countries would be better." It had only been a year since Fateh's mother died. Of course it still bothered him and other than wanting to go home and see the remains, he didn't want to stay in Felinheli. Tabor talked about having a house there, but the thought of staying in the town was too painful.

"Good, then we'll make a world traveler out of you yet." Tabor grinned and then faced the others, who were waiting for them and he turned to Marisa. "I'm counting on you to light the pathway to where the trolls are."

"I know the way." Marisa's tone promised assurance. "We'll make our way to Randi and the trolls and a battle will ensue. Be wary of them going unseen. Light the empty places where you think a troll could be."

"Great, invisible trolls." Fateh made a face. "This is getting better and better all the time." If Randi wasn't such a good friend, he wouldn't even think of doing this.

"Don't worry, you'll have plenty of help." Hana reassured him. "Once you gain the power of water, then we'll have all elements to use against the trolls. A united front is hard to stand against."

Tabor shrugged and looked at the almost comically large group. "Everyone hold hands," he ordered. "I've never taken this many people through the shadows before. I don't know what's going to happen."

"We trust Marisa to light the way." Sam spoke for all of them. "Having a Seer in the dark makes it not so bad, no matter how many people we have with us. You'll be fine, Tabor." He gripped Hana's hand, who in turn held onto Haruki. The others grasped hands, until they were standing in a circle. Tabor took a step back into the shadows.

Like before, a soft light came from around Marisa, whose eyes were closed. She obviously saw something no one could see and she tugged on the hands she held. "This way." She began walking and the circle of people broke off into a line, Marisa at the head. "Be wary."

When a Seer told you to be wary, they should keep an eye open. After all, the darkness stretched around them, with only a thin strip of light leading them towards their destination. Fateh remembered how the Shadows liked to hide near the light and in patches of shadow.

When nothing happened for several minutes, Fateh relaxed a little.. Of course, the Shadow chose to strike.

"Be careful! The Shadow walks." It was all the warning they got before the shadows loomed up ahead of them, forming a human shape, moving like water. Of course it would be water, when they didn't have anyone who manipulated water on their side yet.

Fateh decided to try what he could anyway, thrusting fire at the Shadow, hoping to overwhelm it with heat. Water boiled didn't it? And this Shadow was filled with water, and had made the water a part of it.

"Ow, damn!" The Shadow hissed and spread out the shadows around the group, making them come alive. "You people are attacking a traveler, you know."

"You're a Shadow, one that consumes." Hana spat. "You do not travel." Fire lit in the palm of her hands. "What have you eaten so you are so full of life?"

"Wouldn't you like to find out firsthand?" The Shadow sneered and lunged at her, water wrapping around her and forming a loop. It tightened and put her fire out and there was a whip lash of shadow along her hand.

Hana growled, ears going flat and tail flicking madly. She changed shape and escaped the watery knot. She unsheathed her claws to slash at the Shadow. Her claws made a mark and the Shadow staggered back. He was remarkably solid for being filled with something as fluid as water.

Haruki stood beside Hana with his sword and Tabor put a hand on it, sheathing it in fire. Haruki grinned and slashed out, aiming for the head. With one quick, effective swipe, the head went flying and the Shadow dissolved into water.

Fateh blinked at the remains of the Shadow, feeling sorry for whatever water fae or yokai had gotten sucked into the Shadow's power. They would no longer power the Shadow and Fateh wondered if there was any chance one could come back from being consumed. Tabor said the Shadows stole his magic, little by little, after all. No shape formed in the water, but there was a sense of release.

"Well killing the Shadow turned out easier than I expected." Sam watched the fight with respect. "I thought they would be scarier than this guy."

"We were lucky, this one recently fed so he was filled with power and solid from it." Hana said, licking at the wound the Shadow managed to inflict on her. "Normally, they are not so easy to attack." She looked at the water sadly. "We honor who gave their life so we had a chance to end this Shadow."

Fateh nodded and ran a hand through his hair. "Most of the Shadows I know of are shadow. There are a few that are solid, but they're super strong and terrifying." Fateh thought back to the long-ago day when he bargained for his dinner and how the Shadow bled. "I think if you use their words against them, though, you have a chance. You have to be really clever. They're really smart and have had a long time to perfect deceptions."

"I'd rather cut them in two." Haruki sheathed his sword, now devoid of fire. "I would rather use my weapon than play with words."

"We won't always get a chance to cut them to ribbons." Tabor reminded them "There are only a handful I know of who have filled themselves with power to the point of bursting, Others take dribs and drabs and are only solid for a short period of time."

"Take the advantage while we can, feed them power and then attack." Fateh crossed his arms against his chest. "Use the metal Marisa brought; we can make weapons out of it." He missed the metal he used to carry around for luck and safety, but it would only hurt him now. "A rebel group in my town made a bomb out of metal before and ended up killing a bunch of Shadows."

"Using metal as a weapon has merit, but I doubt they'll fall for such a trick again." Haruki mused. "Still, we can keep the bombs as an option, as long as you three don't get involved in it." He indicated Sam, Tabor, and Fateh. "Metal hurts you in a way which does not hurt us. I'm sure shrapnel will not be fun, but it won't poison us the way it does you."

"You have to have some limitations." Fateh complained. "It's not fair if there isn't something that weakens you."

"Iron can weaken me," Hana admitted. "It is not poison, but it can limit me. And for whatever form I choose, I am vulnerable to the form's weakness. So if I decided to turn into a tree, I would fear fire."

Sam shuddered at the mention of fire and trees. "I hope we won't be setting any forests on fire." They looked at Tabor and Fateh. "You're going to keep your fire contained, right?" They asked.

"No burning down of the greenery." Tabor promised. "Our fire will be regulated to our enemies, not the trees."

"Should we be talking in the shadows like this?" Fateh asked, looking around. "Another Shadow can be lurking and we'd never know."

"I'd know." Marisa's expression and words serene. "The shadows do not walk where we are. We are safe for now. Our path is lit for another enemy, though." She gestured to where the light led. "Are you ready to fight trolls?"

"We have to gather water first before we fight trolls." Fateh was reluctant and his words showed it. "Hana and Haruki said we needed all the elements to fight the trolls and we haven't gotten to Wales and the gwragedd annwn yet."

"Now that I think about it, the water maidens might not be the best choice. We might need something with a little more oomph." Fateh pursed his lips in thought. "The maidens seem a little too gentle for fighting Shadows and trolls."

"They can drown a man on land." Tabor pointed out. "They work better in their home ground of course; you saw what was possible with Mokosh."

Fateh made a face at the mention of Mokosh. She was an afon, a fiercer form of the gentle water maidens. She had decided to stick in her pond, though she could expand the waters, as she proved at the prison.

"I still don't want to do anything with water." Fateh muttered rebelliously, but then reluctantly sighed. "But I know it'll help us out."

"Good." Tabor turned to Marisa. "We need a pathway to the gwragedd annwn before the trolls. Can you light the way? I don't have any pathways to water, other than to Mokosh's domain."

"And we don't want to go to Mokosh or Jonathan." Marisa said serenely. "That's a body of water you won't return from if you go into its depths again."

"Good to know." Fateh shook his head. "On to the gwragedd annwn."

Chapter Eleven

They emerged from the shadows at the bank of a gently flowing river, where a group of women were lounging, combing their long, dark hair. One of them noticed the rather large group and gasped. "How did you come here?" Her smile turned coy as she focused on Haruki. "Not that we mind."

"Sorry, I'm taken." Haruki said cheerfully. "Plus, not human. Don't you girls usually like human men?"

"We can make an exception, even if you keep company with fire users." The rest of the women giggled and splashed water at Fateh and Tabor. Fateh made a dismayed sound, but Tabor took it in stride, using his heat to dry the water from his skin.

Hana crossed her arms over her chest. "We wish to ask for your assistance," she said in accented English. "We are fighting a great evil and your assistance would be greatly appreciated."

"What great evil?" One of the other maidens came closer. Her wide-set eyes and round face showed her youth compared to the other women. Short cropped hair framed her face in a riot of curls.

"The Shadows." Fateh's expression softened. "We know they've spread into the water and stolen the lives of those who are water." The Shadow they fought proved the theory. Whether it had been a maiden, an undine, or some other water creature like Mokosh, Fateh didn't know.

"We've heard of them." Her words were low and raspy. "They taint the water, darkening it with shadow and making it foul. Darker fae live in those waters, making it unsafe for us to inhabit."

"Don't get involved, Uisge. They only want to lead you away from your river and into danger."

"We walk into danger every time we search for husbands." Uisge tossed her hair back. "Humans are dangerous creatures and there is only one human in this group." She gestured to Marisa. "The others are fae-touched." Her nose wrinkled. "There is only one pure fae among them and that's him." She indicated Tabor. "What use do you have with the drips that inhabit these children?"

"Not a child." Fateh snapped and tried to stand up straighter. "I'm seventeen."

More giggles from the entire group this time.

"Oh, yes-- you are a child. Young in power and in age." This came from an older woman, wrinkles at the corners of her eyes. She was full figured, despite her age and her long flowing hair hid her nudity.

"Fine, in human terms I'm not a child." Fateh wanted to pout, but he knew it would make him look even more childish. "But I guess for the ever-living fae, I'm pretty young." Fateh knew he was young compared to Tabor and especially Etana, even if they didn't look it. Fae aged differently and he wondered if he'd stay looking this age for centuries or if he'd grow and mature first. The latter would be preferable

Uisge stood up, shedding water from her hair and body. "I don't want a husband, but I do want to rid our waters of the Shadows which taint it. We've lost several dens due to the scáthach."

"We've lost the chance for husbands, too." Another muttered. It came from the general crowd of women. "The scáthach block our way and some even consumed the husbands we were going to take."

"So see?" Uisge crossed her arms over her chest. "I say I go."

"You'd come with us so easily?" Sam asked. "I thought you'd be more stubborn about it." They shrugged. "I didn't think you'd volunteer. You don't even know us."

"Water is easy, we ... go with the flow." Uisge gave a graceful shrug. "And like I said, this is a problem we are aware of. Why shouldn't we send a representative to fight? I bet your little fire-users are the leaders of this expedition. They're the most stubborn."

"I always thought earth was more stubborn than fire." Tabor spread his hands "But I'm rather biased on my own behalf. Yes, we're the leaders, if you want to assign us a title. This is a partnership, no one rules over the other."

"So you say, but I guarantee one of you came up with the idea of fighting the scáthach." Her gaze landed on Fateh. "You. You're the one. You've got enough human in you to care about what the scáthach get up to."

"And you're not invested?" Fateh shot back. "You're the one that's passionate about fighting the Shadows. Your brethren don't seem nearly as excited as you do."

"My sisters are lazy. I want to go out and do more than just lounge on the bank of a river, combing my hair." One of the girls stopped in the middle of running a comb through her hair, a hurt expression on her face.

"Not that it's not fine for you to do what makes you happy, Abhainn." Uisge reassured her, trying to soothe away the hurt of her words. "It's not for me."

"You always like to kick up the water." Abhainn muttered sullenly. "You were never content with our lives. You always wanted to move from stream to river to the big lakes. Maybe it's best you go with these strangers. There will be more peace with you gone."

"Glad to know I'm so wanted." Uisge rolled her eyes. "I don't mind going with this group. At least they're doing something about the scáthach. It may all end in tears, but at least I'll have tried something."

"We're going to face trolls first." Fateh said helpfully."My friend got trapped by them and we're going to rescue her before we do anything else." Fateh didn't think he was ready to face the Shadows yet, not even with Uisge's help.

"Trolls?" Uisge wrinkled her nose. "They're not dangerous, you just have to know how to fight them. During the daytime and with something heavy to break their bones." She examined her fingers. "Of course, I'm not suited to breaking things like rocky trolls. I can drown the trolls that are awake, though." She created a globe of water in her hands, showing it off to Fateh.

"No thanks, I believe you." She could create water as easily as he could create fire and he reluctantly, silently, agreed she could be an asset.

"You're no fun." She pouted and clapped her hands, the water vanishing with a soft popping noise. "So how are we going to get there? Wherever there is. I assume the trolls aren't right around the corner or else we would have heard."

"No, their path lies far from here, in a land of snow and ice." Marisa's words held a dreamy quality. "Ice lays on the horizon, we best be wary or else we'll freeze where we stand."

"Good thing I'm immune to being frozen. I've been in much colder waters." Uisge said cheerfully. "Don't know about the rest of you surviving a frost."

"Spark and I will be fine." Tabor rested a hand on Fateh's shoulder. "But yes, we should be careful. So a land of snow and ice? Sounds ... absolutely delightful." His tone soured. "I think we should pack warm." He gestured to the pack Fateh held. "We came prepared, did the rest of you?"

"When we heard we were to fight trolls, we assumed they would be in frozen lands. They like such environments." Hana's tone was matter-of-fact. "We packed warm clothing for the trip, as well as many other outfits. One does not know where we'll end up, after all. We can travel the world."

"I suppose I should put on clothes if I'm going to be wandering in the world." Uisge dove into the water without warning, leaving the rest of them baffled.

"She is retrieving clothing we wear when we go out searching for husbands." Abhainn explained. "It's in a waterproof bag and simple compared to what you are wearing, but it will suffice."

"Simpler than him?" Fateh jerked his head towards Tabor, who happily rummaged in their bag for clothing to wear. "He's only wearing jeans."

"Simpler even than those that contain zippers and buttons." Abhainn confirmed. "We eschew complications."

"Easy-going, huh?" Sam asked with interest. "You seem like a very chill bunch and I hang out with trees for fun."

"We are steady as the tide on the ocean." The older woman spoke. "We have that much in common with the earth. Both are sure in what they do; but we are more loose about how we go about things. Water will always make a path, even through the most stubborn stone."

Fateh wanted to ask more when Uisge appeared again, clutching a bag that resembled clear plastic. In it he could see a bundle of clothing; but nothing else.

Uisge stepped onto the bank again and opened her bag, sliding a simple dress over her head. There were no buttons or ties; a shift of a dress, molding to her curves. "There." Satisfaction filled her tone. "I am ready to go out into the world."

Her hair was already drying, the water dripping onto the ground. Her dress stayed dry, a feat that impressed Fateh.

Tabor nodded towards a patch of shadow. "You asked how we travel? I open the gates to the shadow pathways and out little Seer lights the way. Her ability means we won't get lost on the way to where we are going and we get there with relative ease."

"I've never walked the shadows on land before, but there are shadows in the water where one can travel from one stream to the next." Uisge looked intrigued. "I didn't know you could go without water to connect you."

"It's been interesting." Fateh gave an expansive shrug. "It's a little cold and dark on the shadow paths, but like Tabor said, Marisa lights the way so it won't be so bad. The first time I went on the shadow paths, I was sick, though, because the shadows rejected me. But if you've traveled the shadows before, you should be fine."

The others were fine on the shadow paths and Fateh had to wonder if it had to do with Marisa more than anything. Tabor opened the path, but Marisa kept it open and habitable to those who walked it.

"I guess we'll see." She reached out a hand to Haruki and winked. "I promise not to tease you too much, since you say you're already claimed by another. But hold me hand tight while we go into darkness?"

Haruki laughed and took her hand, his free hand taking Hana's. They went in a line again, stepping into the patch of shadow that waited by the bank. This time, there were no warnings by Marisa, no Shadows waiting for them in the dark.

Fateh hoped the upcoming travels would go easy; they'd find Randi, break some trolls and be on their way through the shadows. He didn't know if the trolls could follow through shadow, though and he wasn't keen on the idea of leading the trolls to the sanctuary. They would have to destroy all the trolls to be safe.

What on earth have I gotten us into?

Too late for second guessing. The pathway opened up and then were abruptly in a clearing, snow on the ground. No use walking into the middle of a group of trolls unprepared. It would be much more strategic to come upon them when they were stone.

They saw a circle of stone trolls, each of them frozen by the bright sunlight overhead. Randi was in the middle of them, frozen in place with a terrified look, but while the others were stone, she remained human.

Fateh reached out and gripped her shoulder; she was stiff and then her eyes widened and settled on him. "Fateh?" she whispered in shock. "How are you here?" She still didn't move and Fateh wondered how they were going to get her out of here. Other than bodily carrying her out like a rock, he didn't see a way until the sun went away-- and then they'd have a whole new host of problems.

"I couldn't leave my friend with trolls." Fateh tried to smile through his worry; he eyed the stone statues like they'd come to life any second now and squash him flat. He was aware of the others around him, assessing their enemy and he knew they were working out their own strategies.

"It's dangerous!" She warned him, eyes moving wildly in her face as she tried to take in everything she could see. "The trolls will wake up once the sun goes down and they're fast and mean and they like eating humans." Her face went pale as she obviously relieved some terrible memory which had to do with the trolls eating habits.

"We're going to try and break the trolls before they have a chance to turn into flesh." Fateh explained. "Which one is the king troll? The one that...?"

"Married me?" Her words came out scornfully. "He's the one who doesn't look like the rest of the trolls. He's a King; they have their own magic.. The troll king is who opened the shadow paths and led us all here. They were tired of Wales."

"So where are we now?" Fateh asked, but Randi only frowned.

"I don't know, they didn't exactly stop and ask for directions." She huffed, rolling her eyes. "All I know is that we aren't in Wales anymore. I didn't understand the language of anyone passing by..." She didn't say what happened to those who passed by, she didn't have to. There were piles of bones strewn across the clearing that spoke more loudly than words.

"It doesn't matter at the moment where we are." Tabor spoke up. "Spark, let loose the fireball you were practicing. Nice and fierce, imagine you're a feisty redhead ready to burn a town."

Fateh snorted. "I think someone has a favorite anime." He couldn't help but tease. "Sure, sure, I'll channel chaos incarnate and try and blow up the statues." He wanted to start with the biggest and meanest looking of the trolls, but Randi mentioned the troll king didn't look like a troll. It would be smart to start with him and then hopefully the organization of the other trolls would fall apart and they would be able to fight them easier, if it came down to a fight in the end.

Sam already worked on the trunks of trees, lifting them from the ground and wrapping them around a statue of a troll, tightening their grip until the stone cracked and fell into pieces. It was a large troll, with huge bulging features and thick muscles. The broken stone of the troll gave Fateh comfort. It would have been hard to fight something so huge.

Fateh imagined the fireball in his hands like a bomb ready to go off and threw it as a clump of trolls. It exploded on impact, shattering into large pieces of stone. He beamed up at Tabor, excited about what he managed.

"Good job. Channel your power." Tabor lobbed his own explosive fireball and destroyed another clump of trolls. "This is easier than I expected. I'm glad we came here during the day."

Fateh was still holding onto Randi, wondering if he could bodily move her away from the remains of the trolls and to a safe place. He wished he could open the shadows the way Tabor could. It ceased being creepy and became a useful tool.

"You have to worry about troll magic." Randi said as clearly as she could. "The king troll--eep!" She couldn't gesture but her shriek rang out, announcing to everyone they weren't alone any longer.

Chapter Twelve

"Breaking my loyal trolls, trying to steal away my lovely wife." Someone spoke from a tent, its shadows heavy and enclosing. No sunlight penetrated the heavy folds of fabric. "Aren't you the little nuisances?"

"Oh, we're much more than nuisances." Haruki stood at attention, sword held at the ready. "We're taking this girl and you are not going to stop us."

"She's my bride, you shall not be taking her anywhere." The troll, wearing a glittery suit of what looked like braided metal, gestured at the ground and frost spread everywhere, creeping up the trees and those who were standing there. It moved rapidly, sliding up their legs and freezing them in place.

Uisge didn't react to the frost and she stood her ground, forming globes of water and throwing it at the troll king. He batted the water away as if she were tossing toys at his head. Uisge frowned and shifted her focus to creating a water globe around the troll king, but it was obviously slow-going as she tried to do it without him noticing the water and destroying it.

Hana hissed and shifted into a bear, shaking off the frost and bellowing a challenge at the troll king. He actually backed up a step, retreating further into his tent and Fateh decided to get rid of the tent entirely--it wouldn't do for the troll king to have a place to retreat to. He was met with resistance, though, when he tried to set fire to the tent.

"Not going to make it easy for you." The troll king taunted. "You think I would not have my home fireproofed? It's my sanctuary, of course I wouldn't let it burn so easily."

Tabor smirked at him. "You haven't seen the type of fire we can produce. I bet it can overwhelm your paltry spells." He threw his own stream of fire towards the troll, who hissed as sparks landed in the bones braided in his hair.

"You're dangerous. I don't like you. Go away." The shadows rose up around Tabor and swallowed him and for a moment, Fateh's heart stopped. He had seen this trick before with the Shadows; nothing lived after the shadows consumed it.

It seemed to take hours, but Tabor stepped out of another patch of shadow, glaring at the troll king. "Sending me into the shadows wasn't a nice trick."

"Neither is setting me on fire, but then again, I don't think we're friends. You broke my loyal subjects and intend to steal away what is mine."

"She was never yours to begin with." Fateh shot back, wondering if he could melt the metal the troll wore with a hot enough fire. It was obviously magical and protecting him, but it had to have a weakness.

Hana the bear swiped at the troll king, opening a gash on his cheek. He glared at her and threw his hand out, a wave of energy rushing at Hana and knocking her back. She growled and tried to get to her feet, but she was forced to change again. She changed into a fox, lithe and quick, but the troll king didn't let her near him this time. He threw her back with another wave of energy.

Marisa stood outside the clearing, away from any of the fighting when she spoke. "Unravel the strings and you'll have your chance."

"What on earth is 'unraveling the strings' supposed to mean Can't you give a direct answer?" Fateh groused. He couldn't see any strings to unravel, unless she talked about his clothes. What strings were there in woven metal?

"Set his hair on fire and drop the bones which are the source of his power." Randi managed to get out the useful information before she was knocked back as well, magic visibly wrapping around her, sealing her mouth shut. Unable to block the attack, Randi slid across the ground, still as stiff as a board.

Nearly knocked over as well, Fateh managed to avoid being flung. His hands lit with fire and he threw it at the head of the troll king, hoping to catch his hair on fire. He didn't know how hot fire had to be to destroy bone, but surely it wasn't as hard as stone.

The troll king dodged adroitly, making the fire go wide and hit the tent instead of him. The king's eyes widened in shock as the tent began to burn, cutting him off from his safe haven. "You think a little bit of sun will hurt a king?" He stepped fully into the light, staring them down.

Fateh noticed the troll king moving slower; the sun may not have hurt him, but it did affect him. Like Randi being frozen by it, the sun was enough to sap the troll king's power. Uisge's water closed around the head of the troll king, cutting off his air. He batted ineffectively at it, but his hands went straight through the water. His hair streamed out from the water, giving Tabor and Fateh a target to aim at.

Fateh wasted no time in throwing another fireball. It went out with a fizzle when the water absorbed it, but he managed to light a braid on fire, cracking the bones wrapped in it. The troll king staggered, face turning red as he tried to get air.

"You're scary." Tabor said with appreciation, giving Uisge a look of respect. "I didn't know you could drown a man on dry land."

"You'd be amazed at what I can do." Uisge giggled and batted her eyes at Tabor. "You're not half-bad yourself, you and your little protégé."

"We try." Marisa joined in the circle with Randi now, pushing at her through the rubble of trolls. The sun went behind a cloud and Randi stumbled, nearly falling over. The troll king faltered even more, but he made a few gestures and the water globe instantly burst, showering him with water.

As soon as Fateh had a clear shot, he threw one of the harder, more explosive fireballs at the troll king. He winced at the scream that followed; he knew he had to kill the troll king, but he hoped it would have been a stone king, not a flesh and blood one.

"You are annoying as well." The troll king snarled at Fateh, opening up a pit underneath him, causing Fateh to stumble into a hole filled with snow and ice.

He gasped as the cold bit into him and he stared upward, trying to find a way out.

The earth moved underneath him and he went to his knees as the ground heaved and grew, spilling him out of the hole. Sam looked over at him with a pleased look on their face. "You okay there, Fateh?"

Fateh nodded and gave Sam a determined look. Even half-drowned and on fire, the troll king was strong.

"Spark, now would be a good time to work with Uisge." Tabor gestured. "Do what we were practicing before. I know you've got a big spark in you."

Fateh blinked and then nodded, shaping the lightning in his hands. Uisge saw what he was about immediately and formed a stream of water toward the troll king, encircling him, Fateh shot the lightning into the water and the world seemed to light up for a moment as the electricity charged the water. The bones in the troll king's hair collapsed into dust and he fell to the ground.

Fateh gave the troll king a cautious look; Randi said destroying the bones would destroy the king but did it mean his power or his life?

"You are all nuisances!" The troll king howled and tried to get up, but without his power, the sun, which had come out again slowly turned him to stone, just like his minions.They all watched in silent horror as the troll king fought the transformation, wiggling as much as he could towards the remains of his tent.

He wasn't fast enough and soon one more statue littered the ground, this one with its mouth open in a rictus of horror.

"Aw, I didn't get a chance to cut off his head." Haruki sounded truly disappointed. "Ah, well. Maybe our next enemy will be more accommodating."

"I think we need to break the statue before the sun disappears behind a cloud again." Sam spoke quietly. "I don't want to fight him again. It took a lot of strength to use the forest against him."

"And saving me from the pit of despair.." Fateh joked.

"Saving you took strength, too." Sam grinned. "Couldn't let you miss all the fun, hiding in the hole. You might have gotten buried by snow and frozen to death and then we'd have to deal with a moping Tabor."

"As if I'd let him freeze." Tabor protested. "Granted, I couldn't get him out of the hole, but I could at least melt the snow."

"Then I would have been surrounded by water." Fateh shuddered. "Being in frozen water wouldn't be any better. The snow and ice was bad enough."

"Less talking, more breaking." Randi spoke up from where she crouched next to Marisa. "I'd like to be able to move sometime soon. Even though he's stone, he still survives and nighttime will release him. I don't want to be around when he is no longer stone, do you?"

Fateh shook his head quickly and tried to prepare one of his explosive fireballs, but he found he didn't have the energy for it. The fire he did produce was weaker and barely scorched the rock.

"Looks like it's up to me." Tabor reached his hands back like he wanted to throw a fast ball and instead delivered a blisteringly hot and explosive fireball. It exploded on contact with the stone, scattering stone pieces across the clearing.

Fateh heaved a sigh of relief; the trolls were all dead and they could take Randi to a safe place. She would like the Sanctuary; he would have to tell her it wasn't like the prison they escaped, but a true home. A home he would gladly stay in, if he didn't have other things on his agenda.

"So what next?" He asked into the silence. Everyone was recovering from using their magic, all except Haruki, who pouted he didn't get to actually cut down any trolls. *He's a bit bloodthirsty.* Fateh realized. *I'm glad he's on my side.*

"We go back to the Sanctuary." Hana said simply. "Your friend can use the safe harbor and we can all rest and recharge before our next adventure. We are not ready yet to fight the Shadows, as we barely fought trolls. We need to get stronger before facing such fearsome enemies."

"Randi is weak as a kitten being born." Marisa said quietly. "I don't know if she can move through the dark quite yet." Everyone turned to look at her, amazed she spoke clearly. "What? I can't talk in riddles all the time."

"Yes, but speaking incoherently is all you've ever done, so we're a little surprised." Sam looked her over. "You should do it more often."

"It's easier to speak in riddles. The words come out every which way and it's hard to put them together."

"If you say so." Fateh moved over to Randi, kneeling next to her. "Are you okay?" he asked quietly. She was able to move now, but she didn't move with the frenetic energy Fateh half-expected. She moved slowly, testing each limb as if surprised at what she was able to do.

"I've been better." She gave Fateh a weak smile. "But I've also been much worse. Thank you for saving me, Fateh. I didn't think you would, since you got connected with him." Her eyes flicked to Tabor in silent question.

"Yes, he's still here with me and it's ... more complicated than just a simple contract."

"You made a contract with him?" Her expression filled with shock. "Last you said, you were totally against contracts, especially since...."

"Since what happened to my mother, I know." Fateh spoke quietly. "But I had no choice. It sounds cliche, but it keeps me safer than I would be if I didn't create a contract." He looked away, ashamed. "I'm not exactly human, Randi. Tabor keeps my power in check."

"Just like I'm part troll." Randi's face fell. "I heard the troll king talking about me. He was so excited to have a part-troll as his bride. He said I'd have the advantages of the troll's strength and magic, without being turned to stone." Her bitter laugh showed what she thought. "Too bad being tied to him made me freeze in the sunlight. I could barely blink. Now...I don't know what will happen to me."

"Well, you're not frozen anymore." Fateh pointed out. "You can move in the sunlight. I don't know about the benefits of being a troll, though." He sounded doubtful. "I bet you're really strong at night. You could probably break rock if you tried."

"I have," she said shyly. "Jord wanted to test my abilities. The fact I could be stronger than a regular human and more versatile than a troll pleased him." Her gaze flicked over to the remains of the broken king. "I'm glad he's dead. The things he made me do..." She shuddered and covered her face with her hands, sobbing quietly.

"Jord?" Fateh asked in confusion, then saw where his gaze had gone. Ah. The troll king. Fateh could only wrap an arm around Randi in a one-armed hug, trying to offer her as much comfort as possible. Marisa was on the other side, hugging her as well. Sam wandered over as well, kneeling in front of Randi.

"It will be okay. We're going to a safe place." They reached out a hand to Randi. "Just one little trip through the shadows."

"I got sick the last time I went through the shadows." She made a face. "Jord said I was too human to walk through the dark."

"I light the way so that no one is lost in the dark." Marisa said quietly. "When you're with me, you're safe. Tabor opens the paths and I am the candle."

Randi looked up at Marisa's words and sniffled once more, wiping at her eyes. "And we're going somewhere safe?" she asked. "I won't be alone with …"

"You'll be around other half-yokai." Hana came up beside the little group. "It is a safe house we have, guarded by the trees."

"It's not like Mokosh, is it?" Randi asked, her face pale.

"No, it's a much gentler agreement we have with the local tree spirits." Sam's smile was reassuring. "I work with them and they watch over us, without a contract to put us in danger like we did with Mokosh."

"Okay." Randi stood up slowly. "I'm ready to go."

Chapter Thirteen

They arrived at the Sanctuary without incident. Randi looked around at the trees which surrounded the house and her shoulders slumped in relief. "Mountains are better, but trees are good. I feel comfortable here."

"You're probably tied to the earth in some way." Sam gave her a speculative look. "I could teach you things about plants. I think you could do well here."

"I hope so. I'm tired of being scared." Randi's voice softened. She turned to Fateh. "Are you going to stay here?" She reached out a hand. "I would like it if you did. It could be like old times, only without metal and fear." She smiled tentatively.. Inviting Fateh to return it.

"No, I'm going to fight the Shadows." Fateh squared his shoulders. "Fighting the trolls is just the beginning, I want to free my town from the Shadows. There's a nest there and they're spreading out from my town to other parts of the world."

"Fighting the Shadows is dangerous." Randi said, eyes widening with fear. "The Shadows are impossible to kill."

"Not impossible, just very difficult." Fateh gave her a weak smile. "I'm going to have help. I'm not doing it alone."

"Good." She gave him an impulsive hug. "You were too much on your own in Mokosh's place. You hardly leaned on anyone. Now look at you." She gestured to the group. "You've got quite the collection."

"Hana is a half-kami and Haruki is a yokai. They come from the Sanctuary." Fateh gestured to the two of them and they bowed in Randi's direction. "You of course know Sam and Marisa from Mokosh's and you met Tabor when we were outside of the pond."

"Yes." She gave Tabor a nervous look and lowered her voice. "Are you sure you can trust him? He's a full fae, not half like the rest of us."

"We're stuck together." Fateh shrugged. "We've got a contract which goes both ways, so we can't hurt each other." He kept his words quiet as well. "He's not as bad as some of the other options out there. He helped me out these last few weeks." He didn't mention Etana, he didn't want to confuse Randi by mentioning even more people.

"Well as long as you're happy." She patted his hand. "I worried about you when I first saw you going off with Tabor."

"If I had known you were going to be taken by trolls right after I left you, I wouldn't have left you alone." Fateh shook his head, the trolls were behind them now. He couldn't change the past. "But you'll be okay here. From what I've seen of the place, it's really nice." Fateh looked forward to exploring the Sanctuary more. They had time; the others wouldn't want to leave right away and they weren't ready to face the Shadows.

"Tabor wouldn't have let me come along." Randi was matter-of-fact. "He wouldn't want to have a troll bride around and besides, it's obvious he's attached to you."

"Whatever." Fateh flushed and waved Tabor's clinginess off. "I still would have fought to have you with us. Maybe we could have found the Sanctuary faster and neither one of us would be stuck where we are."

The fact the Sanctuary existed could be unfair, in a place far from their home. They never would have made it here unless they walked the shadows and they couldn't walk the shadows unless one of the fae was with them. Fateh wouldn't begrudge those that lived here their safe haven, though. Everyone deserved to have a safe place to live.

"Spark, come here." Tabor gestured for Fateh to come next to him. "We need to talk."

"I don't want to." Fateh didn't like the look on Tabor's face. It didn't bode well that he wanted to talk to him, just when Fateh was getting ready to relax in the Sanctuary. He deserved a bit of rest after the trolls.

"Now, Spark." Tabor's tone brooked no argument. "It's important. We have to discuss what happens next. You can't stay here, even as much as you want to. I want to get you more training and we're not going to get it surrounded by trees."

"Please don't train around my trees." Sam said fervently. "I don't want this whole place to go up like a torch and trees explode when exposed to too much heat."

"I want to rest." Fateh's tone flattened. "I'm tired, we have a safe place where we don't have to worry about loyalties and we have allies here now. We should get to know them better before we drag them off on some other adventure." Fateh narrowed his eyes at Tabor. "And we are not leaving them behind, we might run into more dangerous situations and we'll need them. We can't resort to fireballs as our only solution to everything."

"It's a good solution." Tabor pouted. "You seemed to have fun using them against the trolls."

"Yeah, it was a good use of fire, but we also had everyone else working to help us. We need all the elements, even water." Not that Uisge hadn't been useful. She almost managed to kill the troll king with water alone.

"I want you to meet some of my cousins." Tabor insisted. "We can work on your finesse and it'd be good for you to meet more of your kind."

"My kind is right here." Fateh could be stubborn. "Full fae aren't my kind, half-fae is what I am and what they are here."

"Technically, they aren't fae at all." Tabor pointed out. "They're yokai. Japanese spirits. You are decidedly not Japanese."

"No, some of them are kami, gods. But I am a fire elemental, aren't I? That's closer to being a spirit than it is to what I know of the fae to be."

"You have a point, but it doesn't change the fact you can't stay here, anymore than we can stay with Etana. I like him, he's a good ally, but it's not a place we can stay. The same is true for here."

"I'm not asking to stay forever." Fateh rolled his eyes. "They would be too uncomfortable with us around, especially you, since you're full fire fae. I have a feeling they don't trust the pure-blooded."

"Fine, we can stay for a little while, so we can all recover and get to know each other, since you think learning about your allies is so important." His words held a teasing note, as if he understood the necessity.

"We're going to be working closely with them." Fateh pointed out. "It only makes sense. We barely know anything about Uisge, for instance and since she's our opposite, I'd like to know more about her before we get too tangled up."

"What if I don't want to share you?" Tabor pouted. "I rather liked it when we were just ourselves and no one else."

"Yeah, you had me to yourself all of half a day." Fateh snorted. "You dragged me to Etana right after Mokosh, remember? Then we picked up Marisa after we were done with Etana. Face it, you're going to have to deal with sharing me."

"Unfair."

"Safety in numbers." Fateh countered. "Come on, we'll go and meet your cousins later. Right now, all I want to do is sleep. I don't have the type of oomph you do. Using so much fire and lightning wore me out."

"Maybe we can meet more than just your cousins." Haruki looked interested. "It might do us good to meet the pure-blooded people of our ancestry. They might be able to give us tips on our power we might not have thought of."

"Or they might reject us completely." Hana put in. "Still, the idea has merit." She yawned, covering her mouth with her hand. "Still, Fateh has the right of it. We need to rest before we do anything."

"Rest is good." Sam agreed. They were still next to Randi, helping to support her. "Some of us are more tired than others and have been through a lot more. Randi's dead on her feet."

"Is there a lake or a river I can rest in?" Uisge asked politely. "I can sleep without it, but I would prefer to be resting in water that isn't salt water."

Hana nodded and took Uisge's arm, waving at the others to go inside. "I'll show you to our stream. It is always good to have a good, clean source of water. There might even be some water spirits there you can get to know."

Fateh didn't think he had to go with. He still had nightmares of drowning. He faced the house again, better able to appreciate the sprawling estate. The trees framed the buildings, which had high roofs covered in slate. The buildings were paneled in wood and there were sliding doors made out of paper. Elegant and cozy would be how he described it.

Sam led Randi inside, taking off his shoes outside. Randi fumbled with her boots, her movements still clumsy, Marisa right behind them. Fateh was left alone with Haruki and Tabor. "Well, should we go in?"

"Just waiting for you." Haruki said cheerfully. "It would have been rude to leave you alone out here. Not that it isn't unpleasant. I quite like the peace the trees bring."

"Then let's go. I would love to explore more of the Sanctuary, but I'm exhausted." His

look toward Haruki was filled with envy. "How are you able to look so refreshed after what we did?"

"I didn't do as much as you did." Haruki reminded him. "I fought the Shadow, but the fight was fun, not exhausting in any way." He grinned broadly. "I have fun using my sword and having your power added to it made it even more exciting. We'll have to practice combining our power so it is as easy as breathing for us."

Fateh gave him a surprised look. "You want to work with me more? You don't think I'm too weak?" He rather thought someone as strong as Haruki would want to work with Tabor. He didn't have as much strength as Tabor did and he thought Tabor would be a better match for Haruki.

"You're stronger than you realize, Fateh." Haruki was serious as they and Tabor started walking toward the Sanctuary's doors. "You can do a lot if you put your mind to it, you just have to work up to amazing feats."

Tabor nodded. "For being so young, you're obviously got talent in spades and can use the power you were gifted with. Remember, it's not been so long since you even realized you could use fire. There's going to be a learning curve."

"Huh. Glad to know I'm not dragging down the team or anything." Fateh paused in front of the sliding doors, toeing off his shoes before heading inside.

"Using all the fire and lightning wore me out. I don't know how useful I'll be against the Shadows."

"You can use your power more efficiently." Haruki reassured him. "It takes time and practice to be good with what the gods have blessed us with."

"You never said, but what is a tengu?" Fateh asked. "I didn't study many of the Japanese yokai; my grandparents were more focused on the fae which were native to our part of the world."

"Full-blooded tengu are like miniature gods." Haruki said this without a hint of self-consciousness. "We're the best swordsmen out there and can control the wind."

"Wow. No wonder you weren't exhausted by the fight." Fateh tried to absorb the information that Haruki was basically a demi-god. "Can I ask how old you are?" Haruki looked to be in his early twenties, but his age could be anywhere from sixteen to hundreds of years old.

"A hundred and sixteen." Haruki looked unruffled by the question. "You said you were seventeen?" he raised an eyebrow. "You have a long life ahead of you. You have time to learn and grow into your power. Don't start running before you can walk."

"The thought of living longer than a normal human lifespan is scary." Fateh admitted. "I don't think I've ever thought about it before, but Tabor is in his hundreds, but he's a full-blooded fae."

"Etana is older than me." Tabor sounded as if he were offended that Fateh called him old. "Fae are long-lived, even half-fae."

"You keep on saying fae." Haruki mused as he led Fateh through the sprawling expanse of the house, past cats and people, on the way to his room. "But you are an elemental, yes? You're closer to the spirits than you are to what you would be considered fae. I have heard stories about them and met some of the higher courts. Forgive me, but you are nothing like those shining creatures."

"After a hundred years, I guess you would have." Fateh took this at face value. Haruki probably traveled and met fae as well. "You're right, though. We're elementals, but in Wales, we would be considered one of the tylwyth teg, even if we are a lesser form."

"And no matter what the power of the strength of the blood, the denizens of this household are considered yokai and kami. There are many different types of yokai and kami, both ill and good, but that is the Japanese name for such spirits blessed—or cursed—by the gods."

"And let me guess, you only have the good here." Fateh stated blandly. "How do you screen for someone's nature? How do you keep the bad out?"

"What is bad?" Haruki asked with a shrug. "Tengu are not considered the best natured, yet here I am. We're mischief makers, which is why I get along with Hana so well. Kitsune are tricksters, but she is not of the malicious sort."

"She seems like a good person." They paused in front of the room Fateh stayed in before. "I appreciate the help you, Hana and Sam have offered. It means a lot to me to have such allies." He gave Haruki a shy smile. "And maybe we can become friends? I'm rather short of those these days."

"Friends." Haruki smiled and bowed to Fateh. "I think we can manage such a feat."

Chapter Fourteen

Tabor hovered outside the doorway when Fateh stepped inside. "Are you going to be okay, Spark?" he asked. "Need me to stay with you?"

"I'm not a child, even if I am leagues younger than the rest of you." Fateh huffed and crossed his arms over his chest. "I haven't had a nightmare about fire since the first night. Mainly, it's nightmares about drowning."

"I'd rather you didn't have nightmares at all." Tabor gave him a slightly worried look. "But I suppose you're too exhausted to do much anyway. You used a lot of power. Next time, don't drain yourself."

"I'll work on it." Fateh agreed and yawned. "Now, if you'll let me sleep? You don't have to cling to me. I'll be fine and I'm obviously not going anywhere. You're the one who controls the shadows not me. And I don't even know where we are, so it's not like I'm going to leave the Sanctuary on a lark to go to town."

"Good, keep sticking around." Tabor patted Fateh on the head, who swatted the hand away. "I'll see you in the morning, Fateh."

"Get some rest yourself." Fateh ordered. "You still used power, even if you have more than me." Tabor would be the type to act as if he were infallible, untiring and capable of doing anything.

"Yes, sir." Tabor snorted and gave Fateh's hair another quick tousle before he headed to his own room, next door to Fateh's. He whistled a tune under his breath as he walked, until the door shutting behind him cut off all sound.

Fateh flopped down on the bed. He could finally rest. He closed his eyes and was asleep in moments, untroubled by dreams.

***

The next day Fateh found himself down a large dining area, surrounded by the residents of the Sanctuary. There weren't as many of them as Fateh thought. It seemed some of the cats who lived here were ordinary cats, not shapeshifting yokai.

Akio looked relieved Hana and Haruki returned mostly unscathed, except that Hana had a scratch the Shadow had inflicted. Haruki was in fine shape, practically buzzing with energy from the fight. Fateh had to wonder if he even went to bed.

"So what was it like, fighting trolls?" One of the girls asked, her long, dark hair sweeping into her eyes. Her almond-shaped eyes were golden and intense as they focused on Fateh. He and Uisge were the only ones of the 'team' downstairs, other than Haruki and Hana. Tabor still slept, along with Marisa, Sam, and Randi. Fateh translated for Uisge.

"Easier than it could have been." Fateh admitted. "They were all stone, except the troll king. We mainly blasted them apart with fire and Sam crushed a few with tree roots. Uisge nearly drowned the troll king." He could give her the credit for what she did. She still gave him the shivers, but as long as she wasn't using her magic on him, he would have to learn to live with her.

"It was a simple task." Uisge couldn't toss her hair back; being as short-cropped, but she did sit up straighter. "I created a globe of water around his head so he couldn't breathe. Any water-worker could do the same."

"Can you show me?" The girl asked, eyes going wide. "I can see the future in water, but I can't create it out of nothing." She held out a slim-fingered hand. "My name is Chisakou. You are Uisge, yes?"

Uisge nodded and took the hand, turning it over in hers. "Yes, I can see your hands don't hold the water in them, but there is water inside of you." She pulled her hands away to form a glove of water between them.

Fateh pulled away, not wanting the water to collapse and splash on him. It wasn't like he would melt, but he preferred to stay dry. And who was to say she couldn't shift the water around him without warning? It was in the nature of water to put fire out. He didn't want to give her an opening.

Uisge turned to him with a frown. "You do not trust me." She accused him sharply. "I have done nothing to you, yet you are apprehensive of me."

Fateh grimaced. He really had been obvious. "I am scared of what you could do." His admission came out slow, words uncertain. "You're made of water and I nearly drowned in water a few weeks ago. So yeah. I am nervous around you."

"But I did not attempt to drown you." She sounded politely puzzled. "I can do it if you want to experience what it was like for the troll king--" She gestured slightly and the globe of water moved closer to Fateh, who cringed away from it. "But no, I would not harm you. You said we were allies. Allies do not harm one another."

"Sorry." Fateh went quiet. "It's instinct, I guess. You're water and I'm fire. Our natures are opposite."

"We are not controlled by our natures." Her voice sharpened. "We have free will and it lets us move beyond the base instincts of our inner selves. I, too, am half-human. Maybe it is the human part of us that allows us to work together."

Fateh looked at her in surprise, but it shouldn't really be a surprise. She was unlike the other water maidens. Outspoken and fierce and eschewed their traditional look. She didn't even want to look for a husband among the humans and it was something he heard of all the maidens wanting to do at some point. Whether they stayed with the husbands was another thing altogether, but Uisge didn't even want to try. If she could fight against her nature, Fateh could do the same.

"I guess you're right." He still gave the globe of water a nervous glance, but he held out his hand. "Let's work together properly. I can't promise I won't be nervous around you, but I'll work harder to see you as you, not just as a water fae."

"Good, because I am my own individual, not a collection of stereotypes." She took his hand and shook it. Her hands were slightly wet from the water she manipulated and steam rose between the two of them from Fateh's nervous heat.

The others in the room looked on in fascination, as if they expected them to fight. They ooh'd at the steam, leaning in closer. Chisakou seemed especially interested.

"Do you think you could teach me to manipulate water?" she asked. "You said I have water in me, is it enough to react with fire?" She grinned. "It would be a useful talent; to put out fires before they start."

"I can work with you and see what you can do." Uisge promised. "We may be staying here for some time, so we can talk over plans of what we are to do next. I do not think we are ready for the Shadows."

"We're all in agreement there." Fateh made a face, staring down at his hands and waving away the brief cloud of steam remaining. "I'm not about to go rushing in without a plan. We... we might need the help of the local humans there." His tone showed his reluctance. "When I left, there were a few rebel groups fighting against the Shadows, using metal as their main weapon."

"I cannot use metal, it rusts in my hands." Uisge shook her head. "Salt poisons my waters. I cannot fight with the weapons of the humans." She eyed Fateh. "Neither can you, I suspect. Is that the reason why you have gone abroad to find allies who can use metal?"

"Marisa brought metal with her and Haruki and Hana can use iron, even if it weakens Hana."

Hana nodded and held out her hands. "The touch of iron does not poison, but it saps my strength. I am also adverse to dogs." She shuddered. "If we are talking about our weaknesses, dogs are my main one. Dogs can scent out my true shape and scare me back into it. I cannot use my magic when I am so terrified."

Fateh nodded; it made sense. Dogs were used to hunt foxes, after all. "Any other weaknesses you feel comfortable sharing?" he asked. "We're all friends here, we won't use anything against you." He turned serious. "It's best to know what each of us can't do, so we can compensate."

Hana hesitated and then gestured to the necklace she wore, with a glowing ball at the end of the chain. "This is my hoshi no tama, my star ball. It holds my soul and powers. It must be guarded at all times."

"Knowing about your power source 's good to know." Fateh whistled low. "We'll protect it." He could see the power shimmer from it and could feel the strength. Hana had to be as strong as Haruki in her own way.

"And you? What is your weakness so we can watch over you?" Hana asked. "Water, obviously. Iron?"

Fateh nodded. "I also can't lie." He muttered, rubbing the back of his head. "I can bend the truth and get around things, but I can't outright lie. None of the fae I know of can lie."

"Ah, another sign of how we are different in nature." Hana smiled. "Kitsune are notorious liars. We have to be, so we're able to trick people so often."

Fateh didn't ask if he could trust her; she hadn't done anything that was untrustworthy yet. He felt slightly ashamed; Uisge hadn't done anything to earn his distrust, either and yet he judged her so easily.

"So we'll count on you and Haruki to lie our way into whatever danger we're going to be putting ourselves in, got it." Fateh said with a smile. "Good to know there are at least a few of us who can lie." He didn't know if Marisa was capable of lying; she seemed more inclined to the truth than anything else.

"You must be devious in your own way." Hana waved his inability to lie away. "There are other ways of getting around the truth than outright lying."

"I've always been an honest guy, though." Fateh admitted. "It's gotten me in trouble with people before, because I had trouble keeping things back." The inability to lie caused Meira and Tobias to be so suspicious of him, since he advocated the fae weren't all bad.

"We'll cure you of being so forthright. Honesty can be good, but it doesn't always have its place." Hana's smile turned mischievous. "We'll get you twisting the truth so badly that the person you speak to doesn't know which way is up."

"Twisting the truth would be a neat trick." Fateh admitted. "I've always wanted to be able to hide what I was really thinking."

"You're with an expert." Haruki grinned. "Don't worry so much, Fateh. You don't always have to speak your mind and when you do, it doesn't have to be everything. Holding back is something which will come with age as well."

"I hope it doesn't take me a hundred years. We don't have a hundred years." The Shadows were spreading and Fateh didn't want to let them run unchecked for longer than he had to.

"We might have more time than you think. The Shadows are long-lived fae as well, are they not?" Chisakou asked. "You could easily have twenty or thirty years before they make their next move."

"Except they haven't been moving slowly in the town I'm from." Fateh frowned at the memory. "They were quick to consume, quick to make contracts. They used to be human, but their souls got taken after an unfulfilled contract."

"Ah... so they are quick in their movements, because their human-fueled nature leaves them unable to do anything but." Hana shook her head. "No wonder why they spread like a blight across the land."

"But they are settled and comfortable now." Tabor spoke as he walked down the stairs. "They're in their nest, they're not inclined to move very fast now they've established a base. Not saying we have fifty years, but we don't have to rush right away. We can gather our strength and our intelligence."

"We also have to gain more human allies." Fateh said reluctantly. "We can't just have Marisa, she's not a combatant. I think we have to ask Meira and Tobias for help."

"Those are the ones who were involved in your mother's murder?" Tabor sounded shocked. "Why would you want to ask them for help?" He clearly liked Fateh's mother.

"Because they're connected with the rebels." Fateh sighed. "I don't know of any other connections; they hide themselves for good reason. I don't want to work with them, either, but desperate times call for desperate measures."

"The enemy of my enemy is my friend." Hana quoted. "I am sorry to hear these people were complicit in your mother's murder. I know it will be hard talking to them. But you are now surrounded by new friends, ones who understand you in a way they never could." She sounded calm and gentle.

"Yeah, I know--but they were my friends all my life. Their betrayal was worse than simply hurting my feelings." He looked down at the food one of the other boys in the house set in front of him. It seemed now that other people were gathering, it was breakfast time. "I don't know how it'll go. They're the ones who sent me to the prison with Mokosh, the water fae."

Chapter Fifteen

The food smelled delicious, it was some type of rice with fried tofu around it, along with eggs and soup. A small strip of fish completed the set. Fateh hesitantly picked up the chopsticks that went with the meal and awkwardly used them to pick up one of the tofu-wrapped rice balls.

"Inari-sushi." Hana supplied with a wink. "It's a favorite of kitsune."

"Yeah, but we also have miso soup, eggs, and fish as well. We can't have kitsune udon and inari-sushi all the time." Chisakou laughed and dug into her own meal with more finesse than Fateh. "We sometimes have a bigger spread, but we didn't want to overwhelm you with too many weird foods."

Fateh couldn't remember the last time he ate and he soon polished off the food in record time. It had taken a lot of energy to do what he did yesterday and it subsequently made him hungry. He wasn't the smoothest at using the chopsticks, but after watching Chisakou and a few of the others eat, he got the hang of it enough so he could eat without too much trouble.

The rest had trickled in by this point. Randi looked much better; rested and moving without any problems. Marisa and Sam were by her side, the two of them obviously feeling very protective of her.

"This place is so elegant." Randi said, sitting down and accepting a tray of food from Chisakou. "I can't believe you want me to stay here. I feel so out of place."

"We want you safe." Hana patted her hand. "A sanctuary is what this place is, a safe haven for those of mixed blood. The trees protect us from the Shadows, their roots are deep and strong to keep out unruly influences."

"Yeah, but I'm just a half-troll from Wales. I don't even speak the language here."

"Don't worry, a great many of us speak English, so you'll have no fear of being left out of a conversation." Hana reassured Randi, still gently patting her hand. "Even if you meet someone who does not speak the language, they can find someone who does and work as an interpreter for you."

"Are you staying?" Randi asked hopefully. "You seem so nice..."

"No, unfortunately I am not staying, not for long, at least." Hana looked regretful. "I have pledged my help to Fateh. Haruki and Sam are coming as well."

"Why didn't you want to take me along?" Randi asked slowly. "You think I'm a weak link because I'm weak in the sunlight?"

"No. You're not a fighter." Tabor shook his head. "We deemed it prudent for you to stay here, after all you have been through. Fateh doesn't want you hurt."

"I'm stronger than I look, especially at night." Randi protested, but it was a weak protest. "Not like I want to go and face Shadows though; from what Fateh said of them, they're terrifying. I've never seen one myself, but even the trolls hate the Shadows."

"Anything with sense hates the Shadows." Haruki nodded. "I don't know how much sense trolls have, but they're aware enough to be wary of those that consume. Although I wonder if a Shadow consumed a troll, would they have the same limitations in the sunlight?"

"Let's hope we don't have to find out." Fateh shuddered. "I'm just glad the trolls we fought were stone, except for the troll king."

"Jord had his own magic for protecting his people." Randi spoke quietly. "It wasn't enough during the daytime, where we are all weak in some way, but during the night time, no one had to fear Shadows in the dark."

"They're more of a daylight creature anyway." Tabor shrugged. "Gotta have light to create shadow, after all."

"So you're saying if we fought them at night, we'd have a better chance?" Sam looked up at the information, interested and Tabor considered the merit of this.

"You have a point, they're numerous at night, especially the smaller Shadows, but it's true they're not as strong without daylight to fuel them." He made a face. "They like brightly lit places for that reason."

"They picked the wrong place to settle down in, then." Fateh muttered. "Wales isn't exactly known for its sunny days." It was cold and foggy in Wales most of the time. The fog rolled in from the sea and it rained more days than not.

"True, they picked it because it was my home." Tabor pointed out. "They liked their little revenge. They're spiteful because I escaped them."

"No wonder they travel so far." Sam muttered. "They go all over the world. I'm surprised they don't go to America or Australia. I've heard there are places there that get over four thousand hours of sunshine a year."

Fateh couldn't imagine so much sun, it sounded terrible. He liked the cold, foggy days, because he liked the atmosphere of it. He never got cold; now he knew why. "How can you live with so much sun?" he asked in shock.

"For all we know, the Shadows thrive there as well, but I'm not about to go make a trip to sunshine hell just to see if the Shadows are there." Tabor made a face. "I like the weather in Wales, too."

"You're practically surrounded by the ocean, it's cold, foggy, and rainy and doesn't get above 21 degrees in the summer. How can you like it?" Sam demanded. "At least in Japan, there are more seasons than just autumn and winter."

"And you'd know about this in the two weeks you've been here?' Fateh asked. It was summer in New Zealand, but winter in Wales and Japan. He wore clothing more suited for warm weather while with Etana, but now switched to ones more suited to the colder weather here. . It hadn't just been where the trolls were.

"I read about the area." Sam protested. "And the others have told me what it's like during different times of the year. They say it's humid in summer, but really nice in the fall." They looked up at Hana. "They have a tree called a cherry blossom which blooms in the spring. People used to come from all over the world to view them."

"A tree?" Fateh blinked. "People traveled to see a tree bloom?" It sounded strange to Fateh, but he wasn't connected to the trees like Sam.

"It's one of our national landmarks and treasures." Hana said calmly. "It's a calming sight, seeing the pink and white blossoms in the wind. If you are still here in the spring, we will take you to see the cherry blossoms and you will see what we mean."

Fateh doubted Tabor would want to wait until spring to get moving; he was already impatient enough that he barely let Fateh rest yesterday. "Spring sounds nice." He couldn't help but agree; they both looked so earnest about showing him this. "I hope we're still here. I'm sure Tabor can settle down long enough for us to really make plans."

"Hey, I wanted to leave yesterday." Tabor protested. "There are things we need to get done."

"Nothing needs to be done right away." Fateh could be more stubborn than Tabor. "It'll be better traveling weather if we wait until spring. I'm not sure where you want to go, but unless it's on the other side of the world again, winter sucks for travel."

"It wouldn't if you would learn how to regulate your heat better."

"And I can learn to control my fire here, not on the road on some half-baked journey you have in mind. I know Hana and Haruki have to put their affairs in order before they go galavanting off with us. Fighting the trolls was a quick thing. It didn't take any planning, other than 'wait until the daytime'."

"Spark...I'm afraid the longer you stay here, the more you'll want to stay here. We can't stay."

"And where are we going to go?" Fateh demanded. "We can't go back home yet; we're not ready for it. You mention these 'cousins' but I figure we can meet them at any point."

"I think it's important you meet the cousins." Tabor looked decidedly un-moved by Fateh's logic. "They're your cousins, too and you can learn a lot from them. Who knows what you can be taught with the right person?"

"Learning from other fire elementals can wait, too." Fateh crossed his arms over his chest. "And don't you think we should be visiting all of our progenitors? I'm sure meeting full-blooded kitsune or more tree spirits will help us out. Maybe a full-blooded tree fae will let us travel between the forests, where Sam can only travel by himself now."

"We don't need to add to our already ridiculous group." Tabor protested. "We already have a circus as it is."

"I didn't say they had to stay with us, just open a pathway for us." Fateh rolled his eyes. "Look, I get you're a lone wolf sort of person, but I need allies and friends and I can't just have you. Not if we're going to do what we need to do."

"I know, I know." The rest of the group watched their exchange with interest. "But you can't blame me for wanting to keep you all to myself."

"Yes, I can." Fateh snapped. "It's unhealthy to want to keep someone, no matter if they're chained like we are." There was dead silence after Fateh's words.

"Your chain is pretty." Marisa suddenly spoke up into the silence. "It shines with all the colors of fire, reds and golds and whites and blues." She giggled and reached out as if she could touch the chain. "But the chain goes both ways. One can't control the other."

"Yeah, a partnership is how we set it up." Fateh scowled at Tabor. "So you can't make me come with you."

"The chain will grow taunt if we're too far apart." Tabor pointed out. "It will eventually hurt us if we're separated for too long."

"Still, having to be close to each other doesn't mean you can make me go any-where." Fateh pointed out. "Unless you want to drag me kicking and screaming into the shadows."

"No, I'm not going to kidnap you." Tabor looked frustrated. "This place isn't for me, it's for you, okay?" he asked. "You can be very comfortable here, with your soft beds and good food and surrounded by people like you."

"But I'm not going to stay forever. I'd get bored, being trapped inside four walls all the time." Fateh pointed out gently. "If I go outside to the town—wherever we are—" He looked at Hana.

"Ise." She supplied the name. "The cherry blossoms are especially famous here, along with our autumn leaves."

"But if I go to Ise,there might be more danger. The trees protect the Sanctuary from the Shadows, but what if there are Shadows in town, just waiting for a tasty meal? You said I'm vulnerable. Well, I want to be able to rest, let my allies do whatever they need before they go and then we can go see your cousins."

"Ise has no Shadows." Haruki spoke up. "It is an ancient and sacred place, dedicated to the Sun Goddess Amaterasu. You are safe to wander there. We go there to buy food. We can't grow everything here, no matter how hard our earth kami try." He considered Fateh. "It may do you good to visit one of our shrines and pray to the gods. It can't hurt and with you being close to the spirits yourself, you might get an answer."

"Fine." Tabor sighed and ran a hand through his hair. "We'll stay for as long as we need. Maybe it won't be so bad, not having to look over my shoulder all the time." He was especially scarred by the Shadows. Fateh wasn't sure why he wanted to go headlong into danger so quickly.

"Good." Fateh sighed as well and deflated, the fight going out of him. He looked up at Haruki. "A shrine? Is there one close by?"

"Not so far away you can't get there by walking." He winked. "I would recommend against using the shadows to travel. As I've said, it's a sacred place and using mmm...unconventional means of travel may not be the best."

"Got it, no walking through shadows in sun goddess territory." Fateh nodded in understanding. "I think I'd like to visit one of your shrines. I don't mind getting a bit of help." He didn't know what he'd do if the gods actually answered him; it seemed to be a little too much.

"Then we'll plan a trip to Naiku." Hana smiled at the group of them. "It is traditional to get the blessing of the gods before such adventures. If Amaterasu smiles upon us, then we will be lucky indeed."

"Does she often answer prayers?" Sam asked curiously. "I don't think I'm ready for the personal attention of the gods. I'm just a simple plant fae."

"Don't worry, she hasn't come down in person in centuries." Hana reassured them. "I don't think we have to worry about having our prayers answered in person."

"Good." Fateh wiped at his brow in mock relief. "I can stand to pray and believe that something is hearing my voice, but I don't need a god coming down and telling me personally I'm doomed or something."

"Oh yes. If we get an obvious sign this venture is doomed, I will not be continuing on it." Hana spread her hands in apology. "I hope you understand. I take signs from the gods very seriously."

"You'd be better off praying to Inari." Haruki snorted. "He is your patron god, after all. Not that Amaterasu isn't a worthy god to pray to. I'm just saying we're more likely to get an answer from Inari than someone as high as Amaterasu."

"Inari would probably show up in person." Hana snorted. "Just because he would think it was funny."

"You have a point." Haruki laughed. "Wouldn't it be a sight?"

"Please no." Fateh begged. "I don't need to see any gods in person. My life is weird enough as it is."

"Embrace the weirdness, Spark." Tabor laughed. "Your life isn't about to get anymore normal, especially with what we have planned."

"The unusual is what I'm afraid of." Fateh grumbled. "I went from being an ordinary kid, to being Shadow-touched, to being half-fae in the space of the year. I don't know if my heart can take anymore weirdness right now."

"I agree with Fateh." Randi whispered. "It's enoughI became a troll bride and part troll, but talking to gods? That seems a bit weird, even for what's happened to us."

"Like I said, Amaterasu is not likely to answer us personally. She'll speak through one of her priests and we'll get an answer in an indirect way."

"Will they even let us on the ground, since we're only partially human?" Fateh had to wonder. Weren't spirits forbidden on shrine grounds?

"No, we're blessed by the gods. Our presence is an honor." Hana explained. "We will get many greetings and bows to honor us."

Haruki looked uncertain. "Tengu do not have the greatest reputation with priests." He admitted reluctantly. "I can go, but I'll ask Hana to disguise me, just so we don't worry the other patrons."

"I'll be weaving my own disguises." Hana nodded, gesturing to her tail. "There are natural defenses against people seeing the true nature of kami, but they are not fool-proof. The rest of you should be just fine. You look human enough to pass. The priests and shrine maidens will know, but they won't kick up a fuss."

"So I guess we're expanding our culture." Fateh said with a laugh. "Who would have thought I'd be exposed to so much in such a short amount of time?" It hadn't even been a month and he'd seen more of the world than he had in his entire lifetime. Books didn't cut it.

"Stick with me and you'll see wonders you've only dreamt of." Tabor rested a hand on Fateh's shoulder. "Come on, let's get ready for this shrine."

Chapter Sixteen

They truly weren't really far away from the shrine; it seemed the Sanctuary was built in proximity to the shrine to give it added protection. Fateh gaped up at the large gate preceding the large wooden bridge. "It's huge."

"This is the Uji bridge. It stretches over the Isuzu river." Hana looked like an ordinary Japanese girl, her flowing hair in two pigtails down the front of her clothes. There was no sign of her tail or ears, but if Fateh squinted, he could see the outlines of them. "It is the connection between the ordinary world and the sacred one. We go over this bridge to get to Naiku, the inner shrine. There are multiple shrines but we can't go... " Hana stopped.

"I wonder if we showed our true natures if we would be let into the inner sanctum. Usually only the Imperial family and senior priests can go in there, I've always wanted to see what the fuss is all about."

"Better not risk it." Tabor said wisely. "I think we can stick to the rest of the shrines around here." He looked around. "There sure are a lot of buildings." He whistled appreciatively. "And I've got to admit it's beautiful."

There were throngs of people about, talking in hushed voices and some were praying near the gates of a large inner shrine. That must be the inner sanctum Hana talked about. There were smaller buildings next to the large gates.

"This is where we pray to the gods." Haruki gestured. "Come on, don't be shy. If you get a personal response, then you'll be hailed for inciting a miracle." He pushed Fateh forward.

"I don't even pray at home." He wanted to visit the shrine because it sounded like a good idea but among all these people who obviously believed in the gods and their prayers, he didn't know about his surety. "What am I supposed to do?"

"Go to a priest and say you're going on a journey, seeking the blessing of Amaterasu. Or if you're not picky, we can pray to one of the wind gods."

"No, better go for the big guns." Fateh grimaced. "I really hope I don't get a personal response. Please don't give me a personal response, whatever god is up there." He said the last part in Welsh, so no one would be able to understand him. He still got funny looks for the foreign language.

"Come on. I'll speak for us." Hana dragged him to a priest. His eyes went wide when he saw Hana and Fateh and he bowed deeply to them.

"What do I owe the honor?" he asked. "It is not often we have the gods come to visit us."

Fateh wanted to protest they weren't gods, but Hana elbowed him. Oh yeah, she wants to speak for us. I'll just keep my mouth shut.

"We are visiting here to get guidance from our higher brethren." She bowed back and Fateh followed suit. "We are here to pray to the great Amaterasu and seek her counsel in the matter of a journey."

"A journey?" The priest led them to a small shrine, paneled in the same wood as the rest of the shrines were. "What sort of journey do the gods take?"

"A journey to fight evil, what else?" Hana asked airily. "It is a perilous journey and we want to make sure we have Amaterasu's blessing before we rush headlong into danger." She gave a quick smile. "Even the gods must tread lightly when facing a darker evil."

"Ah, yes." The priest looked thoughtful. "Let us pray and ask for guidance from the mighty Amaterasu. I am sure she will hear your prayers and offer you her blessings."

Fateh watched as the priest closed his eyes and hummed under his breath, chanting something he didn't quite understand. He wondered if he should close his eyes as well, but he didn't like to be blind to everything around him when he was in an unfamiliar place, even if it was a shrine.

The priest stopped his chanting and held out his hands. As if conjured by magic, a beam of sunlight lanced down from the sky to pass between his hands. The priest smiled brightly at the two of them. "It seems you have a good omen for your journey. May you travel well."

Fateh blinked. A ray of sunlight? He expected a little more fanfare, but grateful all they got was some sun. He bowed when Hana did. "We appreciate your speaking to the goddess on our behalf. Sometimes the voices of the little gods do not reach those which are higher."

"I understand. We are blessed by your presence nonetheless." The priest bowed one more time and then left them. Fateh stared after him, bemused. "That's it?" he asked.

"Did you expect the goddess to come down and tell us 'yes, go on this incredibly dangerous journey'?" Hana laughed at Fateh's expression. "The priest interpreted the sign of the sunlight as a blessing from Amaterasu. His reading is enough for me."

"Things are a lot simpler than I thought."

"And your priests at home, do they not pray for a sign as well?" Hana asked.

"Don't know, never went to church." Fateh admitted. "Our grandparents thought it was a quackery and mom never got in the habit of going because of their beliefs." He considered it. "From what I can remember, though, I'm not missing much."

"You should pray more to the gods." Hana scolded. "They are the guideposts in our life, they lead us to where we need to go, they watch over us--"

"It sounds like you know them personally." Fateh stuck his hands in his pockets and people watched. A place untouched by the Shadows, a place where people were free to come to ask for help. It was a good place and Fateh was sad to know he wouldn't be staying here or at the Sanctuary for very long. "Oh that's right. You said you know Inari."

Hana nodded in affirmation. "Come, let us go back to our companions before they think we have run away. Tabor is most protective, it wouldn't do you any good to have him think I ran off with you."

"He could just tug me back with a yank on my chain." Fateh muttered. He hated the chain, he hated it had to be there. It thankfully wasn't visible all the time for him, but it shimmered in and out of focus like a bad special effect.

"You should renegotiate the terms of your agreement if you find it too restricting."

"We're already equal partners, or so he says." Fateh spotted Tabor in the crowd and started walking towards him.

"Then you can yank his chain as easily as he yanks yours." Hana gave him a mischievous smile. "Why don't you try it and see how he reacts?"

Fateh blinked at her suggestion; he never thought of using the chain in reverse, The chains had always been a one way thing. He wasn't used to it going both ways. He gave Tabor a wide-eyed smile, took his hands out of his pockets, and then tugged on the chain, feeling the power of it slide through his fingertips.

Tabor staggered forward and gave Fateh a wounded look. "If you wanted my attention, all you had to do was call out. You didn't have to use the chain. What's so important you had to give it a tug, especially when I'm within shouting distance?"

"I wanted to see if it would work both ways." Fateh shrugged and tried to look innocent.

Hana giggled next to him. "You yanked my chain before, I wanted to see if I could do the same to you, partner."

"I see. You either had a bad influence," he looked at Hana, "or you didn't trust me when I said it worked both ways."

"Hey, I'm the type that needs to test it out. I just never thought of it before today." Fateh shrugged. "Sorry if it hurt you."

"More like shocked me. I've never been chained before either and I didn't expect to feel like my insides got yanked out." Tabor grimaced and rubbed his midsection.

"Well, now we both know what it's like." Fateh grinned. "You did it to me and so I returned the favor. Now let's not do that again, hm? If you need me, you call for me, you don't go grabbing the chain to get my attention."

"I only yanked your chain once.." Tabor protested, but acquiesced immediately. "Fine, fine-- no more playing with the chain." He managed to look disappointed and amused all the same time. "I'll just have to call for your attention like a normal person."

"Yeah, imagine if you grabbed the chain while we were fighting." Fateh pointed out. "You'd get my attention, but you'd also throw me off guard and make me lose whatever concentration I had going."

"You've made your point." Tabor shook his head at Hana. "And I'm sure I have you to blame for Spark deciding to investigate the limits of his power."

"Of course, he needs to know there is not an imbalance, not just take your word for it." Hana was unruffled by Tabor's glare. "It's only fair he knows what he is capable of and what his limits are with you. You are partners and are going to be bound together for a very long time indeed. It's best to nip these sort of things in the bud before the perceived imbalance grows."

"Don't belabor the point. I got it, okay? Spark can use the power that connects us, just as easily as I can. Next thing you know, he'll be picking up all sorts of useful talents you're going to encourage him to try."

"Best he grows instead of stagnates like still water." Uisge put in, having coming up

behind them at the last part of the conversation. "He needs to grow and he is not going to do it if he thinks you are the one in charge. He is his own power and being connected to another person isn't going to change what he can do."

"Is this gang up on Tabor day?" Tabor asked rhetorically. "I get it, okay? Sheesh."

Fateh grinned up at Tabor. "It sucks to be the one being picked on, doesn't it?" he asked. "Now you know how I felt all the time with you annoying the hell out of me."

"I only teased you because you were interesting and I didn't want you to lose your interest in me." Tabor protested. "Teasing is different than everyone ganging up on me."

"Who's ganging up on you?" Haruki asked, a bundle of charms hanging from one hand.

"If you're anything like me, you probably deserve it. The best and brightest always attract the most ire. We can't help it, we're that fabulous."

Tabor snorted at Haruki's matter of fact words. "No, they're just picking on me because they can." He looked hurt. "I'm devastated I tell you, devastated you all think I'm an idiot who doesn't understand I want the best for Spark. It's why I want us to travel to see the cousins, he can learn a lot from them and grow in his power."

"A good point." Hana allowed. "But I am interested in meeting these cousins of yours as well. I think meeting more spirits of fire and other elements will be an exciting adventure and like Fateh pointed out, may give us advantages we otherwise would not have had."

"It's going to be a circus by the time we get to the Shadows." Tabor moaned. "I know it. We're going to be dragging half a town with us."

"Better to be over prepared than under prepared." Haruki shrugged and started handing charms to the group. "I personally don't think we need anymore in our core group, but it's good to make allies along the way. Who knows what they can do in our hour of need?"

"What are these charms for?" Uisge asked, turning hers around in her hand.

"They're good luck charms, blessed by the priests of the temple." Haruki shrugged. "I figured we could use as much luck as possible, considering what we've committed ourselves to."

"Buying a charm is a good idea." Fateh approved. "I'm not about to turn away a little luck." He tucked away the charm in his pocket, where it left a comforting presence. Luck from the gods, hm? It certainly couldn't hurt.

Chapter Seventeen

They stayed in the shrine area for a good part of the day; just exploring and sight-seeing. Fateh wished he had a camera so he could capture what he saw. He saw other tourists with smartphones, capturing the expansive area of the shrine--where they were permitted to do so--and it felt so weird watching them use a technology he hadn't seen for years. The kids at the Sanctuary had smartphones as well and Fateh felt a brief stab of envy. The Shadows had stopped smartphones from working in their purge of technology, but he had sometimes played with his as if it would work they way it used to.

He hadn't exactly felt the need for a camera of a phone when he shopped with Tabor for the essentials, but now was different. This was a gorgeous place and filled with so much peace. He'd just have to depend on his memory alone and perhaps a chance to visit here again. Besides, even if he had a smartphone, who would he call? Etana may have a phone, but he couldn't see ringing him up for a casual call. Maybe there would be the games he could play on the phone again and the aforementioned camera function, but really, he had been without one for almost three years. He didn't need one now. Although reaching the kids at the Sanctuary... it was a thought he pushed into the back of his mind.

He could already see himself coming back to the Sanctuary, if only to have a dependable resting place and allies to depend on. Tabor would just have to deal with it. Fateh liked this place as much as he hated Mokosh's. It felt comfortable to him in the same way Etana probably felt for Tabor. Safe harbor and allies were nothing to discount out of hand.

It was strange to feel so comfortable in a foreign country and Fateh wondered what his life would have been like if the Shadows never came. Would he have traveled the world and explored all new destinations or would have stayed in Wales, comfortable in his home and with his friends and family? He liked to think he would have been the type to explore; he enjoyed it so far.

"So where are these cousins of yours?" Fateh asked. "Please don't tell me Wales again. I won't believe a bunch of fire-fae have decided Wales is the best place to live."

"What's so surprising about it?" Tabor asked in mock-surprise. "Don't you love Wales?" He liked teasing Fateh and it earned him a scowl. "I kid. Wales is great, but the cousins live in a place a bit less damp?" He shrugged. "Wales is my home, but the cousins live in nicer climes than the human world. How do you feel about visiting the fae realm?"

Fateh stared at Tabor in open-mouthed shock. "The fae realm?" He repeated. "Am I even allowed there?" He gestured to himself. "Still partially human, you know."

"Less human than you think you are, you're fae enough to visit the fae side of things." Tabor shrugged. "It can be dangerous, but so is the human world right now, hm?"

"You have a point." Fateh acknowledged the point. "And the biggest thing to worry about is someone trying to make a deal with me, right? And I'm already contracted to you, so I don't have to mess around with that sort of thing."

"Exactly." Tabor looked over the rest of the group critically. "The only one we really have to worry about is the little Seer, but she already proved adept in the shadows, so the fae realm may be safe for her as well."

"We aren't fae, though." Hana pointed out gently. "We're yokai and spirits. How will we fare in your realm of fae?"

"It's more of a spirit realm we're going to." Tabor admitted. "It's not where the high fae live, it's sort of a... corner of the world where elemental spirits of all kinds live. My cousins find it more palatable than the human world and there are no Shadows there." His smile was grim. "We have more than enough power to keep them out. If we weren't so numerous there, it would be like a buffet for the Shadows."

"Good to know." Fateh didn't ask why they didn't go there instead of with Etana; Fateh probably would have been overwhelmed to have so many fae around, rather than the singular Etana. "How do we get there? More shadows?"

"Have you ever heard of the hollow hills?" Tabor asked. "It's a doorway we have to find, not the shadows. Those are pathways which cut through your world, we're going to the overworld."

"Can we access these doorways from anywhere or do we have to be some-where specific?" Fateh raised an eyebrow. "This traveling circus of yours would like to know how far we have to travel before we can get to where you want to go."

"There are doorways all over the world." Tabor reassured him. "I just have to find the one here in Japan, so we don't have to travel across countries again." He grinned. "The language barrier is starting to get interesting. Not all of us have the same language capabilities."

"How kind of you." Hana smiled. "Not that your Wales would be a problem, Haruki and I speak English. We are the odd ones out when it comes to your home country; if you would feel more comfortable leaving from Wales, then I don't see the problem."

"How many times do you want to travel through the shadows?" Tabor asked in return. "I'm sure such a holy place such as this has a doorway we can use."

"Probably in a torii gate." Haruki looked interested. "They are said to be gateways to the spirit realm. I'm sure you can key in your destination somehow so we end your spirit realm and not ours. There is a large torii gate on the bridge we crossed."

"Using the gate is a good idea." Tabor looked relieved they wouldn't have to go far. "We don't need anything special for the fae realm. What you're carrying will be enough. The main thing to remember is to be polite."

"Will they welcome me?" Uisge asked delicately. "Fateh is already apprehensive of me. What will a clutch of your kind do when faced with a water spirit?"

"They'll have to deal with it." Tabor's words were firm. "You're a part of this group now and we're not going to leave you out of it. Besides, the water spirits live where we are going. Maybe you can meet more of your kind and get ...pointers on what you can do." Tabor clearly thought Uisge was competent enough on her own and didn't need the extra help. His tone said it all.

"And us?" Haruki asked. "Are you able to open up a doorway where we can meet our erstwhile relatives as well?" He indicated himself and Hana.

"I love how you think I can do anything at all." Tabor huffed. "It really builds my confidence. I don't know if I can, but I can certainly try. I don't want to leave you out of this little adventure either."

"Sounds like we're going to be visiting as many places in the fae realm as we have in the human realm." Fateh noted. "We're not only going to meet our elemental cousins, but we're going to cross over and meet the Japanese ones as well." Fateh shook his head. "I'm really going to need a vacation after this. It's a lot to take in."

"Vacations are for after we do what we need to do." Tabor pointed out. "You decided on this little mission, now you have to see it through to the end."

"You're a terrible person." Fateh complained. "Don't you believe in rest?"

"You got to rest for a year in prison." Tabor looked unconcerned and a little mischievous.

"You said it yourself, a prison, not the Sanctuary." Fateh protested. "I wore metal for more than half of my time there and according to you, slowly being poisoned. I wouldn't call what I went through a vacation at all."

"I'll grant you that much." Tabor gestured around him. "But you've spent some time in the Sanctuary before we went on this little jaunt. Don't worry, we won't stay overly long with the cousins. I don't want you entirely overwhelmed."

"Too late for not being overwhelmed." Fateh groaned. "It's been not even a month and I've already experienced more than I have my entire life."

"Aren't you glad for the experience?" Tabor asked. "You're a regular world traveler now and very cosmopolitan in the types of people you've met. We just have to expand your worldview a little more."

"As long as we're not going back to the land of snow and ice." Fateh shivered. "Although I don't know; wont' a fire realm be too much for everyone except us?"

"It's not like it's fire there." Tabor shook his head. "It's just not damp and cold, but it's a perfectly respectable and comfortable corner of the world. I just don't live there full time because Wales is my home."

"Picking Wales over something less damp is definitely a story you'll have to tell one of these days." Fateh pointed out. "How damp, chilly Wales became the home of a full-blooded fire fae. It's not like me; my family grew up in Wales for centuries."

"And I've been here for over a century." Tabor pointed out. "I can stay warm even in cold weather, so the atmosphere of Wales doesn't bother me. I like the people and the culture. It has a good history, too."

"Huh." Fateh filed Tabor's love of history away for later. "It is a nice place, isn't it?" Everyone except Hana and Haruki nodded; they were all from Wales. It was their home. Despite its flaws, they would always return home.

"We will have to visit." Hana said with a smile. "For more than just the bank of a river. I'm sure there is a lot of Wales that is beautiful and you'll want to show off."

"Oh, you'll get to see Wales when we visit the nest of Shadows." Tabor said grimly. "Won't be the nicest area of Wales, but we're not there to sightsee. It's going to be a battle."

"And I say after we visit these cousins, we figure out a plan." Fateh said stubbornly. "We're not just going to rush into fighting the Shadows after we meet them. We're not ready yet." He stared at his hands, imagining the fire that appeared there. "I get too exhausted too quickly. I think it'll take time to build my strength."

"I know, I know." Tabor sighed. "Look, I'm not about to throw you into danger. I want you to get stronger as well. You're going to be in the line of fire and I'm not going to lose you to the Shadows just because I was impatient."

"Good." Fateh relaxed marginally and looked around the temple grounds. "Alright. I guess we've done all we can get done." They had good luck charms, they got the blessing of a priest for a goddess and they had a gateway to go where they needed to go. It was all settled. "I guess we're seeing Tabor's cousins--and a lot of other spirits along the way." They all deserved a chance to get the help from their progenitors. Tabor might think it was all about the fire elementals, but Fateh knew he wanted to get a broad education. He was overwhelmed yes, but also fascinated by the sheer scope of what he was going to see.

"I'm interested to see more of the earth fae." Sam spoke up, sounding a little shy. "Maybe we can spread to the four corners of where we need to go and meet up back here after we're done?" They shrugged. "It seems the most logical, we can cover more ground that way and no one will be bored."

"Are you sure it's a good idea for us to be wandering around alone?" Marisa asked, tilting her head to the side. "I will not wander alone, for there are too many traps in the paths we will walk."

"You'll stay with us." Fateh said firmly, looking up at Tabor. "Isn't that right? We're not going to let Marisa out on her own?"

"Of course not. A human-- a Seer -- wandering the fae realm alone? She'd go mad." Tabor looked insulted. "I'm not a monster. I'm tempted to let her stay at the Sanctuary as well, it'll probably be safer for her."

"Insteads of traveling with us, staying at the Sanctuary may be a good idea..." Haruki bit his lip. "Humans are rare in the spirit realm, it might be too overwhelming for her. And a Seer? She'll See too much." He shrugged. "It's going to be a struggle even for us and we're half-spirit. It's the human half of us that'll be in danger."

"Okay, so it's decided. We're going to take Marisa back to the Sanctuary. Then we'll come back here to the torii gate and try and key our way through to where the elemental powers are, then a side trip to where your kin are." Fateh looked at Haruki and Hana. "This is going to be interesting."

"We're certainly getting our walking in for the day." Sam muttered under their breath.

"And we'll probably do much more." Fateh snorted. "Okay, the game plan is in order. Let's get it done."

"Yes, sir." Sam saluted Fateh with a grin. "We'll follow your lead."

"Anything but following my lead" Fateh snorted. "I'm just--"

"Just acting like a leader." Sam waved him off. "Someone has to. Glad it's not me."

"Tabor should be our leader." Fateh insisted. "He's the only full-blood around here, he knows the shadow roads and the pathway into the fae realm." He didn't know where he started depending on Tabor, but it wasn't a surprise anymore.

"You're a natural leader, Spark." Tabor patted him on the head. "Just roll with it."

The others were nodding as well and Fateh flushed, scraping the ground with the toe of one shoe. "Alright, whatever." He muttered. "I still don't think we need a leader. It's best we all speak up and lead when it's needed."

"And right now it's your turn." Haruki said cheerfully. "When we wander into the yokai realm and I try to keep you all from being eaten, it will be my turn."

"Being eaten is not encouraging." Fateh stared at Haruki. "I don't want to go to a place where something will eat me. I have enough danger of being consumed with the Shadows."

"There are worse things out there than Shadows." Haruki looked unphased. "They just choose to stay in the realm of nightmares, rather than interact with the human world. Luckily, it's relatively safe where I want to go. We won't be going to the realm where it's dangerous; it's going to be nicer."

"That's still not super encouraging." Fateh made a face. "Maybe I'll decline going with you to your realm."

"You're no fun." Haruki pouted. "I'll make sure you're safe. It's really not as bad as it could be. The tengu realm is filled with large-nosed, feathered morons who admittedly like to use a sword. Just set one of them on fire and assert your dominance if they try to skewer you."

"Yeah, not the best plan." Fateh retorted. "I only plan on setting my enemies on fire and I sure as hell don't want to make enemies out of minor gods." He shuddered. "I have more plans for my life, thank you."

"Again, no fun."

"It will be easier meeting my kitsune relatives." Hana put in. "They are Inari's messengers and thus more well-behaved than some rowdy, wind-using tengu. I think you'll like them, they're more calm." She frowned a little. "Not that I have ever met them in large numbers, only my mother, but she is an example of her kind."

"If they're anything like you, I think I'll like them a lot." Fateh smiled at Hana. He really did like her. Calm and collected, with power and just a hint of mischief. He thought of her as the leader. If he was going to be vetted as the leader, he wanted to emulate her.

"You flatter me." She hid a smile behind one hand, waving his compliment away with the other. "Let us go and get who we need to safety, while we prepare to enter the spirit realm. There are items at home I think will be useful for when we enter the land of the yokai."

"It's a good thing we're going back to the Sanctuary first, then." Fateh nodded. "Alright, let's go."

Marisa smiled brightly and twirled around, clearly happy with the decision she wasn't going to the spirit realm; either fae or Japanese. "My eyes will be open when I stay within the tree-lined walls." She said. "I will not spill any secrets, though. The cats may wander where they will and I will not stand in their way."

"There's more shapeshifters than just the cats." Haruki said mildly. "You'll see through a whole lot of illusions and no one will be grateful if you speak of what they are hiding."

"My lips are sealed." Marisa's eyes were wide as she promised. "No secrets spilled, no shapes revealed."

Chapter Eighteen

I t didn't take them long to go back to the Sanctuary and set Marisa up; they also carried more charms to protect against the yokai, for when they traveled to Haruki's tengu realm. Fateh felt like he was going into battle, with the amount of protections he had. Haruki and Fateh were alone in Haruki's room, gathering what they needed.

"You're not wrong." Haruki agreed with Fateh when he brought it up. "You have to go into the yokai realm prepared for anything. My people are usually okay, but there are realms which touch ours which aren't so nice. So we're preparing for those realms."

"You make it sound so enticing." Fateh had to laugh. "But I suppose there's danger in everything." He looked away for a moment. "I wish the charms would work against the Shadows. It would be nice to stick one to a Shadow and have them dissolve into mist."

"Who's to say it won't work?" Haruki asked with a shrug. "You've never had the opportunity to try it yet; you never know what our magic can do to solve your problems."

"Our problems." Fateh pointed out. "The Shadows are your problem, too. You're just safe here at the Sanctuary. But what if your defenses fall? You'll need to fight."

"Aren;t you the brightest ray of sunshine." Haruki wrinkled his nose. "We have centuries of magic protecting this place. The lack of protection in your home made it easy for the Shadows to move in. But with our help, we'll build up the magic to protect, as well as root out the problem at its source."

"I hope so." Fateh said, expression troubled. "I'm willing to throw anything at the Shadows."

Haruki gave him a hug around the shoulders. "You should be more positive. Have a brighter outlook on life instead of being so much doom and gloom. I know it's been hard for you these past couple of years, but things will get better. You have a lot of strong allies on your side to fight and we're going to get help from those much more powerful than us."

Fateh didn't say if they'll help, because he didn't want to be more negative. He didn't want to depress Haruki with his negative thoughts. He was so used to looking on the practical side of things and recently 'practical' had meant negativity.

"Tabor's itching to get going." He changed the subject. "I don't know why he's so obsessed with meeting these cousins of his, but he's determined to have me meet them." Fateh had a sudden vision of an endless group of people who all looked like Tabor and he grimaced.

"He's concerned for you and wants you to meet those with similar power to yours. Maybe he feels he can't train you as well as a group can; there may be tricks they know that he does not. He may even be seeking advice for himself. He is young, as you said. He will not admit he needs help, but it is a need all the same."

"I didn't think of him needing help." Fateh considered Tabor was looking for help for himself, not just for Fateh. "It makes sense, though." Maybe he wouldn't be so hard on Tabor for wanting to go to his cousins.

"It's why I am willing to meet with my relatives." Haruki shrugged. "They can be temperamental, but I'm willing to bet they can teach me some swordsman-ship and magic I don't already know."

"You're decades ahead of me." Fateh pointed out. "It's a shame we don't share the same kind of magic; you could probably teach me loads."

"There's probably some magic I could teach you." Haruki looked interested in the idea. "There is charm magic anyone can do and like I said, it could serve you well during the fight with the Shadows."

"I'm willing to try anything." Fateh admitted. "Even if it's using magic I'm unfamiliar with."

"And how much magic are you familiar with?" Haruki asked with amusement. "I have a feeling you're not used to a great deal of magic. You have your fire, but that's a natural part of your being. Learning actual spells is different."

"If you're willing to teach, I'm willing to learn." Fateh said.

"Hana is better at magical spells than I am. It may be good to ask her for help, especially with illusions. Your fire can create them and she can help you refine them."

"Like I said, I'm a willing student." Fateh repeated. "I need every trick I can think of to fight the Shadows." He was willing to learn magic, learn about his fire and if it came down to it, he'd learn how to use a sword so he could fight on a physical level.

"Well, we better get back to the others before they wonder where we've run off to." Haruki said cheerfully. "I think we have all we need here." He dumped half the charms into Fateh's arms. "Come on."

Fateh nodded and followed Haruki through the house to where the others were waiting.

***

In less time than Fateh expected, they were in front of the large torii gate again. Tabor looked at it critically from every angle he could reach and finally nodded to himself. "Alright, this is a possible doorway." His tone brightened. "Just have to do some manipulations--" He stood in the middle of the gate, obviously concentrating on something. The minutes ticked by until a flash occurred and there was a pathway that wasn't the bridge on the other side of the gate. Fateh gaped at it, but the others were already moving and Tabor gestured for him to move as well.

"I can't hold this gate forever and the priests are going to start investigating." Tabor warned. "Stare later, go now."

Fateh got the hint and hustled through the gate, right behind Hana and Haruki. Sam and Uisge brought up the rear and Tabor stepped through with them, closing the gate with a quick gesture of his hand. The torii gate was gone and in its place, a simple wooden door.

"Guess that's our doorway back home." Fateh observed. He didn't try the door; he didn't know what would be on the other side of it. Even if the door seemed to go nowhere, it could lead anywhere.

"We'll find our way back here or we'll find another doorway." Tabor looked a little tired after his big working. "There are dozens of them all over the realm." He kept a hand on Fateh's shoulder. "Now, to get on with what we're here for."

"How? Are you going to call them?" Fateh asked with a raised eyebrow. It seemed like a pretty ordinary landscape on the other side of the gate, with a city not far in the background. "You live in houses?" he asked in bemusement.

"What did you think, we lived in the trees?" Tabor snorted. "Everybody likes a solid place to live and maybe we copied from the humans or they copied from us, but yet, we have houses. Quite nice ones, actually. That's where we'll be going. There will be a community of my cousins there. It's similar to the Sanctuary, only we live in houses of stone rather than flammable wood."

"Stone houses make sense." Fateh peered at the city spread out and shook his head. "I don't know what I expected, but this wasn't it."

"I live to defy your expectations." Tabor gave a wide grin as he bowed to Fateh. "It's good to surprise you. Keeps you on your toes." He led the way down the cobbled street to where the city lay.

There were trees lining the road and gently rolling hills surrounding the city. In the distance, Fateh could see other cities, but they were much further away. He could have sworn he saw the shimmer of sun on the water and resolved to be on his best behavior when they inevitably went that way for Uisge. He didn't want to go, but he also didn't want to separate the group anymore.

"So what are these cousins like?" Fateh asked when they were close to the entrance of the city. "Do they look like you?"

"They're as varied as me and you." Tabor laughed. "Some have actually fire for hair, instead of just strands of hair which resemble fire." He ruffled Fateh's hair. "Of course, you grow fire in your hair, but it's not the same."

Tabor hummed cheerfully to himself, waving at various fae peeking out from windows and doorways. Some on the street openly stared at the motley group. One young woman ran up to them, fire streaming down from her head, forming a waterfall of flame.

"Tabor! You've returned!" She hugged him tightly. She barely came up to the height of his nose. "And you've brought...friends." She looked the six of them over, curiosity in her expression.

"Nia!" Tabor laughed and swung her around, earning a laugh of delight. "It's been awhile." He observed her with a hand on his hip. "You look taller," He teased her. "Have you been drinking milk?"

She wrinkled her nose. "As if I'd drink something that came from a cow."

"Could have been a goat." Tabor grinned. "I don't know your preferences.It could have changed since the last time I saw you."

"Not enough to be drinking milk." She protested. "You know me too well to know I won't drink cow or goat milk."

"Yes, only plant juice for you." Tabor sighed heavily. "Maybe if you drank milk from a cow, you'd grow as tall as me."

"Not a high bar to reach." Fateh muttered under his breath, but it caught Nia's attention.

"And who are you?" Her tone belied her curiosity. "You're traveling with Tabor and he doesn't like that many people," Nia's look turned scrutinizing. "Ah, you have fire in you!' She was clearly delighted by this. "Tabor, this child has a lot of fire in him, but he's human, too! What did you bring us?"

"I'm a who, not a what." Fateh crossed his arms over his chest. Etana called him a what as well. It aggravated him. "My name is Fateh and Tabor says I'm half aodhamair. I take it you're full-blooded, like Tabor?"

"Did the hair give it away?" She ran a hand through the flames and looked smug. "You can't pull off this trick, but Tabor can if he wants to do more than just blend in with humans." She eyed the rest of the group. "Who else have you brought?"

The rest stepped forward to introduce themselves. Nia's eyes went wide at the sight of Uisge and she slightly edged behind Tabor, as if afraid of the water fae. Still, she waved politely enough when she gave her name.

"What a diverse bunch you have here, Tabor. What are you planning to do with such a group?" Nia examined them. "You have all four elements, even if they are in slightly different forms than we're used to." She gestured to Haruki and Hana. "What are you, if I can ask?"

"We're half-yokai," Haruki bowed, "and half spirit-fox." Hana bowed next and smiled. "We have decided to lend our power to the cause of defeating the Shadows."

Nia's eyes went round with shock. "Tabor, you can't fight the Shadows! Not after what they did to you last time." She wrapped her arms around him and looked up pleadingly. "I don't want you to get hurt again. We almost lost you last time."

"I know, but now I'm stronger than I used to be. I have Spark, who has the ability to do some things I can't, and his host of friends." Tabor's smile went cold. "They won't know what hit them."

"Still, it's dangerous." She protested, still clinging to him. "They nearly drained you last time and I heard they took over your territory. We lost a few cousins already to them." She looked down at the ground. "We lost Deri when he tried to save you."

"I know what happened to him." Tabor's tone went grim. "I've met the Shadow that subsumed him and took his power."

"Then why are you going on this fool's errand? Why don't you stay here and be safe? The Shadows can't reach here; we have too many protections in place."

"Because Spark wants to rid his town of a nest of them." Tabor rested a hand on Fateh's shoulder. "And I want to get revenge for what they've done to me, Deri, and Alys." Alys had been Nia's sister and she was taken early on. She had barely been old enough to hold her majority.

"Oh, I want you to get revenge, especially for Alys." Her hair flared with a brighter intensity as she talked about her missing sister. "I just don't want you to put yourself in danger doing so."

"Don't worry, we're not going to rush over right away and fight them." Tabor reassured Nia. "We're going to build up our strength first, learn some tricks from the cousins here and meet the family of some of my compatriots. We're going to learn all the tricks we can before we go fighting the Shadows."

"I'm sure I can teach you something." Nia promised. She looked over Fateh. "Have you learned how to manipulate lightning yet?" Her palms crackled with it and she tossed the living balls of electricity from hand to hand in a juggling motion.

"Tabor taught me how to create it, but we haven't done much with it yet." Fateh admitted. "I can throw lightning, but I can't manipulate it."

"Oooh, it means I can teach you to throw a lightning spear or a ring of lightning around someone." Nia was suddenly bright and cheerful. "I'm very good with lightning."

"Can you teach me how to make a rope out of fire as well?" Fateh asked with curiosity. "I can throw explosive fireballs, but I haven't done much more than fireballs and streaks of lightning."

"Oh, don't worry. I'll teach you and Tabor plenty." She rubbed her hands together with glee. "Tabor only knows fireballs, which is why he hasn't taught you much more than forming lightning and throwing fire, I bet."

Fateh nodded and Tabor pouted. "Fireballs are a perfectly acceptable use of combat." He protested. "But if you want to get fancy, I suppose we can do fancy shit, too." He looked reluctant. "We can teach Spark how to use a fire tornado as well, now that we can practice in a place which can handle it."

"And what about the rest of your little gang?" Nia asked. "Shall I show them the guest quarters so they'll have a place to rest while we play with fire or do you think they'd be interested in seeing what we can do?"

"The more we know about Tabor and Fateh's ability, the better." Sam spoke up. "Fire and I don't get along well-- something about trees being extremely flammable--but I am interested in what they can do. I think knowing each of our own strengths will be an asset. This way we're not surprised at anything he does and not disappointed when a task can't be performed."

"Watching is a good idea." Nia said approvingly. "If you're going on this fool's errand, at least you're going about it as sensible as possible. I'll show you the spectator stands so you can watch and not get burned. We have a training ground for our children, when they're just getting used to their powers."

The way she said children made Fateh flush with embarrassment, but he was a child to Tabor and it seemed to be Nia as well. Unaware of her age, he didn't want to ask. She'd probably be centuries old or something and he would just feel like an idiot.

"You just graduated from those training grounds, so don't act like it was a long time ago." Tabor chided. "You may be a prodigy when it comes to lightning, but you're not that much older than Fateh, technically speaking."

"Oh, ruin the image I've been cultivating." Nia pouted. "I could have pretended I was much older and wiser and your little -- Fateh? Fateh wouldn't have known the difference. I'm still older than some half-human teenager, though."

She's right about me. Fateh kept his thoughts to himself, Maybe he should stop assuming and just ask next time. "What are you, fifty?"

"Ah, you're so kind to think I'm as old as fifty." She winked at him. "I'm only thirty, but I'm advanced for my age."

Fateh blinked; she really wasn't much older than him. She was younger than his mother had been. "Oh--well, I'm sure you're quite accomplished and I trust you to teach me what you know."

"Good." She took his hand and smiled over at him. "Come along, Fateh. I'll take you all to the training grounds and we can see what you can do, as well as teach you a few new tricks,"

Fateh could only nod and follow along. He wanted to learn more, but he knew the more he used his fire, the less human he'd become. Etana said fire burned away everything and he wondered if it meant his humanity as well.

Chapter Nineteen

I t didn't take them long to get to the training grounds; they were situated on the edge of town for safety reasons and were a wide, open space, devoid of any plant life. There were wooden dummies peppering the grounds, a lot of them blackened with fire.

"We try to replace what we destroy." Nia explained as they walked past a particularly fire-blackened dummy. "Here are some untouched ones." She led them to a corner of the training ground, where stadium seating was nearby. "It will be a good gauge of what you can do when you see what you do to the dummies."

"Tabor had me exploding cinder walls." Fateh thought it was only fair to warn her.

"Oh, so you're a bit of a loose cannon." She laughed. "I'm going to teach you finesse, so you can use your fire in more versatile ways." She twisted her hand in a circular motion, making a throwing gesture at the same time. A fine rope of fire settled around the dummies head, cutting into it and burning through the cloth and charring the wood underneath.

"See what I did?" she asked. "You have to envision the rope and throw it where you want it to land." She stood behind him, ignoring Tabor's splutters that Fateh was his protege, not Nia's.

Fateh tried to envision the rope, but the throwing motion reminded him too much of the fireballs he and Tabor created and he sent one flying towards the dummy, nearly knocking its head off. "Oops."

"Don't worry, no one gets it on the first try." She reassured him. "Well, I did, but I'm a special case." She sounded both pleased and smug at the same time and Fateh made a face. It was good to be proud of what you could do, but you didn't have to be an ass about it.

She demonstrated the twirling motion again, forefinger and thumb pressed together. "Here, try again." She encouraged. "You're bright, I'm sure you can get it right on the second try."

"You have a lot of faith in me." Fateh grumbled, but looked towards the group in the stands, all of them watching avidly. All they needed was popcorn and it'd be a real show for them.

"Because I know you can do it. Now, try again." Nia was unrepentant in the way she pushed him. "No excuses,"

Fateh made the twirling motion and a fine rope of fire appeared, but it was several feet short of the target. He groaned and made a face. He somewhat succeeded; he at least made the rope.

"Now we just have to work on your aiming skills." Nia laughed. "You're not doing bad for a half. Not that I've known any halves, but you're not as strong as a whole, I'm sure. You're doing fine with what you have."

"I'm not sure if you insulted me or not." Fateh complained. "Look, I made the rope and it only took me two tries. I can practice getting it over the dummy's head."

"And aiming is what you're going to do." Nia was short, but she had a lot of determination packed in her tiny frame. "Once you master the fire rope, we'll work on other tasks."

"You're bossy." Fateh said bluntly.

"You came to me for help." She retorted. "Can't ask for help from me and think I'll do it by halves." She shook her head.. "It's not the way I work. I go all the way or not at all and if I chose not at all, we wouldn't even be talking."

"Weren't you going to teach Tabor, too?" Fateh asked desperately. "I know I'm not the only one you wanted to focus on."

"True. Tabor, get over here." Nia pointed to a spot next to her. "You're not getting out of this lesson."

"I used to teach you." Tabor muttered sullenly, but did as he was told. "Until you outpaced me and started learning fancy tricks."

"You can't just expect I would have been satisfied with a fireball or a tornado, did you?" Nia asked, eyebrows arched. "I like manipulating the fire in a finer way." She flicked her fingers and fire danced in a circle, miniature figures holding hands. "You can have fun with it, too."

"I'm sure little dancing flames will be very useful against the Shadows." Tabor rolled his eyes. "Those sort of tricks are for entertaining children, not going against the scáthach. It's like my firebirds, pretty for entertainment, but not for fighting."

"You can make them bigger." She rolled her eyes right back at him and increased the size of them, until they separated into full-sized men made of flame. They were terrifying and Fateh could appreciate how it could scare an enemy.

"I stand corrected." Tabor waved away his earlier comments. "Your dancing figures can morph into walking men of flame and terror. It's not a bad trick, I'll admit."

"Glad you approve." Nia huffed and crossed her arms against her chest. "I do know what I'm doing. You could trust me a little more."

"I'm just grumpy being on the training grounds again and not as a teacher." Tabor admitted. Fateh elbowed him in the side.

"Give up and just take her lessons. I think we'll both learn a lot." He turned to Nia. "Can you teach me how you made the flaming men?"

"After you finish the rope trick." She promised him before turning back to Tabor. "You practice it as well. I want you to be as good at it as I am, so that when you're inevitably teaching Fateh on your own, you know what to do."

"You really are pushy." Tabor muttered and flicked his hand in the twirling motion she showed Fateh, landing the rope over the dummy's head with ease. "I'm not a child like Spark is."

"But you're just as stubborn." She raised a single eyebrow. "Fine, then. You know how to make a fire rope. Let's see you manipulate it like a whip. I want to hear the crack, Tabor."

"Fine." Tabor swung the rope out, changing the width of it so it was thicker on one end like a handle and thinner at the end, just like a real whip would be. He flicked the fire whip, making a loud cracking noise. "This is actually fun. I never thought of using the rope trick like that before."

"And sometimes I have good ideas, I know." Nia stuck her tongue out at him. "Good job, Tabor. I hereby graduate you to making fire men. Remember to start small and then increase their size. You can sneak them into an enemy camp and suddenly surprise them."

"Pushy and a tactician." Tabor mimed being shocked. "When did my Nia grow up?"

"I run border patrol to make sure the Shadows don't come into our lands." Nia said grimly. "You learn tactics the hard way." She let her flaming men vanish into smoke. "Which is why I'm still against you fighting the Shadows. They're too dangerous, Tabor. You have a handful of half-blood children as your backup?"

"Etana, too." Tabor felt compelled to point out. "He's thrown in his lot with us, because he likes Spark."

"Oh so maybe you're not as dumb as you seem. Etana's the one who saved your bacon before. Hopefully he can do it again and without you incurring a large debt this time." She pointed to Fateh. "Pin it on him."

"I like Spark too much to saddle him with such a debt so large." Tabor snorted. "What sort of partner would I be if I let him be in debt?"

"Partner? You became partners with a half-blood kid?" Nia stared at him. "You must really like the kid." She grinned wider. "You like him, don't you?"

"Yes, I do. Yes, he knows. And no, he hasn't returned my affections." Tabor made sad eyes at Fateh. "My heart is forever being broken by Spark. If only he'd acknowledge me."

"Notice me, senpai?" Fateh teased.

"Now who's giving away his favorite anime?" Tabor shot back. "And besides, I'm the older, more experienced one. You should be noticing me, not the only way around."

"I told you I don't dislike you, not anymore." Fateh pointed out. "I'm not exactly falling all over myself for you, but I think we're at least friends again." He tilted his head to the side. "Isn't it enough for now?"

"Yeah, I guess it's going to have to do." Tabor gave a dramatic sigh. "For now."

Nia just laughed at the two of them. "Alright, let's get back to work. Fateh, let's see you master the rope trick before we go onto anything else. Rope around the dummy and then pull it tight."

Fateh was so eager to learn the whip and the other forms of combat that he managed the rope trick--correctly--on the third try. His eagerness showed with how he tugged on the rope and the dummy's head came off with a pop. "Oops."

"No, no, you're good. You're a bit enthusiastic, but you've got the trick. Try doing it without beheading the dummy this time."

Fateh saluted her and faced the dummies again, taking a deep breath. He could do this; if he could do this, he could learn to do so much more. He needed to learn everything he could to fight the Shadows. He wouldn't have iron to use like Etana or the full humans did. He would need to use nothing but his fire and perhaps the charms Haruki gave him. He wondered what other magic he could use.

As he beheaded another dummy, Fateh realized this would be a long day.

***

They took a break for lunch; Nia provided them with a spread of fresh vegetables, fruit, creamy nut butter, and fresh baked bread. Fateh wasn't surprised at the lack of dairy; not after Nia's comments about drinking milk.

A vegan fire fae? I suppose weirder things have happened...you'd think they'd like everything well-roasted, including their meat. It still tasted delicious and filled up the empty corners, providing fuel for what he needed to do next. He'd finally graduated from the fire rope and currently tried to manipulate the rope to become a whip.

Tabor worked on firing arrows made of pure fire. He shaped his fire to the image of a bow and created arrows out of the extra fire. It was amazingly effective and got applause from the group watching them.

"So Nia--have you always lived here?" Sam asked politely, taking a strawberry and eating it slowly. "You said you were only thirty--have you ever been to the human realm?"

"The human world is a mess." She wrinkled her nose. "It's filled with short-lived humans. The moment you make a friend, you turn around and next thing you know, they've either forgotten all about you or died."

"Made many friends, have you?" Tabor asked. "You gotta get them when they're young, like Spark here." He ruffled Fateh's hair. "Then you keep bugging them and don't leave, so they know you mean serious business. You can't make a friend of a human and just vanish for ten years at a time. They won't understand."

"Is that why you were so annoying?" Fateh asked dryly. "You were hanging around all the time so I wouldn't forget you? Next time, try to be less annoying."

"But look at where we are now!" Tabor's grin widened. "You never would have come with me unless I showed my persistence."

"Sure, keep telling yourself it was your persistence." Fateh snorted. "You were damn annoying and I only went with you because of my desperation and the fact I nearly died. You were--" he shrugged and stared down at the ground. "My mother trusted you. So I had to trust you."

"Oh, your mother is the one that made you trust me?" Tabor was solemn for a moment. "She was a good woman. We'll avenge her, too."

"How?' Fateh asked, stabbing at a tomato. "By killing the humans who killed her? I don't want to kill them. I want to save them." He closed his eyes and slumped over his knees. "Somehow I want to save the people who got my mother killed. Am I insane? Why am I doing this?"

"Because even though they hurt you, you're a good person." Tabor sighed. "And you're not just doing it for them, you're clearing out a nest of Shadows infecting more than just your town."

"Tabor''s right." Hana put in. "You're going to help with the Blight that is the Shadows. It's more than just your town you're saving." She frowned. "I would not save those specific people who killed your mother, but I'm sure there are innocents in town."

"I just have to keep those who committed the crime and those who were adjacent in mind." Fateh sighed as he ran a hand through his hair. "Save those that had no hand in what happened to my mother. It just all happened so fast and there were so many people in the mob..."

The day had been a blur; filled with fire and pain and loss--then getting taken away to a prison on top of it. He couldn't remember the faces of those who surrounded him, but he would always remember the person who held the knife.

Meira and Tobias had been leading the mob; Meira wanted him to kill Tabor. What if I actually tried to? He thought glumly, not for the first time. Would he have saved his mother if he had taken the knife from Meira?

He hated he'd probably have to talk to Meira and Tobias again, just to get the help he needed from the humans. He didn't trust them, but they were his only link to the rebels. He would have to pretend to be perfectly human. He would have to go alone, without Tabor there. If he showed up at the door with the entire gang in tow they would do more than just get the door slammed in their faces. Meira would waste no time in making sure Tabor died this time. He didn't want to think of what she would try to do with someone like Hana or Haruki.

Not that she'd get very far. They're both very good at defending themselves, especially Haruki. Meira would end up dead if Haruki decided she was a threat. Metal and salt don't hurt him like it would hurt a fae and he's very good with his sword.

He'd mourn the idea of the friend, but Meira was no longer his friend. He hoped she could end up being an ally. A reluctant one on both their parts, but the rebels in town were needed.

Chapter Twenty

He realized he was staring into space, recollecting the past and letting his voice drift off. The people here knew the basics of what happened to his mother, he didn't need to rehash it.

"Anyway." He coughed and waved away his trailing words. "So Tabor, I've only met one of your cousins. Don't tell me Nia is the only one you wanted me to meet."

"No, Nia is just the one that's the most talented when it comes to fire and lightning." Tabor grinned. "There's Kynan, Treyvn, Efa, and Cassian who I want you to meet. Not because they're talented, but because they're family and they'll get a real big shock from seeing you."

"You're just showing me off now like some sort of weird prize you've won." Fateh accused him. "Have you given any thought about how I feel about this?"

"I told you I wanted you to meet the cousins." Tabor shrugged. "It's good to meet family."

"They're not my family." Fateh protested. "They're your family."

"Family by fire, Spark." Tabor grinned. "And who's to say you don't have a relative among them? You don't know about the fire side of your heritage at all."

"You have a point, but it doesn't mean you aren't still showing me off. I'm not some sort of exotic creature you've found. Look at us here." He gestured to the group of them. "I'm not the only one that's a half-blood. I'm not as unique as you thought I was at first."

"True. I get to show all of you off." Tabor looked unrepentant. "You have to realize in all the world, the Sanctuary and places like it are unusual. Fae and human don't always mix, as you've seen. Humans are usually too scared of the fae or they're making deals which go south."

"Hence, the Shadows." Fateh shuddered. "I see what you mean. So it means my father--"

"Is fae. Didn't you ever wonder why he wasn't around?" Tabor asked curiously.

"I stopped asking pretty young." Fateh admitted. "It made my mom sad when I brought it up and she just said Grandma and Grandpa didn't approve of him." His smile tightened. "Guess I know why now. They were always cautious of the fae and they are the ones who taught me everything I knew to protect myself against the Shadows."

"I hope you find them one day." Tabor's words were sincere. "You said they vanished before the Shadows came, right? They got out of town?"

"Yeah--I wonder if I could ask Marisa to help me find them." Fateh perked up at the thought; he cared a lot for his grandparents and wondered what they would think of him using fire. They probably already knew of his half-fae nature. He wondered why they never told him.

"She could probably find them." Tabor tilted his head to the side, as if in thought. "She could probably find your father, too. If he's not already here." He said the last part casually, but Fateh froze at the very idea. His father had been a myth for as long as he could remember. He hadn't thought about him in years; not since his mother stopped answering questions about him.

"I--" Fateh swallowed hard. "What should I do if I find him?" He didn't even have the words in his vocabulary to describe a father's role. The closest he'd gotten to it was Meira and Tobias' father and he hadn't seen that much of him.

"You say hello and demand to know why he hasn't been in your life." Tabor raised an eyebrow. "He owes you seventeen years of your life. I'd be demanding answers if I was you."

"You have a point, but it's just so weird of an idea. I don't even know." Fateh made a face. "I don't even care about having a father. I don't think I want to know."

"You may be surprised." It was all Tabor said before he stood up, brushing his hands free of crumbs. "Okay, let's meet some people before the day gets too far from being over. It was a nice break, but it'll be an even nicer one with more spectators in the stands to heckle me and Spark."

"You mean the group of people coming by now?" Fateh asked dryly, pointing to the distance where there was a small knot of people. All of them were fire fae; he could tell even from this distance. Only one didn't have the flaming hair Nia had, and even his dark hair smoldered like hot coals on a fire.

"Exactly like those!" Tabor said cheerfully, waving them over. "I didn't have to go hunting them down. They must have heard we were doing a practice here and came to watch."

Fateh watched warily as the group came up. It wasn't an overly large group, but overwhelming in its own way. It was the largest group of pure-blooded fae he had seen and Tabor called them 'cousins'. When he thought of it, Etana called him a cousin as well. Maybe Etana just used it because of Fateh's heritage?

The man with curly black hair like coals stopped and stared at Fateh, his eyes gone wide. His eyes were the color of honey, the same as Fateh's and he was short and thin in the way of Tabor and him. Dressed in a long tunic and tight pants, Fateh thought he looked ridiculous.

"Fateh?" the man asked and Fateh's heart plummeted to his toes. He stared back at the man, trying to find a hint of himself in him. This man knew his name and he'd never seen him before in his life.

"It is you." The man gave a sigh of relief and reached forward and hugged him tightly. "I knew you'd live to be an adult. Your grandparents thought you'd die as a baby, but I knew they were wrong. Your mother wouldn't let me take you."

The man babbled and Fateh blinked as he tried to take in the rush of words. "I--who are you?" he asked, as if he didn't already guess. He just wanted to hear it.

"I guess I deserve your question." The man looked sheepish. "I'm your father. Long time no see?" he asked.

"More like long time, never see." Fateh shot back. "You couldn't have shown up at least once? Mom missed you, even if she stopped talking about you when I was a kid."

"How is Enfys?" The man asked; Fateh didn't even know his name and he certainly wasn't going to start calling him Da.

"She died." Fateh's tone didn't allow for warmth. "Humans killed her because she tried to save both our lives with a contract." He looked over at Tabor. "The contract didn't save her, but it did save me."

"You didn't tell me you have a son, Cassian." Tabor stood in front of Fateh protectively. "Why haven't you been in the human world with him?"

"Enfys parents warded the place against me." Cassian made a face. "They didn't like the idea that their daughter was with a fae and locked me away from Fateh and her. Then the Shadows came and I wasn't strong enough to face them."

"You could have shown up long enough to get Fateh's mother and him to safety." Tabor stared at Cassian. "They lived with the Shadows for two years, fighting and surviving."

"Fighting is going a bit too far." Fateh muttered. "We survived for two years. We left the fighting to other people." He swallowed. "But Tabor is right. Why didn't you come and save us? Grandpa and Grandma vanished and you had the chance to come."

"Their wards are still up. They knew how to make them properly." Cassian looked sad. "You think I didn't want to be there for you? I was proud as anything when you were born. I saw the fire in you right away and I wanted to see what would become of you." He looked closely at Tabor. "So you've partnered with Tabor?"

"Is it that obvious?" Fateh asked dryly. "Yes, I contracted with him so he could save my life, but he calls it a partnership."

"It is one. It's a good one to have; Tabor is stronger than he seems and he'll be able to look after you." Cassian spread his hands. "I'm sorry I wasn't able to. How can I make it up to you?"

"Teach me what you know." Fateh said bluntly. "We're going to fight the Shadows."

"You're going to -- but they're--you're not strong enough!" Cassian blurted out. "You're only half, the Shadows are dangerous and tricky and can suck the energy out of you without you even noticing."

"That's why we have friends to help us out." Fateh gestured to the group on the bleachers. "Even went overseas to get some of them. They have a different way of looking at magic and they're not fae. They're Japanese spirits and they're really strong."

"You've already made up your mind." Cassian made a face. "I can't dissuade you from fighting the Shadows, but I can give you more fire and tricks so you can use them to fight the Shadows. I'm your father, gifting you power is something that can be done."

"Like a fairy godparent?" Fateh snorted. "You're about seventeen years too late to show up for the birthing ceremony."

"I told you it wasn't my fault." Cassian looked hurt. "I tried, really I did."

"You should have tried harder. My grandparents did not ward the town. You could have shown up there when the rest of the fae did."

"Every time I showed up, your mother saw me." Cassian grimaced. "I couldn't hide from her and she didn't want you to meet me. She said it would be too confusing."

"So you did see my mother." Fateh looked over at him and sighed softly. "I'm glad you saw her, even if you never tried to meet me. She never talked about you, but I guess it would have been hard to explain my father is fae."

"It explains a lot though, doesn't it?" Cassian raised an eyebrow. "The inability to lie, the aversion to metal--"

"The weirdness didn't happen until after I met Tabor and he was annoying." Fateh made a face. "I could handle metal just fine all my life until just recently. I used to carry metal with me to guard against the Shadows."

"You're growing into your power." Cassian looked interested. "What can you do now?"

"I can throw fire and lightning." Fateh grinned widely, suddenly proud of what he could do. "It's been fun and we used it against a Shadow and some trolls. Nia is teaching me some finer use of my fire. Like ropes and whips."

"He's an outstanding student." Nia put in, beaming. "He's picking it up quick, but you were always a quick study, so it makes sense he is, too."

"I'm older than you." Cassian said flatly. "You don't have to act like you were at my training; I finished long before you were even born."

"But everyone talks about how you were a quick study." Nia countered quickly with a disarming smile. "I wanted to be like you, so I studied hard. Some of my techniques are ones you passed down to students. You're a legend, Cassian."

"Oh. I didn't know people thought of me as a legend." Cassian blushed and waved the praise away. "I just did my work and lessons and thought others should know some things I invented. It's part of what I meant about pow-er--there are a number of things I can do with fire that normally isn't done."

"Like what?" Fateh asked with curiosity. "Is the fire whip your idea?"

"The fire whip and making the little dancing figures grow into an enormous figure." Cassian looked proud of himself. "Also I can juggle fire, but juggling is more for fun than it is used for combat. It is useful as a distraction, though. While they're staring at the dancing balls of flame, you can lob them at the person you're fighting against. You would be amazed at how effective it is."

Chapter Twenty-One

They went back to training after their meeting with Cassian, although Fateh couldn't help but cast looks at his father. His father. He never thought he'd have a father in his life. Fathers were mysterious quantities.

Fateh practiced the loop of fire until he got it around the practice dummy without looking. He wanted to try more of what Tabor was doing and paused, his reluctance to not use his abilities. Fateh couldn't help but think that Etana would be proud of how far he had come. It was a long way from having a nightmare and setting his bed on fire.

Maybe he'll think of me as more of a worthy ally and be more willing to help when push comes to shove. Etana didn't seem inclined to move from his comfortable home, because his presence kept the Shadows away. But the Shadows were spreading like a stain, and Fateh wondered just how far they would go. Would they end up on the other side of the world, using shadows to make the trip easier?

He hoped Etana would lend a hand when it came down to the last battle.

"So what are we planning to do next?" Fateh asked into the pause of them firing fire arrows. It took energy and concentration to form something he had never used before; he copied what Tabor did, but Fateh stood awkwardly and the arrows didn't fire as clearly.

"We are going to train more." Tabor said firmly. "I want to cram as much learning into you as possible before we go on our next impossible request. I do warn you, when we visit the water worlds, you'll be more vulnerable, since your fire is so strong now."

"And my humanity?" Fateh asked, suddenly growing cold. "How much have I burned away using fire?"

"Less than you think but probably more than you'd like." Tabor was honest. "You have less humanity than what you started with, but you're not fully fae yet, either." He rested a hand on Fateh's shoulder. "Do you regret it?"

"If I say I do, will it change anything?" Fateh asked tiredly. "Can I cancel out the humanity that's gone and gain it back?"

"What's gone is gone." Tabor sounded brutally cheerful. "You've burned it away, your humanity is nothing but ashes now. You have to be careful in what you do in the future. These little tricks won't use up your humanity, so you should be fine to learn how to protect yourself. But big feats of magic are where you have to worry."

"Great." Fateh slumped. "By the time I go home, I won't even recognize myself."

"You'll be more of yourself than you ever have before." Tabor rested a hand on his shoulder. "Just wait and see, Fateh. There hasn't been as much change as you think you have; you can just do a little more with your talents."

"Not that I have anything to go home to." Fateh's mood plummeted. "My friends have betrayed me, my mother is no longer alive, and Shadows have infested the town."

"Because you're saving it for other people." Hana stood next to him, having added her illusions to what Fateh was trying to 'attack'. "The Shadows are spreading, you're cutting it off from one of its sources."

"One of?" Fateh squeaked.

"Of course; not all the Shadows in the world stem from your small town in Wales." Hana rolled her eyes. "Additionally, there are other nests that require our attention. There are other nests we should take care of as well. The Shadows in

Japan need to be taken care of, as well as other parts of the world. A lot of work needs to be done."

"I never said anything about clearing away other nests!" Fateh said, panicked. "I don't even know if we can handle the Shadows in my town." The idea of going after unfamiliar Shadows in unfamiliar places sent a shiver down his spine.

"And I said I would help, but not just your small corner of the world.. There are Shadows in every corner of the world, Fateh. I am making a commitment to eradicate as many of them as possible." She frowned. "If it were only possible to reason with them, then we wouldn't have to destroy them."

"Maybe some you can reason with." Fateh tilted his head. "I know you can make deals with them. What if we bind them with their own words so they're caught in the tangle? They can't resist making a deal."

"Making deals with them is dangerous." Tabor shook his head. "They're crafted from deals, they are masters of the craft. It's best to just destroy them at the source. Take out their leaders and their core of power and watch the rest crumple into dust." His stance tensed and voice harsh.

"Not going to argue with you. You know them better than me." Fateh rubbed at his head. "What do you think of this plan of going after other Shadows?"

"I think you're setting yourself up for a long, hard fight that will only get harder as it goes on, as they get craftier and stronger, more resilient to our magic." Tabor was serious. "I will support you, but I can tell you it won't be easy. Better to focus on the Shadows which lay in your town. Don't worry about fighting the war until the initial battle is over with."

"You're right." Fateh took a deep breath, calming his racing heart. He didn't have to worry about anything other than fighting the Shadows that overtook his town. Fateh would worry about the rest of the dangers after he took care of his initial problem. "One step at a time."

"Just as long as you don't forget the bigger picture." Haruki said gently. "We need help as well and we are offering help to you so you can help us in return."

"Yeah, I know. I get it." Fateh bit his lip. "Let's just see how we handle what we have in front of us first." He flicked his gaze to Cassian. "Are you coming with us? My mother is gone, my grandparents are missing and my town is under siege. You can do something to help."

"I have to protect the borders here." Cassian sounded regretful. "You have a powerful teacher in Tabor and excellent protectors in the friends you have gathered. I believe you can do anything you set your mind to. You always have a home here, though. Some place you can always come back to. I will try to be a better father for you, Fateh."

"Having a place to come home to means a lot." Fateh said softly. "I'm glad I have a parent left."

Cassian suddenly hugged him tightly. "Don't get yourself killed, Fateh. If all hope is lost, flee and find a safe harbor."

"Where will be safe if the Shadows think they have the upper hand?" Fateh whispered against his shoulder. "I can't lead them to safe harbors, the people inside them don't deserve to have their lives upended because I'm a coward."

"I want to say your life is more important, but you'd never agree with me. That's why you're going on this fool's errand to begin with."

"Yeah, I guess it is a fool's errand." Fateh admitted. "But I got a bunch of fools to agree with me, so I guess we're doing this."

"Not before we gather more help." Hana put in. "You are not the only one who gets the training montage." Her lips quirked up at how she poked fun at his training. "We want help from our own allies. Not that this hasn't been amusing and educational, but it's hardly useful for us."

"I know, I know." Fateh pulled away from Cassian, running a hand through his hair. "We won't stay here much longer. I know we have other places to visit, other people to visit and things to learn." He looked at Cassian. "You'll guard the border here and keep it open for us?" he asked. "So we can access it from anywhere?" He rolled his eyes. "I have no idea where we're going to end up."

"My doorway is always open to you." Cassian confirmed with a smile. "You and your merry band of misfits."

"Glad to know we're included." Tabor said dryly. "I'd hate to be on the other side of a door Spark is on."

"Mmhm." Cassian looked at Tabor seriously. "You've got to take care of Fateh, Tabor. I trust you."

"Spark and I will take good care of each other." Tabor reassured Cassian. "I'll make sure nothing happens to him, even if I have to drag him out from beneath the Shadows myself."

"Don't get yourself killed." Cassian said flatly. "My son will not thank me if that happens. How about none of you gets killed?" he asked. "That's the best plan of all."

"I'll vote for all of us all surviving." Haruki raised his hand. "I'm not looking to die with this little venture." Uisge nodded from her spot on the bench. She kept herself far away from the fire, not wanting to cause an accident with her own inherent magic.

"I didn't volunteer for any dying, either. I'll go back to my river if that's the case." Uisge stood up and brushed herself off. "Can we go now? I can scent the water from here and there is power in it."

Fateh looked at Tabor and Nia. They would be the ones to determine if he was ready to leave. "I think I've got a handle on things. The only thing to do is practice more." He didn't want to be surrounded by water, but Uisge probably felt just as uncomfortable around him and his family.

"You're that eager to leave?" Cassian looked disappointed. "I hoped you'd at least stay the night, see my home and rest before you went on another adventure."

"As long as it doesn't involve more fire, I am fine with staying the night." Uisge proclaimed. Hana and Haruki nodded in unison, and Tabor shrugged.

"I'm happier here, but I know we should only stay the night and then get going onto our next venture in the morning. Spark is right, practice is what he needs to know and we can practice on the unsuspecting targets we find in the dark." His smile turned sour and Fateh knew what targets he meant.

"Great, then it's settled." Cassian clapped his hands together. "Everyone, follow me. You'll get some good food and rest and be ready to face anything tomorrow."

***

It was a large house Cassian took them to; fully large enough to keep all of them. "Wow. my dad's rich." Fateh's voice went dry, trying to keep the impressed tone from his words.

"This is nothing." Cassian waved off the house. "It works for what I need. It lets me host plenty of family and friends; I also like the space."

"And it's a lot of space." Fateh agreed. "I guess it's good you have it, though. I'd hate to see us all squeezed in a space that would fit half of us." He plopped his bag down on the couch and flopped down next to it. "How normal is this?" He gestured around him. "I could be back home, except the place is a little outdated."

"Did you expect it to be a pit of fire?" Cassian asked. "We like our minor comforts and it includes human inventions." He pouted. "What do you mean by outdated? I thought it was fashionable."

"Maybe a hundred years ago." Fateh grinned. "You really have to go to the human world and update your furniture. I think this was fashionable in the 1900s. The early 1900s." Still, it somehow exuded comfort, and he stretched out, yawning. "I could fall asleep here easily."

"Well, you don't have to. We have a bedroom for you." Cassian laughed. "You'll have to share it with someone, but there's a space for you to sleep." His gaze flicked to Tabor and then back to Fateh. "I'm sure it won't be a problem."

"I'm sure it won't be." Fateh barely kept the words this side of polite. "Planned it all out for us, didn't you?" He didn't move from his spot on the couch. "You know, it's a little weird having my dad approve of whatever it is that Tabor and I have going on."

"I know he's your partner." Cassian looked over at him with an innocent expression. "Is there something more I should know about?" His grin said there was nothing innocent about his question at all, and Fateh flushed.

"The idea of being with Tabor it's just wrong." He said flatly. "Look, Tabor and I are partners, but there's nothing frisky going on between us. I'm asexual, damn it and I like being asexual!"

"Doesn't mean you can't like him." Cassian went triumphant. "I've met some asexual people in my life. They have perfectly fine relationships, even if there isn't any sex."

"Double yuck." Fateh made a face and covered his ears. "I am so not hearing someone who is supposed to be a parental figure talking about sex."

"Didn't your mother have the talk with you?" Cassian asked in surprise.

"Yeah and when she figured out I had no interest in it, she dropped the subject." Fateh scowled at Cassian. "You can drop it, too. Whatever I feel for Tabor is for me and him alone. I don't need to hear anything about it from anyone else, especially my father."

"Fine, fine--I'll drop it and I won't worry about what goes behind closed doors." Cassian relented and Fateh relaxed.

"Good." He stood up and gave Cassian a bright smile. "You mentioned something about dinner?"

Chapter Twenty-Two

I t felt strange being with his father, Fateh thought. Here was someone he hadn't thought about in forever/ Now he served up food and drinks, like they were a normal family. They were an odd group to have around the dining table, but Fateh just shrugged it off and rolled with it. These were his companions now and they were going to be with him for awhile.

"So after this meal, we are going to the water, yes?" Uisge looked up from her food and fixed Fateh with a look. "There is more out there than just the maidens and I am eager to see about getting some help in my water craft."

"I'm sure we can find someone to help you with your magic." Fateh propped his chin up on his hand. "I mean, I'm not going to offer anything, since we're kind of opposite and all. Same reason why you aren't comfortable here. I can see why you want to get going."

"Yes." Uisge didn't mince words. "While it's nice you had your training, there are several more of us who need assistance if we are to help you."

"Not going to argue with you. After we eat, we can get going." Fateh looked at the rest of the group. "Does getting going after food work for you? Track down more water spirits so Uisge can get a handle on what she needs to do?"

"Preparing to go is fine." Hana spoke calmly. "As long as we visit my relatives as well, I have no objection to going to Uisge's errand first." Haruki nodded as well, but the both of them were in agreement more often than not.

"We'll make the full rounds." Fateh looked at Sam. "If it's alright with you that we take a trip to water land."

Sam shrugged. "I don't have any problems with the water." They grinned at Fateh, "Being allergic to water all you and Tabor. Water actually helps me. You know how plants love water."

"It's not all water." Fateh protested. "It's just overwhelming amounts of it." Fateh looked up at Tabor. "Will you be fine?" he asked. "You're fully fae, unlike me. Will the water bother you or do you want to stay here?"

"And be away from you?" Tabor put a hand to his heart. "I won't melt in the rain and water country won't disable me entirely. I'll be okay, Spark. There is an advantage of being full fae, sometimes you have protections you otherwise wouldn't have."

"So you're going to pretend like nothing is bothering you, got it." Fateh rolled his eyes. "You could just admit to having a problem, you know. We're not going to judge you. We're not the Shadows, looking to exploit a weakness."

"No, but one does like to be seen as being stronger than they are." Tabor made a face. "How does it look if you're willing to help and go to a deadly water hellscape and I'm not? I tell myself it's like dealing with Etana and make precautions."

"What sort of precautions are you going to take?" Fateh asked, interested. He wondered if he could take the same sort of precautions.He didn't want to be caught unawares either. If Tabor knew something, then Fateh wanted to be let in on the secret.

"You have to create a fire shield." Tabor shimmered with power, practically glowing with nascent fire. It didn't burn anything around him, but he gestured to Uisge. "Hit me with water. Not too rough, but a little splashing wouldn't hurt."

"Huh." She eyed him and formed a water globe in her hands, before lobbing it at Tabor. The water broke up in a cloud of steam and Tabor grinned widely.

"See?" He asked, spreading his hands wide. "It protects you." He waved the steam away from his face. "I'll teach you to produce one so you won't get overly wet."

"I'm glad to hear it." Fateh gave the shield an appreciative look. "I wish I had something like a shield when I was back home. It would have saved me from a lot of wet mornings."

"You can't just use this power whenever you want." Tabor snorted. "Or else I would have been covered in this twenty-four seven when back home."

"You didn't have to stay in Wales, you know." Fateh gave Tabor an amused look. "There are plenty of other places to live that aren't damp."

"But they wouldn't be home." Tabor let the shield go. "You know how important home is as well as I do. You're able to try new places; Etana would always welcome you in New Zealand and the country is sunny and warm."

"Yeah, it is." Fateh shrugged. "But like you said, it isn't home." He looked wistful. "I miss home."

"This is home now for you, too." Cassian spoke up. "Whenever you find a gateway, you can come and visit me. There will always be a place for you."

"Having a safe place to come to is good, having more than one is great. If Tabor teaches me how to open gates, then I'll take you up on your offer." Fateh was quiet for several moments. He had been away from home for over a year now. Even that time spent in the prison had been in Wales, but he hadn't been properly home to Felinheli since he had been kidnapped from it. He wondered what changed there since he had been gone.

"You're assuming you won't be with Tabor." Cassian's brows rose. "But yes, he should teach you magic and the magic of shadow-travel. If he's even incapacitated, it will be good for you to have an avenue of escape."

"Your dad has a point." Tabor looked at the group as a whole. "It might not be a bad skill for more than one of you to learn."

"We'll leave learning of shadow travel to Fateh." Sam's words were hasty. "Traveling with shadows reminds me too much of the Shadows. It's enough to walk through them when we have a guiding light, but we don't have Marisa here at the moment."

"My fire can light the way." Hana said softly. "It's not as good as Marisa, but between me, Fateh and Tabor, we can make sure the pathways aren't completely dark." She tilted her head to the side. "I could open up gateways, but I don't think I'm suited to opening shadows. I'm fine with walking them, however."

Fateh made a face, he agreed with Sam, it felt too much like the Shadows to manipulate shadow, but he could see how using the shadow roads could be a useful tool. He didn't think he wanted to learn, but Tabor and his father both thought he should.

"What about closed pathways?" He looked to Tabor, "You mentioned you had to get permission to visit Etana and there were your own pathways you created. Could I create my own pathways? Like opening a direct one to the Sanctuary?"

"You could, with time and practice." Tabor shrugged. "It's easier to use already open pathways, which is harder to find when there is not a Seer lighting the way, but you will get a feel for what's open, what's safe, and what will end in horrible disaster."

Fateh gulped. "There are pathways that end terribly?" He demanded of Tabor. "You'll teach me about those first. I don't want us to walk one way and find out there are knives at the end."

"Don't worry, I'll teach you everything I know about shadow travel." Tabor waved Fateh's worry away as inconsequential. "Now, I'm done eating. Cassian, it's been great catching up and finding out all sorts of information, but we should go while the day is still going."

"It won't be going for long." Cassian warned. "Are you sure you don't want to stay the night and head off in the morning? There's plenty of space for you here."

"I'm done with staying in places that are unfamiliar." Tabor shook his head. "Uisge's itching to get going and I want to see what will happen next. You already said you can't come, so dragging this out won't do any of us any good."

"What if I wanted to spend more time with my son?" Cassian retorted. "Can't I have him with me longer?"

"You should have thought of your son years ago." Tabor shot the idea down quickly. "You don't get to take all this time to make up for the past. Fateh said he'd visit you when we had the chance. Don't know when we'll be back this way again, but I suspect we'll have time before we go and face our fears in the Shadows."

"Yeah, I'll see you before things go south." Fateh promised. Cassian was actually trying to be a parent, he wasn't going to look at this unexpected gift sideways. He appreciated the opportunity.

"At least someone appreciates me." Cassian pouted, which looked frankly ridiculous on a grown man, but Fateh just snorted.

"Yeah, yeah. I'm glad you're around and I hope I get another opportunity to get to know you better." Fateh's face went slightly red; he wasn't used to expressing his feelings so openly anymore. He did it with his mom, but other people were different.

"You sound real thrilled about it." Cassian's tone went extra dry. "Love you too, son." He rested a hand on Fateh's shoulder, but it seemed to be more than just a fatherly gesture. He shared fire with him so Fateh would have more on his side when it came down to the battles ahead.

Fateh looked at him, smiling and grateful for the gift. Cassian couldn't come with him, but he could offer help in this simple way. "Thank you."

"I wish I could give you more."

"You've given plenty." Fateh reassured him. "Well, I guess it's time to go." He looked at the others, focusing on Uisge. "Can you find your way to the water from here?"

"It calls to me." Uisge said comfortably. "I don't think I'll have any problem." She stood up, facing the door, poised to go.

"I guess that's our cue." Fateh laughed and looked up at his father one last time. "We'll be back."

"Don't you forget it."

Uisge gave him an impatient look and Fateh just shook his head. "Bye, Da." He followed Uisge out the door, the rest of the group following suit.

***

There was another portal, this one watery and shimmering and Fateh shuddered to have to go through it. The fire lands weren't all fire, hopefully the water lands would have land as well as water. Fateh did not look forward to the idea of being covered in water. They came out of the portal and on a bank of land. Still, they were surrounded by water and Fateh whistled lowly. "Well, Uisge, you must be in heaven."

She smiled brightly at him. "Yes, this is more acceptable than the fire tricks you were doing in your lands."

"At least the fire lands weren't covered in fire." Fateh grimaced. This would put out his fire for sure if he fell into one of the oversized ponds. Ponds. His blood suddenly went cold. What if Mokosh or creatures like her were here?

"Hot enough, not that you noticed." Uisge shrugged. "But we are here now, it is time to find some help." She stood at the edge of one of the ponds and looked as if she pondered diving right in.

"Maybe you should call out to someone of your kind first?" Hana suggested. "We don't know what is in the water, it may be dangerous."

"And calling out is safer?" Uisge raised her brows in question. "We don't know what will answer, after all. Not everything that comes out of the water is as nice as me." She smiled fiercely and Fateh backed up a little. She had a point.

"It seems we're at an impasse." Haruki crossed his arms over his chest. "We have to take the chance and call out. I'm sure Uisge can determine what is safe and what is not."

"And we are no slouches either when it comes to fighting if it comes down to it." Tabor pointed out. "It may be water, but we can all do something. We did before with the Shadow that was filled with water magic."

Chapter Twenty-Three

"Are you going to keep talking amongst yourselves or are you going to talk to us?" An unfamiliar voice spoke up and all heads turned towards the water, where a person emerged from the water. "I assume you are here to speak to us."

Fateh blinked at the person emerging. She was covered in scales and looked like what he had envisioned mermaids to look like. She stayed in the water, but her eyes were fixed on Uisge. "Hello, cousin." She murmured. "It's rare to see one of the maidens leave their domain and in the company of such ... unusual guests." Her gaze flicked over to Tabor and Fateh. "Aren't you uncomfortable here, little fire sprites?"

"Hey, we're more than just sprites." Tabor looked insulted. "And we're fine, as long as we don't decide to go swimming."

"You are in water territory. Coming here is hardly a wise move for someone made as much as fire as you." The person shrugged. "But you are in the company of one of my cousins, so I suppose you have your reasons for being here."

"We've come to ask for help." Uisge said bluntly. "I know tricks of the water, but I need to know more. We're fighting the blight known as the Shadows and I am afraid what knowledge I have from my time with my family is not enough."

"You are wise to figure out that we, the spirits of the water, know more than just the maidens." Her face darkened at the mention of the Shadows. "We have lost many cousins to the Shadows. What knowledge do you seek?"

"How to better use my water as a weapon." Uisge said immediately. "I can make water globes and daggers of water, but I am limited in what I can do. I would like to be able to manipulate all forms of water, including water not native to myself."

"You're off to a good start. I am Ran. I will help you with the knowledge you seek, but you have to come into my waters to gain the knowledge. Water speaks to water and it's much faster to let you absorb the knowledge rather than just me speaking it to you."

"Why couldn't I just absorb the knowledge?" Fateh muttered to Tabor. "It would have been more efficient."

"But not as much fun." Tabor grinned to him. "Besides, what do you think about Cassian's gift? Not just fire but knowledge in the fire you can pick apart when the time is right."

"Huh." Fateh took the information and then shrugged. "Uisge, I think you should do it. It sounds like you'll gain all you need without having to jump through the hoops I did."

"Of course." She stuck her nose up in the air. "Water is more mutable than fire, it flows through everything. Even you have water in you, even if your spirit is fire." She took a step towards the pond, only hesitating briefly before stepping in fully, dissolving into the water.

Hana made an aborted sound of worry, but when a hand reached up and waved them away, she stood back, watching with wide eyes, Ran had her hands in the water, eyes closed as she hummed a song. It entranced him and Fateh found himself taking a few steps forwards towards the water to better hear it.

Tabor snatched him back before Fateh could actually step in the water. "Uh, no." His tone brooked no argument. "No splashing in puddles for you. It's bad enough we're surrounded by all this water. Your fire will not like it if you decide to go swimming."

Fateh winced at how close he had come to the water. "Yeah, dousing my fire would not be good." He gave Ran a suspicious look. He didn't know she could enchant people and wondered if she was teaching Uisge how to do the trick. It would be interesting to have her be able to drown the Shadows, assuming they could be drowned and wouldn't just absorb the water like evil sponges. Maybe if they were stuffed with enough magic that they were solid. He pondered this as time ticked by slowly.

"This is boring." Haruki looked disappointed. "All the knowledge is going on without us seeing it. At least with your fire, we were able to see what you were learning and perhaps pick up a few tricks for ourselves."

"You can come into my water and learn the same way." ran suggested with a wink. "I promise I won't drown you."

"Thanks, but I can't turn into water the same way Uisge can." Haruki made a face. "I'd just get wet and it would take forever for my wings to dry out." He shook them as if shaking off invisible streams of water.

"Ah well. We can't all be superior beings." She smirked at the group huddling together on the shore. "Maybe I can teach you a few tricks which don't involve you coming into my waters."

"Learning new magic would be useful." Hana said softly. "I don't know what water can teach us, but I'm sure we can adapt our powers to what you teach."

"No knowledge is ever wasted." Haruki agreed. He stared out at the expenses of water all around them. "Are you a true cousin of our Uisge or merely a cousin-in-power?"

"A cousin in power." Ran said simply. "My sisters and I are not water maidens the way Uisge is. We are ningyo."

"Ah, you are Japanese mermaids." Hana looked pleased. "We are cousins in a way, then. I am a kitsune, one of the Japanese fox spirits."

"Yes, cousins in a way, we come from the same country." ran kept her hands in the water Uisge had come a part of, still obviously 'teaching' her, even if the song stopped. "But while our natures are amiable to each other, they do not mesh in the same way it does for my cousin."

"We're not water." Hana agreed. "I am more akin to the earth than I am to the water. But we are allies at least."

"An ally is something good to have." Ran agreed. She took her hands out of the water and made a shooing motion. "There, you can have your companion back. I have given her the knowledge she asked for."

"All of it?" Fateh asked skeptically. "I think she asks for a lot."

"You have been here longer than you realize." Ran spoke matter of factly. "Time moves funny within the realms and water flows all around you, distorting time further. Trust me, Uisge has been in my waters long enough to absorb a wealth of knowledge."

Uisge appeared in the water again, eyes flashing as she focused on Ran. "I thank you for the information." She spoke formally and with great respect towards Ran. "I shall use what you have given me to fight the Shadows."

"Use it well, little cousin." Ran smiled at her and shooed her out of the water. "My sisters will be here if you require more knowledge."

"I think I'm stuffed full for now." Uisge gave her a bright smile. "I don't know what else you can give me."

"There is always more than you can learn and I am not the only water spirit here." Ran pointed out. "There are other, darker paths you can take if you were willing to taint your waters."

"I don't think I need to go that far." Uisge shuddered. "Dealing with the Shadows darkens it enough. I'm not used to using my water as a weapon."

"We all have to make sacrifices." Tabor said firmly. "You chose to walk this path with us. Don't do anything you don't want to do, but be aware that using your powers as a weapon is something we'll all have to do." He made a face. "I'm not normally a fighter, either. This is new territory for all of us, I think."

Sam gave a fervent nod. "It's true." They said. "I'm a nature loving sort of person. I didn't think I'd ever use my powers for offense. Defense is what I'm good at."

"Then we could use you for defense." Hana looked at them, unconcerned. "Everyone needs a shield and the earth shields more than most." She looked pleased at this idea. "I worried everyone would be using their powers to fight and we would be left defenseless."

"I'll do my best." Sam looked relieved at not having to fight outright. "I can put up rock-hard shields but if I need to, I can use the land against the Shadows."

"Creating shields is all we ask of you." Haruki put a hand on Sam's shoulder. "Sometimes the best offense is a good defense."

"I can defend." Uisge looked put out. "I am not normally a fighter, either. This goes out of my basic nature. Water is not normally an offensive element."

Fateh threw up his hands. "We can all take turns defending and attacking. I hate fighting, but I'm going to do what is needed to fight the Shadows." He crossed his arms over his chest, looking stubborn. "You all agreed to this."

"It's true, we did agree we could work together on ending the Blight." Hana kept her words soothing. "It may make some of us uncomfortable, but we will all do what we can to fight."

Ran looked on all of this, vaguely interested. "You're really planning on fighting the Shadows? This small group of you? Are you sure this is not a fool's mission?"

"We can only try." Fateh looked determined. "The Shadows hurt all of us and they spread like a disease. We can do what we can to cut off the source in this part of the world." He didn't want to think about other nests of Shadows. They would cross that bridge when they came to it.

"Well, my blessings upon this little venture." Ran smiled at them. "I don't know what it's good for, but anything which can stop the Shadows is good in my book. They haven't spread to this land yet, but our guardians on the other side of our borders are getting overwhelmed and overtaken. I would not lose any more cousins, if at all possible."

"We'll try not to be lost." Uisge promised her.. "We have a few more stops to make along the way, but then we're going to do what we can to fight."

"Yeah, we'll see how well we can recruit more people to our cause." Haruki grinned. "My clan is a bunch of troublemakers and this is something I think they'd enjoy." He side-eyed the group. "I still don't know how safe it would be for you to venture into yokai territory. It's not like the elemental lands. There are a lot of dangerous creatures about who love to snack on humans."

"I think I'll pass." Fateh shuddered. "I'm just glad the yokai aren't an invading force at this time. The Shadows are bad enough."

"Who's to say they aren't making their own mark on this world?" Haruki asked. "You may not have seen them, but they cause their own sorts of disasters the priests are hard-pressed to fight."

"Okay, I stand corrected. Let's hope they won't join forces with the Shadows and make all of our lives more difficult." Fateh looked at Ran and smiled weakly. "Your help is appreciated. I'm sure Uisge gained a lot of knowledge we can use in our journey."

"Ah, you already know not to thank me outright." Ran looked vaguely disappointed but shrugged it off. "You are an interesting creature, little fire sprite. Make sure the Shadows don't smother your flame."

She vanished back into the water without another word.

Chapter Twenty-Four

"Well, I think it's time we parted ways and let us go on our own journeys to the realms we need to go to." Haruki said with a smile. "Unless you want to court certain death by coming with me to the yokai realm."

"You could have left for the yokai realm at any time." Fateh pointed out. "I think you want us to come with you." He raised an eyebrow. "Do you have something to prove?"

"Maybe I want to see if I can keep you all safe." Haruki looked unashamed of his admission. "My sword skills are unparalleled. I can fight anything which comes my way."

"If you're so strong, why do you need to go to the yokai realm anyway?" Sam asked curiously. "It seems like a waste of time if you're not going to learn anything."

"I'm looking for people to come and fight with us." Haruki shrugged. "They might not come with us right away, but at the zero hour, they may appear and cause havoc. It's what my kin does best and we're all good with a sword. Have ten of us at your side and the Shadows won't know what hit them."

"And the reason why they haven't fought before?" Fateh looked skeptical of this whole venture. "If they're so strong, they could have fought the Shadows at any point."

"The Shadows don't threaten them. I told you, there are worse things in the yokai realm than Shadows. They're used to fighting bigger enemies than the remnants of human souls. The thing is, they might see it as fun to harass the Shadows. Ever see crows play with someone? It's the same principle."

Fateh blinked at the mental image and then pushed it away. It wouldn't help to laugh at this moment, but the image of Haruki and a dozen of his kind circling the Shadows and dive-bombing them made him laugh.

"I hope whatever portal we use to get to your kind opens directly to them." Fateh muttered. "I don't want to end up fighting things that are worse than the Shadows. I don't think we're ready for something worse."

"Aw you don't want to do a trial run?" Haruki grinned. "You can see how strong you can be as a group. The Shadows will be nothing if you can defeat yokai."

"Let's not put our lives on the line just yet." Sam pleaded. "I don't even necessarily want to fight the Shadows, much less yokai. Yokai are supposed to be in manga and anime, not in my real life."

"I am a yokai and this is my real life." Haruki protested, but he eventually relented. "Alright, no dangerous trips through the yokai realm. I'll try and get us right where my family is."

Fateh wanted to thank Haruki for that, but the words stuck in his throat again. He just nodded and held out a hand. "I look forward to meeting your family and I hope they'll be on our side."

"We're creatures of the air. We may walk in darkness, but it doesn't mean we fight along the side of it." Haruki's expression was cocky. "You'll see."

"I guess we will." Fateh looked towards the horizon. "Onto certain doom."

"It won't be that bad." Hana smiled at Fateh. "I've been to his realm before and while it's filled with feathers and chaos, it's ultimately not a bad place. You just have to keep on your toes and don't let the tengu intimidate you. It's a good thing your friend Marisa is not here with us. They would not be able to resist someone as enticing as her. A full human who can see beyond the tricks we all employ? Priceless."

"Yeah, it's best she stays at the Sanctuary." Fateh shuddered at Marisa being in a place awash with spirits. Having her in the elemental realm would have been bad enough.

"We're going to need her when we face the Shadows." Tabor pointed out. "She can see within the shadows to see where the scáthach are hiding."

Fateh wanted to protest that Marisa had done her part, leading them safely through the shadow roads, but Tabor spoke the truth. They would need her clear eyes. Fateh could see through the illusions as well, but he wasn't a natural at it and he hadn't been practicing. Having a Seer with them would be better.

"We'll visit the kitsune after we visit the tengu." Hana smiled brightly at Fateh. "You'll see how much less chaotic it'll be. Fur instead of feathers and a bunch of foxes that'll fawn over someone as adorable as you." She pinched his cheek and Fateh scowled. He didn't want to be seen as "adorable".

"Let's just go." Fateh wasn't looking forward to being in a realm full of self-proclaimed monsters, but he didn't want them to get separated, either. He squared his shoulders and prepared himself. This might end up being more dangerous than anything he had done before.

Haruki nodded and made a motion like he opened a door in the air. Cool, scented air wafted out from the slice in reality. Haruki held open the 'door' and walked inside, sticking out a hand to gesture to the others to come with. Tabor shrugged and tugged Fateh along with him, the others following in their wake.

***

The first impression Fateh got was lots of feathers. There were people--bird people--nesting in all sorts of spaces, others facing off with swords, others sand-wiched together and eating something Fateh didn't want to identify.

"Ah, my home away from home." Haruki gestured grandly at the crowd of tengu spread out around them. Their sudden appearance garnered attention and Fateh became suddenly aware of several pairs of eyes looking at their group.

A few tengu broke apart from the crowd and surrounded them. They must have looked so alien among the giant bird creatures. They were taller and broader than Haruki and Fateh realized how young and small Haruki looked next to these full-blooded tengu.

"Hello to you, cousins!" Haruki didn't seem intimidated at all and instead smiled cheerfully at the menacing creatures. "We're just here on a friendly visit and looking to ask for help. You've heard of the Blight, the Shadows?" he asked.

"Small fry." One tengu crossed his arms against his chest. "Nothing to be concerned about." He raised an eyebrow at Haruki. "Don't tell me even a halfling like you is having trouble with them."

"They're a nuisance to those around me." Haruki shrugged. "And they're starting to encroach on the human territory I live in. We've found where a group of them are nesting and spreading and thought to ask for your immeasurable strength in fighting them." He spread his hands wide. "You are the best of the swordsmen and can cut down any foe who opposes you."

"Flattery will get you everywhere." The tengu gave him a broad smile. "But what do we have to gain from fighting enemies which are not our own? You'll bring misfortune to our steps and rile up the surrounding yokai. They would be all too happy to band together with them."

"All the more reason to fight them now, before they become a nuisance at your

door." Haruki became earnest and cajoling. "We could use a hand with the outer defenses, for those who try to run and spread their darkness elsewhere."

"You make a compelling point." The tengu held out a hand. "Arata." He gestured to his companion. "Isamu." He considered Haruki and then his gaze slid over to Fateh and the rest of the group. "You travel with strange people. Are these the humans you want to help?"

"They're not quite human, but they're not yokai, either." Haruki shrugged. "They're a type of hybrid elemental spirit."

Fateh supposed it was the best way to describe them. They weren't fully fae and as time had proven, they weren't human, either. The more time went by, Fateh felt more of his humanity slipping away. He decided to step forward and gave the tengu as brave of a look as he could manage. It reminded him of how you dealt with the Shadows. You didn't want them to see you were intimidated by them, or else they'd lose all respect for you.

"I'm Fateh." He kept his eyes on them and watched them shuffle nervously.

"Fire and feathers don't always get along." Isamu's smile went crooked. "But your fire is stronger with the wind we use. Working together can cause a firestorm." He looked almost thoughtful. "Something so grand could be good or bad, depending on the type of destruction you're aiming for."

"I want to burn the Shadows so there's nothing left of them." Fateh said fiercely. "They shouldn't exist in the human realm. They've caused too much pain." He fiercely reminded himself if it wasn't for the Shadows and their stupid contracts, his mother never would have been caught up in the whole mess that killed her.

"So you'll let them roam in some other realm?" Arata asked, looking blandly curious. "Aren't you worried they'll cause trouble there?"

"The fae realm has defenses the humans don't." Fateh spoke bluntly. "We don't have magic we can use to fight."

"You have other weapons." Arata countered. "I've heard stories of humans fighting off the Shadows and besides, you have magic of your own, being a hybrid." He gestured to Fateh and his companions. "All of you have magic of a sort which can fight the Shadows."

"We're only a small group." Hana spoke smoothly. "The Shadows are more numerous than we can fight comfortably, which is why we're coming to you for assistance. With your ability to use magic and fight, it could give us the edge we're missing."

"It doesn't answer the question of why you don't want to eliminate the Shadows completely, so that they don't bother other realms as well." Arata spoke directly to Fateh, who flushed.

"They were once human. If we could purge the Shadows from them, then maybe they'd be free." The thought just occurred to him and he sounded wondering, even to his own ears.

"Kid, they're lost. Nothing about the human remains in them. They're corrupted--" Tabor made a face. "But I see your point. If they're corrupted, maybe you can un-corrupt them." He eyed Fateh. "I don't know how we'd do it. I still say we burn them until there's nothing but ashes left."

"I mean, I'm for your plan, too. Burning away the entire Shadow might free the soul that's trapped in the darkness." Fateh felt uncomfortable. "Look, I just thought of this. I don't know how it'd work or if it could even work. But I'm willing to try. At least burn away the Shadows from the Shadow-bound. They don't deserve to have their souls taken."

"Taking care of the contracts is something easier done." Tabor looked relieved Fateh had another suggestion. "We can break the magical connection between human and Shadow."

"We can't stab shadows." Arata pointed out. "I hope you have a plan for us being able to use our swords/"

"The Shadows become solid when they consume the magic of an elemental spirit or fae." Tabor said quietly. "That's why they're so dangerous. They can absorb entire creatures, humans and fae alike. I'm sure they wouldn't stop at yokai if they were given the chance."

"Is this supposed to entice us?" Isamu laughed. "I don't want to get absorbed by Shadows."

"You're too fierce of fighters to go down." Haruki snorted. "Your magic is too strong, your swords too swift to be taken down by mere Shadows."

"Again with the flattery." Arata laughed. "We already said we'd do it. Where and when do you need us?" Other tengu came around to listen and they were all murmuring amongst themselves, eyeing the small group with interest.

Haruki practically beamed at them and spread his hands. "At the crossroads betwixt this realm and the human. We'll have lights to mark the paths where we'll need you on."

"We'll exact the payment from you once the deed is done." Arata smirked. "We are not going to fight for free, but we are fair in our terms." He said something to the waiting tengu in a language only Haruki would understand and the flock of tengu nodded, examining their swords and looking as if they were ready for this fight.

"My thanks to you." Haruki bowed and Fateh flinched. But thanks didn't mean the same to the yokai as it did to the fae and there was a part of him that regretted he wouldn't have his old level of politeness again.

"Until we meet on the pathways." Arata nodded and took off without so much as a goodbye. The rest of the flock followed.

Hana looked at them and shook her head. "At least they can be counted on in times of battle, if not in terms of societal niceties." She smiled at the group. "Do you feel like you're ready to come to the realm of kitsune?"

Fateh shook his head, feeling it swim lightly. "I think we need a break," he muttered. "Can we rest somewhere where we won't get eaten, charmed or drowned?"

"Don't forget getting boiled alive." Uisge pointed out. "Your fire-home wasn't exactly welcoming to those that weren't fire inclined like you."

"Yeah, good point. We need to find our way back to the Sanctuary and regroup a little bit." Fateh felt exhaustion pulling on his bones. "A nap wouldn't hurt, either."

"We have been doing a lot of gate traveling." Sam pointed out "You all may be used to it, but us poor halfsies are getting worn out by it." They shook their head. "We don't even know how much time has passed between now and the time we left. I've always heard time runs funny when you're on the other side of a gate."

Hana looked disappointed. "I'm sure you'll get rest with the kitsune. Feather beds--" She grinned at Haruki's appalled look. "And food and drink which is safe to eat. It won't be so bad, Fateh."

Fateh took in her pleading look and sighed. "I suppose one last trip won't hurt."

Chapter Twenty-Five

Fateh got used to gate travel by now and he could say he preferred it over the shadow roads. It could be instantaneous, instead of traversing a dark path with unknown enemies lurking in the darkness. It was a pity they couldn't gate travel home, but at least they could transport themselves to the Sanctuary. Still, at least they could get around without having to resort to more dangerous methods. There were even connected doorways within the realms, like with the fire and water realm, or with Haruki and the tengu.

"The tengu and kitsune realm are connected." Hana gestured down the pathway. "It's hidden by illusions, but I can find the way in. Seeing through illusions is something I'm very good at. At least kitsune-crafted illusions."

"Seeing through illusions is a handy talent to have." Sam looked interested. "Can you craft illusions that can fool others who aren't kitsune?"

"I think I can, but I want to learn more illusions while I'm here. If I can get my soul stone ... mm. .. updated, then it will make it so my magic is expanded. It will be like with Uisge. The majority of our time in my family's realm will be spent resting and resupplying."

"Are the things we are getting resupplied with illusions as well?" Fateh asked dryly. "I heard of kitsune illusions, They're supposed to be real enough to touch. I don't want a bag or clothes or even food to melt away just when I need it."

"It will be real." Hana promised him. "We can't subside off of rainbows and moonshine. We need solid food as well, even if a lot of us hunt for our meat." Her teeth were very sharp. "We have free range chickens so we don't go robbing farmers."

"I miss fresh chicken," Fateh said wistfully. "And fresh milk, cheese, and butter." He looked hopeful. "Is there a chance...?"

"Oh, for sure." Hana reassured him as they continued walking down the path. The air seemed to shimmer slightly and with a feeling like popping a soap bubble, they were on the other side of the illusion.

"Nice trick." Sam said appreciatively. "I bet if you weren't with us, we would have continued wandering the tengu realm and never entered the kitsune lands."

"You got it." Hana looked very pleased with herself. "If you weren't a kitsune, the illusion wouldn't break," The lands drastically changed from the tengu lands of windy mountaintops and scrubby trees, to rolling fields and forests. The temperature was like a pleasant spring day.

"This is nice." Fateh gave the area a curious look. "I can see how it reminds me of the Sanctuary."

Sam nodded eagerly. "This is good land." They reached down and spread their fingers in the grass and sniffed the air, "You've been good custodians. The earth is happy to have the kitsune here."

"We try." Someone spoke directly behind them and they all whirled around, startled at seeing a strange kitsune there. Hana beamed and threw her arms around the stranger. "Shikomoe, it's been forever!"

Shikomoe grinned and hugged Hana back, obviously happy to see her. "Hana, you naughty girl, always staying away." She stepped back and rested her hands on Hana's shoulders, examining her from top to toe. "Are you here for a reason or just for fun? Her gaze flicked over to the group behind her. "You brought guests."

"I thought they should see our hospitality." Hana shrugged. "Could've come without them to do what I need to do, but we'd rather not get separated and where's the fun in living people alone?" She quickly introduced everyone.

"Mmm, you have a point." Shikomoe grinned. Her gaze zeroed in on Sam. "Aren't you an interesting specimen?" She tapped her lip in thought. "You smell of the wild, of growing things."

"I have a connection with the earth." Sam shrugged, keeping their expression neutral as Shikomoe pressed up into their personal bubble, sniffing at their hair and skin. "I also don't like people this close to me, so if you could please?"

Shikomoe huffed as she stood back, arms crossed against her chest. "I didn't mean any harm by it. You're just like a kitsune in the way you smell, but you're obviously not one." She tilted her head slightly. "Not that you're human, but you're definitely not one of us." She gestured to her and Hana.

"No, I'm a gwyrddni." Sam outright grinned at the baffled look on Shikomoe's face at the tongue-twisting Welsh. "It means I'm a forest fae, in tune with nature, but I'm mostly at home in a forest." They spread out their hands. "Do you live in the forest or in the fields?"

"We have proper homes within the forest." Shikomoe laughed. "We hunt mice and other small animals in the fields, but we have other food as well, so you don't have to worry about what you eat. I think you'll like the udon, ramen and inarizushi." She licked her lips in anticipation. "I'm the welcoming committee, so let's go to the village and see how we can help you, Hana."

Uisge twirled around and smiled. "There is good water near here, too." She observed. "Why did you leave, Hana?" she asked. "It seems like a perfect place to live."

"These are kitsune who are messengers to Inari. I can't be a messenger, because I am only a half-kitsune." Hana shrugged, but there was true regret in her eyes. "I'm dedicated to Inari, but I can't work for them the way my brethren can."

"Them?" Sam looked interested at the phrasing. "Your Inari is a they?"

"Of course. We can be male or female, so Inari reflect our dual nature." Shikomoe looked nonplussed at the question. "We're very fluid in our gender." She looked at Sam again. "You are so very much like a kitsune. But you can't do shapeshifting or fire magic, can you?"

"Fire is kind of my anthesis." Sam shuddered. "You ever see a forest fire? They spread fast and they're deadly. Not many people survive them and they're devastating to the forest."

"Our fire isn't wild." Hana reassured Sam. "It's half illusion, so it can't cause any forest fires. Good thing, too, since we light our homes with it."

Shikomoe nodded and walked next to Sam, still obviously fascinated with them, even though they weren't a kitsune, or perhaps it was because they weren't one. "We do indeed. You'll see the lights here shortly." They were deep into the forest by now and Fateh wondered where this village was, when Shikomoe stopped and whistled a tune. The air seemed to vibrate and then the homes appeared, carved into the large trees and surrounding hillside.

"It's cozy and it's home." Shikomoe looked proud of the small village which spread out around them. He saw kitsune fire burning in the windows of all the homes Fateh could see and Hana was right, it didn't burn like normal fire did. When he reached out with his power, he didn't feel it the same way he would regular fire. "Can you make your fire burn? Or will that be up to me and Tabor?"

"I can light the way in the dark, if we don't have Marisa with us, but I'll leave the burning of Shadows to you and Tabor." Hana tugged Fateh's hand towards one of the hillside houses. "My mother lives here. She'll have plenty of space for you and Tabor, and I'm sure Shikomoe can find places for everyone else to stay."

Shikomoe nodded and beamed at them. "Several of you can stay with me. Especially you," she said to Sam, tweaking their nose. "I want to get to know you more. It's not every day a cutie like you drops in on my doorstep."

Sam actually blushed, looking rather pleased at the unexpected attention. Fateh hid his shock. He didn't think Sam could get flustered. They always seemed so together. It was nice seeing them complimented, though. He had a feeling some people thought they turned off their emotions based on their gender, but Fateh knew it wasn't true. Fateh remembered Sam showed interest in all genders, but didn't get the chance to date much. Maybe this little meeting with Shikomoe would do them some good.

"Then it's settled." Hana clapped her hands together. "Uisge and Sam can go with Shikomoe; Tabor, Fateh and Haruki can stay with me." She eyed Haruki. "Unless you'd prefer to nap in the trees like you did the last time you were here?"

"I don't want to be underground." Haruki shuddered, "You like dens in trees and hills, the air doesn't flow around you the way it does in the open air."

"Hey, it's not like it's stagnant air or anything!" Hana protested. "We get plenty of airflow. It's just not the open air." She snorted. "You're such a bird sometimes."

"Your point being?" Haruki didn't look insulted. "I am related to birds, after all." He fluffed his feathers. "You notice I didn't offer any of you a place to rest in the tengu lands. You wouldn't have liked the high eyries we live in. You would complain about potentially falling out and you'd never get any rest."

"You're not wrong." Hana laughed at his reasoning. "I never would have gotten a wink of sleep, thinking the ground would be rushing up to reach me."

"So don't judge me for not wanting to be in a cave. I'm sure it's a very nice cave, but I don't think I want to close myself off."

Uisge raised her hand as if it would give her permission to speak. Everyone turned towards her and she rubbed the back of her head in embarrassment. "I would rather sleep in the lake I sense nearby. I think it would be more comfortable for me than staying in a cave or a tree."

"So much water!" Shikomoe shuddered. "Not that it doesn't have its uses, but I wouldn't want to get all wet." She peered at Uisge. "But you're not quite all human either, are you?" she asked. "Hana, you brought a very strange bunch with you."

"Yeah, we're all a little weird." Hana shrugged. "Okay, so Uisge will go sleep in a lake, Haruki will nest up in a tree, while Sam stays with Shikomoe. If that's okay with you, Sam?"

Sam shrugged, still looking slightly dazed. "Yeah, staying with Shikomoe is fine." Their voice firmed. "I don't want to crowd your mother anymore than she'd already going to be with those two crowding in." They winked at Fateh to show they were joking.

Fateh wrinkled his nose and poked Tabor in the side before he could do anything detrimental. "Sounds like a plan to me. Hana, you'll be looking to do that thing you want to do?"

Shikomoe looked curious and Hana shrugged. "Just looking to expand my magical abilities."

"Well, you're in good hands here." Shikomoe nodded. "There are plenty of people with magic nd tricks enough to spread around. I'm sure they won't mind sharing their knowledge."

"I'm counting on it." Hana'a expression went solemn.

***

To Fateh's delight, fresh bread lay on the table, along with the promised milk and cheese. The main dishes were some sort of ramen dish with fried tofu in it, something the other kitsune around him seemed to enjoy a lot. There were double helpings of the fried tofu and Fateh grinned at the way the collective kitsune all looked at him when he nibbled on his. He wanted to savor it.

Hana's mother was a full-blooded kitsune, with dark, shining hair and eyes to match. She wore a kimono and her tails peeked up from the bottom of it. She didn't speak English, but whatever Tabor and Fateh couldn't pick up, Hana translated.

"Aren't you just adorable, all filled with fire the way you are." She stared directly at Fateh and Tabor, a broad smile on her face. "You shine as bright as stars, the both of you."

Fateh started in surprise, the only other one who noticed the fire straight off had been Marisa and she could See things which other people couldn't. "You can see a lot about me." he said instead, keeping his tone casual. "How did you know I am fire-inclined?"

"The illusions which make you seem like a normal human boy are laced with fire." She said easily. "Your ire is what I'm seeing. Most kitsune can see through illusions as well as weave them." She beamed at Hana. "Are you here to learn how to manipulate stronger illusion and magics?" she asked.

"Yes, that is what we have planned, Mother." Hana's tone was both casual and formal, the words at odds with the fond way she spoke with her mother. "I have been remiss in studying and absorbing knowledge and I am here to fix my lack of knowledge."

Fateh wished it could be so simple for him-- even Uisge had it easier when it came to learning her powers. His powers were all flash and lightning and it could be damn dangerous to practice. Wouldn't it have been nice to just say a spell and know what he had to do to harness his fire?

Tabor grinned at the look on Fateh's face. "Aw, don't be like that, Spark, Isn't it fun, playing with fire instead of just getting it through a stone or water?"

Fateh made a face. "I'd rather not risk blowing up things because I wasn't able to control myself."

"You think I'll just gain knowledge and be able to harness it right away?" Hana asked in surprise. "I will have to practice the illusions and magicI have learned so I am proficient in it. I can't snap my fingers and be able to perform on command. It's like reading a book. You learn how to do it, but you really gain proficiency by actually doing."

"I didn't think of it that way." Fateh admitted. "It just seemed like you'd be able to go after getting the magic lessons. I'm sorry." He could at least give his apologies, even if he couldn't thank Hana and her mother for their hospitality. What if... "I appreciate your explaining this to me." He got the near thank you out without any problems, so it must be a way of skirting around the forbidden 'thank you'."And for letting me stay here."

Hana gave him a surprised look. "I promised you a place to stay to rest and re-energize yourself. What better place than my own home?" She shook her head. "You don't have to worry about thanking me for something I offered, but your words are appreciated."

Fateh nodded and turned to Hana's mother. "Now, what can I do to help?"

Chapter Twenty-Six

Hana and her mother left Tabor and him alone in their rooms white they worked out the details of the magic Hana would need to learn. Fateh was just relieved to be laying flat. Not that he hadn't gotten to rest at his father's house, but this seemed different. He had been so wound up about having a father in the first place, not to mention all the work he had done with his fire.

"So, Spark--" Tabor sat next to him, "You've had some shocks lately, Are you truly prepared to go home and face the darkness there?" He obviously didn't just mean the Shadows.

Fateh flung an arm over his head and sighed. "I don't know," he admitted. "It'll be the first time going home and not having my mother there. I don't even know what's left of my house. If I'm lucky, they only robbed the place, Worst luck is that Shadows moved in." Shadows taking over his house wasn't something he prepared for. He'd rather the people in town burned the place down rather than let Shadows move in. The thought of them running their hands through the mementos that he and his mother collected filled him with coldness.

"Are you sure you want to go home?" Tabor asked seriously. "It must be worse for you if you go."

"It'll be worse not knowing." Fateh spoke stubbornly. "I'll eat myself up worrying what happened to the place. It's best to just get it over with." He wanted to see if he could salvage anything--he wanted something to take away with him to remind him of happier times.

Going to town and seeing Meira and Tobias would be its own type of hardship. Seeing the people who killed his mother would be worse. He would be exercising every bit of restraint he had to not return the favor.

Tabor must have seen something in his expression because he sighed. "If you're sure, Spark." Tabor rested a hand on Fateh's head. "I'll be with you every step of the way."

"You just don't want to have me away from you." Fateh's accusing tone was half-hearted. "You're already chained to me, why the need to be with me all the time?"

"Why, you don't like my company?" Tabor asked, pressing a hand to his heart. "I'm wounded, absolutely devastated you don't want to spend all of your time with me." His tone grew more serious. "Once we get back home, I'm not letting you out of my sight. You're especially vulnerable now, having come into your power and being so young. You'll be a tasty snack for one of the Shadows."

Fateh shuddered. "Is getting overwhelmed what happened to you?" he asked, lifting his arms from his eyes to look up at Tabor.

"Yes. Young and new in my power and fell right into their trap." Tabor's face closed off. "I hope you never have to experience what they did to me."

"What I've seen them do is bad enough." Fateh pointed out. "I won't forget what happened when the Shadows first appeared in town, remember?"

"Yes, you saw them come, but you weren't touched by them," Tabor shuddered. "It's worse when they pretend to be friends at first. It's easy to lure you in when they're friendly." He shook himself out of his mood. "Which is why we're going to be cautious and use every trick we have up our sleeves when we fight them."

"Yeah, it's not like we're going in with guns blazing," Fateh shifted to give Tabor a confused look. "I think it's going to be a lot of magic and illusions and sneaking around in their base so we could attack them on the sly. As much fun as it would be to blow their central ground sky-high, they'd probably escape."

"Not if we use metal." Tabor spread his hands. "Using metal is where our little humans and yokai friends come in. They can handle the metal we can't and our magic can make it volatile enough it will become a weapon."

"I think after we get Marisa from the Sanctuary, it will be time to visit Etana again. We probably can't get him to leave his town, but he said he'd help. I bet supplying us with metal is considered help."

"Right you are." Tabor smiled. "It will be nice seeing him again. I don't see him nearly as often as I'd like to." Obviously he had a good time with Etana last time, the details of which Fateh didn't want to know. Especially now that he didn't know exactly where he stood with Tabor.

"What if he's not our friend when we go to see him?" Fateh asked nervously. "He did say he could change without warning."

"Then we buy metal in town--Etana's got loads in for sale--and then we leave without saying a word." Tabor wrinkled his nose. "Etana as an enemy would be a bad thing. But he's on our side more often than not, so odds are good he'll welcome our group with ... well, I wouldn't say open arms, but at least he won't be throwing metal darts at us."

"He wouldn't." Fateh looked at Tabor in horror. "That'll hurt like a bitch if he hits us."

"And Etana has very good aim." Tabor pointed out. "Where he wants his metal to go, it goes."

"What a gamble." Fateh muttered. "Well, I guess there's no helping it." He knew they'd definitely need Hana, Haruki and Marisa for the metal. It could be spread out between the three of them so they could split up if needed.

"Nope." Tabor said cheerfully. "Etana's place is one of the few which have pathways open to have the metal we'll need. We don't want to open pathways to places which are clean of magic and Shadow."

"There are still places out there which are normal?" Fateh asked wistfully. "Must be nice for them."

"Very few." Tabor sighed and leaned back against the bed. "Magic is only in fairy tales." He poked Fateh's cheek. "And no, you can't go there. You need the ambient magic in the air to survive."

"Yeah, well, I'm used to magic now." Fateh muttered. "I think life would be boring without it." He wouldn't admit out loud about how he'd hate not having his magic any longer. He had grown accustomed to the power and it had become an integral part of his identity.

"Good to hear because it's here to stay." Tabor got up, ruffling Fateh's hair as he did so. "Don't sleep the day away. You'll want to explore the town and maybe learn some magic tricks of your own."

Fateh looked up, interested. "You really think I can do magic other than just my fire?" He was interested in the concept of magic and reading books about wizards used to be some of his favorites. The fae never were--the fae had always been a warning from his grandparents. Fairy tales were lessons, not amusement.

"Sure you can. It's just spells and humans have been using spells for ages. You just haven't seen many spells until lately." Tabor sounded as if he knew some of these humans personally and he gave Fateh an expectant look.

"But I'm not human." Fateh protested. Tabor pointed it out to him quite enough times he wasn't, even if he sometimes still felt that way. Seventeen years of life didn't get erased so easily, even with all the fire magic he learned.

"Part of you is and we'll use that part of you just as much as we did the fire aspect of your nature. You can never have too many tricks at your disposal." Tabor spread his hands wide in emphasis.

"And you?" Fateh asked. "Are you going to learn magic as well?" He rather thought the idea of Tabor using magic could be a scary one. He already could do so much damage, slinging about spells like some magical gunslinger didn't set his mind at ease.

"I'm not even a bit human, so all my magic is in my fire." Tabor sounded regretful. "We'll gather Sam and see if they're willing to learn some magic as well."

"Good plan." Fateh sat up and looked down at the fluffy bed with regret. "I guess you're right that we can't sleep now. We have too much to do."

"That's the spirit." Tabor nodded. "Kitsune are some of the best at magic. I'm sure you can learn something."

"Let's hope they'll be willing to teach us." Fateh stretched and stood up, holding out a hand to Tabor. "Let's see what we can find."

***

They didn't have far to go before Shikomoe found them. She slid an arm in the crook of Fateh's and beamed up at him. "And here I thought you'd be like Sam and sleeping away."

"Thought about it, but then Tabor pointed out I can sleep tonight and better use my time while I'm here." Fateh gave Shikomoe a curious look, she thought she showed interest in Sam. They would be disappointed to find out it wasn't the case, but Shikomoe's next words surprised him.

"Oh, I knew I'd find you sniffing around here and thought I'd be your guide. Are you looking for magic? Most humans do look for learning spells when they're here." She frowned. "But you're only partly human. Are you sure you can learn magic?"

"Tabor seems to think the human part of me will allow me to do magic." Fateh shrugged. "I still feel mostly human and I thought I was human for sixteen years of my life. It has to count for something, right?" He gently disengaged himself from Shikomoe, not wanting to burn her with his elevated temperature.

Shikomoe pouted at him, but didn't try to grab him again. "I think Sam might want to learn some magic, too. They're partially human, aren't they?"

Fateh nodded. "Tabor is the only one who is full blooded fae, Hana and Haruki are halfsies like Sam and I are." He tilted his head. "But Hana can do kitsune magic with no problem, right?"

Shikomoe nodded. "Yep and she's learning it all right now, to be stored for later use. I'd show you what she's doing, but it's really boring. She's just sitting there, meditating with her soul stone."

"Sounds riveting." Tabor's words were dry. "I say we skip it and focus on Spark here learning some magic. We can wake up Sam and see if they want to come on this adventure with us. I don't know if Uisge can do magic, but we can ask her, too."

"They seemed so tired, though." Shikomoe chewed on her lower lip thoughtfully. "I guess it wouldn't hurt to ask, They can always throw a pillow at my head if they don't want to wake up." She sounded almost cheerful at the idea of getting a pillow lobbed at her.

"Sounds fair. I think they would be hurt if we left them out of the potential of learning magic." Fateh knew he would feel the same way if the tables were turned. He just wished he could learn fun magic, instead of needing it for a reason to destroy what he saw as an evil. Hana and Haruki were right to call the Shadows the Blight. He couldn't think of a more apt descriptor for them.

"I'll show you to my place, then." Shikomoe skipped ahead of them, leading them to one of the large trees which held a home. The size of the tree staggered and Fateh couldn't help but gape at it.

"How on earth?" he managed to ask. It was the size of a small house. There were windows carved in the walls of the tree and a doorway sandwiched between them. Kitsune fire burned in each of the windows, glowing a cheerful blue.

"Magic, of course." Shikomoe giggled at his flabbergasted look. "We couldn't grow the trees so big without it and boy was Sam excited when they saw my home. They couldn't stop talking about how exciting it could be to stay in a giant tree. They could feel the tree had accepted this and still grows around the intrusion that I've made into it."

"I bet Sam was excited." Fateh shook his head. "Color me impressed." He examined the tree closely. He wanted to see how it all worked, but Shikomoe already pulled him inside. "You can examine the outside of my home later. We want to talk to Sam before they get into too deep of a sleep."

"Yeah, I guess so." Despite his disappointment, Fateh found the inside of the house fascinating as well. Built like a studio apartment, it held a loft in the corner. Sam slept in the bed in the loft.

"Did you give up your bed for them?" Fateh asked curiously.

"Or were you planning on sharing it?" Tabor returned with a grin. "I don't blame you. Sam is very attractive, if you like tall, dark and handsome."

"Maybe a little of both." Shikomoe admitted without shame. "I wasn't just going to jump in without asking them, though. That would give Sam an open invitation to smother me in my sleep." She gazed up at Sam fondly. "What a way to go, though."

"Okay, you're officially weird." Fateh snorted. "You want to wake them up or do you want one of us to do it?"

"I got it." Shikomoe climbed up the steps nimbly, skipping rungs as she went. Fateh couldn't hear what she said to Sam, but she slowly woke them up with a gentle hand on their shoulder. Sam didn't throw any pillows, but they did look adorably rumpled as they sat up in bed and squinted down at Fateh and Tabor.

Tabor waved and grinned widely. "So you want to become a wizard?"

Sam blinked in confusion and then nodded with a wide smile. "Where do we start?" They squeezed Shikomoe's hand as they got out of bed. "And you mean we can learn real magic? More than just what we do with our elements?"

Sam hadn't gone to see anyone in any of the elemental realms, but they were getting training from full-blooded earth elementals back at the Sanctuary. Fateh thought something like this would give Sam something fun to do.

"I guess we'll learn kitsune magic." Fateh shrugged. "Maybe illusions?" He looked to Shikomoe for help.

"I'll be helping Sam since they're earth and I'm an earth kitsune." Shikomoe tilted her head to the side. "But I can teach both of you how to create illusions--how to hide yourself and your nature, as well as hide other people or things." She raised an eyebrow. "Our magic is inherent, so there's not a lot you can perform yourself--but your elements should lend the oomph you need to do simple spells."

"I'm eager to learn anything." Sam spoke with conviction. "Teach away, oh wise Shikomoe."

Shikomoe blushed and her multiple tails twitched from side to side. "We'll see how wise you think of me after I finish teaching you."

Fateh frowned a little. "You said you can teach Sam because of their element. What about me?" he asked. "I thought we were using the human part of us to learn magic. What does affinities have to do with anything?"

"You're right, I can probably teach you both." Shikomoe looked disappointed she wouldn't have alone time with Sam. She grinned. "Other than illusions, how would you like to learn how to fly or appear in the dreams of others?"

"Sounds like it could be fun." Fateh stretched out his arms and smiled at Shikomoe. "Should we get started?" He could use dreams to talk to Meira and Tobias before he saw them in person and hopefully soften them up for his visit. Did Shadows dream? They were once human, so perhaps they dreamt of their time as a human.

"Let's get studying." Shikomoe gestured for them all to gather on the couch in the middle of the room. "I'll get the books."

Chapter Twenty-Seven

Learning took most of the morning and part of the afternoon, but by the time they had a late lunch, Sam and Fateh were able to spin passable illusions.

"It won't fool a kitsune," Shikomoe cautioned, "but it should fool humans. They don't look past the initial reality of a situation and they'll take what they see at face value."

"Mmm, you may be wrong there." Tabor spoke up. "Humans have been through a lot in the last few years. They're starting to question things. Those illusions better be more robust if you don't want them seen through right away."

"It's not like this comes naturally to us." Fateh complained, massaging the back of his neck with one hand. "We're not kitsune. When I thought we were going to learn magic, I thought it would be something like teleporting." He sounded wistful. "We could forgo the shadow roads if we could teleport."

"We can't teleport, but we can work on invisibility next." Shikomoe was cheerful and encouraged by their illusions. "You can sneak in places this way and not have anyone the wiser."

"Being able to be sneaky will be very useful trying to get past the Shadows or any guards which are in the town." Fateh mused. "I don't just want to pop in out of the shadows and have something stab us because they have a gut reaction."

"Being wouldn't be ideal, no." Tabor grimaced. "Well, I can get us to the outskirts of town and then we can make our way into it, hopefully under a cloak of invisibility." He stared down at his hands for a moment. "It's a shame I can't use magic the way Sam and Fateh can. I'm counting on you to make the rest of us invisible."

Fateh snorted. "No, I thought I'd let you just wander in without any disguises, you being public enemy number one there, among the Shadows and the humans."

"Not quite that bad." Tabor sniffed. "I left on good terms, but I'd still rather not show my face until we're on our way to fight the Shadows. Some humans might be overzealous and decide to attack me out of principle. They last saw me with you, after all. Your old friends might not be accommodating."

"They're not going to want to see me, especially if it comes out I'm not human." Fateh made a face and turned to Shikomoe. "Can I enter someone's dreams and try and convince them I'm okay to deal with?" He didn't want to deal with them; they hadn't held the knife, but they were part of the reason his mother was killed. But they were going to be necessary for intel.

"You can say whatever you want in a dream. Whether or not these people you want to convince will believe you is another story." Shikomoe shrugged. "Sucks to hear, I know. But I can tell you people are more susceptible in their dreams and it;s likely to carry over into the waking world." She held out another book to Fateh, this one smaller than the one on invisibility, but not by much.

Fateh took it and studied the cover of two foxes touching noses, surrounded by stars and moons. He flipped through a couple of pages, taking in the illustrations that demonstrated what he would have to do to engage the dream state and walk in someone else's dreams. "It seems complicated."

"Not as hard as you think." Shikomoe reassured him. She took the book page and turned the pages until it came to the main instruction of what to do once you got into someone's dream. "It may be a little bit of work, since you're not naturally inclined to it, but I think the reward will be worth the work."

Sam craned their head to read to see what the book contained. "I think I'll concentrate on learning illusions and invisibility. There isn't anyone whose dreams I want to invade."

Fateh reluctantly put the book aside. "You said our illusions weren't perfect yet. I guess we should work on those before I try anything with dreams."

"Good plan." Shikomoe rubbed her hands together. "Let's see you start from the top. I want to believe you're a kitsune. Let's see those cute ears and tails of yours." She winked at Sam. "I especially want to see you as a kitsune."

Sam blushed again and mumbled something under their breath, before concentrating on the illusion. They could get most of the basics right, but the illusion had to go deeper, more than just on the surface. That meant disguising their own magical signatures so it seemed like an affinity, rather than an intrinsic part of them.

It was almost dinnertime before Shikomoe pronounced them 'good enough to fool everyone except Seers and kitsune'. Fateh would take the compliment; no one could fool a Seer., "Maybe we can greet Hana this way." Fateh said with mischief. "It will at least make her double-take."

"Trying to fool her is as good a judge of your well your illusions are. It depends how much she has learned, but it might be fun. Come on, I'm tired of sitting around. Let's get moving and get some real food."

Sam and Fateh didn't argue; Tabor grew bored watching the two of them silently reading and constantly moved in and out of the room. "Let's show each other how much we've learned." Fateh knew they weren't done; there were still a few lessons to learn. He especially wanted to learn invisibility, so they could sneak into town and past the Shadows.

Tabor shook his head. "If I didn't share a bond with you, Spark, I wouldn't know you." Tabor bowed to Shikomoe. "You're a good teacher."

Shikomoe waved the compliment away, but gave them a pleased smile. "I've never taught anyone but kitsune before, so it was a pleasure seeing what the two of them could do." She grabbed their hands and beamed. "Let's go."

***

Hana finished her own training for the day and when she saw Sam and Fateh, she giggled. "Oh very good." She clapped her hands together. "You could almost pass, if it wasn't for the fact I can see through your illusion." She patted them on the head, tweaking an ear. "Very nice, you can even feel the illusion."

"Shikomoe made sure it covered all senses." Fateh nodded, twitching his imaginary tail with amusement. He carefully took down the illusion, one piece at a time to make sure he got it all. "Next thing is invisibility and for me, dream-walking."

"Oh, good. The more we are able to do invisibility, the better. A cloak will only stretch so far and I can't cover the entire party." Hana led them all into the kitchen, where her mother finished up dinner. "If you and Sam can cover as well, it will make things much easier."

Sam dismantled their illusion as well and smiled at Hana. "We'll do our best."

"You guys get to have all the fun." They all turned to see Uisge standing there, looking disappointed. "I don't have any fire or earth blood, so I can't participate."

"But your magic is amazingly strong and you can do illusions with water. I need to use human magic to be able to do an illusion." Fateh reassured her. "You don't need extra tricks like Sam and I do." Uisge could drown someone on dry land; it was no mean feat. She could also pull all the water out of someone, slice with water and create ice spikes. Fateh wouldn't want her as an enemy.

"Yeah, I know." Uisge didn't blink at his words. "I'm pretty awesome and all. But I wish I could learn kitsune magic. I think it would be fun."

"Glad to see you're so sure of yourself. I need to have the sort of confidence you do in my life." Their words held nothing but amusement.

"You'll get there." Uisge patted Sam's shoulder and gave them a reassuring smile. "Once you get to be my age, you'll gain lots of confidence." She gave them all a severe look. "But no, you don't get to know how old I am. A lady never reveals her true age."

Fateh held up his hands in denial. "Wasn't going to ask. Mom raised me to be polite." She also taught him to accept most things and have an open mind. Uisge could be anywhere from twenty to two hundred and just played as if she were ancient. He had a feeling she had that type of confidence from the moment she accessed her magic.

"Good. It will serve you well if you ever have to deal with the higher fae. Politeness is part of what makes them." Uisge's tone held nothing but politeness.

"Me and Spark don't plan on seeing the higher fae anytime soon." Tabor was serious. "We're simple elementals; catching the gaze of anything higher is asking for trouble. I'll keep Spark away from that sort of nonsense for as long as possible."

It could be inevitable they meet the higher fae at some point, but like Tabor, Fateh didn't want to see them. There were stories about the regular fae and then there were the clear warnings about the higher fae his grandparents instilled in him. He wouldn't be sticking his hand in the bear trap if he could help it.

"You should always be prepared." Uisge gave a graceful shrug. "But that's not my concern right now. What's for dinner?"

***

The next few days went much the same. Sam and Fateh learned kitsune spells, things that would be useful when they confronted the Shadows. Shikomoe knew some human magic as well, and had fun in teaching them how to do binding spells. Being able to tie someone up magically would be particularly useful when fighting against the Shadows or Shadow-bound. Fateh hated the idea of fighting humans, but there were those who went with the Shadows willingly and worked for them, sowing discontent and mischief.

Besides, if he just bound them, it wasn't actually hurting them, unlike his use of fire against the Shadows themselves. One spell he found particularly useful was an enhancing spell. Who couldn't use extra speed when dealing with the Shadows? All of these spells came at a price; it used their own internal strength and vitality and to use a little speed now would slow them now later. Fateh put that under 'spells as a last resort' because as much as he wanted to be faster, he also didn't want to be caught with his defenses down, either.

All in all, they ended up staying two weeks with the kitsune, learning and relaxing and prepping for their own private war. Fateh came out of it feeling much better prepared for what they were going to do. He could also. He'd already admitted out loud that learning magic had been a childhood dream of his. Fateh thought fleetingly of Meira and Tobias, and how excited they would have been to learn magic. They certainly played enough fantasy games growing up and they all loved the magic users.

Then everything changed when the Shadows came to town and ruined it for everyone.

"So Fateh, Sam." Shikomoe looked very pleased with her students. "How do you feel now about going into battle against your chosen enemy?" She hesitated a little, giving Sam a sideways look. "There's no way I can convince you to stay, is there? It's safe here and we all adore you."

"I'll come back." Sam promised, squeezing Shikomoe's hands. "If I'm still alive at the end of all of this, I'm going to come back and see you again." They obviously felt about Shikomoe in the same way Shikomoe felt about them.

Fateh averted his gaze. He didn't want to intrude on what could be a private moment between the two of them. Still--"I'd come back too, if you'd have me." He said with a grin. "It's nice and peaceful here and the company is great. I've never had so many people pinch my cheeks and tell me I'll be adorable when I grow up a bit."

"You both are young compared to the rest of us." Shikomoe nodded and released Sam's hands. The moment between them passed, but it wasn't forgotten. They still gave each other occasional glances, but nothing like the one they shared previously.

Fateh felt guilty about taking Sam away from someone who understood them. It was so rare to find someone. Fateh wasn't sure he'd ever be able to find a person who understood he wouldn't ever be in a relationship for the sex. Tabor and Etana were in a relationship and they seemed happier for it.

"Well, we're pretty young in general." Sam laughed. "We have a lot of growing up to do. They looked at Fateh. "Are you ready to go? I know you're eager to fight these Shadows and from my understanding, we have a few stops to make along the way before we actually go to your town."

"Yeah, I want to go back to the Sanctuary, see if there is any news and update the people there on what we've learned, then I want to go see Etana about getting metal to defend ourselves with. If we go into town, looking for help, having a cache of metal will help our cause enormously."

"Alright, then." Sam took Shikomoe's hand again. "It might be over before we know it and I'll be back here, living the good life with you. Don't forget me, hm?" They leaned forward and kissed Shikomoe lightly, before pulling away. Shikomoe reached up, dragged them back and kissed Sam more enthusiastically.

"Kissing is how you say goodbye." She and Sam were both out of breath and Fateh couldn't help but smile. It was good they found one another; Fateh just hoped they would all survive facing the Shadows.

Chapter Twenty-Eight

The trip back through the gate held no problems and the early morning sunlight shone down on them when they emerged. When they came out of the empty air on the bridge, it was empty. They wasted no time in making their way to the Sanctuary, urged by an internal clock, ticking down the minutes until things went all to hell.

The first person they saw as they came up to the Sanctuary's walls was Marisa, waiting for them calmly with a drink in her hand. "I knew you'd be back today." Serenity suffused her features. "You were gone an awfully long time and people thought you already went to battle the Shadows and lost."

"We weren't gone that long, were we?" Fateh asked, eyeing Marisa in confusion. Marisa looked different from when she had been the last time they saw her. If Fateh didn't know any better, he would say she had aged.

"You were gone for a year, fourteen days and twenty-five minutes." Marisa sipped her drink, unconcerned by the bombshell she had just dropped among the group. "Did you go beyond the gates? Time can run funny there; you could spend a day and emerge ten years later. You're lucky you weren't gone for that long."

"A year?!" Sam rushed forward to the Sanctuary, Hana and Haruki hot on his heels. "They're going to be so worried about us!"

"I told them you were safe." Marisa frowned, irritated as if she hadn't been believed. "I knew you were coming back here on this day."

Fateh watched the others run with bemusement. "So we were really gone a year? It wasn't even a month for us." He shoved his hands in his pockets, frowning. "I wonder how much worse things have gotten over the past year."

"The Shadows still spread their reach, but they haven't penetrated these walls." Marisa looked wistful. "I wish I could stay, but I know you need me to see through the darkness and shadow to the real truth."

"We don't have to take you." Fateh felt the guilt gnaw at him again. Marisa spent a year here, in safety and care, Dragging her out to an uncertain future seemed cruel. He wondered how much Marisa knew of what was coming, but he wasn't sure about asking. What if he didn't like the answer of 'rocks fall, everyone dies'?

She caught his look and patted his hand. "It's not all bad news." She reassured him. "We've sent people to your town and they've reported back that while the Shadows are numerous, there is still life in the town and in the resistance which fights there. You will have companions who will fight by your side when it comes down to the end."

"At least they won't be fighting us." Fateh mumbled. "I'm sure they won't be thrilled at fighting with us, but it will be good to have humans on our side."

"More than just humans will join the fight." Marisa took his hand and led him back to the Sanctuary, Tabor and Uisge trailing behind. "This is more than just a fight against human and Shadow; the fae are in danger as well and they will lend their strength to the cause."

:"Please don't tell me it's high fae." Tabor spoke behind them. "I don't think I could deal with those snobs, taking over and running roughshod over all our plans."

"You will meet the high fae, but not in this battle." Marisa said calmly. "Your destiny lies far beyond the places you've been and the places you've yet to travel are numerous and varied."

"Traveling to numerous places isn't bad, but the way you phrase it doesn't fill me with hope." Fateh grimaced; he didn't want to meet the high fae either. There were way too many stories about them and their divided courts to want to mess with them. He wasn't even a full fae, only half. He could only imagine the snobbery that would arise from such a meeting.

"It's not meant to." Marisa raised an eyebrow at him. "It's meant to fill you with knowledge so you're better prepared when the other shoe drops and you find yourself in an unfamiliar landscape. This way, you have been forewarned of events."

'Well, let's worry about what is to come later." Tabor shook his head. "One step at a time; we're going to see an old friend of mine; if he's still a friend. I want to pick up some metal from him so our clever little humans can use it in the same sort of destructive ways they've done before." Tabor had witnessed the bombing of the restaurant, where several Shadows perished. Fateh only saw the devastating aftermath.

"Good. First thing you need to do is take me with you to see Etana." Marisa said the name without a hint of doubt. "Then we'll come back here to pick up the rest of the people and head to Felinheli."

"Why not bring everyone with us?" Fateh asked. "That way we're not doubling back."

"I think your friend might be overwhelmed if an entire group of strangers showed up at his door. It might cause problems in town and then he'd definitely not want to be your friend any longer."

"You talk as if you know him." Tabor's words were filled with amusement. "I mean, you're not wrong, but how do you know him so well?"

"I've dreamt of us meeting him." Marisa shrugged. "It's always the three of us, except when I dream the whole gang is there and he gets super pissed." Her expression and tone didn't change as she spoke. "It goes best when it's just the two of you, but then you couldn't carry away the metal you need." She gestured to herself. "This is where I'll be of use."

"And the fact you can travel the roads to Etana's home doesn't hurt, either." Tabor observed. "Hell, I always wanted to see Etana's reaction at seeing a true

Seer. He thinks they're all fakes or fae. I don't know what he'll do when confronting a human one."

"Guess he'll be in for a shock on multiple levels." Fateh snorted. "Us showing up a year later with a human in tow that isn't puking her guts out on the shadow roads." He wished he could take a gate to Etana's place, like they did with the elemental and kitsune realms, but Etana very much lived in the human world.

"Aw, Spark, being sick only happened once and you weren't recognized yet. Now you've come more into your power, you'll be fine. You haven't had a problem with all the traveling we've been doing, right?"

Fateh nodded in agreement. It helped with Marisa lighting the way with her Seer abilities, but the other times he traveled the shadows, it hadn't bothered him like it the first time he had gone on them.

"We shouldn't waste anymore time." Marisa said seriously. "Make your goodbyes and explanations and let the others get into the rhythm of things before we haul them away to dangerous waters." Her gaze flicked to Uisge. "Even you can't come with us. I'm sure you'll be fine here or even back in your own waters until we come back."

"Always left on the outside. I should have just stayed with the kitsune." Uisge was faintly bitter. "I hope I'm not just being used for my powers. I hoped we would be considered friends after all we've done together."

"It's not like that at all." Fateh hastened to reassure Uisge. "Etana is touchy and territorial and barely allows Tabor to come. I think the more people come, the less likely he will be to help us. That's why none of the others are coming, either."

"I understand." Uisge's expression barely flickered. "I hope I won't be left out of many more things. I may have to rethink my position in his little group."

"I promise, we won't." Fateh reassured her. "After we come back from seeing Etana, all of us will go to my home together. You won't be left out of anything from there on out."

Uisge gave Fateh a faint smile. "I appreciate it, Fateh." She twirled on her toes once and headed towards the large lake in the Sanctuary's grounds. "I'll be resting in the waters while you explain to the others why they can't come along, after all they've done so far."

Fateh grimaced at the reminder. They had been through a lot together already and a side trip to Etana's shouldn't warrant cutting them out of it. Still, they might be happier at home for a time, since they lost a year. They were probably reassuring everyone they were fine. Uisge's smile turned wicked. "Have fun."

***

Telling the others about their trip to Etana's went better than he expected; there were no more arguments after Marisa stated what she Saw. Fateh noticed relief on Haruki and Hana's faces. They were probably glad to be back home, even if it wouldn't be for a long time.

"Things are going to move fast after we get back from Etana's." Fateh bit his lip. "We'll shadow-travel to my town and meet up with some of the leaders of the resistance there. Even if it's not people I know, there will be people we can work with to help bring down the Shadows. They've been working at it for four years now." They had to have a grasp on the situation by now and had to have lots of solutions that would be better executed by having the proper weapons at hand.

Hana nodded, looking grave. "We've had our reprieve, staying with my relatives, but now the real work begins. I'll spend my time here taking care of things while you are gone and we'll look for you soon. I know you're eager to get on your way."

Fateh didn't know if he wanted to go home, to confront his demons and destroy those who took so much away from him, from all of them. "Not in so much of a hurry that I can't let you settle things here first." His tone was direct and honest. "I have friends here as well and I want to make sure they're taken care of." His look grew anxious. "How is Randi, by the way?"

"She's thriving here, from what I've learned." Haruki spoke up. "She is the little night owl, only going out in the daylight when it's overcast. I don't blame her; I wouldn't want to get frozen in place, either." He gave Fateh a reassuring look. "Randi is fine here and she doesn't need to go with you to know you're doing your best to save us all."

"Good. I didn't have plans to bring her along. She's been through enough already, she doesn't need to be dragged into the middle of the mess all over again." Between Mokosh's domain and the trolls, Fateh rather thought Randi had her fill of being hurt. She would be defenseless against the Shadows and Fateh would never put her in danger, simply because he wanted a friend next to him.

"Alright then. It's decided. You guys stay here and get everything sorted, while Tabor, Marisa and I travel to Etana's." Fateh crossed his arms over his chest. "We'll get what metal we can and head back here so we can all travel together to Felinheli."

"I hope your Etana can be useful to us." Hana hugged Fateh tightly. "Be safe and come back soon. I don't want anymore year-long absences."

"Me either." Fateh said fervently. "One year lost is enough." He gave her a hug back, then leaned back to rub the back of his head. "We won't take forever. We should be back within a week's time. It all depends on Etana."

"Etana and the Shadows." Haruki sounded dire. "We don't know what the situation is there. You may be walking into a trap."

"Thanks for the vote of confidence. Marisa didn't see a trap, so I'll take her word for it. She hasn't been wrong yet." He looked up at Tabor. "If you'll do the honors of getting us to Etana's?" he asked.

"I thought I'd let you try." Tabor was all innocence and Fateh snorted out a laugh.

"I haven't learned how to manipulate the shadows into a road yet." He wouldn't trust himself to do it any further than the backyard of the Sanctuary, even when he did learn. Traveling all the way to New Zealand would be beyond his capabilities, even if he knew how to open the shadows.

"You have a point. That'll be our next lesson." Tabor gave a huge sigh, as if it were a huge thing to open a shadow road. "You're a fast learner, though. I bet you'll pick up the trick of it once you watch me do it enough times. Pay attention this time, though, hm? I want us to have a backdoor in case things get hairy."

"If something happens where you can't manage it, how do you expect me to handle it?" Fateh demanded. "I'm nowhere near your level and I don't think I'll ever be. I have a long way to go to understand what I can do. You're at least a century older than me. Even you don't have it all together."

"Thanks for the faint praise." Tabor couldn't keep the irony out of his words. "Please, hold back with the compliments. I simply can't handle it."

Fateh grinned. "If I compliment you too much, you'll get a big head."

"Oh, no. You don't want to see me all confident." Tabor snorted. "Fine, fine--I'll make the pathway and let our little Seer light the way so she doesn't get sick."

"Then let's get going." Fateh gestured to the bright sunlight streaming inside the room. "We have plenty of light to create a shadow."

"Don't teach me how to make shadows. That's what I'm going to be teaching you." Tabor stepped into the pool of shadow and gestured with his hands to form a door. The shadows rippled around him until an archway formed.

"Ohh getting fancy." Fateh quipped. "Making it all official looking."

"Well, I have to impress the lady." Tabor grinned, gesturing to Marisa, who did look as if she was going to enjoy this walk into the shadows more than their last trip.

"Old men first." Fateh pushed at Tabor as he grabbed Marisa's hand. He waved goodbye to the group as the shadows swallowed them.

Chapter Twenty-Nine

They arrived in the same woods as they had the last time. It was just as quiet; no sign of Shadows, big or small. Fateh counted the lack of Shadows as a good sign. The little Shadows liked to burrow in the woods. It was why they had been so numerous around his house up in the hills. He automatically looked up, but no Etana was waiting for them this time. It didn't necessarily mean anything. Etana had an entire city to watch over, he couldn't just wait for Tabor and Fateh to show up. Especially if it had been a year since they last saw him.

Fateh couldn't help but think of what Etana said about being enemies, though. How he could switch loyalties easily, since it didn't matter that much to him. He felt a shiver crawl down his spine. Having a miotal on the opposite side of you couldn't be good for your health. No matter what Marisa said, there could always be the possibility Etana wouldn't want to help them.

"So do we go straight to Etana's?" Fateh asked, looking up at Tabor. "Or should we be more cautious?" Tabor hesitated and Fateh knew he thought the same thing.

"I think it would be best if we scouted around town first." Tabor said finally. He looked around the woods and shook his head. "I wish your friend Sam was here. They could tell us what the woods have seen lately and if it's something we need to be concerned about." They both turned to Marisa.

She gave them a bland smile. "The forecast has changed. Chance of rain likely; better avoid areas where lightning strikes."

Fateh winced. Her references, while vague, were clear to understand this time. "Change of plans then. We find metal in town and take it away with us; Etana isn't hurt by the stuff, so there should be plenty in town."

"I'd say we avoid certain factions in town, but they may be the ones we need to go to to get the metal." Fateh didn't look forward to running into the gangs of kids that hated the fae, especially now his power showed that much more and it made him more vulnerable. They could really do some damage to him if they tried.

"Aw, you're not going to come see me?" Fateh's gaze shot around to see Etana standing in the middle of the path, covered in more metal than he had been the last time they saw him. "I'm truly hurt; it's been so long since we've seen each other." His smile sharpened and Fateh took an automatic step backwards.

"I take it we're not friends today, Etana?" Tabor asked casually, one hand on Fateh's shoulder and keeping him in place.

"Not today, but maybe tomorrow." Etana said cheerfully. "You shouldn't have brought a human here with you; they're ever so much more fragile. Although I can't hurt her like I can you with metal."

"You said you would help me." Fateh said desperately. "You said you'd provide metal and help and to not worry about you."

"Friendship was a year ago. Things have changed." Etana shrugged and took a step closer to the three of them. "I told you my loyalties change and you can't trust me on days I tell you I'm not your friend."

"What are you planning to do with us?" Fateh asked, eyeing Etana with a wary expression. He could do a lot of damage, even with a simple touch. The metal that was a part of him would burn.

"Not much. You're not that much of an enemy. Not like the Shadows." Etana spat on the ground. "They tried to infiltrate my city. I lost a few people until I called in the cousins and they helped take care of the problem."

"Well, if the Shadows are your enemy, then we're not." Fateh spread his hands in supplication. "We're working on a way to eradicate the Shadows, so they don't invade anymore towns."

"You and what army?" Etana laughed sourly. "You're only half a fire elemental, you can't do much against shadow."

Fateh didn't say there were more than just the three of them or volunteer Marisa was a Seer. Not everything had to be given to someone who proclaimed they were an enemy at the moment.

"Fighting the Shadows is why we need your help." Tabor tried for reasonable. "With your metal, we can work with humans to wreak havoc on the Shadows."

"Oh, is that the only reason why you came to see me?" Etana demanded. "So you can use me?" He flung out his hands and metal shot out towards Fateh, who barely managed to dodge out of the way.

"No, you great big idiot." Tabor's tone sharpened with his frustration. "There are other places we could have gotten metal; one of the human towns that doesn't have fae, for instance. But we're coming to see you for your company. But you're being an ass." Tabor dodged the next missile, but not enough, it grazed his skin, causing him to hiss in pain.

"I'm being an ass?" Etana demanded. "You're the one who promised he'd visit and help with the Shadows and you decided to screw off for a year?"

"It wasn't a year for us." Fateh kept a wary eye on Etana and his weapons. "We were gone for maybe a month, tops. We were in the fae worlds."

"You didn't create an anchor so time would pass by normally?" Etana looked momentarily disgusted. "It's the most basic of rules to follow. Especially if you have lives outside of the fae realm."

"Time didn't mean so much to me before." Tabor shrugged. "So I didn't think about it. It's my mistake and now we're dealing with the fallout. Are you seriously saying you're an enemy because you haven't seen me for a year and you're throwing a fit? I know it's not because you want to sell us out to the Shadows."

"The Shadows aren't the only ones that are interested in you." Etana smirked and settled back against a tree, apparently getting comfortable. "I know of several bidders who are interested in a half-fae brat and the one who escaped the Shadows."

"Are you talking about the higher fae?" Tabor blanched. "They don't deal with us, we're usually beneath their notice."

"Apparently, having a half-fae in your entourage is something that piqued their interest. Your half-blood nature and the fact you survived the Shadows with only a little damage." His eyes were half-lidded. "Well, we don't count the emotional damage."

"Yes, why would we count emotional damage?" Tabor rolled his eyes. "Hardly consequential."

Fateh looked between the two of them. "Are you saying he's sent the higher fae after us?" he demanded. "I don't want to deal with them. They're part of the reason we have the Shadows in the first place!"

"Granted, human greed is ultimately what caused the Shadows to exist," Tabor pointed out. "The higher fae just gave them the oomph they needed to exist."

"I haven't sold you out yet." Etana admitted. "But I do have people asking about the half-fae who have been cropping up lately. They offer a lot of protection in exchange for information. It's something I can't afford to turn down." His face twisted slightly. "And I admit, I was a little put out. You ignored me for a year and then showed up looking for handouts."

"That's not the only reason why we're here and you know it." Fateh crossed his arms against his chest and frowned at Etana. "We came to see you. If we just wanted metal, I'm sure there's half a dozen shops selling it we could have gotten it from."

"You really didn't mean to abandon me?" Etana asked, hesitant now. He stood up from his slouch against the tree and gave them a closer look. "I understand if Tabor decided to ignore me for a year or more--he's done longer--but I thought Fateh and I had something."

Fateh wanted to demand what exactly the 'something' was; They hadn't bonded romantically or anything. Fateh liked Etana, but it wasn't like Etana and Tabor's relationship. He instead just raised an eyebrow at Etana. "Well, I swear a year hasn't passed by for us. We came back to you as soon as we could."

"Hmph." Etana looked mollified and held out his hand to Fateh. "Come on back to my place. You can rest there before you go world-hopping again." His grin changed to being just as broad as it had before. "So you've traveled in the outer fae realms? Did you like it??"

Fateh explained the fire realm, but neglected to tell Etana about his father or the other half-fae kids he traveled with. Etana may not have sold them out yet, but Fateh was sure that with enough information, it would be enough to tilt him over the edge from friendship to enemy again.

He had to be more cautious than ever around Etana. He turned to Marisa, who observed this whole exchange without a word. "Are you okay?" He acted cautiously, hoping she wouldn't go into one of her 'Seeing' moments. He put a gentle hand on her shoulder, which she shrugged off easily.

"Oh, I'm as fine as the day is short in the winter." She gave Fateh a brilliant smile and twirled around, her scarves twisting in the wind. "I told you it would be fine if I just showed up. But you see now why it was not wise for the rest of our group to come." She grew quiet, her words meant for his ears alone.

A handful of half-human kids and Fateh shuddered at the thought of putting so much temptation into Etana's hands. "Yeah, I get you." He murmured back, just as quiet. He turned back to Etana. "We're ready to go."

"Why don't you try opening the shadows to my place?" Etana suggested with a wicked grin. "It's only a short distance. I'm sure you can manage something simple like opening a pathway." He leaned into Fateh's personal space. "Or are you scared?"

"Scared that I'll turn everyone inside out." Fateh said bluntly. "I'd rather not practice with a human along." He winced at his own words. He still wasn't used to referring to himself as not human.

"Aw, practice would be good for you." Etana protested. "But I guess I can understand wanting to end up at the destination, rather than taking an unexpected detour." He made a grand gesture at the pooling shadows all around them, until a doorway formed in them. "Kids first."

Fateh hesitated, it wasn't as if he didn't trust Etana-- well, no. Honesty with himself compelled him to admit he didn't trust Etana at the moment, especially when he spoke so casually of selling their information off to the higher fae.

"Fine, I'll go first." Etana rolled his eyes. "I have to do so to keep the pathway open to my place, since I kinda removed you off the list of welcome visitors about half a year ago."

"Am I going to be sick again?" Fateh asked dryly. "I'd hate to throw up all over your floors."

"Don't worry, with me to open the way, my guests can walk freely." He walked into the shadows, vanishing into the darkness, but a moment later, he thrust out his hand, waving at the others impatiently.

Tabor and Fateh exchanged a look. "Guess there's only one way to find out if he's going to sell us out." Fateh took a deep breath and took a step into the shadows, Tabor and Marisa on his heels.

It was different from how he usually traveled with Marisa. Whatever she did to usually light the way, she didn't do this time. Perhaps she also found it wise not to shout out all their abilities to someone who could be a potential enemy. The air tasted strangely of metal and Fateh breathed as shallowly as he could, worried that the taint of the metal air would hurt him in some way. However, as Etana promised, it was a short trip and Fateh blinked in the strong light in Etana's main room.

"Expecting someone?" Tabor asked dryly, looking around at the almost clinically neat house. "Don't tell me you've kept it this clean just for me and the kid." The house changed since they were last there; the bed Fateh scorched with his first nightmare was replaced and the appliances in the kitchen were all new.

"Can't I just enjoy new things?" Etana flicked off the light, taking away the shadows with it. Normal sunlight poured through the window, casting its own dim shadows. "Plus, the bed stank like firewood from your firebug's little episode. It had to go, I figured while I replaced one thing, why not replace it all?"

"You live more like a human than most fae I heard of." Fateh looked around and shook his head. "I thought you'd power everything by magic."

Etana gave him a sly smile. "Who's to say I'm not?" he asked. "I'm nt exactly registered on the power grid. They ask too many questions I don't want to answer." He patted the side of his fridge. "I have a few favors from different fae from around the world. Their magic powers my kitchen quite nicely. Even my stove is powered by magic Tabor leant me ages ago." It was the only appliance that didn't look updated.

Tabor shrugged. "I owed you a favor, lending you magic was the least of what I could do to start repaying it."

Marisa observed everything around her with an intense look on her face, as if she committed it to memory. "You've guests recently." She looked matter of fact. "Guests you didn't want, but still supped with anyway. Where have they gone?"

"Gone back through the shadows and good riddance to them." Etana huffed. "I told you, I didn't want the Shadows here. They're more of a nuisance than I thought they would be. They tried to shut down my commerce." He rolled his eyes. "They didn't like all the metal I had everywhere, though. Every house is laced with it."

"How welcoming for your other guests." Tabor snorted. "Remind me to be careful where I step in town."

"If you didn't have any problem last time you were here; I wouldn't worry about it." Etana shrugged it off. "But I have protection for my people and it's all of my metal, so I can reach anyone whenever I want."

"So far of a reach is a little creepy, not going to lie." Fateh shivered a little at how easily Etana could have tracked them down in town, if they chose to go there first. It was the right decision to show up in the woods where they first met. It might not have gone too well for them if they had decided to ignore Etana. "I know there are a few gangs of kids and maybe some adults in town who wouldn't like protection." He thought of the group of kids he met the last time he showed up in town and grinned. They definitely wouldn't accept being protected by a fae.

"Apples to oranges." Etana looked unconcerned. "What they don't know won't hurt them."

Fateh had his opinions about keeping people ignorant, but kept it to himself. He instead flopped down on the couch.. Unease hung in the air, as if something was unsaid and Fateh just needed to be observant enough to pick it up.

Tabor looked as uneasy as he felt, but Marisa looked unconcerned about their situation.

Fateh took heart from Marisa's mood and relaxed minutely. If Marisa wasn't worried, then he would just have to trust in her. Marisa had shown to be the best early-warning system and he kept a close eye on her. All their safety depended on it.

Chapter Thirty

"As much as I would like to stay for as long as we did last time, we need to get to Fateh's town sooner rather than later." Tabor did sound regretful. "We've already lost a year of time we could have used to get an edge on the Shadows."

"We can still have some fun if we send the kids out to get the metal you so desperately crave. I'll even give them directions to the best metal smiths." He grinned. "Although Fateh may turn a little green there."

Fateh wasn't willing to leave Marisa alone; either in town or with Etana. "I'll manage. Metal only hurts me a little, not like it does Tabor. He'd be useless on a shopping trip."

"You may be surprised at how much metal bothers you now." Etana held out a hand to him. "C'mon, give it a shake and we'll see how you do."

Fateh cringed away from all the metal in Etana's hands, but wasn't it just proving a point? If he couldn't even shake Etana's hand, how could he stand to be around all the metal they needed? He reached out a trembling hand and wrapped it around Etana's. It didn't burn, but it was uncomfortable, as if an invisible force tried to push his hand away. When he pulled away, his palm pinkened slightly, as if he held someone hot briefly.

"Huh, you're less affected by it than I thought you'd be, especially with coming into your power." Etana looked almost disappointed and Fateh inwardly shuddered. Apparently they couldn't fully trust Etana, even now.

"Guess I can handle metal for small periods of time." Fateh brushed his hand against his pants, trying to ease the slight prickling. It really wasn't as bad as he imagined it would be, but it wasn't something he wanted to do on repeat. He'd leave the carrying of the metal to Marisa.

"When you go shopping, tell them I sent you." Etana opened the door for them, apparently eager to be alone with Tabor. "It'll give you a discount." He held out money for them. "Still, you'll need some cash. Don't go crazy kids and don't come straight back. Give us an hour or so."

"So little time?" Tabor joked, but there was faint unease in his eyes. It seemed as nice as he would find the time with Etana, he felt slightly worried about what could happen to himself at being left alone with Etana. Not that Fateh would have been much use, but it was the thought that counted.

"I'll make it worth your while." Etana promised, showing Fateh and Marisa out the door and shutting it firmly behind them.

Marisa and Fateh looked at each other and Fateh shrugged. "Might as well do what we meant to do here. It'll be better for us in town."

"Tabor can handle himself," Marisa agreed. "He's stronger than you think."

"Having Tabor on his own does not fill me with comfort." Fateh protested, looking as if he wanted to go back inside, no matter what Etana had implied would be happening.

Marisa shrugged. "I meant to tell you the truth. But you're right, we won't want to be in there. There are some things even Seers ignore."

Fateh snorted and took her hand. "Let's go, then." He would worry about what Etana was going to do to Tabor, but only so much. Marisa said he'd survive Etana. Fateh would rather not think about it.

***

The first thing they did once they reached the city was search for a metal shop. It wasn't hard. He spotted a metal shop on the outskirts of the city, but Fateh figured they'd get better deals the further they went into the city. He'd never noticed that many shops selling metal the last time he was here, but then again, he hadn't been looking for them.

Halfway through the city, Fateh stopped at one smaller shop, tucked in amongst a place selling burgers and another a clothes shop. "Might as well try here." He looked at Marisa. "What do you think?"

"Keep your hands to yourself." She warned him to be careful not to touch anything. Fateh nodded. He didn't plan on handling the merchandise. He just hoped he could be in the shop without revealing himself as being one of the fae, even if he was only half. He pushed open the door as carefully as possible and stared around at all the metal displayed on the shelves. His jaw nearly dropped and he could only think of how Meira and Tobias would be like two kids in a candy store at seeing all the metal. The possibilities were endless.

Marisa handled several pieces carefully, examining them from all angles before picking one. She did this around the entire shop and soon the basket they grabbed to hold their purchases filled with raw metal pieces. Most of it wasn't worked metal, but cheap and direct and Fateh could only imagine the damage they could do with these. Marisa picked just enough worked pieces to add variety. The raw metal would do the most damage, but it seemed the most obvious.

"Setting up a home protection, are you?" The man behind the counter eyed their basket of metal with an upraised brow. "Lots of metal for some kids."

Fateh bristled at being called a kid, but Marisa just gave him a bland smile. "We're going to put the metal to good use." She kept her tone serene. "Etana sent us to collect."

The man brightened at the mention of Etana's name. "He's my best supplier; I'm surprised he's not selling it to you wholesale."

"He thought going into the city was a better idea." Fateh shrugged, skin prickling at the proximity to all the metal. "Besides, he didn't have any spare metal to give us when we saw him." All of Etana's metal was on him and Fateh doubted he could just peel it off and hand it over that easily.

"Well, if Etana sent you..." His tone indicated Etana would find out if he lied. "Then I'll have to give you a discount. Let's see what you have there and what it'll come out to be."

Fateh handed over the basket, trying not to seem too eager. He could hold the stuff while in the basket, but handling it raw made him queasy. It was one thing to shake Etana's hand, it was another to practically juggle the stuff.

The man hemmed and hawed over the metal pieces, weighing them on a scale he had on the counter. He finally finished his tally and named a price. They had enough to pay for it and money left over to buy something to eat for the both of them. Fateh gave Marisa an impressed look, not sure of how she managed it.

They were given another basket to carry the metal in; it was useless to wrap it and a bag would just rip underneath all the weight of the metal. Fateh hefted the basket and he and Marisa left, Fateh slightly giddy at the potential weapons they now held.

"We can't go back yet." Marisa turned her face in the direction where Etana's house stood. "But we're about to have company."

Fateh opened his mouth to ask who was going to find them here of all places, when a familiar voice sounded in his ears. He gave an internal wince. He remembered it, even if she sounded older than she had before. Meg and her little group of friends; the ones who tried to recruit Fateh into joining their gang to fight against the fae.

"Well, look at what we have here." Meg stood taller than before, obviously having a growth spurt in the last year. Despite being younger than Fateh, she now stood taller than him.

"I'm flattered." Fateh wanted to edge away, but he remembered the persistence of this group. They'd just follow him if he left and if they remembered him, they remembered his edging around words and away from the supposed safety of their group. "It's been a year."

"Yeah, and you don't look any different." A girl with frizzy hair spoke up next, green eyes sharp on him. "You just perpetually runty? I thought you stopped looking differently once you got to be older."

"Guess I'm just lucky." Fateh flicked his gaze over to Marisa, who was just smiling at the group as if she knew a secret.

"Yeah and I'm sure you're not anything we need to be worried about, either." Meg took a look at what he held. "Metal?" she whistled lowly. "We've got metal in our houses, but not like this, What sort of rich boy are you, that you can afford the raw stuff?"

"Came into some money, thought I'd put it to good use." Fateh kept his tone light. "I'm traveling and where I'm going, they need this metal." He held the basket closer to him, holding it protectively.

"Calm down. We're not going to steal your metal." Meg snorted and tossed her hair back. "Even though we don't have the fancy stuff, we're in a place that's covered in the stuff. You could come and see for yourself. It's a step up from the last place we were in."

Fateh's skin crawled. Maria's reaction said it would not be a good idea to go to where

there was so much metal, but they couldn't exactly go back to Etana's yet either. They were stuck between a rock and a hard place.

"I told you, I'm traveling." Fateh said instead. "I don't really have the time to stop by your safe house." He didn't think he'd survive stopping by their safe house, but he survived the metal shop, so maybe? He chewed on his lower lip. "Maybe just for a short while."

Meg gave him a broad smile. "Not that we were going to just let you go this time, but it's

nice you agreed." She gestured to the rest of the group around her. "We'll go over introductions when we get to the safe house."

He gave another glance toward Marisa, but she just shrugged. "In for a penny, in for a pound." She spun around and around, causing the others to give her funny looks. "You get dizzy when you spin in circles."

"Yeah, you do." Meg's stance showed her uncertainty and Fateh hid his grin. It was fun

watching Marisa unnerve people the same way she had him when he first met her. "Don't do it if it makes you dizzy."

"Sometimes you can't help it." Marisa gave one last twirl before falling in step next to Fateh, the two of them following Meg and her little group. Fateh hoped he wouldn't get 'dizzy' when surrounded by all the metal, but he had a feeling Marisa wanted to warn him.

Although he wondered what these kids would think of their safe house being invaded by

Etana. All the metal would call to him like a beacon. They would be safe from the higher fae--Fateh suddenly found a good reason for going. He still didn't know what Etana was planning. Perhaps a little dizziness was a small price to pay for being invisible.

***

They didn't have to go far to get to the safe house; it was encircled by a wrought iron fence and Fateh carefully brushed his hands against it. He didn't want to announce to the group how wary he could be. He would pay for it, so he would play his part. He would pay for it later, but he concentrated on the human part of him as much as possible this time. If he could channel the fae part of himself, he could channel the human part as well. It seemed to work, because other than a prickling, the metal didn't burn him. I can do this. Marisa held his hand tightly, as if imparting some of her humanity, and thus her protection on him.

The metal door swung shut behind them as they walked in and Fateh saw the normal furniture and breathed an inward sigh of relief. He didn't think he would have been able to stand it if all the furniture was metal, too.

"See?" Meg gestured grandly at the door and the windows, which had metal shutters over them. "The fae can't get in here; there's too much metal on the entrances."

"Good idea." Fateh had to admit it could be seen as a smart move, if the fae in town wasn't a metal fae. They didn't know that though, and it wasn't his place to give up Etana's secrets. He wanted to be his friend, not sell him out. What could these kids do against a metal fae, though? Their entire protections lay in metal.

"Well, let's introduce ourselves." Meg smiled at Fateh, as if pleased he hadn't burst into flames going over the doorway. "You already know I'm Meg, or I hope you remember."

Fateh nodded, eyes flicking over the rest of the group. "Yeah, I remember you but no one else introduced themselves when I was here last." Maybe one or two more kids joined since Fateh saw them last.

Meg pointed to each kid in the group, naming them as she went along. "Ava, Willow, Charlotte, Thomas and Leo." She gestured to Fateh, "And remind me of who you are and your friend?"

"I'm Fateh and this is Marisa." He was glad it was just the two of them, he couldn't imagine having the entirety of his group here and trying to explain them. Marisa had a good idea in making sure they traveled alone.

"Fateh." She nodded. "So what brings you back into the city? You said you were traveling, but we haven't seen you in a year. Where are you traveling from?"

He couldn't say Wales or Japan. It wasn't like there were flights any-more...were there? He admitted   to himself he didn't know. There had to be flights from town that held no fae at all, Tabor said there were entire places which were normal, where the fae were only fairy tales. Unless there was a reason for technology failing them, life had to have gone on as normal, right?

Marisa spoke up. "We came from further away from the city." She said easily. "We're visiting a friend and he wanted to be alone with a friend, so he sent us away to buy metal and give him some alone time."

"Huh." The frizzy haired girl--Ava--looked contemplative. "Where were you before you were visiting this friend of yours, then? You don't sound like you're from here, you sound like you come from pretty far away."

Fateh shrugged. "Yeah, well I guess I do." He admitted. "But where I came from, we don't have metal like this." There were fae, but no metal and there all metal had vanished because of the Shadows. "Say, have you seen the Shadows here?"

Chapter Thirty-One

The group exchanged uneasy looks. "They say walking shadows tried to come into town, but all the metal scared them off." Willow shuddered. "I saw one of them when I visited my Dad outside of the city. It looked like it ate the sun and dripped light from the darkness. I hightailed it back to my mother's before it could see me."

"Where I come from, there are those Shadows everywhere." Fateh quieted. "It's the reason why we have the metal, so we can fight them. "It's the reason why I can't join your fight here, I have an important mission to do."

"You're going to fight them?" Meg asked. "I thought you were a coward, not wanting to fight the fae with us and running away, but you're going to be doing something incredibly dangerous." Awe filled her words. "I'd offer to help, but I don't know how to fight the Shadows, other than lobbing metal at them."

"Lobbing metal at them works." Fateh smiled. "They're allergic to the stuff, they can't

touch it. Salt works, too." He shuddered a little. "I hope you don't have to fight them, they're dangerous creatures. I hope they stay out of your town."

"We have enough problems without walking shadows." Leo spoke up. "The fae creep around the edge of town and prey on those that don't live in the city. People make deals and don't come back from it."

Fateh shook his head. "The only thing you can do is warn people to not make deals. Get

the word out to as many people as possible. Read fairy tales as to what you might expect." Fateh didn't want more Shadows to appear and they would, once the human who made the deal died and their corrupted soul changed to form into a Shadow.

There were nods all around. "This is how we stay safe in town. We know metal repels the fae. We're also not dumb enough to make any deal with the fae, but not everyone is as smart as we are. Adults are especially dumb."

Fateh agreed with the sentiment, but kids could be taken in, too. "Just be careful," He went quiet.

"If you see them, be polite, but don't fall for any of their tricks. Don't eat their food or drink anything they give you and never enter into a bargain with them."

"You're preaching to the choir here." Meg snorted. "We know all the warnings, I'm just glad you do, too. If you're not staying in this city, you're vulnerable. Are you sure you don't want to stay here? Let someone else fight the Shadows?" She gave him a tentative smile. "We can tell you're a good person, Fateh, and you're smart. We need more smart people on our side."

"They took over my town, it has to be me." And half a dozen friends. "I'll be careful." He nodded in acknowledgement of her compliment to him. "Maybe I'll even come back here after." if there was an after. He would like to see what these kids did, if they had luck repelling the higher fae and what they could do to save those who lived outside the borders of the city.

"Well you keep to your word." Charlotte said softly. "Don't get yourself captured or killed." She grimaced faintly. "Actually, it might be better to die than be captured. Who knows what they'll do to you if they catch you?"

Fateh had nightmares about the very scenario and shuddered briefly. "Trust me, it's not on my agenda."

Marisa tugged on his hand. "We should go. Tabor is waiting for us." She sounded definite about it and he nodded.

"Our friend is waiting to take us." He didn't say where or how; they didn't need to know the details and frankly wouldn't believe any good of him if he told them the specifics. "Maybe we'll meet again one day."

"Meeting again would be nice, Fateh. We see you in the city again, we'll find you." Meg held out a hand and Fateh gave it a hesitant shake. "And hey, you see people making a deal outside of town, you save them, alright? We can't be everywhere."

Neither could he, but he made his promises before he headed out the door, leaving Meg and her small battalion behind iron doors. It was just in time, too. He started to feel sick from all the metal.

"Dizzy?" Marisa asked sympathetically. "You couldn't stay in there much longer without giving the game away."

"Yeah, I figured." Fateh wiped his brow, wiping away the sweat that gathered there. "Their intentions more than the metal kept me on edge. They were really determined to keep the fae away. It makes me think humans have magic of their own and they just don't know it."

"Could be. Why should the fae have all the magic in the world?" Marisa asked. "Aren't there a lot of stories of wizards and witches? There are as many of them as there is about the fae."

"I never thought of it that way." Fateh considered her words. "Although it makes sense. I appealed to my human side when I learned magic with the kitsune."

"So you see? They probably have magic that works on intent." Marisa said this matter-of-factly. "They may or may not realize they can do it. They'll be more effective if they do it on purpose, though."

"I'll steer clear of them in case they realize they can." Fateh could only imagine the repelling charms they'd have around their safe house. He wouldn't be able to get near it and he'd probably break out into a rash.

"It's good that humans might reclaim their magic." Marisa walked as she talked, hand still tucked into Fateh's. "It gives us protection we've been lacking."

"Yeah, we all want to be able to protect people and ourselves." Fateh agreed. "It's why I don't mind--" he gestured with his free hand. "You know." The people flowed around them, not paying attention to their conversation, which Fateh was grateful for. He didn't need any pointed fingers at him and cries of 'fae'. Although they didn't have the problem with fae here like outside of the city. It must be all the metal...and Etana's influence. There were no fae around Mokosh's domain, after all. She must've been powerful enough to scare them all away.

Marisa squeezed his hand in response. "We do have to get back," she said. "I didn't lie.. We have our metal and the others are waiting for us."

"It's time I went home." Fateh agreed, closing his eyes briefly. "I'm not looking forward to it, but it's been beyond time. The year I spent in the prison and the year that was lost when I went to the fae realms adds up."

"You're brave and you're going to have to use all that bravery facing your demons from the past." Marisa turned down a side street and stopped in front of a bakery. "Let's get some food before we go. Etana likes the peach-filled croissants."

Fateh didn't ask how she knew Etana's food preferences, but he was willing to believe it. "One last errand before we hit the road."

***

All was quiet when they arrived back at Etana's house, such as no screaming, which Fateh counted as a plus. Whatever happened, it was over and done with and he didn't have any desire to ask any questions. Not when Etana could hear, anyway. He'd ask Tabor plenty once they were on their way.

"Spark! Good, you're here." Tabor opened the door and he ushered the two of them inside. "We were just about to go out looking for you, I was afraid you ran into the same kind of trouble you had last time you were here."

"Some of it." Fateh admitted. "I'll tell you more about it later. Marisa has an interesting theory we can probably use."

Etana poked his head out of the kitchen, sniffing the air. "I smell peach croissants." He held out his hand to them. "Gimme."

Fateh snorted and handed over the dessert. "Marisa was right. She said you'd like the peach croissants."

"They're my favorite. You even went to the right bakery." Etana sounded impressed around his mouthful of flaky pastry. "Smart girl. How'd you know?"

"I got lucky?" she asked. "Finding the bakery was luck, but I know you have peaches here and you seem to be the type to like sweets." She shrugged as she munched on a blueberry muffin, handing the bag of pastries to Tabor. He pulled out a blueberry and cream cheese danish and practically beamed.

"I'm keeping you around." He ate with clear delight. Fateh was left with his favorite type of pastry, a sweet cream and apple croissant. He didn't have the chance to eat anything like it in years and he savored every bite. He would have bought more, but they only had enough money for each of them to have a single treat.

"Hmph. I think there's more to you than meets the eye." Etana ate his treat with great delicacy, hardly shedding any crumbs. "Good thing you won't be here, causing trouble. I can only think of the type of mischief you'd stir up in town if you were left to your own devices."

"We behaved ourselves." Fateh wrinkled his nose. "We bought the metal and met some people in town. Your metal comes in handy to keep the fae out." He popped the last bite of his food into his mouth and finished eating before he spoke again. "Some people are using the houses to stay away from the fae. Yet you said you're dealing with the higher fae?"

"Don't worry about my past dealings." Etana waved it away. "I told you, I won't interfere with your plans."

"And after?" Fateh asked cautiously.

"Who's to say there's going to be an after?" Etana asked cheerfully. "This could all go down in flames and not the kind you'll be safe from."

"Glad we've got your vote of confidence." Tabor rolled his eyes as he shook his head. "You make a terrible motivational speaker. You'll see, we'll come out of this just fine."

Fateh was quite aware Etana didn't answer his question and Tabor helped him evade the question. I'm definitely going to be having a conversation with

Tabor after we leave here. There's something that isn't being said and it all has to do with the higher fae.

"Yeah, yeah. I'm sure going against your natural enemy is going to go swell for you. Don't forget to stop by once it's all over. I don't want to be waiting a year to see you again."

"I'd hate to see the missiles you'd sling at us if we ignored you a second time." Fateh made sure Marisa held the basket when he faced Etana. He didn't want him to absorb the metal. He didn't know what the metal elemental could do. "I promise we'll stop by if we survive this madness we're embarking on."

"I'm holding you to your word." Etana smirked and flicked on the bright light again, creating the dark shadows they needed to travel in. "Don't forget, little Fateh. You made a promise."

Fateh shuddered at the look in Etana's eyes. He didn't know how yet, but he knew he was going to regret this.

Tabor gestured to the shadows and they came alive, forming an archway. "You're always welcome to come and help us out." Tabor offered. "We could use your talents."

"You already have my strongest weapon--my metal." Etana looked regretful. "Besides, someone has to be here to keep the riff-raff out. My presence makes it so that no one invades. No one wants to tangle with my kind. I've got to protect the people in this town somehow."

"Ah, it was worth a shot." Tabor gestured for Fateh and Marisa to go first through the shadows and Fateh looked over his shoulder at Tabor, giving Etana a light kiss before he followed them into the darkness.

Chapter Thirty-Two

The trip to the Sanctuary was short this time; they only stayed long enough to gather the others and then Tabor created another shadow road for them to walk on. Their entire group came this time, with Marisa lighting the way.

For the first time in two years, Fateh found himself in the woods where his house once stood. It was burnt down to the foundation. The garden was razed and what plants there were left were weed-choked and buried under a mountain of greenery.

Oddly enough, the barn still stood and Fateh looked at the ridiculous amount of junk stored above the spot where the cow had once stayed. "They could have left me the house." He whispered. "What did they have to gain by burning it to the ground?"

"They were erasing you from the world." Tabor put a gentle hand on his shoulder. "They thought if they burned your home, they'd get rid of the memory of you."

Fateh shook his head, not in denial of Tabor's words, but in what he saw. He hoped his house would still be here so he'd be able to walk through the hallways one more time, grab anything from his bedroom. He immediately turned away from Tabor and climbed the ladder to the storage area. Pictures. He could get pictures of him and his mom; they'd be up in the storage area.

The others stood around as he rooted around like a madman, looking for the box of photos. He finally found them after a half-hour of searching and he clutched the precious box to his chest as he descended the ladder.

"They didn't destroy everything." He sounded fierce as he held back tears. He held up the box where a few photos lay. "I still have a picture of my mom." It was taken several years ago, but his mom still looked like he remembered. He scrubbed at his eyes, keeping the tears at bay.

"I'm glad you have a picture." Sam seemed sincere and they gave Fateh a hug around the shoulders. "I only wish I had pictures of my parents. Treasure what you have."

Fateh nodded and tucked away the photos in his bag and then squared his shoulders. "It's time to go into town. I know where we can meet with at least two members of the rebels that are in town." It didn't occur to him that Meira and Tobias could have been killed by now, as reckless as they were.

"Good. We'll need inside help." Uisge looked concerned. "But these are your old friends?" she asked. "The ones who betrayed you?"

"They're our best bet." Fateh stubbornly did not think about what they did to him and his mother. How they got his mother killed and sold him out to the children's prison. "As much as I hate to have to deal with them..." There had to be other rebels in town, but Fateh didn't know who they were.

"We better get walking." Tabor pointed to the overgrown pathway. "I don't want to open a shadow road right in the middle of town. There's being cautious and there's announcing our presence with bells and whistles."

There was snickering all around them and Fateh went cold. How could he have forgotten about the little Shadows, the ones that flourished in the woods? They were more like pests, but he didn't know if they stood as sentry and could warn the larger Shadows.

"Relax, they're not actually Shadows." Tabor looked around. "They're just the little fae, harmless and they don't report to anyone."

"One less worry." Fateh looked around at the ruins of his old life and sighed. He wouldn't be coming back here; there was no point. He looked around at his small, hopeful group. So much rested on them and what they planned.

One last walk into town and this time, it wasn't with his mother. One last trip to see Meira and Tobias, but not as friends. So much the same, yet so much had changed. Fateh took a deep breath and took the first step back towards town.

***

It didn't take as long as Fateh remembered it taking to get there, before he knew it, they were at the outskirts of town and he took a moment to take it all in. It hadn't changed on the surface; but when he looked closer, there were gaps where houses and business once stood. There were people all about and all of them Fateh saw had the delicate chains going from them to an unknown spot.

The contracts were connected to everyone he saw. He winced; what if Meira and Tobias had fallen and were now contracted to a Shadow or fae? The thought never even occurred to him and he berated himself for being an idiot. A lot could have changed in two years.

He found all eyes on him and his small group. Haruki and Hana stood out like flowers in a snowstorm among all the humans, but they seemed uncaring. No one outright pointed, but there were whispers behind hands as they walked by.. Fateh led them to the familiar door where he had last known Meira and Tobias to be. He knocked on the door and took a deep breath, Here went everything,

The door swung open and a familiar-not-familiar Tobias stood in the door-way, Meira right behind him. For the first time in over two years, he faced Meira and Tobias. So much changed since their last time together. Fateh swallowed nervously, unsure of what to do and not wanting to make the first move, although he supposed he already had, just by knocking on their door.

"Fateh, you're back!" Meira looked nervously at the group gathered behind Fateh. "And with friends--I didn't know you knew so many fae. Is it because of the school we sent you to?" Her brows knit together with confusion. "There wasn't supposed to be any fae there." She gestured for them all to come inside and it was almost comical how they all crowded inside.

Fateh felt strangely compelled to tell her the truth. "Some of them aren't fae." He gestured to Haruki and Hana. "They're Japanese spirits." He quieted a moment. "And it's partially because of the safe house you sent me to. I met some of my friends there."

"Spirits or fae, you're keeping strange company these days, You wouldn't go near the fae when you were here last. What happened to you?"

"What happened to me?" Fateh demanded. "Having my mother killed in front of me happened to me, being locked away in the so-called safe house happened to me. The people there and here accepted me for who I am. Can you say the same?"

Meira looked startled. "You're blaming us for your mother?" she asked. "It wasn't me who held the knife, things just got out of hand." She tossed her hair back. "Your mother would have been just fine if you had killed the Shadow."

"You were the one threatening us! You and Tobias!" Fateh's breath hitched in his throat, he saw it all like it was yesterday. The shouting, the uncaring crowd of Shadows, the burning--

"Fateh." Hana's tone calmed his spiraling mood. "Remember why we're here."

"Oh, did you have a reason to come and see us other than berate us? It looks like you're doing just what we predicted you would do; hanging out with the fae and losing your humanity." Did the Shadows finally corrupt you? We sent you away so you'd be safe. We did it for your own good, Fateh."

"For my own good?" Fateh's voice rose, but Hana's gentle hand on his shoulder steadied him. "It turns out you can't corrupt someone that's already different." He kept his words as casual as possible, but his heart beat loud in his ears. "It turns out I'm not quite..."

"You're not quite all you seemed to be." Tabor interrupted him. "And I've been protecting Fateh. Saved him from a dangerous situation where he would have died. You sent him to die."

"What exactly happened to put Fateh in danger?" Tobias demanded. "It is a no Shadow zone. How did you get there?"

"Simple, I'm not a Shadow." Tabor lifted an admonishing finger. "Not all fae are Shadows, but all Shadows are fae. You'd do well to know the differences. The lesser fae have been in just as much danger as being corrupted and killed as humans."

"But not all fae are good, either." Fateh's tone went flat. "A water fae took over the house you sent me to. Flooded the place and nearly drowned everyone in there. I got out by sheer luck. A student who was changed by the fae helped me get out."

"And how have you changed, Fateh? And why come back here, of all places? You must already know there's nothing left for you here."

Had Meira supervised the burning of his home? Fateh's fists clenched at his side and he took large, calming breaths. The last thing they needed was an explosion of any sort because he lost his temper.

"Even with everything that happened, I still want the Shadows gone." His tone went matter of fact. This is still my home and I want them gone." He shrugged a little. "You two are the only ones I know who are in the rebels. We need your help to get rid of them."

"You and what army?" Tobias crossed his arms over his chest. "We don't even have the weapons we need to fight."

"Like metal?" Fateh gestured for Marisa to come forward, and she held out the basket so Meira and Tobias could see the wealth of metal inside. "We brought something to help."

Meira almost lunged for the metal, but Marisa danced out of her way and held the basket close to her. "You don't get this unless you agree to work with us." She sounded prim. "Not that you won't join us, we're too valuable of a resource to waste."

"So you've come to fight? You have changed, Fateh." Meira's eyebrows went up at Marisa's matter of fact tone. "You wouldn't ever fight before, it was all 'the Shadows aren't all bad.'"

"I never said the Shadows weren't all bad. I hate the Shadows. The fae, yes--but I hate the Shadows and always have, ever since they came here. I just didn't want people to get hurt in the middle of all the fighting."

"People will get hurt, Fateh." Meira faced him, lips turning down into a frown. You have to accept that if you're coming to us for help." She paused. "And before we get too far into all of this and making grand plans, why don't you introduce your little group? I don't want to call out 'hey you' when we're trying to do tactics."

Fateh introduced everyone quickly, but left out what they were. They could choose to tell Meira and Tobias their lineage themselves, Fateh wasn't here to spill any secrets. The only ones he had said were definitely not human were Haruki and Hana, and they were obvious with their inhuman parts.

Meira nodded politely, but her gaze lingered on Hana and Haruki. "Japanese spirits?" she asked.

"Yes, we are not fae as you know the term." Hana said in careful English. "We are from Japan and we do not have fae there, but the Blight has crossed the ocean and invaded our homeland." She inclined her head. "You would call the Blight a Shadow."

"We're here because we can bring more firepower than what you have already." Fateh gestured to Marisa. "We have metal so you can make more bombs and we want you to make them so we can get rid of the nest of Shadows here."

"Did you really just say 'firepower'?" Sam demanded. "Cliche, much?"

Fateh turned red. "I didn't do it on purpose, I swear." He was doomed to make fire-themed puns for all of his life. Was this what it had come down to? He groaned internally at the thought of it.

Chapter
Thirty-Three

The air went still as Meira and Tobias stared at him. "We wanted to just fight the Shadows, but you think you can actually get rid of them? You and what army?" Tobias indicated the small group. "It's not like the actual army helped." He went bitter. "Nothing can stop a Shadow except metal and you're holding a king's ransom."

"We found out elemental powers are effective to fight the Shadows with." Tabor spread his hands. "You already know metal and salt work against the Shadows." Not that metal and salt wouldn't hurt the ordinary fae, too, but they had to use what weapons they had at hand. Meira was right, there would be casualties, and not just human ones.

"We have all of what you need." Hana spoke briskly. "Metal and salt does not hurt us and we are bringing elemental powers to the forefront of this fight."

"What, with all your powers combined, you're going to form a superhero?" Tobias looked disbelieving. "What sort of drugs have you been smoking?"

"You already know fairy tales are real." Fateh snorted. "What, magical elemental powers are beyond you?"

"I'm more concerned with the metal and salt you have, then some magic that doesn't exist unless it's from the fae. And you may have been weird all this time, Fateh, but you were never fae."

"We'll lend you the metal as long as when you make your bombs, it's not in a public place like before." He sounded terse and unyielding. So many people get hurt and regular fae, too. The fae are a part of this world. The Shadows are the Blight we need to get rid of."

How many other half-fae were taken by the Shadows? Fateh doubted he was the only who was partially fae or had magic of their own.

"Shadows and their supporters filled the place." Meira scowled at Fateh for bringing up old news. "We don't need Shadow sympathizers."

Fateh scowled right back at her. "And what if we were in the restaurant that night?" he demanded. "It wasn't that long ago before the bomb went off where we were in the restaurant."

Tobias wouldn't meet his eyes. "We checked to make sure no one human was in the building." He didn't mention the Shadow-touched or those those who had their souls taken by the Shadows and forced to work there. Maybe they were already lost, but they still deserved a chance.

"Just because they were chained to Shadow, doesn't make it right to kill them. There are probably more people chained than not right now." He didn't mention he could see them; Tobias knew, but Fateh hoped he forgot.

"Yeah, well-- like I said, there's going to be casualties." Meira looked almost tired. "We are operating with a small team here; like you said, there's a lot more people who are chained to the Shadows than before and while we recruit who we can, we have to be careful." She looked over Fateh's friends again. "So as weird as you all seem to be, your help will be appreciated."

"What's to say he won't team up with the Shadows?" Tobias didn't look convinced. "You're still bound to the Shadow--"

"Tabor's obviously not a Shadow." Fateh rolled his eyes. "You can see him and feel him as a solid presence. He's fae." He swallowed and looked away for a moment. "I'm half fae." He was defiant. "So yeah, I guess you were right in thinking I was weird or wrong."

"Oh, fae. That's so much better." Tobias looked even more stubborn. "The fae caused their own problems and when the Shadows came and ran us over, they didn't help us." He stared at Fateh, half horrified. "What type of fae are you?"

"The Shadows hurt the fae as well. We could only offer so much help when we were being overrun ourselves." Tabor looked tired. "And Fateh's like me. He's a fire elemental."

"And the rest of you?" Meira asked. "You mentioned elemental powers, so I'm guessing your friends aren't any more human than you are."

San and the other exchanged a look. Uisge shrugged. "I'm half human," She sniffed. "I'm what you would call a gwragedd annwn. I'm here to help Fateh take care of the Shadows. They poison the water."

Sam spoke up next, since Hana and Haruki had already introduced themselves. "Half gwyrddni. Not that it should matter to you, but I stayed in that so-called school with Fateh and a few others."

Marisa looked cheerful. "I'm human." She held out the basket of metal again. "I'm here to light the way and hold the metal. I was also in the school of Mokosh's." Her expression darkened. "And good riddance."

"So we're down to a handful of kids who aren't even human to help us fight the Shadows." Meira looked resigned. "I guess we better start planning this out, but I promise you, if you betray us, you'll regret it. We have metal, too and we'll make sure you get a face full of it if you prove to be untrustworthy."

"Glad you're as enthused to have us along. I'd say we'd do it without you, but you have information we need and we have the resources you lack." Fateh sighed as he ran a hand through his hair. "I don't like this anymore than you do."

"Guess the saying 'the enemy of my enemy is my friend' is true." Tobias snorted. "Let's get planning. First off, what can you do?"

***

Several cups of tea later and a quick run to the market to grab some food, and they had a semi-decent plan in place. Tobias and Meira knew where the Shadows nested, but they didn't have the resources to take them on. They didn't know how you could fight a shadow, except for repelling them with salt and metal.

"The key is to give them enough power so you can negate the power with your own." Hana said calmly. "There will be an element of danger in this; giving them strength is a risky move, but we defeated a Shadow who had absorbed a water fae by using the element against him. They're solid when they've taken from somewhere else."

Meira and Tobias looked stunned. "We've been keeping them from taking power, because they're much stronger when they have fire or lightning." There were a few Shadows Fateh avoided for just that reason. "You're saying we could have actually hurt them when they're more dangerous?"

Fateh grimaced. "Yeah, it gives them an anchor to the world we can exploit. It's not the most ideal of situations, but it's what we have."

"So who's going to be the one pumping them with power?" Meira looked around all of them. "I sure as hell don't have magic." She smirked at the group, "One of you planning on being a sacrifice?"

"No." Fateh's tone went flat. "We're not sacrificing ourselves." He bit his lip in worry. "Although we probably have to sacrifice some of our magic." He didn't want to and couldn't wait for a Shadow to consume some innocent fae just so they could save everyone else. "But the Shadows we're going after have already absorbed magic. They're the leaders we need to get rid of."

"Assuming they're vulnerable is a lot of speculation." Tobias looked thoughtful, though. "You are right, the leaders seem to be the most...solid." He gave Tabor a look. "It's why we thought you were a particularly strong Shadow. You didn't look like the other fae and you hung out with the Shadows." He flicked his gaze to Fateh. "Are you sure we can trust him?"

"I've trusted Tabor with my life." Fateh shook his head in denial of Tobias' words. "He can't harm me and by extension, can't harm those I've pledged loyalty to." He grinned. "Not that he would even try. Tabor's a pretty decent guy. You liked him before we found out he was a ... well, before we found him mingling with the Shadows."

"He's deceptive, but I guess we have no choice but to take the weapons and help that's offered to us." Meira sighed as she untangled a knot of hair. "So the basic plan is we lead you to the nest of Shadows and you fight them?"

"A couple of those metal bombs tossed in the center of all of this --before we go in--wouldn't hurt." Uisge wrinkled her nose. "It's distasteful stuff, but if you soften them up beforehand, it will be easier for us to fight them. A wounded animal snaps back fiercer, but they're also weaker. An advantage is what we need."

"We've just been waiting until we had the materials," Meira nodded along with Tobias. "We've been planning to attack the main cluster for years now. We just didn't have the metal and couldn't get close enough. We got a couple of high-rankers in the restaurant attack, but most of them were weaker Shadows."

"How many people can we count on to help us?" Sam directed the question to Meira, who seemed to be the obvious leader. "I hope it's not just you and your brother."

"We have a small group of Shadow-held holdouts." Meira promised him. "It's been tough, since so many people are chained to the Shadows and it comes with special privileges, but our group manages to get by." She shrugged. "Pretend to play their game, make your trades and deals and you'll skate by." She eyed the group again. "Well, maybe not some of you. You stand out as you are. Can't you do some magic and make yourselves seem normal? Not that you won't stick out anyway, being strangers, but you could try a little harder."

Hana and Haruki nodded and there was a shimmer around them and their wings and tails faded out. They were dressed as they were before, but they looked ordinary. They could blend into the people in town much easier. "We can say we're visiting from the next town over." Hana ran a hand through her long black hair. "We don't fit in, but Fateh said you haven't had contact with the outside world in a long time. We can't just say we appeared from nowhere."

"If people came to visit us and see how we were doing." Tobias grumbled. "No one has come to check on us since the Shadows came. The ones that were here when the Shadows originally attacked fled and no one's been back since. It seems like they spread the word we weren't an ideal place to be."

"Enough time has passed where I am sure curiosity will get the better of people," Hana sounded absolutely sure of herself. "Trust me, where I come from, we are isolated as well, but it is our own choice." She looked wistful. "It's a shame we can't offer you the type of protection we have at home. Maybe after the Shadows are gone, we can extend our magic to make this town a safe haven."

"You can make this place safe?" Meira asked eagerly and even Fateh stared at Hana.

"It will take you cooperating with what you call the fae." Hana warned. "You don't have the same relationship with the land as we do, but you do have fae who are connected to the land." She nodded towards Sam. "If you can manage to co-exist, then you have a much better chance of repelling invaders in the future."

"We'll think about it." Tobias spoke gently. "We haven't had a good relationship with the fae, either. We were warned not to make deals with the fae." He looked at Fateh. "Are we going to be in debt to you and your little group of friends because we're making a deal?"

Tabor shook his head. "This is a mutually beneficial relationship. There are no contracts, no tricks. Just two groups of people helping each other out. You have the intelligence, we have the metal for your weapons, and we ourselves are a type of weapon." He grew serious. "I don't know the outcome of all of this, but we're going to give it our all."

"Some of you may die, but I'm willing to make the sacrifice?" Tobias snorted. "Great pep talk."

"We've only got one real chance at this." Meira summed it up. "So don't screw up any of our parts."

The rest of the group looked fairly uncomfortable at this, but there were nods all around. The message delivered a harsh truth. They would have to all do their best. Fateh didn't hold high hopes of them getting out of there alive, but he was going to fight with all he had.

Chapter Thirty-Four

Meira and Tobias kicked them out after that encouraging speech, stating they had to connect with the rebels they worked with. "We'll meet you by the site of the old restaurant tomorrow at noon. Try and blend in." Meira begged. "I know you're all so weird you won't be able to, but you could at least try."

"Hey, most of us are Welsh." Fateh pointed out. "We won't stick out so much." He gave Haruki and Hana an apologetic look. "You two will stand out, but it's not like there's a lot of variety in my town. There used to be..." he sounded wistful. "But a lot of people left and we were left with the holdouts who hadn't left their town in centuries."

"The holdouts and the fighters." Meira put in. "Some of us wanted to stay and fight for our home. Now scat. We're going out as well, but don't follow us. We don't want to lead an entire group of outsiders to our safe house."

Hana looked confused at this. "We're going to be working with them. Wouldn't it be better to get to know them now, before we're in the heat of battle? I'd rather know who my allies are."

"We'll have you meet them, but we're also trying to stay somewhat incognito." Tobias explained. "Having your group march up to where we're based is just putting a big red flat on the place. I'd rather not get raided. We're careful about when and how we go." He held up a hand. "And don't ask to see the place. You'll meet the rebels, but a few at a time."

"Sounds reasonable." Tabor shrugged and wrapped an arm around Fateh's shoulders. "Come on, Spark. Let's see if my place is still standing and if the Shadows have sniffed it out yet." He led them out the door and waited for Meira and Tobias to vanish into the crowd of people in the middle of town.

Fateh shrugged and looked at the others. "Well, we need a place to stay while we're in town. I hoped it would be my house, but that's gone now." He hadn't asked if Meira and Tobias were involved in setting fire to the place and now he was going to work with them, he didn't want to know. He didn't need another reason to want to fight them, instead of with them.

"Lead the way." Marisa said graciously, but her tone said she knew exactly where Tabor's place was and didn't need any help finding it, no matter how carefully Tabor tucked it away. Tabor snorted and nodded.

"At least they can't burn the place down." Tabor lowered his voice, as if he was trying to keep from being overheard. "I have magic against fire being used to burn my own place down."

"As is appropriate for a fire elemental." Uisge nodded in approval. "My house has charms against fire as well. We'd douse it straightaway, but it's best to guard against our opposite element." She gave him a curious look. "Are you scared of drowning, Tabor?"

Tabor gave a full-body shiver at the mention of drowning. "More than you know." He wasn't afraid to admit it and Fateh nodded in sympathy. He nearly drowned and would have died if it hadn't been for Jonathan. "Water will put out fire without a thought. So we always have to be careful." He gave her a look. "Why, planning on killing me, little water maiden?"

"No." She sounded calm. "But it's good to know that if a Shadow absorbed your magic, they'd have the same fears."

"Hoping they have the same fear is not unreasonable." Tabor allowed.

Hana looked fascinated. "So we can use our own fears against them if we give them a taste of our magic? So if I gave them any of my magic, they could have a fear of say... dogs?" She sounded tentative.

"More like they're going to have a healthy fear of fire if they take any of Sam's powers." Tabor explained. "It's trickier when you don't have the same elemental weaknesses. You can still fight them with your magic--" That much had been clear; Hana and Haruki were a formidable pair. "But you can't use your fears against them. It's an innate thing which comes with the elements."

"Not that there is much which can fight a tengu." Haruki looked self-satisfied. "Give me one solid Shadow and I'll cut them into ribbons."

"We have to get them solid first, or else all you'll be slicing is air and mist." Hana patted his shoulder. "Don't get too ahead of yourself."

"Yeah, you're right." Haruki deflated slightly. They were talking while Tabor led the way and now he looked around, sniffing the air. "I smell magic."

"Good, then we're close." Tabor stopped in front of an ordinary looking house, flicking his gaze around to make sure no one watched them. "The outside looks like it's intact..." He pushed open the door and a ripple of magic washed over the group.

When Tabor led them inside, it was a much larger space than the outside led them to believe. Tabor shut the door behind them and Fateh whistled faintly. "I've seen this trick in sci-fi shows, but never in real life. This isn't really in town, is it?"

"Nope, but it's anchored there." Tabor looked pleased with himself. "If the rebels had this space, they wouldn't have to worry about people finding them. It's a shame they're so close-mouthed and secretive."

Hana looked impressed. "You have an anchor in the real world so time doesn't slip by like it did for us before, but your real home is in the spirit world?"

Tabor nodded as he stretched his arms above his head. "Yep. It gives me my own space and safety. The Shadows haven't breached it yet and I intend to keep it that way." He led them to the back door. "Out there is the fire-lands, where we stayed with your father."

"So we could have just short-cut our way back home?" Fateh asked in disbelief.

"Yes, but we had other places to be." Tabor reminded him. "We had several other lands and people to visit and I don't think it would have worked with us just popping out into town with no plan and no real magic at our disposal."

"Yeah. I guess that's true." Fateh grumbled, but he was too busy looking around Tabor's house to be angry for long. "You've lived here a long time," he observed. "How long have you had this anchored to Felinheli?"

"Since before you were born." Tabor snickered at the look on Fateh's face."I told you, this is my home, too. I came here before any of the Shadows or other fae. Etana in his city is the same way. I wanted to be enough of a deterrent to keep the Shadows at bay, but they caught me when I was much younger and sapped most of my power. It's taken me this long to get it back. I was around Fateh's age when it happened.

"So with you, like with Fateh, it's personal." Hana spoke quietly. "You must be careful to not let your emotions overwhelm you when you go to fight. Half of the enemy's work will be done if you go in there without thinking."

"Oh, I've been planning a strategy for a long time." Tabor reassured her. "I didn't think it'd involve bombs made out of metal, but metal figured into my plans from the start." Of course, the metal would have been supplied by Etana and he would have been the one fighting at Tabor's side, but that ship had sailed. They were lucky they got what they did.

Fateh knew all of this, of course--Tabor talked about Etana being there for him when it came down to revenge, but neither of them counted on Etana wanting to be not-quite enemies. They had both been looking forward to having Etana on their side when they fought the Shadows. At least he's not working for the Shadows. Fateh would take the news and count it as good as they were going to get.

"Good. As long as you go into this with a level head, then there won't be any problems." Hana seemed satisfied. "Your hospitality is appreciated and having a backdoor to one of the spirit doors is even more so. You could have left at any time, you know." She gave him a curious look. "Why did you stay?"

"This is my home, too." Tabor was quietly fierce. "It should have been mine to protect, but they took the chance away from me. I won't fail the humans here again."

Tabor flopped down on a couch of indeterminate origins and closed his eyes. It was clear the conversation was over, at least the part which had to deal with Tabor's past. Fateh sat down next to him, expressionless.

"So you'll stay here forever?" he asked quietly. "It seems kind of lonely."

Tabor opened one eye to peer at Fateh. "Did you miss the part with the fire lands being in my backyard?" he asked. "I can visit my relatives whenever I want and one of them can take over guardianship if I find a need to travel somewhere. I do have you to think of now, after all and you can't possibly want to be stuck in the same town all your life."

"No." Fateh went quiet. "I always wanted to travel and see the world. I guess I could say I got my fill of it, traveling to so many different places in such a short amount of time, but there's still so much out there I haven't seen yet."

"Best stick to the center of the places you visit and avoid the coast." Tabor grinned. "You don't want to test what's so close to the water. You can be hurt by the ocean, more than the normal person."

"He'd be safe with me." Uisge spoke up. "Would it be so bad if we all continued to travel together?" She sounded wistful, as if even she wasn't expecting to come out of this with a whole skin.

"You don't want to go back to your home?" Fateh looked over at Uisge in surprise, but she shrugged.

"There's a reason why I left. Life was boring where I was, with the same things happening all the time. I wanted to see more of the world as well." She gave Fateh a shy smile. "You're not as bad as I heard fire-walkers are."

"Thanks?" Fateh tilted his head in confusion. "I didn't think water was bothered by fire. It's usually us who's scared of you." '

"You could boil our water until we died from the heat." She said matter of factly. "You could heat our waters to steam, among other things." Uisge shook her head at Fateh. "You need to know these things, so you can fight better if you ever get trapped by one of the water fae again. They're not as nice as me."

"I...I guess the knowledge will be useful against a Shadow that's absorbed water magic, too." Fateh spoke slowly as he thought out Uisge's words and the vivid images which came with it. "And if I ever see Mokosh again, it will be nice to know I have some sort of defense against her."

"Not Mokosh." Tabor's brooked no argument. "She's too old and too strong to mess with. Even I won't fight her and I've got a century on you and a lot more power. She's fine where she is and I'm not going to have you square off with her just because you got a head full of ideas."

"Didn't plan on it." Fateh said with feeling. "Just if I had the bad luck to run across her, I could at least go down fighting."

"Mm. Well, concentrate on the fight we have coming up. I agree with Uisge about boiling water. She can turn them into ice cubes for us to shatter easier than it will be for us to remove all the heat, though."

"And what about me?" Sam asked, crossing their arms over their chest. "I can grow plants and stuff, but--"

"You can poison them with plants." Fateh thought about it. "You can do a lot with plants, why not grow poisonous ones or bramble or something that will trap the Shadows?"

"Using my plants is a good idea!" Sam stopped looking so doubtful and instead excitement lit up their face. "I can pull a Sleeping Beauty on the place where they're holed up so they can't escape."

"Just make sure we can get back out." Uisge warned. "What can be a trap for an enemy can also work against an ally."

"I'll put the brambles up after we carve them up." Sam said decidedly. "Then those humans of yours can throw metal bombs at the place and make sure no one gets out."

"You want us to do the metal after we fight the Shadows?" Fateh asked. "Not before?"

"We'd have to walk over the scraps of metal and shit in the air." Sam shuddered. "I don't know about you, but that's not something I'd like to dance with."

Chapter Thirty-Five

They had a plan, now Fateh just needed it to be put into motion. There were a lot of 'what if' factors involved and a lot of hope the rebels would come to do their part. The only part he worried about were the rebels taking them out after they had killed the Shadows. It was a valid fear. Meira and Tobias didn't like the fae anymore than they did the Shadows and Fateh didn't know what the other rebels thought of them. This could all end with them getting blown to bits by the very metal they offered as a weapon.

"How will we know when they're ready for us?" Sam asked, looking around the group. "It's not like one of us volunteered to go with those two to suss out the situation. We're at a disadvantage here."

"We have a safe place to run to if things don't go in our favor." Tabor pointed out, gesturing to his house. "But I agree, we don't have a clear timeline of when things are going to start."

"Meira said to meet her at the site of the old restaurant tomorrow." Fateh reminded them. "I guess it's as good of a landmark as any. No one's built over it so it'll just be a big, gaping hole where a building once stood."

"It's also a place where the Shadows would avoid." Tabor reasoned. "Since so many of them died there." He looked pleased at the fact. "Your little friends are fierce fighters, I'll give them that much."

"They're not my friends any longer." Fateh turned intense. "They lost the role when they orchestrated my mother's death and sent me away to prison. They're allies under a temporary truce." He looked up at Tabor. "Are you sure you want to stick around here after the Shadows are gone? It doesn't seem like it'll be a very welcoming place and you can't hide in plain sight like you did before."

"No, you're right." Tabor sounded regretful. "This will always be my home to come back to, but I may have to wait and have another guardian here until people forget who I am. Tricks of illusion only work so well and I don't like possessing people anymore than I have to." He winked at Fateh. "Although your face when I spoke through the old man was priceless."

Fateh turned red at the reminder. "I definitely wasn't expecting your voice from someone ancient." He ran a hand through tangled curls and sighed. "There's nothing left for me here, either. I'd rather travel and see the world rather than be stuck here, where people hate me just because of what I am." He didn't say he wished he'd never found out the truth about himself. He might always think his mother might still be alive if he had never found out.

"You're always welcome at the Sanctuary." Hana smiled at the two of them. "Marisa and Uisge as well. There's plenty of space and you'd be a wonderful addition to our little family."

Going back to the Sanctuary sounded nice as well, Fateh had to admit. A place protected by the trees where no Shadows could follow? A group of half-fae or Japanese spirit kids who would understand him. He looked up at Tabor hopefully, but Tabor only shrugged.

"It's a possibility, but you'd probably get bored after too long." He grinned down at Fateh. "You have a pretty bad case of wanderlust. You took to traveling the shadows with ease." Tabor considered Fateh. "You know, right now might not be a bad time to practice shadow-walking. Say, from one room to the other to start out?"

Fateh gulped. It was one thing to walk the shadows with Tabor opening the pathways and Marisa lighting the way, another to do it on his own. "Just from one room to another?" he asked nervously.

"You're the one who opens the door and sets the path." Tabor said cheerfully. "It's a simple test. You should be able to know how to open the shadows in case we need to make an escape and I'm not able to help you."

Having a need to escape made him even more nervous; he needed Tabor to be able to whisk them away if necessary and he certainly didn't want to be the one to get them lost in the dark. But..."I guess I'll never know unless I try."

"That's the spirit." Tabor clapped him on the back. "Now, face the shadows in this room--" There were plenty of them, shadows cast by furniture and the bright light which came through the windows on the fire-lands portion of the house. "Picture a doorway, a path opening up through the dark. Picture your destination on the other end. You're just stepping over the threshold, You're just taking a shortcut to do it."

Fateh made a face and faced the shadows, feeling like an idiot. Shadows were just shadows, except when they were Shadows. "Has anyone ever tried opening a shadow road through the Shadows?" he asked absently, stalling for time.

"Yes, and that's how they got absorbed by the Shadow." Tabor shook his head. "It is not a trick I'll see you try. I like you too much to see you become part of the Shadows you came to fight. Now, no more delaying. Concentrate."

Fateh tried to imagine the doorway Tabor sometimes created out of the shadows. He moved his hands and for a long moment, nothing happened. He turned away, feeling like an idiot and about to tell Tabor he was too human for him to manipulate the shadows the way Tabor did. As he turned away, though, one of the shadows rippled like water in a pond. Fateh stared at it, fascinated and gestured with his hands again. Another ripple appeared and Tabor clapped him on the back.

"The shadow is ready for you. Now, just imagine the next room over. Close your eyes if you have to, but you've got this, Fateh. Just a little more."

Fateh pictured the entryway, the only other room he had been in and stepped into the shadows. It was cold and dark, like he expected, but it only took a moment before he was in the entryway, the rest of the group peering around the corner of the doorway to stare at him. "I did it!" He said excitedly. "It was weird, but I did it." His stomach didn't even rebel at such a short trip, but since this was his pathway he supposed it wouldn't have made him sick.

"Now, you just have to practice more." Tabor said in satisfaction. "I knew you could do it, it just takes time and effort for your first real traveling. This little blip--it's good, but you'll need to know how to travel much further distances in the future."

"I think practicing is a good idea." Fateh sounded reluctant. "Like you said, it's good to have a backup, especially if we get separated."

"Good. Now, I want you to explore the house thoroughly, so you can picture each destination in mind. Once I deem you're proficient enough, you'll be able to take a passenger."

When Fateh looked alarmed at the idea of bringing someone with him, Tabor laughed. "It'll be me, of course. I can find my way through the shadows and to a safe place. You won't have to worry about losing me on the shadow roads."

"So I guess that's how I'm going to be occupying my time until tomorrow." Fateh wasn't too happy. "What about the rest of you?"

Uisge shrugged. "I'd say I could find a nice pond or lake to stay in, but I don't know how welcoming the fae are in these parts to share a bit of space, and the fire-lands are what lies beyond the back door. Not exactly a place where I can take a cool dip."

"I can explore the woods around here and get a feel for the fae who are living here." They spread their hands. "As long as I can make my way back here, there shouldn't be a problem with doing some scouting."

Marisa nodded in agreement. "Traveling the paths we're going to travel on is a smart move." She spun around in circles. "You won't get lost, but you may come across some surprises along the forest path."

"Surprises are not exactly comforting." Sam complained. "They can be good or bad. I hope you're talking about the good kind of surprise."

"I'll be with you." Marisa giggled. "And I don't put myself in danger."

"Even with you coming with us to fight the Shadows?" Fateh asked in interest. "Does it mean we're going to come out of this okay?"

"I did my part." Marisa's eyes met his. "I brought the metal and lit the way and I can show you the path to the Shadow-nest so you don't need Meira and Tobias. You will still need them, but you can make your way alone. It'll just be harder."

"That's the clearest "nope, not me, I'm not fighting" I've ever heard." Fateh laughed. "Okay, so we can find our way to the nest where the Shadows lay, but you won't be coming inside where all the danger is going to be. Good. You're only human."

"I can See more clearly than you can." Her tone admonished him. "But you're right. I'd only be a liability if I came with you."

"So Marisa can stay here once all the fighting goes down. It's the safest place for her. Hana, Haruki?" Tabor turned to the last members of their group. "What are your plans?"

"We'll stay here and practice our magic and sword fighting." Hana said calmly. "There's no reason for us to go around town, sticking out the way we do. We'll make our way to where we need to go once the time is right." She looked at the door to the fire lands. "I can open a pathway to my kitsune relatives from here if need be. I just have to tweak the door a little." She gave an unabashed laugh of delight at the look on Tabor's face. "I'd put it straight back to where it goes," she promised. "I just like having my own back doors to safety if needed."

"So let's split up and meet back here after everyone's done their exploring or whatever they need to get done." Fateh said. "After I practice more shadow walking, I think I'll go out into town and see who's been chained and who is safe to talk to." He looked at Marisa. "Are you sure you don't want to come with me? You'll be awfully useful with seeing the chains on people."

"Your offer is appreciated, but I want to explore the woods with Sam." She gave Sam a cheery smile. "If it's okay I'm there."

"The Seer thinks she has to come with me?" Sam asked. "I'd be crazy to turn down the offer. Who knows what we're going to find in the woods?"

Marisa just smiled and didn't say anything. Sam shook their head and let the subject drop. "Meet back here in a few hours?" They suggested.

"Sounds like a plan." Fateh waited until everyone scattered and looked up at Tabor. "Guess it's time to get to work."

It took Fateh less time than he thought it would to manipulate the shadows. Once you had the trick of it, it was easy. He didn't dare go any further than the confines of the house, but he soon traveled between floors and even brought Tabor with him with minimal mishap. Once an hour passed, Fateh called for a break. Tabor had other ideas.

"Spark, before we get too far into it all, I think it's time I told you more of what happened to me when I was your age."

Fateh looked up in surprise; Tabor had been pretty close-mouthed about his past and always cut off Etana when the other brought it up. "You don't have to tell me anything." He wanted to be cautious. He wanted to know, but he also knew it was painful for Tabor to bring up. Mistakes were made and no one liked to admit how vulnerable they were.

"No, it's beyond time I told you what happened." Tabor's voice showed his pain. "You have to know what you're getting into, fighting the Shadows on their home turf."

"It's my home turf, not theirs." Fateh growled out. "They're the interlopers here."

"Yes, but they've made it a base of operations that will be hard to shake them from, unless we destroy the main core." Tabor raised an eyebrow at Fateh. "I hope you weren't thinking this was going to be easy."

"I think it's going to be terrifying and we'll probably die in the attempt." Fateh said frankly. "If it's not the Shadows drinking our power like milk through a straw, it's going to be metal bombs going off we can't escape."

"At least you're realistic." Tabor snorted out a laugh. "If a little morbid and cynical." He sobered up as he ran a hand through his hair. "Come on, Spark. You know you've been wanting the details for awhile now."

"Yeah, doesn't mean I'll get the pony I've always wanted, either."

"Well, buckle up. It's a sad tale, but one that you need to hear." Tabor settled on the couch and patted the seat next to him. "Alright, Spark. Here it is." He took a deep breath. "It all started when I first set myself up away from the fire lands..."

Chapter Thirty-Six

Tabor liked the look of the town he decided to set up shop in. It was quiet and there weren't a lot of people. Tabor had a good feeling about the place, even if it was nothing more than a village. It held potential. The damp weather was the only downside and it was also windy and cloudy. He didn't melt in the rain, but he didn't like it, either.

"Better yet, there's no one here but me." He rubbed his hands together gleefully. His family would come later, but he was going to be the one to set down roots and be the protector of the town from the start.

Tabor disguised himself enough so he'd blend in with the locals and made his way through town. He needed to establish himself as someone benevolent, but who had to be respected. He didn't need idle riff-raff making its way into town and disturbing the peace he set up here. It included the small twyleth teg. Enough of them could band together and it could be a real headache.

He got curious looks from the people he passed by, but no one outright called him out on being other. Tabor didn't want to shout from the rooftops he wasn't human. Let them discover his nature over time, when he was ready to let them know. By then, he'd be so established as part of their lives that they wouldn't think to harm him. He'd be respected, powerful and able to protect this little slice of life he discovered.

Tabor knew he was young for the job, but he could handle anything that came his way.

****

Tabor ran into his first bit of trouble when he saw the first of the scáthach. They were small things, lingering around human establishments and trying to entice the people there to make a deal; any sort of deal. They would be rewarded for it, came the promises. Tabor frowned to see it. The scáthach were dangerous creatures, feeding off of human desires. It was no wonder, since they were the product of those same human desires. Their greed landed them in the mess they were in. Still, Tabor felt confident he could get rid of them easily. There were so few of them and he was fire. He could burn away the shadows which formed the scáthach.

He wasn't about to go burning creatures that hadn't earned it, though. While it would be easy to scour the town free of the little scáthach with one fell swoop of his power, he didn't feel right attacking them when they did nothing to him. Even the humans ignored them; but humans were finicky these days, their belief in the twyleth teg having faded.

The twyleth teg hadn't gone anywhere, except perhaps their homelands, but they were still about in the world. He hadn't seen any of the higher ones, though and he didn't want to. They kept to their own spaces and didn't interfere with small fry like Tabor. If they decided to make a visit to this little village of Felinheli, he was screwed, but he felt confident enough they'd go to much grander places than a Welsh village on the edge of nowhere.

Tabor would keep his protections up and his senses sharp for any danger. This was all under control.

****

The scáthach grew more numerous and even the locals started to get wary. Tabor made the choice to let the scáthach know he was the one in charge here, not them. He wondered if he should wait for back up from his family, but he decided against it. If he couldn't handle such a small problem as this, they wouldn't let him be on his own. He had to handle this himself.

He made his first confrontation outside of a small wooded area, where the scáthach were gathered. Tabor let his power flare at a show of dominance and strength; he was going to show them he was superior here. Shadows could be burned away by flame, if the fire was hot enough. They were becoming the nuisance he didn't want them being and he wished that he had less scruples than he did. He should have burned them out before they became so numerous.

They weren't exactly the little slips of shadow they were before. They were full grown now, vibrating with power. Still, Tabor was stronger, even if there was only one of him and several of them. He could even reason with them, get them to leave his village.

"Oh, look, the little firebrand has come to say hello." There were titters all around the ground at the sally and Tabor scowled at being made fun of.

"I want you to leave." He said boldly, keeping his expression as determined as possible. "This is my territory and you're becoming a problem. Find some new area to haunt."

"Oh, but we like it here." The leader stepped forward and Tabor wondered at the wisps of lightning that flickered in its being. Where did it get lightning to absorb? It surely didn't stand out in a storm and wait for lightning to strike it. "We think you should go."

"Not likely." Tabor stood his ground, arms crossed over his chest. "I came here first and this is my land. You're nothing but a blight that humanity is exposed to."

"And you, oh, the benevolent ruler is so much better?" The leader taunted and shifted its form in such a way that it became vaguely feminine. "You are not native to this town, either. You hail from much further away and I'm sure the humans don't want you here anymore than they want us."

"I'm not offering them deals and threatening to take their souls as collateral!" Tabor snapped. "You're only going to corrupt them until they turn into shades of you."

"And why shouldn't we offer the weak-minded humans deals?" The leader taunted. "They get something which will make them happy for the rest of their short lives and at the end, we expand our numbers. Why shouldn't we grow?"

"I'm telling you now to leave. I don't want to have to hurt you, but I will burn away the Shadows which form you."

"Ooh, you're going to fight us?" Another one piped up, this one more masculine. A malicious grin split his face. "Please, give it a go, small fry. Your elders couldn't fight us, what makes you think you can?"

"What do you mean?" Tabor asked cautiously. He could be cautious when he wanted to be. "There haven't been any elders of mine here. I'm the first." He made sure he was the first to come to this damp village; most of his kind wouldn't come to a place so perpetually rainy.

"You can't think you're the first of your kind we've met." There were more giggles and Tabor tensed, not liking where this was going. "How do you think we got such tasty treats in power?" The lightning flickered again and Tabor blinked at the leader stupidly, not wanting to get it.

"Don't worry, it won't hurt ... much." The leader reached out of him, faster than Tabor could counter and wrapped its arms around him. "Shhh, little firebrand. It will all be over soon."

No matter how much Tabor struggled, he couldn't get free of their clutches. He felt his power draining away and his first futile attempts to burn away the arms holding him only lead to his power being bled out faster.

It didn't end in a day, either. They dragged it out, letting him go far enough so he thought he escaped, only to fall back into their clutches yet again. Several days--or weeks--later. he wasn't sure about how time passed any longer. He just knew he was going to die, sucked dry by the scáthach which held him.

He was about to give in when he smelled the distinct tang of metal and something sharp burned along his body. But while it only grazed him, it caused the scáthach to shriek in pain and release him. Tabor lay on the hard ground, panting and feeling as weak as he had ever felt. He didn't even think he could get up to crawl away from the scáthach. He didn't have to, though, because someone already dispatched the scáthach with what looked like flattened strips of metal. Wherever it touched the scáthach, they shrieked in pain and faded away to wisps of smoke in the air.

Tabor looked up to see just who had saved him and was surprised to see one of the moital there, standing over him with his arms crossed.

"You've gotten yourself into a fine mess, little one." The moital looked unimpressed with Tabor and Tabor grimaced. If this man wanted to finish him off, he could do it easily. Metal burned and purged and deadly when used under the right circumstances. He was a sitting duck.

"I'm not little." Tabor growled out, trying to sit up, to move, to do anything that would make it seem like he had this vaguely under control. He could hardly move an inch and the moital's lips twitched in amusement.

"You're little enough to me." He grinned widely. "Now, more of those scáthach are coming. I can play with them all day long, but I can't always keep an eye on you. Do you want my help?"

Tabor grimaced; asking for help put yourself in debt and he couldn't afford a debt, not in his weakened state. Still, he was easy fodder for the scáthach that were going to come investigate the loss of their companions. The moital could burn him and make his life miserable, but it would take more than a few shards of metal to outright kill him. He didn't really have a choice. The scáthach would suck him dry.

"Fine." Tabor growled. "We have a deal; please help me." It was as broad a deal as one could even imagine and Tabor knew he would be paying off this debt for a long time. How long would help last? Would it just be this one time and the moital would leave him to fend for himself? Or would it last longer and give Tabor time to recover?

"Take a deep breath and try not to get too sick when we land." The words were his only warning before the stranger yanked into the shadows, right before he saw the smaller scáthach come up to where he sat.

He felt like his insides had been turned out when they landed in the middle of an unfamiliar wood and Tabor was sick from the little adventure through the dark and cold. "What about the people in town?" he asked muzzily, feeling disconnected from his body. "The scáthach are going to go after them..."

"The scáthach are too weak to feed upon humans yet." The man who rescued him stood far back, wrinkling his nose at the mess Tabor made. "They can make deals, but when you don't believe in mysterious shadowy figures offering you the moon, it's not likely you'll be able to see the creature that wants to make a deal with you." He rested his cheek in his hand. "I'm Etana, by the way. You are?"

"Tabor." He gave the shortened version of his name; this Etana didn't need to hold any more power over him than he already did. He took a deep breath and said the forbidden words. "Thank you for helping me."

Etana preened. "Oh, it was nothing. The scáthach ran at the first sight of metal and they were drunk enough on power. I severed their connection from this reality. They won't be coming back anytime soon."

Tabor tried to lever himself up again, but to no avail. "They're going to come back?" he demanded. He couldn't go home if they were going to come back. They would have a vendetta against him and he already proved he was powerless against them.

"Not for at least half a century, if not longer." Etana reassured him. "You can go home and be fine and live your life as you always have, but right now, you're vulnerable to anything that comes around. Why don't you stay with me a bit and recover?"

"What's it going to cost me?" Tabor asked wisely. He was already in debt, he didn't need to make it worse.

"This falls under the category of 'help'." Etana leaned down and helped Tabor to his feet, supporting him the entire way. "I'll ask for your payment later."

Tabor groaned; he didn't like having a debt hanging over his head, but he didn't really have a choice, either. "Fine." He grumbled. "I'll accept your help and we can work out the details later."

Chapter Thirty-Seven

"And that's how I met Etana and got into his debt." Tabor finished, spreading his hands wide. "So you see, it just takes one touch for them to get their hands on you and they can drain you like water."

Fateh quieted after Tabor's story, digesting it. "So you're saying we're definitely not allowed to go and fight alone. If we get separated, we retreat?" He shuddered at the mental image of having your power sapped away. It wasn't even power than he originally asked for, but it was a part of him now and the idea of losing it to the Shadows terrified him.

"No heroics." Tabor said firmly. "The only way we're going to get through this is by using all of the power we have at our command, combined. I don't want anyone sacrificing themselves for the cause. You're definitely not strong enough to face them on your own, even with all your fireballs and lightning strikes. They'll drink up your power and go for the source."

"But we want them to have some power, right?" Fateh asked slowly. "It's the only way they'll be solid enough for us to attack."

"I don't think you'll have a problem attacking those we're going after. They've already absorbed power from other fae and are stronger for it. If they have guards around which aren't so well-fed, then we feed them power and cut them down before they have a chance to sound the alarm."

"Sounds reasonable." Fateh looked down at his hands. "I wish we could have gotten Etana here to help us. It sounds like he would have been a lot of help, with his metal abilities and all."

"It's why we have metal of our own." Tabor said firmly. "Etana is holding down the fort at his home, we've got to defend ours." He smiled. "It's a good thing Hana and Haruki can handle the metal we can't."

"Yeah, it's good." Fateh sounded absent-minded. "Once we're out, we're out, though and we promised we'd give some metal to Meiria and Tobias and their little band of rebels to use as weapons."

"They only need one or two pieces to make a bomb, if they're smart." Tabor shook his head. "We don't need to give them our whole supply."

"Wasn't planning on giving them that much ammunition." Fateh ran a hand through his hair, tangling his fingers on a curl and making a face as he tugged it free. "Tabor, what if this doesn't work?"

"Then we die." Tabor said bluntly. "Or became fodder for the scáthach. Either way, it'll take a miracle to save us if we don't win. So count on winning."

"I doubt that this was what my mother wanted when we contracted."

Tabor quieted for a few moments, then he gazed at Fateh with a wistful expression. "Your mother would be proud of all you're doing."

"Yeah, I think she would be." Fateh shook his head, the pain of her memory still hurt, but not like it had a year ago. So much has changed since he last saw her alive; he'd gone through a radical transformation of the self that he was sure wouldn't have surprised her. She always did see more than what was good for her, even if she pretended otherwise around Fateh.

"You sure you want me around you, cramping your style?" Tabor asked.

"If anyone asks if I'm contracted, I can point to you and honestly say 'yes'." Fateh pointed out. "If they're not chained, then you're just my friend."

"I'm glad you finally admitted out loud we're friends." Tabor said honestly. "I didn't think you'd ever do it."

"Well, some things don't need to be said." Fateh muttered, ears red. "OF course you're my friend, Tabor. We would have stayed friends if you hadn't decided to hang out with the Shadows and confuse me all those years ago."

"Yeah, survival is a beast of a burden." Tabor sighed as he ran a hand through his hair. "Let's get going."

They said their goodbyes to those who remained in the house, promising to be back within an hour or so. If they didn't return within three hours, they were to assume the worst and use Marisa to find the Shadow-nest and take them out. Fateh hoped it wouldn't come to being rescued. Taking a deep breath, he stepped into the blustery, rainy day which was typical for Wales and sighed. This wasn't going to be easy.

***

Despite the weather, the town was busy with people, but the Shadows were conspicuously absent. Fateh didn't know why, but he'd take the blessing as it came. Still, even without the Shadows lingering about their chosen humans, the number of contracted humans was high. It seemed like almost the entire town was strung with glittering chains only Fateh and Tabor could see.

"It's insane." Fateh looked around and wondered if there were a free human around. He had visions of Meira and Tobias being the only ones free and he shuddered. Not only would it be bad for Fateh's group--they needed more firepower--it also put a target on Meira and Tobias' back. The Shadows could see the chains, even if humans couldn't. They could pretend all they like with other humans, but if a Shadow came around, they'd notice straightaway the two weren't contracted.

"Things have definitely ramped up since the last time we were here." Tabor agreed. "At least you know the rebels will stand out. You can probably pick them out on your own without the help from those former friends of yours."

"If I can see them through all of this." Fateh grumbled and crossed his arms over his chest. "I'd swear the entire town is contracted." He peered through the rain and the crowds and was relieved to find a few standouts who weren't linked with a chain. Those would probably be the rebels, but Fateh wasn't about to go up to them and ask them if they worked with Meira and Tobias. It was the quickest way to getting shut down and losing their chance to work with them at all. He'd let someone else do the introductions.

"Let's just get some food, see who remembers me and then go back to your house." Fateh looked around for familiar food stalls and was relieved to see places he recognized still there. "I mean, it's a gamble, but we need to eat."

"It's been two years for these people." Tabor reminded him. "They probably remember you, but as to the events that led you out of town, it's going to be not as prominent in their minds."

"Thanks for the reminder." Fateh shuddered. The people who cornered him and his mother were out there still--they could have given in and been contacted, or they were part of the rebels that Fateh needed to connect with. "It's not going to be pleasant, seeing those people all over again. I know the ones who instigated the murder of my mother will remember me. I just hope they don't try and kill me out of hand."

"You can protect yourself now." Tabor patted him on the shoulder. "You're not as fragile as you were when you thought you were just a regular human." He kept his voice low so it wasn't overheard. Not that people were paying any attention to them. They were hurrying from place to place, ignoring everyone around them. There were clusters of friends who talked and laughed loudly, even in the middle of a crowded street and Fateh's heart twisted. He missed the friendship. The group he collaborated with now was fine, but they didn't share the same history or acquaintances. They shared a common bond about being half-human and the need to destroy the Shadows. Although Fateh was certain they'd become closer friends as time went on.

"You know, it's the memories which are important, not the people." Tabor gave him a knowing look. "You can mourn what you lost and cherish the memories you once had, but you can still distance yourself from the people that gave you so much pain."

"Yeah, I guess you're right." Fateh stuck his hands in his pockets and sighed. "I can't forget the good times, but I sure as hell don't have to want to be friends with Meira and Tobias again. That ship sailed when they worked with those that had my mother killed."

He didn't even want to work with them, but they needed to. They had resources and information Fateh lacked. He could probably gather intelligence, like he did now, but it would take longer and they didn't have the time to waste.

"Fateh?" Lira, who owned the stall which sold the seeds and seedlings used to buy from, for his garden at home, spoke out to him. "You're back! I didn't think you'd ever come back." She reached out to give him a hug and Fateh tensed slightly, uncertain of how to react to the affection she gave him. She hadn't been a part of the crowd that surrounded him and to his delight, he noticed she wasn't contracted. He relaxed a moment later and let the hug happen.

"Well, I'm eighteen now." Technically. "I thought it was time to come back home."

"I'm surprised you came back after all that happened." She spoke frankly. "I wouldn't have come back here." Her words went low. "I see Tabor is still attached to you. He was always interested in you."

"Don't make it sound gross." Fateh laughed. "Tabor and I are friends. Once I learned he wasn't a Shadow, it became easier to talk to him."

"Oh yes, he was always one of the tylwyth teg. I'm surprised you didn't know." Lira raised her brows in silent question and Fateh wasn't sure what she asked. She saw his confused face, laughed and clarified. "How did you find out about him? You and your group of friends didn't seem to be inclined to want to mingle with Tabor or any of the tylwyth teg at all."

"I learned a lot during my time away from home." Fateh couldn't lie. "I learned they're not as bad as the Shadows, but you still have to be careful." Like dealing with the higher fae, for instance. He wouldn't touch the possibility with a ten-foot pole.

"It's good." She smiled at him and squeezed his hand. "The tylwyth teg are our allies and they've been good to us." She eyed Fateh. "It's good you have Tabor as your protector. You need one here or else you'll be an easy target." Her expression shadowed and he wondered what sort of problems Lira had.

"You should get a protector of your own." Tabor said smoothly. "I"m sure one of the tylwyth teg wouldn't mind standing in for you."

"Oh, I don't make contracts." Lira said firmly. "I've read enough stories where people make contracts and it never ends well. There's being friends with the tylwyth teg and there's contracting your soul to them." She looked sad. "Too many people here got contracted and while they seem happier, I can tell it takes a toll on them."

"But they're contracted to Shadows." Fateh said, puzzled. "Isn't being contracted to one of the tylwyth teg different?" He looked up at Tabor questioningly, but Tabor shook his head.

"Not so different, depending on who you contract with. I wouldn't contract with the higher fae, that's for certain."

Lira shuddered. "They haven't come around here, it's only the minor tylwyth teg who come around. I don't know what I'd do if we had Shadow and the higher fae here at the same time. It would turn into a war zone."

Fateh didn't tell her it still might turn into a war zone, with what they were planning, but hopefully it would be very localized fighting. He didn't want to involve the other people in town with the fight; he wanted to keep them out of it as much as possible. He didn't want any more casualties like there had been with the restaurant.

"Well, keep an open mind." Tabor gave her a sympathetic look. "Contracts for protection are different from asking for the moon and stars, so you should be safe enough, as long as you're savvy about how you go about it."

"I'll think about it." Lira promised. Fateh could only hope that if she did decide to contract with one of the tylwyth teg, it would go good for her and she'd have some protection. He wouldn't be surprised if he saw her with the rebels, though. She had views that the tylwyth teg weren't all bad, but she was against contracting. Fateh hoped he'd see her there. It would be nice to see one friendly face amongst all the hostility.

Chapter Thirty-Eight

When they got back to the house, Sam and Marisa were waiting outside, looking uncertain as if they should have just gone inside instead of waiting for Tabor. They had expressions of relief on their faces when Tabor and Fateh walked up.

"We thought you'd be gone forever." Sam complained. "Marisa and I finished our scouting of the woods and it's amazing the number of tylwyth teg that are hiding out there."

"I'm not surprised." Tabor shrugged it off as he let everyone inside. "There are a lot of Shadows in town and the tylwyth teg don't mix well with them. They're hunted and they don't have the 'benefit' of being contracted to a Shadow for protection. A lot of them are just fodder."

Fateh shuddered; he was fodder to the Shadows, or at least he would have been more of a target if it hadn't been for Tabor and his pseudo-contract. He was marked as being protected, even the protection came from one of the tylwyth teg and not a Shadow. "Did you talk to any of them?"

"Some of them. Most hid from us, but a few of the wood tylwyth teg came out and talked to me once they noticed I had the same power as them, but there were a lot more who stayed hidden." Sam looked disappointed they didn't have more success. "I did find out they're planning a rebellion of their own, though. Not quite as flashy as ours, but they're willing to add their strength to ours when it comes down to the fight. They're leery about the metal, though."

"Hell, I'm leery about the metal and it was my idea." Fateh snorted. "I don't want to mess with the stuff, but that's what we have Meira and Tobias for." He looked at Marisa. "I don't want you in combat. You're going to be like a lit candle to them."

"I told you, I don't want to fight." Marisa spoke calmly. "I lit the beacons, but you don't need me to find the Shadows. They're all around."

Fateh immediately spun around and looked at the innocent looking shadows on the floor, but Marisa shook her head.

"Not here. This space is protected by fire and magic. The Shadows cannot cross. If we stayed here all our lives, we wouldn't have to worry about the Shadows any longer. We could escape out the back and let them run rampant over the human world." Marisa sounded very confident and Fateh relaxed.

"We can't let them take over." Fateh was very firm. "We said we'd take care of what we could and we're going to hold to our deal."

Tabor gave him a sly smile. "I wonder if your friends know that by working with you, they made a deal with the tylwyth teg."

"Let's not remind them of the fact." Fateh huffed. He still didn't like thinking of himself as being part of the tylwyth teg, but it was hard to see himself as human anymore. "We don't want to antagonize them any more than we already have. We actually want to work with them, not against them."

"I don't see why we have to work with them." Uisge spoke up. "We have Hana and Haruki who can lob metal at the Shadows. They won't be bombs, but do we really want bombs going off while we're there and hurting us?"

Fateh grimaced. She had a point, but still..."They know where the Shadows have holed up." He pointed this out, rubbing the bridge of his nose in thought. "And we can do a lot on our own and will." He looked at the others. "I don't like the idea of the bombs, either. There's too much potential for friendly fire."

He had a very vivid image of being trapped in the room with the Shadows when the bombs went off.

"Exactly. I say we go in with Marisa's help and take care of the Shadows without having to resort to the humans. They might target us next and then where would we be?" Uisge stood with her hands on her hips, facing down Fateh. "I don't trust those humans of yours. They might use the metal we got them to attack us."

Fateh had to admit the plan had merit. Marisa could suss out where the Shadows were hiding, go into hiding after pointing it out. They could go in and take care of what Shadows they could. "We could always tell them about the Shadows we have pinned up in the briars after we get out and are safe." Fateh pointed out. "That way we're not inside when the bombs go off."

"Waiting sounds better." Uisge admitted. "As long as we're not in the line of fire, I'm happier about it. I'm not going to hand over metal to those crazed humans and let them go at it."

"I didn't plan on setting myself up for getting shredded, either." Fateh protested. "Fine, new plan, We find the Shadows ourselves, kill as many as we can and lock up the rest to be pummeled with metal bombs."

"As long as we can take care of the Blight, I don't mind." Hana gave a graceful shrug. "I was against going inside with those humans on the outside with weapons. Waiting until we are out to give them the metal and let them make their little devices sounds like a much safer plan. Metal may not hurt us, but we can still be hurt by explosions."

Fateh rubbed the back of his head. So many things changed and were still changing, but this plan of attack seemed much better than what they had decided with Meira and Tobias. "Good. Let's get on with it."

***

The thing with making their plan was they all had to go out in a group together. It made them conspicuous as hell, but they weren't going to get separated when fighting the Shadows. Marisa, ahead of them, skipped and twirled, but always avoided running into people. Fateh didn't know how she managed it. He barely managed to avoid the crowds and he just walked normally.

"We're not going on a picnic." Uisge scowled at Marisa's back. "She's acting like this is some sort of pleasure jaunt and it's not. We could die doing this."

"You agreed to it." Fateh felt a cold chill run down his back. "Please don't back out now." Well, he was less assertive than he wanted to be. He wanted to order her to stay, not plead with her like a child.

"I said I would do it and I'm not going back on my word." Uisge's voice sharpened with her anger and frustration. "What sort of person do you take me for? You think I'm less trustworthy because I deal with water?"

This conversation definitely wasn't going the way he planned. He'd just insulted her. "No, I don't think you're dishonest." Fateh's face screwed up in frustration as he tried to articulate the words. "I just know this is a lot and it's not really your fight."

"I told you, the Shadows poison all our wells." Uisge shook her head. "It's best to cut off the source before it bleeds into all the water, spreading and corrupting. Prevention is why I'm doing this. It's not to save your little village. It's to save those I love."

"And that's just what we're doing as well." Hana interjected. "We care about the people in our lives, to what the Blight is affecting. Your village happens to be a catalyst of sorts. If we cut off the power at its source, then we will have less problems facing the horrors later on."

"You make a good point." Fateh sighed, running a hand through his hair. "This isn't going to be easy..."

"We already know it won't be." Haruki rested a hand on Fateh's shoulder. "We did agree to this, knowing it would be a fight where we might not have the best of outcomes. But we're doing what we can. I'm just grateful we found a nest we can eradicate. The less powerful Shadows, the better."

"Yeah." Fateh began walking again, catching up with Marisa and her dance through the people. "Here goes nothing."

"Here goes everything." Sam corrected him. "Everything is riding on this, our lives, the people we care about and the outcome of a large slice of the world. We have to go into this with open eyes and a strong heart."

"So no more bickering." Uisge raised her brows at Fateh. "I know we get along like our elements do, but you have to trust us. We're not going to suddenly turn tail and flee back to our safe spaces."

"I know no one is going to run away." Fateh made a frustrated sound. "I just--there's so much at stake here, like Sam said. I don't want anyone to get hurt because of me." He went quiet at the end and the others stared at him, pausing in their walk once again. Even Marisa noticed them stopping and turned around to look at Fateh as well.

"We understand the risks and the rewards." Sam was gentle with their words. "I'm glad you care about us enough--you didn't used to be that way--but we'll either be fine or we won't. We know what we're doing. We have a plan and a back up plan in case this one goes sideways. It may end up with us getting bombed with metal and it'll be the end of us and the Shadows, but we'll have at least fought to the end."

"I hope it won't end with death by metal." Fateh gave a weak chuckle. "I intend to come out of this without one of Meira's little bombs going off in my face."

"That's the spirit. We'll nip in, take care of the Shadows and lock them up tight before they can come after us. We'll leave the rest of the Shadows to your other compatriots and that'll be it." Hana sounded reassuring and sure of herself. Her words made Fateh feel more confident about the whole thing.

They were following Marisa as she made her way through the crowd--she was the one who would know best where the Shadows were holed up. Marisa frowned at them with every stop. "We're going to draw a crowd." She warned. "We already shine like sparklers enough to make us stand out, we don't need any help."

"You're right." Fateh squared his shoulders and began walking. The rest of them fell silent as they made their way to their hopefully not-final destination.

It didn't take them long to get to where Marisa led them and Fateh blinked at the building in front of them. "This is the old city hall." He said in disbelief. "It's where all our records are kept."

He expected a cave, not this cheerfully painted building which had gone back several hundred years.

"What better place to hide than in a place where they know everything about everyone?" Uisge was practical, even as she eyed the building in disbelief. It was an obnoxious shade of yellow that had been recently painted. Even when things had gone to hell in the town, the city hall was being maintained. He couldn't imagine the Shadows painting the building, but he couldn't imagine anyone else keeping the building in working order with Shadows lingering.

Speaking of Shadows-- "I don't see any of them." Fateh scrunched his brow. "Are we sure they're in there?"

"I'm sure." Marisa shivered and her eyes went dark. "They're in there, resting until they can come out and make more mischief. The leaders are in there, the ones who don't go into town. They're old, Fateh. Old and powerful."

Fateh swallowed hard. "Well, we knew what we'd be dealing with. Let's prepare before going in." He meant their shields and tricks and magic. It was best to go invisible, so the humans who were inevitably inside wouldn't raise the alarm. And Fateh knew there would be humans involved. It was a sad fact, but there were probably going to be casualties that couldn't be avoided. He only hoped they'd flee when the fighting really started. He had a feeling these people were Shadow-trapped, Shadow-bound and unable to leave.

He wrapped himself, Uisge and Tabor in invisibility, while Sam took care of Marisa. She wouldn't be going in, but it was best she hid when the fighting went down. No one wanted her to get hurt. Hana used the same spell on her and Haruki. They could see each other, but only barely--their forms wavered like candles on the water. Hana confirmed it worked and she would know the best.

"Is everyone ready?" Her words were hushed as she tried to focus \her gaze on their flickering forms. "There's no turning back now."

Fateh nodded and wished he didn't feel so nervous. They had a plan and they had allies, skewed though they may be. They had magic of their own and metal to protect them. Fateh couldn't use the metal, but he trusted Haruki and Hana to wield what they did have. "Ready."

Marisa moved forward to give each of them a hug and a reassuring smile. "We'll see each other on the other side." She promised and Fateh just hoped she meant on the other side of the door, not on the other side of life.

Chapter Thirty-Nine

It was not quiet when they slipped through the front door. There were at least a dozen humans behind desks and at filing cabinets. There weren't any computers of course--that technology had died with the Shadows coming. Everyone seemed cheerful, though and not bothered by the chains Fateh could see wrapped around them. It wasn't just the light chain he and Tabor shared. They looked heavy, as if it should weigh the humans down. But they moved as if they didn't notice them and Fateh grimaced. He wanted to shout at them to leave, but if they did, they'd set off alarms.

They moved quietly as a group, trusting each other in what they planned together. As they moved further into the building, the shadows seemed to increase and the temperature dropped. Fateh felt a cold trickle of sweat go down his spine as he swallowed nervously. What were they doing? Marisa said the Shadows here were old and powerful. What chance did they have? They were committed now, though-- they couldn't turn back. For a brief moment, Fateh wished they'd stuck with the original plan and bombed them from afar, but that would have meant all those innocent humans getting hurt in the crossfire.

He knew they were close when he saw the shadows pooling out from beneath a doorway, squirming as if they were alive. He took a deep, shuddering breath and pushed open the door.

Shadows didn't fill the room, which made Fateh grateful, but the Shadows that were there were tall and filled with such power they almost seemed human. They had a type of solidity to them that was absent from all the other Shadows Fateh saw before this. One of them looked up at the door opening, but frowned when they didn't see anyone.

"Either we're being haunted," it said in a sing-song tone, "or we've got visitors who are trying to be stealthy." It spread its hands and focused on the small group. "Your footsteps give you away, little sneaks. The shadows may absorb them, but we hear what the shadows do."

Fateh grimaced. They couldn't be seen, but they could be heard. The only advantage they had was the Shadows couldn't see exactly where they were, but it would change once the first attack happened. They'd light up like fireworks with their power.

Nothing ventured, nothing gained. He eyed Sam, who nodded and began turning the wood of the floors into something living, turning into hard vines which wrapped around the Shadows. They were solid enough only where parts of them bled through the restraints.

It wasn't like with the trolls or with the lone Shadow they fought. These Shadows fought back against the magic, pulling it into their skin and glowing all the brighter for it. Fateh swore under his breath; he'd been worried this would happen. Their magic was just fuel for the Shadows and unless they did this correctly, they could find themselves hampered by their own magic.

Hana put a reassuring hand on his arm and nodded. They were still tied down and they weren't absorbing as much magic as they could have been, so Fateh took the moment to let one of the fire loops land over one of the Shadow's head and he pulled tight. It caused the Shadow's eyes to bulge out, and the Shadow hissed in pain and anger as the fire burned through his Fateh neck. Fateh didn't need to encourage the others to move as they bombarded it with their own magics. Uisge surrounded the Shadow with watery bubbles, enclosing it in a sphere of water it couldn't get out of. Eventually, the group of them broke it down to its separate parts, the head popping off last, and the Shadow dissolved like water, leaving only a bright sphere of power behind.

Hana moved quickly to grab it before any of the other Shadows could move towards it and she swallowed it in a satisfied gulp.

"Ah, now that's nice." She murmured and stretched out her hands, facing the remaining Shadows.

They were ready for them this time, though and they were angry. They wouldn't take the death of one of their companions well and it was clear they were angry in the way they methodically broke apart the woody vines that held them hostage only moments before.

"Now the real fight begins." Haruki swung his sword in the ready position, a maniacal gleam in his eyes. "Taking down the one Shadow was the easy part." They caught them unawares, but now the gig was up. They were still 'invisible' to the naked eye, but their power marked each of their spots as clear as if they dropped the spell.

"Oh, little halflings have come to fight." One of the Shadows stood free from their bindings and gave the group a cold smile. "But oh, we have old friends here as well. Hello, Tabor."

Tabor's response was a ball of lightning straight to her face, causing her to scream in agony. The shrieks echoed out from the main room, where the humans were being kept. Fateh felt sick, They were going to end up hurting the humans no matter what. The Shadows had tied themselves to the humans and what pain the Shadows felt, a human would as well.

"That wasn't very nice." The Shadow spat, her face half-melted away from the lightning, the shadows bleeding through and wriggling like snakes. "You've gotten very impolite since we last met, Tabor."

"Yeah, I wasn't feeling very friendly then, either." Tabor eyed her warily, waiting for her to make the next move, but Haruki already moved, not waiting for the pleasantries to be exchanged. With a powerful gust of wind pulling from his sword stroke, he sliced into several of the Shadows surrounding the main one. Fateh started to think of her as the Queen.

The Shadows didn't die with the blow, though-- they were battered and bleeding shadow, but they still moved with purpose and without warning, the shadows around Fateh's feet writhed upward and grasped his ankles, sending him crashing to the ground.

He swore and tried to get up, but the shadows were moving swiftly, lacing around his legs and hands, pinning him to the ground. The 'queen' watched all of this calmly, hands moving in gestures to direct the shadows to her will. Fateh pressed his palms against the floor and created fire to burn against the shadows holding him down, but it was like trying to catch fire to smoke. These shadows didn't have the solidity of the Shadows they were fighting. Still, Fateh could do what he could and he burned away the wood beneath the shadows, until they didn't have an anchor. He shot to his feet as quickly as he could after he did so, heart beating fast in his chest. He was almost taken by something so simple.

"Fateh, get behind me." Uisge warned, before blanketing the area in a wash of water, stretching out in a cube and somehow washing the shadows away. They didn't react well to the water, shrinking back into the hands which held the strings. Haruki moved again while the Shadows were distracted, lopping off a hand of the queen Shadow. She hissed and turned her attack on Haruki, hurting shadows towards him to wrap around his throat.

Hana moved before he could get caught, flinging herself in front of Haruki and dissolving the shadows with a blast of the power she had stolen from the fallen Shadow. It was effective in a way the the rest of their attacks weren't-- Shadow-magic tangled up in the pure magic of the unfortunate elemental that got subsumed by the Shadow's power proved effective. It dissolved the Shadows in a bright arc.

"Clever." The queen gathered her power around her more, using the shadows to rebuild what had been destroyed by Tabor's attack. Her features knit back together, but Fateh noticed she was only doing it with one hand. She still hadn't repaired the one Haruki had cut off.

"We try to be." Uisge had swords of water in her hand, sharp enough she cut through more shadows which came towards them. "Better to be clever than dead."

"But you'll be so much happier dead." The queen lashed out and her two companions on the other side of her worked fast as well and Fateh had to throw up a shield of fire around the group of them so the attack broke up against it and went up in a show of sparks.

"We can do this all day." Sam stood forward, arms crossed against their chest. "You'll run out of shadows before we run out of power." The shadows on the floor were already diminished and Fateh took it as a good sign.

"Are you so sure?" The queen sneered and took a step forward, only to be stymied by the floorboards working against her again, encasing her foot in hardened wood. She made an inarticulate sound of rage and then broke off her foot. She was down a foot and a hand and Fateh grinned to himself, even though the situation couldn't be more dire. This Shadow was willing to take herself apart to fight them.

Uisge moved with quick precision and sliced off the Shadow's other hand, cutting off the queen's access to the shadows on the floor. "Try again." Uisge mocked.

"Not if I take your power first." The queen moved with lightning speed, wrapping herself around Uisge and drinking up her power. Uisge struggled and tried to put out as many defenses as possible, but it was a losing battle. While Uisge distracted her, Haruki moved to stab the Shadow queen right where a heart would have been.

This time the scream echoed throughout the room and beyond and without hesitating, Haruki moved his blade to behead her. She was still screaming as her head fell to the floor, before it dissolved into shadow, along with the rest of her body.

The two Shadows left looked uncertain now their queen was gone. "Look--" one of them held up their hands and shook their head. "We only wanted what we were denied as humans. You can't understand."

"I can't." Fateh's voice went flat. "You send your shadows out into the world and subsume the people living there. You're not just trying to live, you're dominating and destroying." The floor of shadows on the floor stopped momentarily, but Fateh knew this battle wasn't over yet. They may have wanted to talk now, but the Shadows were going to fight.

Fateh spared a look for Uisge looking pale and drawn, all the power gone out of her. She faded fast and Fateh swore, turning back to the Shadows. They killed the queen who had drained Uisge's power-- and probably it was only because of her power they were able to defeat the queen-- but there were still Shadows who remained which posed a danger to all of them.

Some of the metal they had were throwing daggers and Hana flicked her wrist sideways to better throw the daggers in her hand, embedding it in the eye of one of the Shadows. He screamed in pain with the metal poisoning him and Fateh shuddered as he imagined the same fate happening to him. He took a step forward and grasped the arm of one of the Shadows, sending a line of fire up the Shadow's arm, shriveling it.

Uisge gasped out something and Fateh almost turned to see what she said, but all of his attention went to the Shadows that engaged him. Both remaining Shadows decided to go after him at the same time, which ended up being a mistake. Keeping their attention just on him left them open for attacks from the others in his party. Haruki was especially devastating, moving with the speed of the wind and slicing pieces of Shadows off as he moved with his sword.

They fought back, clinging to members of their party and draining their power. Even Fateh got taken at one point, the Shadows wrapping around him and he felt his body shake and his power flow from him to the Shadows. He fought back as well as he could, using fire and lightning in equal amounts. Bit by bit, he wore down the Shadows which clung to him. Sam used their woody trap again and now that the queen wasn't there to supply them power, it was easier to hold them down.

No magic came from Uisge now; it was obvious she did all she could to hold herself together. Fateh wished he could provide her with his own magic, but they were opposites in every way. His power wouldn't mingle with hers. He looked at Hana, who nodded and switched her attention from the Shadows to Uisge, pouring magic into her. Uisge looked a little better, more solid and Fateh breathed a sigh of relief. Maybe she'd come out of this okay.

Then one of the Shadows moved away from him and struck Uisge, taking all the new power Hana gifted her. The parts of the Shadow that were cut off by

Haruki grew back and the Shadow grew more solid. Hana made a cry of dismay and tried to pry the Shadow away from Uisge. Fateh hesitated to use his fire or lightning, afraid he'd hurt Uisge in the process. Haruki was just as hesitant; but he at least was able to channel his move into dispatching the remaining Shadow. Now there was only one left and it grew in power to an extent where Fateh was afraid they were just stuck back in the same position as they had started in, Could the Shadows clone themselves?

"Kill it now! Don't think about me!" Uisge's words rang out strongly from within the darkness of the Shadow. "This is your only chance before it gets too strong."

Fateh swallowed hard; he didn't want to be the one responsible for destroying Uisge, even if she said to do it.

"Stop hesitating." It was given as a flat order and Fateh still stayed his hand. Surely there was another way. Haruki shook his head and Hana met his gaze and nodded. She reached within the Shadow and yanked out the power she had given Uisge, melting parts of the Shadow away.

"Now!" Fateh didn't know how Uisge held so much strength in her words when she was clearly dying. He closed his eyes and took a deep breath, sending his strongest lightning into the Shadow-- and Uisge.

The Shadow evaporated like water and when he looked, there was nothing left of Uisge, either. They had won this round, but at the cost of one of their own. Uisge sacrificed herself so they could have a chance.

"Oh, you got rid of those troublesome three." There was a new voice in the doorway and Fateh's heart nearly stopped in his chest. He knew it better than anything.

"Mom?"

Chapter Forty

It couldn't be...but the Shadow that stepped in the room was unmistakably his mother. She drifted like smoke on the wind, but even the tattered edges of her blurred into a familiar figure. He took a step forward, tears in his eyes. Hana stopped him before he went to her, to step into those welcoming arms.

"Stop, Fateh. She is no longer your mother. She is subsumed by shadow." Hana kept a hand on his shoulder.

"But it's my mom. She died and now she's here--" He reached out a hand again and his mother seemed all too eager to reach out to him as well.

"No." Sam stood in front of him. "You said it yourself. She died, Fateh. What's left is not what your mother was."

"Fateh." His mother's tone lacked any inflection and Fateh hesitated. It looked like his mother, but there was no warmth in the acid-green eyes that marked a Shadow. "Come here. I missed you."

Fateh shook his head slowly. "No. I don't think so." He sounded too timid and he tried to put some conviction into it. "You're not my mother."

"Of course I am." There was the odd, crooked smile he remembered so well. "Just because I'm a little different doesn't make me any less of your mother."

"You've turned into a Shadow." Fateh hissed out, taking a step backwards now. This couldn't be his mother. It has to be a Shadow lie. "My mother would never be a Shadow."

"Oh, silly boy. Of course I can be a Shadow. The Shadows can twist any soul they want into being a Shadow and they had me right there." She shrugged as if it was of no consequence. "I get to live again. Look at you, showing all this power." Her smile turned sharp and predatory. "Now come on and give your mother a hug. It's been so long, Fateh."

Something about her words compelled him. Fateh found himself walking forward again, but Haruki yanked him back this time. He stumbled a bit, nearly falling to his knees, but it would just make him more of prey. He straightened quickly and let his hands light up with fire. "I'll show you power." He was angry. This Shadow used his mother's face to trick him.

"Don't be like that. I raised you better than to raise a hand against your mother." His mother-the Shadow-snapped her fingers and shadows crawled up from the floor and shoved Fateh forward. Fateh stumbled again and it was only Sam's arm around his shoulders which kept him from barreling straight into the arms of the Shadow.

"You're despicable." Fateh hissed. "How dare you use my mother like this? Stop with your tricks and let me see your true face so I can destroy it."

"Ah, you really can't hurt your mother, can you?" The Shadow taunted him now and Fateh growled under his breath. "I told you, Fateh. There's no trick. I am your mother. I have no other face to wear."

"Oh fuck you." Fateh snarled. "My mother would never put me in danger."

"And have I hurt you?" The Shadow sounded way too innocent. "All I want is a hug from my son. I have missed you, Fateh. Come to your mother and give her one last hug before you--" Her face twisted slightly and her tone abruptly changed. "You have to kill the Shadow part of me, Fateh."

Fateh blinked, wondering at this new trick. Uisge's death was still fresh on his mind and he wasn't of a mind to repeat the same action.

"I'll kill her for you, Fateh." Haruki spoke gently into his ear and Fateh shook his head. "Are you sure? I think there's a bit of a conflict of interest here."

"What if it really is my mother?" Fateh asked weakly. "I can't kill her again. It's my fault she died in the first place."

"You can't blame yourself for the act of some vigilantes." Haruki's voice was steady and gentle. Fateh found himself listening. "You heard the true words from her; she wants you to kill the Shadow. I think your mother will be free if you do it."

Fateh shook his head, wiping away the tears which streaked down his face. It was one thing to plunge his power into the formless power of a Shadow, it was another to do it to a Shadow that wore his mother's face. Even watching someone else kill her would be like her dying in front of him all over again.

"If it has to be done, I have to be the one to do it." Fateh wavered slightly, but his expression turned resolute. He closed his eyes briefly, trying to gain the strength he needed to do this. He took several steps forward, until he was within touching distance of the Shadow. He reached out as if to hug her and the Shadow grinned wildly at the movement.

Fateh took a deep breath and then slammed his power into the figure of his mother, the Shadow that had taken her and poured with all his strength. The Shadow screamed with his mother's voice and Fateh closed his ears to it, still crying as he slowly killed the Shadow.

Hana stood behind him, providing him with power and Fateh increased his attack, until nothing was left of the Shadow. A glimmer of something caught his attention and Fateh reached out with a burning hand, but Hana took it away.

"You don't want to burn the soul" Her words were gentle. "Say goodbye to your mother for real now, Fateh."

The glimmer resolved itself until a figure emerged, familiar and not just a twisted replica. It was faint but real and Fateh doused the fire to reach out to the ghost of his mother.

"I knew you could do it, Fateh." She whispered and her words seemed to echo slightly. "You've grown so much." She held out a hand, but it went straight through him. Fateh sobbed. Here was his mother, but he'd never get to hug her again or feel the touch of her hand on his. "I see you're still with Tabor. He'll take care of you."

Fateh nodded as he wiped away his tears. "Yeah, guess I'm stuck with him. It's not so bad."

His mother giggled. "You say that, but I can tell you genuinely like him." Her form grew mistier and Fateh automatically reached out, trying to keep her there with him. "Keep growing stronger, Fateh. The fight isn't over yet, even if a portion of the battle is won. I foresee dark days ahead of you."

And with his mother being a Seer like Marisa, it didn't bode well. "I miss you." He whispered. "Don't go."

"I have to." She was filled with regret as well and she met Fateh's eyes with her own. "Don't worry about me. I'm free now. One day we'll see each other again."

Fateh could only watch as she faded from view and they were left alone in the room that once held such power so it had leaked into the world. Uisge died and the rest of them were drained and feeling battered. "What now?" He asked quietly.

"We go to Uisge's home and let them know of the sacrifice she made." Hana spoke gently. "It's only right they know what happened to her. They shouldn't be left wondering."

Fateh nodded and looked at the space where his mother stood and sighed. "Let's go. There's nothing left for us here."

There were still the humans outside; there was still information to be given and other Shadows to destroy. But they did what they had come here for and Fateh just felt tired. Drained and not just by his power being taken.

Tabor wrapped an arm around his shoulders and directed him out the door to the main room. He got a shock when he saw the humans slumped over their desks or on the floor, unmoving. "What?" he demanded. "We were supposed to free them!"

"Their souls may have been too tangled with the Shadows to be free of them." Tabor sounded sad as he knelt down next to a young woman. "When they died, the shock reverberated down the bond and killed them."

"This is such..." Fateh swallowed the words. "Is there anything we can do?" He thought of all the people in town tied to Shadows and shuddered. Were there any other options besides death for them?

"The other Shadows don't quite have that time of hold on people." Tabor reassured him. "We can destroy the Shadows without destroying the humans that are attached to them." He sounded very sure of himself and Fateh gave a sigh of relief.

"Alright then." He took a deep breath and looked around at the devastation their fight had wrought. "I don't think I could take another human death on my hands. The Shadows I'll kill all day long."

"About your plans--" Their heads all turned at the sound of an unexpected, but familiar voice. "You'll not be killing any Shadows right now, or giving your regrets. You have somewhere to get to."

Etana stepped from a shadow and smiled brightly at all of them. "Oh, what a good little group you've managed to gather. I'm very proud of you, Fateh and also disappointed you didn't bring these lovelies to see me."

"I had my reasons." Fateh tensed, uncertain as to what was going to happen with Etana now. He thought they resolved their issues, but here was Etana, away from his home. He looked and sounded suspicious and Fateh didn't trust him for a moment. "What are you doing here? We said we'd come visit after we were done fighting."

"And you can't lie, so I knew you'd be around eventually, but who's to say how long the fight would last? This isn't the only pocket of Shadows and what if I waited for a year or more like I did last time? Waiting for you all over again would hurt me, Fateh. Especially when I've made promises."

"What sort of promises?" Tabor asked cautiously, standing slightly in front of Fateh in a gesture of protection. "We have places to be and yours is not first on the list."

"I'm wounded. I used to be first for you, no matter what." Etana pressed a hand to his heart, looking hurt. "Before you go off on any jaunts, there's someone I want you to meet."

Hana, Haruki and Sam looked confused at this stranger making their way into their midst, disrupting their plans and spouting cryptic messages. "Who are you?" Sam finally asked.. "And what do you mean, you have someone for us to meet?"

"I'm Etana." Etana showed all of his teeth in a broad smile. "And while you weren't originally on my guest list, my patrons won't be very disappointed at all to have you join the festivities. There's so few chances of them to find halflings such as yourselves,"

Fateh felt cold; he had a feeling he knew where this was going and he didn't like the sound of it one bit. "Who?" he bit out. "Who do you want us to see, Etana?"

"Why the higher fae, of course." Etana looked inordinately pleased with himself. "The King and Queen themselves have an interest in you and will be even more intrigued now that you've gotten rid of a Shadow Queen and her court."

"Oh no." Fateh backpedaled and shook his head. "I am not seeing the higher fae."

"You don't have a choice." Etana said firmly. The shadows rippled behind him, creating an archway which led into a sun-dappled glade. "You don't leave the King and Queen waiting."

Tabor looked like he was going to be sick and Hana and Haruki took a step back. "This is nothing for us to interfere with. We will be going home as soon as a pathway can be opened for us." Hana looked at Tabor. "Can you open a road for us to go back home?"

"Oh, we don't have time for Tabor to help you out." Etana shook his head. "You put yourself into this group, you'll find yourselves at the end of it as well." He held out his hands, knives spinning across the palms of his hands. "My metal can go anywhere I want it to go. I wouldn't want to hurt a pretty lady such as yourself."

"You're unforgivably rude." She drew herself up. "You'll find we're not as big of pushovers as you think we are." She formed a bright arc of her own magic, slashing it toward Etana. Haruki moved with blinding speed with his sword.

He jumped back, looking impressed. "Maybe you are more trouble than you're worth. But Tabor and Fateh don't have a choice. I've already told the Queen and King about you two and if you don't come with me now, they'll find

you later and you really don't want them coming after you. More humans will be caught betwixt and between and how guilty will you feel then?"

Fateh hesitated and looked to Tabor, indecision clearly written on his face. "You're being a real ass." He finally said to Etana. "You're putting us between a rock and a hard place."

"I know." Etana shrugged. "But I already made a promise and I can't go back on my own word." For a moment he looked regretful. "If it helps, I made this promise when I was mad at you."

"It doesn't." Fateh said flatly. He looked at the rest of the group. "I don't know how long we'll be, but we'll return as soon as possible. Go to Tabor's house and find refuge there and there are the backdoors you can use to escape this town. It'll dump you in the fire lands, but you know there are pathways you can open there." He pondered the idea of an escape for a moment. "I'm sure there is someone there that can open a doorway for you to go back home." Fateh glared at Etana. "It seems as if we don't have a choice in where we're going."

"You really don't." Etana said agreeably. "Shall we go?" He looked disappointed that it would only be Fateh and Tabor, but Hana and Haruki were standing in front of the others protectively, so they wouldn't be snatched up. Etana gestured towards the portal again and Fateh shuddered. He didn't know what was going to happen next, but he didn't think he'd like it.

"Fine." He bit out. "Let's go." With Tabor by his side, they followed Etana into the sunlight.

End Book 2

G lossary:

aodhamair- Fire elemental

scáthach- Shadow

Miotal- metal elemental

Caergybi--Mokosh's town

Felinheli--Fateh's town

Gwyrddni- forest fae

gwragedd annwn- water maidens

Twyleth teg- Welsh fae

About the Author

Trisha Thacker is an east coast girl at heart, coming from Virginia, but has sprouted into a desert flower after almost a decade of living in Arizona. Her two cats, Kai and Loki, are the sunlight of her life. She has told herself stories since she was a child. She didn't start writing them down until she was a teenager, which she burned. Trisha recently stepped into the publishing world and her latest book, Sparks, was inspired by her fondness for faerie tales and was a labor of love.

Trisha loves fantasy, anime, and baking shows, but her favorite show to binge is Mythbusters. Who doesn't love a good explosion? You can find her with a cup of tea in one hand and a taco in the other while she hides from the sun.

You can reach her at trisha@trishathacker.com or her website at http://tris
hathacker.com